AS THE U.S. CAVALRY'S LAST MOUNTED CHARGE BEGINS, AN EPIC ADVENTURE TAKES US INTO THE MINDS AND HEARTS OF THOSE WHO BECAME LEGENDS OF COURAGE AND BRAZEN DREAMS

PANCHO VILLA: Hero, killer, womanizer, beloved husband, brilliant military strategist, he was *all* those things and a masterful manipulator of the emotions of those he hated and loved. Now the American Army was chasing him into the most remote terrain of Northern Mexico, where a bullet would find its mark and history would be changed by whether he perished or lived. . . .

GENERAL JOHN J. "BLACK JACK" PERSHING: Having earned his nickname by leading a regiment of black soldiers against the Indians, he was a veteran of the American West, and now he wanted his chance at the raging war in Europe. He also needed to forget the tragedy that took the lives of his wife and daughters, so he threw his very soul into following the President's orders to punish Pancho Villa— but he was ordered to do it with untested trucks and planes, not the mounted cavalry he knew best. . . .

"Fred Bean takes a little known piece of American history and he makes it live and breathe. Black Jack Pershing, young George Patton, and Pancho Villa come alive on the pages of *PANCHO AND BLACK JACK*. Well done!"
    —John Byrne Cooke, author of *The Committee of Vigilance*

WILL JOHNSON: No one knew the territory better than this young cowboy who was dead broke from trying to ranch this dry, remote country. He needed the money the army offered him to find out where Pancho Villa hid. But Will Johnson was no army regular—he wouldn't salute, he wouldn't follow orders, and he didn't relish killing. He'd sleep with the enemy if he had to . . . or just for the hell of it. . . .

ELISA GRIENSEN: Pancho Villa had claimed this blonde trophy for his bed, not knowing the German beauty was really a specialist in pillow talk and playing a dangerous game of espionage. But she had to please her brutal lover to spy on him, and it wasn't until an American cowboy treated her like a lady that she begin to let her heart feel . . . and her guard down. . . .

LT. GEORGE PATTON: Young and ambitious, the hot-headed officer sometimes let his emotions rule, but he was smart, fearless, and tough as armor plate. He saw the potential in America's new war machines . . . and was determined to win Pershing's approval by leading America's first mechanized charge. . . .

"At times humorous, at times brutal, and at all times earthy, *PANCHO AND BLACK JACK* grips the reader from the first page with its rousing account of Pershing's pursuit of Pancho Villa across the deserts and mountains of Chihuahua."

—Elmer Kelton, five-time Spur Award–winning author

HERR MILNOR: Cruelty was his profession, and this German agent had made Elisa a whore and a spy. He told her which lovers to take and which to use, and he thought she was his to control—until she met the cowboy named Will Johnson. Trying to divert America from entering the Great War, Milnor had a role to play in Germany's grand plan . . . and he was cast as the ultimate villain. . . .

TASKER BLISS: President Woodrow Wilson's Deputy Chief of Staff, he felt Pancho Villa, the most dangerous of Mexican revolutionaries, had to be stopped. But it had been hard to convince the pacifist President to send Pershing across the border. Now Bliss was up to his neck in trouble because five prisoners from Villa's supposed raid on New Mexico said Villa didn't do it. . . .

"With *PANCHO AND BLACK JACK*, Fred Bean has reached a new plateau. It will twist your mind and even crack your neck a little. Read this one without delay. You can't help but enjoy the action and enlightenment."
—Max Evans, author of *Bluefeather Fellini*

Books by Fred Bean

Pancho and Black Jack*
Rivers West: The Pecos River
Guns on the Cimarron
Border Justice
Trail's End
Range War
Blood Trail
Gunfight at Eagle Springs
Law of the Gun
Renegade
Santa Fe Showdown
The Last Warrior
Killing Season
Hard Luck
Hangman's Legacy
Tom Spoon
Bloody Sunday
Cry of the Wolf

*Published by POCKET BOOKS

PANCHO and BLACK JACK

FRED BEAN

POCKET BOOKS

New York   London   Toronto   Sydney   Tokyo   Singapore

An *Original* Publication of POCKET BOOKS

POCKET BOOKS, a division of Simon & Schuster Inc.
1230 Avenue of the Americas, New York, NY 10020

ISBN: 0-671-88691-6

First Pocket Books printing July 1995

10 9 8 7 6 5 4 3 2 1

POCKET and colophon are registered trademarks of Simon & Schuster Inc.

Cover art by Darryl Zudeck

Printed in the U.S.A.

PANCHO and BLACK JACK

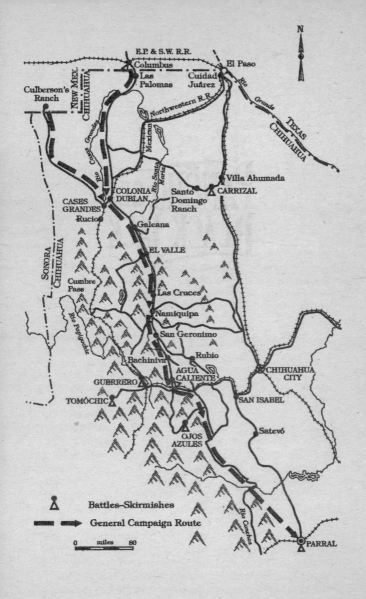

. Introduction .

On the night of March 9, 1916, only a few minutes past midnight, a barbed-wire fence was cut three miles south of the sleepy town of Columbus, New Mexico. Telegraph wires failed to attract the notice of sixty five American soldiers guarding the Texas-Mexico border a short distance away. A few miles to the west, none of the 151 men commanded by Major Elmer Lindsley, also charged with guarding the international boundary, were aware that the unthinkable was about to take place—an invasion onto American soil by a hostile army. Unthinkable because Camp Furlong, an army encampment that was home to the Thirteenth Cavalry Regiment, was just south of the railroad tracks passing through Columbus. Columbus was nothing more than a collection of small adobe and frame houses, a few stores, a bank and a hotel, crowded along a single caliche road running from Palomas in Chihuahua to Deming, New Mexico. Hardly the expected place for an invasion, most everyone agreed. The skeptics would soon be proven wrong.

Colonel Candelario Cervantes, some reports later stated, silently led five hundred mounted revolutionary soldiers through the gap in the fence—some mere schoolboys the age of twelve who only the day before had been attending classes in Chihuahua—toward Columbus and a contingent of U.S. Cavalry armed with some of the most modern weaponry in the world, including French-made Benet-Mercies machine guns. On the surface it appeared to be an act of utter madness, for the invaders were said to be followers of the acknowledged master tactician of the Mexican revolution, the infamous Pancho Villa. During six years

1

of bloody warfare, Villa had demonstrated an uncanny knack for knowing when and where to strike an enemy, earning him the nickname Lion of the North. He was said to be fearless, clever, a brilliant guerrilla strategist. So why would he send a poorly equipped fighting force into the teeth of the American war machine? No one believed he would.

A mile south of Columbus the raiders divided into two columns, one to strike the heart of Camp Furlong, the other to sack the town. What the invaders hoped to gain is still something of a mystery, but what happened next is recorded in the annals of American military history.

Colonel Herbert J. Slocum, the regiment's commanding officer, was sleeping soundly. For weeks there had been rumors of movement near the border by Pancho Villa's raiders, so he had doubled the guard along the fence marking the international boundary. More than two hundred heavily armed men watched this section of the border day and night, leaving three hundred and fifty soldiers to protect Columbus, although Slocum could not imagine why anyone would be interested in the town. He regarded Columbus as a hellhole, of no consequence to an invading army. There wasn't enough booty to interest Villa, of that he was sure.

Lieutenant John Lucas stirred in his sleep, awakened by the sounds of moving horses. He glanced at his pocket watch in the starlight from a bedroom window. It was four-thirty. Looking through the window, he could make out the shadowy forms of men wearing broad-brimmed sombreros. Suddenly wide awake, he reached for his .45 automatic and crept to the back door, only to discover that his small house was surrounded by Mexican guerrillas, each shadowy form bristling with a rifle barrel.

At almost the same time, a sleepy-eyed guard at Headquarters Building in Camp Furlong heard noises from the south. The night was pitch black, and the guard squinted into the inky darkness to see what was making the sounds. Unable to identify anything, he raised his Springfield rifle and shouted, "Who goes there?" He got an answer, although certainly not one he expected.

A thunderous explosion rocked the night silence. A .44

caliber bullet entered the guard's stomach, shattering his spine. When he fell against Headquarters Building, he glimpsed the dim outline of a sombrero-clad horseman only a few yards away. As he slid down the wall he took hurried aim and fired his rifle. The roar of the Springfield seemed distant and far away. He collapsed on his rump beside the building, watching the Mexican topple from the saddle. Then his vision blurred and his eyes batted shut.

Lieutenant Jim Castleman bolted upright in bed when he heard the pair of gunshots. He grabbed his pistol and raced out the back door of his shack. Thirty yards away, a man in a drooping sombrero was dismounting from the back of a pinto horse with a rifle in his hands. Castleman stumbled to a halt and fired.

The Mexican spun away from his frightened horse, a strangled scream caught in his throat. His knees buckled. He went down slowly, choking, landing facedown on the hardpan with a bullet hole through his neck.

A sudden burst of heavy gunfire from across the tracks in Columbus brought dozens of soldiers from barracks doorways and field tents. Castleman shouted, "Bring your rifles!" as he took off in a lumbering run toward town. He ran less than twenty paces before a hail of bullets surrounded him. Bright yellow muzzle flashes winked from another direction, the southern perimeter of Camp Furlong. The noise—the heavy thud of rifles and the lighter chatter of pistols—was deafening. Castleman fell to the ground, whistling lead all around him. A slug plowed a tiny furrow in the caliche near his face, sending grit and dust into his eyes, blinding him briefly. Behind him, men from K Troop began returning fire in rapid bursts. Blinking furiously, he found it was too dark to see a target where the shooting was coming from. Men pouring from the barracks and tents shouted to each other between volleys, asking who was firing at them. All was utter confusion. Castleman prayed that his men weren't shooting at each other.

A private from K Troop stumbled and fell alongside Castleman. "Who the hell's shootin' at us!" the terrified soldier asked, his voice shrill with fright.

Castleman pointed to the dead Mexican a few yards away. "Bandits!" he cried above the booming noise of the guns.

The private aimed his Springfield into the dark. "Bet it's Pancho Villa!" he shouted back, firing at a fading muzzle flash beyond the row of tents housing F Troop, wincing when the rifle blast hurt his ears.

An unexpected lull slowed the shooting. Castleman jumped to his feet, crying, "Forward to the town!" Across the tracks in Columbus, there was no slackening in the staccato of gunfire.

Men from K Troop scrambled to their feet to follow Lieutenant Castleman. At almost the same time, Lieutenant John Lucas ran barefoot toward the barracks housing the machine-gun troop and the guard shack where the Mercies machine guns were kept under lock and key. Lucas passed Castleman and his men in the dark. Fleeting mounted shadows swirled around the encampment, firing at will. Now and then, Lucas heard the piercing cries of the wounded and dying. Spent bullets whacked into the sides and roofs of clapboard barracks, thumping dully when they struck canvas tent walls. It was the first action for most soldiers at Camp Furlong, and it came all at once, in the dark of night, rousing terrified young recruits from sound slumber to the eerie cacophony of battle sounds.

Lucas dodged and darted to the shack and fumbled with the padlock while men from the machine-gun troop struggled into pants and boots. A first sergeant and a corporal were among the first men to reach the shack as the door swung open.

"What the hell is going on?" the sergeant asked, looking wide-eyed over his shoulder.

Lucas, still panting from his dash across the compound, handed him a Benet and four cartridge clips. "Mexican bandits. Probably Villa's men. Start shooting anyone wearing a sombrero. Pass out the rest of the guns and do it quick!"

Armed with a machine gun weighing twenty-seven pounds, Lucas took off for the railroad tracks, almost stumbling into a group of mounted Mexicans about to make the same crossing. He knelt and fitted a clip into the feed slot at the side of the receiver and cocked the gun, his hands trembling. Remembering the fierce recoil of the Benet, he

4

tightened his grip and aimed for the riders, then pulled the trigger.

A stream of bullets blasted from the machine gun's mouth, accompanied by a series of heavy explosions. He was jolted backward by each shot, ruining his aim. It felt as though a mule had kicked him. Spent shell casings flew, tinkling hollowly around the lieutenant's feet, as four of the raiders were torn from their saddles. A horse bearing a fifth rider crumpled, whickering with pain, the flesh across its croup split to the bone. Other horses lunged against their bridle bits to escape the ear-splitting noise. A rider was unseated, tossed sideways when his horse bolted. He fell on his back across one iron rail—Lucas heard the unmistakable crack of bone when he paused to aim in another direction.

A soldier with a machine gun raced up to Lucas, whirling around when pounding hooves sounded from the west. His Benet roared, the string of bullets seemingly endless, its recoil knocking him back a few steps. Running horses fell. Men shouted and screamed, falling from saddles into a growing pile of downed horses and dead or wounded men. Thirty rounds quickly produced a deadly toll before the clip was empty. The machine gun was only accurate when properly set up on its folding barrel forks, yet the soldier's aim had been remarkable, perhaps the product of fear. A wounded horse tried vainly to rise on a shattered foreleg, falling back to the ground with each failed attempt, bawling with pain and terror. Another horse thrashed helplessly on the hardpan, dark blood pouring from a hole in its side. A Mexican set out to crawl away from the flailing hooves, just as the corporal beside Lucas inserted a fresh cartridge clip. The wounded man had crawled less than six feet from his dying horse when a short burst from the Benet jolted through him, flipping him over on his back.

"The town!" Lucas cried. Increasing volleys of gunfire echoed back and forth across Columbus. A fire glowed orange from the rear of a store beside the bank, flames licking higher into the night sky. The dark outlines of mounted men in sombreros raced back and forth between the railroad tracks and the fire. Guns popped and cracked in unison. At times, the shooting grew so heavy that it became a single sound, a wall of noise akin to exploding dynamite that seemed to shake the ground where Lucas and the corporal stood.

Somewhere near the Palomas road, a machine gun came to life. Then two more Benets burst forth strings of molten lead, becoming a deadly trio of barking voices pouring bullets into the invaders.

Lieutenant Lucas took off at a run, crouching as he led the corporal across the tracks. The whine of lead added a singsong to the battle sounds when it passed above them. Men were shouting and cursing. Soldiers from K and F troops could be seen racing among the adobe huts and clapboard shacks east of the train station. A dead horse lay across the iron rails where the road crossed the tracks. When Lucas glanced over his shoulder, another group of attacking Mexicans came galloping across the dark parade ground of the encampment, when suddenly several Benets opened fire from the shadows among the barracks. Men and horses went down in twos and threes, forming a grisly heap around the flagpole in front of post headquarters. Wounded raiders cried out as they fell. A crippled horse floundered a few yards more on three legs, spilling its rider before crashing to the ground on its chest, bawling pitifully when it landed and forcing Lucas to turn away from the sight, his stomach churning.

A second fire flickered. One wall of the ramshackle hotel across the street from the bank was quickly illuminated by flames. Lieutenant Lucas ran faster, leaving the winded young corporal behind. A woman screamed somewhere in the heart of town. Guns roared from all sides now, the rhythmic thump of machine guns near the compound and the pounding of rifles across Columbus. At the railroad crossing, three men from the machine-gun troop ran up the street, then fell down to set the forks, firing irregular bursts from their Benets. Lanterns brightened behind windows of the adobe huts and wooden shacks when the noise awakened everyone—Columbus had no electricity yet and oil lamps were the only source of light.

Running alongside the tracks, Lucas was soon out of breath. Fear knotted his belly as bullets flew all around him.

His right shoulder throbbed from having used the Benet improperly. Few men had the strength to hold and fire one while standing, and yet somehow he and the corporal had.

He saw the silhouettes of a band of mounted Mexicans galloping behind the stores and shops on the west side of the road, a few carrying torches. Diving to the ground, he extended the barrel forks and took careful aim, surrounded by the din of endless gunfire. When he pulled the trigger his Benet stuttered, drowning out every other sound. The dim outlines of men and horses began to fall until his cartridge clip was empty. As he was taking a fresh clip from his waistband, one of the falling shadows suddenly became engulfed by flames when it struck the ground. A rider bearing a torch ignited a clay jug of kerosene tied to his saddle that shattered when his horse fell. Both man and animal were instantly engulfed by a giant ball of orange flame. The downed horse leapt to its feet, its rider still clinging to the saddle despite the fall, fire consuming the horse's chestnut coat and the Mexican aboard its back. The raider, a boy of fourteen from Chihuahua City, slapped his burning coatsleeves helplessly, a ghostly apparition inside the flaming inferno. His horse bounded forward in spite of a useless hock mangled by a machine-gun shell, trying to escape the searing pain of burning kerosene. Lucas watched the nightmarish scene, frozen by the horror of it. His heartbeat seemed to stop altogether until the flaming horse and rider went down a second time.

The rattle of machine-gun fire to his left awakened Lucas from his grim trance. Another group of galloping horsemen charged among the scattered adobes west of the road. The corporal with the Benet, his machine-gun forks resting on a railroad tie, fired into their midst in sporadic bursts. Lucas swung his sights and cocked the machine gun, swallowing bitter bile, trying to forget what he had just witnessed. War was supposed to be hell, he thought. He found a target among the deeper shadows around the adobes and squeezed the trigger gently, prepared for the jarring recoil when the stock slammed into his sore shoulder.

Two riders, one wearing an odd, cone-shaped sombrero, were lifted from their saddles as though they had sprouted wings. Good aim had spared their horses, until the corporal let loose with a spray of bullets that cut down animals and men moving among the huts. Wounded horses screamed. A thin voice wailed as a horse collapsed underneath a young raider. The corporal's cartridge clip emptied, sending thirty deadly rounds through all manner of living flesh, some slugs ricocheting off sun-dried adobe walls amid a shower of pale dust billowing into gently rolling clouds hovering above the masses of bullet-torn bodies. The corporal, caught up in a strange killing frenzy that sometimes befalls men driven by unreasoning fear during battle, cried out, "Yahoo!" when he saw the carnage his Benet had wrought. Lucas grimaced and turned his head. Tonight, quite suddenly, everything around him was utter madness, his worst nightmares becoming grim reality.

Smoke from the fires drifted across the railroad tracks where Lucas lay, still gasping for breath. He was sure he could smell burning flesh and would not look at the spot where the flaming horse and rider had fallen. Gunshots thundered from the business district and behind him, echoing back and forth across Camp Furlong. More machine guns rattled now as the men trained with the Benets took up firing positions.

The clapboard two-story hotel was fully ablaze, casting bright yellow light and dancing shadows upon the buildings of Columbus, providing gunmen on both sides of the fight a better chance to find targets. He could see a number of riderless horses milled about, nickering to each other, seeking ways to flee the noise and the smell of death, turned back when guns exploded in their path only to be turned again when they chose another direction where men were fighting. Lucas knew the death toll would be high when the shooting finally stopped. This was no mere border skirmish —it was a full-fledged war between armies that was sure to awaken slumbering Americans to the growing threat brewing in revolution-torn Mexico. Attention had been on the war in Europe. Until now.

Light from the fires at the Lemmon & Romney grocery and the Commercial Hotel grew stronger as the flames spread. Looking over his shoulder, Lucas saw a huge contingent of Mexicans enter the stable area at Camp Furlong to drive off some of the corralled horses. Volleys of withering rifle fire from the barracks cut down many of the raiders. Shooting erupted at the mess shacks, the deep, throaty blasts of shotguns. Men in sombreros dashed from adobe kitchens, easily within range of Lucas's Benet. Squirming around, he drew a bead on a group of running Mexicans and opened fire. Three men dropped immediately. Two more staggered and fell. A sixth went down on his hands and knees until Lucas sprayed him with bullets, knocking him flat, facedown.

In Columbus, a hail of bullets turned the invaders away from the bank. Some wheeled their horses in retreat, only to be shot down by deadly crossfire from shadows between buildings. Lucas heard the clatter of hooves and glanced that way. A full-scale retreat had begun from the center of town. Mounted men spurred relentlessly to abandon the fight, heading back to the south, shouting to each other in Spanish. Mexicans attacking the encampment started to withdraw, and the din of gunfire slowed to sporadic shooting.

Colonel Slocum, watching the fight from a point south of the tracks, was approached by a running officer. "Shall we go after them, sir?" the soldier cried.

Slocum nodded his assent, apparently speechless after viewing the pitched battle no one expected. The officer, Major Frank Tompkins, wheeled and raced for the stables, shouting to every man within hearing distance to saddle a horse for the chase to the border.

Leading H Troop and several men from F Troop, Major Tompkins gave chase. The retreating Mexicans placed a rear guard on a low hill below the border fence, opening fire when Tompkins led his men within range. Tompkins ordered his men to dismount and shoot anything that moved. A fierce gunfight ended the lives of thirty Mexicans without a single American casualty. Two raiders slipped away from the hill alive, one badly wounded, as dawn brightened the eastern sky.

Only then did Major Tompkins realize he was on Mexican soil. He sent a request for orders back to Colonel Slocum. A short time later the messenger brought back permission for Tompkins's men to continue the chase until the invading army was safely driven off. Riding at the head of his troops,

Tompkins rode south through Palomas at a gallop. The Mexicans had retreated further until, twenty miles from the border fence, Tompkins ordered a halt to return to Camp Furlong, satisfied that the invaders would not come back.

On the ride back to Columbus, almost a hundred dead Mexicans were counted along the road, many dying from wounds suffered earlier during the attack. Crippled horses wandered through the mesquite brush, slowly bleeding to death. It was a scene Frank Tompkins knew he would never forget.

Returning to Camp Furlong about noon, he found a pile of bodies aflame in a huge funeral pyre near the edge of town. A member of the disposal detachment informed the major that the corpses of sixty-eight raiders had been set ablaze with lamp oil by Major Slocum's order. He was also informed that eighteen American lives had been lost during the fight, including ten civilians, some of them women. Only nine raiders had been captured, and to a man, they were seriously wounded. The business district of Columbus had been gutted by the fires, leaving only fire-blackened skeletons where walls once stood. Heaps of ash still smoldered, rendering a thick gray pall of smoke above what was left of the stores and the hotel. Shattered windows were everywhere. Adobes were pockmarked with bullet scars.

A night telephone operator managed to get word of the attack to Deming while the raid was in progress. By morning, news of the invasion had reached Washington. President Woodrow Wilson was informed shortly before noon. He ordered a Cabinet meeting for the following day, knowing full well what the vote would be. The army would be dispatched to Mexico to punish the revolutionaries. The brazen bandit Francisco "Pancho" Villa must be brought to task for his crime against the United States. Even the peace-loving Wilson understood that something had to be done.

• 1 •

Doroteo Arango stirred beneath the bedsheet, opening his golden brown eyes, eyes some said were the color of a cat's eyes when viewed in just the right light. He studied the ceiling briefly, blinking away sleep fog, remembering last night's romp with the pretty girl sleeping beside him. She was a beauty, a tall, shapely blonde with long, curvaceous legs and ripe breasts, her nipples the same pink as rose petals. Ah, but was he not the envy of his *soldados* for bedding her? He could see it on their faces, in the looks Candelario and even the stoic Julio gave him when he left them to spend a night at Elisa's house. All men who saw her desired her, and yet it was only he who could claim her whenever he wanted. She was like clay in his hands, eager to do his bidding, begging him to stay when duty or a desire to see another woman called him away. Bedding many beautiful women was a part of his public image, as well as something he needed continuously to satisfy his ravenous lust for lovemaking. Secretly, he never really cared deeply for any of them, not Elisa, not even pretty Luz Corral who bore him two children. It was no accident that Luz lived in Chihuahua City while Elisa lived in Parral. And there were others almost as dear in many more villages across Chihuahua and Durango, many beautiful young women who were at his beck and call whenever he visited them.

He lay on his back for a time, idly watching flyspecks on the adobe ceiling and walls. Bedroom curtains lifted slowly in lazy currents of mountain air whispering across the Sierras at dawn. He had difficult plans to make, tough decisions, but they could wait until he was finished with the German girl. He also needed a few days of rest. For weeks

11

they had been crisscrossing the state of Chihuahua, eluding the patrols Venustiano Carranza sent out into the mountains to try to track them down. But they would never find him, and he knew this with absolute certainty, unless someone close to him betrayed him to the *Federales*. Such a betrayal was quite possible, however, for he was surrounded by many greedy, ambitious men. It was a never-ending task, trying to find out who was loyal to the cause for reasons of the heart, and who was only pretending to be a true follower of the revolution.

Most intelligent men were very clever, able to disguise their real feelings, and it was an intelligent man he should truly fear, not the simple *peóns* who fought for him so willingly without ever questioning an order. The poor farmers and stockmen who became the best soldiers for the revolution believed in the cause—and much more than that: They believed in the man who led them, in his invincibility. They called him *el León del Norte,* the Lion of the North. They believed he could not be defeated by any army in the world. Superhuman powers were often attributed to him by those inclined toward superstition, and even the doubtful had to admit he was a man's man, both in a gun battle and with the ladies.

It was this image he cultivated, which only added to his growing popularity among the poor. And even *un idiota* could count on his fingers and toes; there were a hundred times more poor people in Mexico than *los ricos*. In a country at war, a wise man sought the support of the impoverished masses who could easily be incited to rise up against oppression masterminded by a handful of rich men. This would soon be the dilemma of Venustiano Carranza, president of Mexico's de facto government, when all of the country's poor rose up against him in a united effort to drive him from power. It was this union of effort that was lacking, as Emiliano Zapata fought Carranza in the south while the far less numerous followers of Doroteo, calling himself Pancho Villa now, nipped his flanks from the north. There were other revolutionary factions, all making a grab for the presidency of Mexico, some who even now claimed it publicly while Carranza's larger armies kept them continually on the run. Should one strong man, an instinctive leader, come forward to unite them and lead them to victory on all fronts, Carranza would fall and his successor would be a president with the popular support of the people.

Staring blankly at the flyspecks above him, Doroteo knew who that man would be. Making just the right moves, *el León del Norte* could soon become ruler of all of Mexico if things went according to plan. If no Judas stabbed him in the back before his time. Doroteo would make it his personal responsibility to ferret out the Judas, since there was no one else who could be completely trusted among his closest associates and confidants, not even Rudolfo Fierro, his bodyguard.

He looked over at the woman. She slept on her stomach, and this position robbed him of the pleasure of fondling her breasts. He loved big-breasted women, when the breasts were firm and high, youthful. Luz once had firm young breasts, until their first child was born. Now her bosom sagged like half-spent toy balloons, scarred forever by ugly stretch marks. She was still a pretty girl, though permanently disfigured, and he only slept with her occasionally when he paid a visit to see the children.

He seized Elisa's shoulder and pushed her over roughly, as though in anger, then he pulled down the sheet until it covered only the tops of her thighs. She awakened suddenly, her eyelids fluttering over emerald pupils, fumbling for the hem of the sheet with sleep-numbed fingers as if she meant to pull it back over her.

"Leave it down!" he snapped in Spanish, cupping a callused palm over her right breast. He took her nipple between his thumb and forefinger, rolling it back and forth, pinching until it grew hard, twisting.

Elisa turned to him, half her face buried in the pillow. She smiled, then her forehead furrowed slightly when she felt pain, until the subtle beginnings of pleasure spread from her nipple and a stronger sensation awakened in her groin.

"Will you ever have enough of me?" she asked in a whisper, speaking fluent Spanish with only the hint of an accent. "Last night you took me so many times I lost count."

A humorless grin raised the corners of his mustache when he heard this admission, for it was further proof of his manliness to make love to a woman many times. Most women would deny that rough, frequent intercourse fulfilled them, made them feel more content or fully satisfied. But not Elisa, and perhaps this was part of the special attraction he felt toward her. No matter how many times he took her, or how rough the treatment, she always told him how pleasurable it was, how perfect. No amount of pain could make her cringe from him, not even when he slapped her face with enough force to knock her to the floor, or ground one of her nipples between his teeth until he drew blood. Those deep green eyes still beckoned to him, asking for more, begging for him to continue until his lust abated. He knew she wanted a real man to make love to her any way he wanted. Although she never said so, he knew pain was a part of her deepest pleasure, bringing her to great heights, before she experienced a powerful release that turned her muscles hard and brought a cry from her throat. Hearing that cry always brought him to a climax. He liked the sound of it, liked knowing that he could hurt her in this wonderful way.

"I want you again," he told her gruffly, "and this time—" He was interrupted by the distant sound of galloping horses, and the pounding hoofbeats brought him fully alert, wary of danger. Two men were stationed outside the house, skilled *pistoleros* who knew how to use their guns if trouble arrived. Elisa's house was far from the village, in the foothills, and it was early for anyone to be running a horse way out here unless there was a very good reason. He let go of her nipple and rolled out of bed to take his pistol from the nightstand. Cocking his head toward an open window, he listened to the approaching horses for a moment, then hurried from the bedroom to peer through the front door before the unexpected visitors arrived.

Below a cloud of yellow dust, four riders wearing dusty sombreros spurred their mounts up the lane toward the house. Doroteo recognized them and lowered the .45 Remington revolver to his side.

"Who is it?" the girl asked from the bedroom as she quickly donned her cotton sleeping dress, worry making her voice sound strained.

He answered over his shoulder without taking his eyes from the horsemen. "It is only Ramon and a few others. Stay inside." He walked out on the front porch completely naked as the riders came to the fence around Elisa's yard, more concerned by the reason for their haste than being seen without his clothes. Slanting shafts of morning sunshine struck him when he stood on the top step, his pistol dangling beside his bare leg only inches from his plumcolored genitals. Sunlight gave his wavy hair a reddish tint, a clue to his Tarahumara Indian ancestry.

Lathered horses bounded to a halt near the fence. Both his personal bodyguards were also watching the four men dismount. Ramon Salas, his spurs rattling over droughthardened earth, trotted to the porch with a worried expression clouding his bearded face.

"Jefe!" he cried. "Someone has attacked the *Americano* town named Columbus! Someone heard the story over a two-way radio in Texas and telephoned the news to Parral!" Out of breath, Ramon paused to collect himself. "There was a terrible battle with the *gringo* soldiers and many on both sides were killed. But here is the strangest part, *Jefe.* . . . The radio said that you were the one who led this raid across the border yesterday, that papers were found on some of the dead, letters from you calling on the poor people of Chihuahua to follow you in a fight with the *Americano* army. We are being blamed for what happened there! It is *muy loco* for anyone to think we would be so foolish!" Then, as though for the first time, Ramon noticed that Doroteo was naked, his eyes falling to the exposed genitals for a moment, returning quickly to the face looming above him, embarrassed that his gaze had wandered thusly.

The news Ramon brought struck Doroteo to the bone. It was outlandish enough that anyone would brazenly attack an American military outpost, but far more puzzling was the bit of information that he was being blamed for it. He had written no such letters inciting the poor to fight the Americans or anyone else. Who would do such a thing? "Perhaps the one who telephoned was mistaken. Surely it is a mistake in the translation."

Ramon wagged his head. "There is no mistake, *Jefe.* I asked again and again. People in Columbus have sworn they saw you there. Now everyone believes the *Americano* army will come after us, to punish us for the attack across the border, even though we were not there."

It was quite possible. The powerful Americans were not likely to ignore such a violation of their boundaries. The American people would demand retribution for it, and now, with absolute clarity, Doroteo suddenly understood what had happened. "They will come," he agreed, fingering his pistol grips while thinking aloud, "like a swarm of hungry ants. Carranza will permit it, a crossing by the United States Army into Mexico, for he knows they will try to do what he cannot accomplish on his own. The Americans will help him look for us. Very soon all of Chihuahua will be crawling with thousands of American soldiers. We will be hunted down like dogs, pursued to every corner of the earth."

"And we are so few now, *Jefe,*" Ramon added softly, for he also understood the gravity of what was about to happen. "The people of Mexico will be very frightened when so many *Americano* soldiers come, for they will fear that it is an invasion of our country, that the *Americanos* mean to occupy Mexico and take control of the government. The poor people will not understand what is happening. They will worry that they might lose their small farms to the invaders. It could be a terrible time for all of us. Only a few brave men will join us now, for the others will be afraid of the mighty *Americano* armies, their big cannons and the machine guns. Only you can put a stop to it, *Jefe,* by announcing to everyone that we are innocent of the attack across the border, that we were here in Parral when it happened."

Doroteo was quickly seeing events in an entirely different way, as a plan began to take shape in his mind. If he were to publicly denounce any responsibility, only a few would believe him and the American invasion would surely come anyway. Carranza would welcome help in putting a stop to the revolutionary movement in the north, allowing him to concentrate his forces against Zapata in the south. Doroteo now suspected Venustiano Carranza was behind the clever ruse to blame revolutionaries for what happened at Columbus.

But Carranza's treachery might backfire if the man who was being blamed were to accept this false guilt, for it was the loyalty and sympathy of the Mexican poor Doroteo needed most. They were his strength, and in the north, he was their champion. If they viewed this battle with American soldiers as an act of uncommon bravery, facing far superior manpower and weaponry with little more than raw courage, it could just as easily rally *more* followers around him. A brave underdog always found widespread sympathy in Mexico among the desperately poor, for they themselves were born to roles as underdogs, their part in the old caste system that had gripped Mexico for centuries. It would be risky, taking the blame for what happened at Columbus, but there was a chance this unexpected event might focus nationwide—even worldwide—attention on the bitter struggle being led by the man who called himself Francisco "Pancho" Villa. Attention to his cause could also bring an added infusion of foreign money. Even now the German government was sending secret payments to Doroteo and Emiliano Zapata, as insurance to protect German interests in Mexico should the de facto government fall.

He looked down at Ramon, knowing a simple man would never understand this complicated logic. "For now, say nothing to anyone about it. Everyone is to remain silent. These are my orders. I must have time to think about this problem, and what will happen to the people of Chihuahua whom I love so dearly. It is our people we must consider, for they are our countrymen, the reason we risk our lives to challenge the evil rule of Carranza. It is my duty to do what is best for them, in what is sure to be a difficult situation. Pass the order of total silence among the men who wait for me in Parral. No one is to say anything about where we were the day of the attack. I will come down to the village later, when I am finished satisfying the woman. Then I will think about what to do when the Americans come."

At that, Ramon grinned weakly. *"Sí, Jefe.* Satisfying the woman is also very important. We will wait for you at the little cantina, and I will repeat the order you have given, that no one is to reveal where we have been."

Doroteo watched Ramon turn and plod slowly across the yard to mount his horse, yet at the same time his mind was dealing feverishly with other matters and he paid little attention to the men as they wheeled and rode away. He wondered if he had just been handed a great opportunity to win what had become a demoralizing war against the

Federales of Venustiano Carranza. Of late it had become harder than ever to recruit men of fighting age from the dry cornfields and goat pastures of Chihuahua. Most everyone knew, even the simplest *peón,* that the revolution was losing momentum. This action, undoubtedly by the hand of Carranza, could be the catalyst Doroteo needed to bring the whole country behind him. He looked up at the sky idly, wondering if *Dios* Himself had just handed him the moment of glory he had been praying for, all of Mexico's poor united under his leadership.

A soft sound behind him made him whirl around suddenly with his gun leveled. Then he relaxed, lowering the weapon, when he saw Elisa standing in the doorway.

"Something terrible has happened," the woman said, as if she understood without being told.

His eyes wandered down the front of her gown, taking note of rounded places. The beginnings of an erection pulsed slowly in his groin as he looked at the outlines of her breasts. "Go inside," he commanded sharply. "I am not finished with you yet."

He cast a final, wary glance over the empty hills around the house, then he nodded silently to one of his bodyguards, Rudolfo Fierro, a mustachioed killer nicknamed "the Butcher" for dozens of bloody slayings he had performed at Doroteo's request.

Rudolfo, standing quietly beside an oak tree in a corner of the yard, returned the nod, his hands resting on a brace of pistols at his waist. No one would disturb Doroteo until he was finished with the woman unless they were willing to pay dearly for it.

• 2 •

John Joseph Pershing paced back and forth across his office at Fort Bliss, hands clasped tightly behind his back, square jaw jutted. He had been planning the expedition for three days, and since his orders had arrived from Major General Fredrick Funston at Southern Command Headquarters in San Antonio, Brigadier General Pershing had hardly slept at all, eating little, consumed by the task at hand. Finding Pancho Villa in the wilds of Chihuahua would be like looking for the proverbial needle in the haystack. Only a carefully executed cavalry campaign of the kind he'd led at Pine Ridge in South Dakota against the last Sioux uprising stood any chance at all of success. Even then it would be a game of chess, requiring planned strategy he'd learned at West Point, and much more: the common sense he'd acquired by experience in Cuba and the Philippines.

Yet the lessons he'd learned as a shavetail in Arizona during the manhunt for Geronimo might be the most valuable here, for in many ways the guerrilla tactics of Villa were not unlike the crafty maneuverings of Geronimo. With only a handful of fighting men, Geronimo had eluded thousands of cavalry in the field, showing up where he couldn't possibly be, never where the limits of human endurance said he must be at the time. Pershing had never forgotten the amazement when he and the rest of his weary cavalrymen learned that Geronimo had somehow defied all logic in crossing impossible distances over equally impossible and almost impassable terrain to strike where no one had believed he could. Villa had earned a similar reputation in Mexico while leading his famed Dorados throughout the Sierras, outnumbered and usually outgunned, yet still winning decisive battles and then falling back, disappearing altogether at times, scattering his forces like the wily Geronimo, making it harder to track him.

Pershing remembered his meeting with Villa and General Alvaro Obregon in August of '14 at the International Bridge between El Paso and Juarez. At the time, he hadn't thought much of Villa personally, neither impressed nor disappointed by his appearance and manner. Back then Villa and Obregon were regarded as friends of the United States, allies against what was then viewed by the War Department as a troublesome insurrection by far more radical men bent on toppling the government in Mexico City. Now Villa was the enemy. Pershing's orders were to find him and punish him for the brutal attack on Columbus. Every available soldier and piece of war materiel in the country was at his disposal, and the campaign strategy was his personal responsibility. If only he could put his mind to it and forget the lingering agony of his recent past.

The terrible fire had changed him, as anyone might expect it should. His loving wife, Frances, and three beautiful daughters had all been lost to the flames. He had been uneasy from the very beginning about leaving them in the Presidio near San Francisco, after orders had come for him to report to Fort Bliss in El Paso with 3,500 men, to take charge of guarding a sector of the increasingly restless Mexican border. Leaving his family behind went against his better judgment, but he had done so anyway because he hadn't had the time to secure proper quarters for them at Bliss. His orders had said to report at once, and as always, he'd followed his orders to the letter whenever he could. Then on the night of August 26, 1915, just over six long, painful months before, fire had claimed his wife, their firstborn, Helen Elizabeth, Anne, and tiny Mary Margaret, leaving their only son the sole survivor. The boy had somehow been spared, rescued by a fireman, the only member of Pershing's family he had left. Warren was with Pershing's sister now, lovingly nurtured through his recurring nightmares about the fire by May, who doted over Warren as much as his father. Was it any wonder he had difficulty keeping his mind on the punitive expedition to find Villa? How could anyone be expected to recover his faculties in so short a time after such a devastating loss as his?

Yet he knew he must, for he was first and foremost a soldier. All his adult life had been spent preparing for advances in rank, and this campaign was a stepping stone toward the very top. The eyes of the nation, perhaps even the eyes of the entire world, were on this forthcoming military effort. President Woodrow Wilson had kept America out of the fighting in Europe with a "watch and wait" policy. But now a real threat had come to American soil, and even the peacemaker Wilson could not ignore the attack on Columbus. Pershing would be commanding the campaign, and at all costs, it must go well. His career depended on it. He had been hand-picked over the more logical choice, Fred Funston, and now those who had insisted upon John Pershing expected quick and sure results from their choice for leadership in such an important military matter.

One bit of news, however, would cripple the most logical strategy to capture Villa. The expeditionary force was forbidden to use the Mexican Northwestern Railway upon orders from President Wilson, and that fact would severely limit what Pershing hoped to do. Villa was most certainly pushing south as rapidly as his horses could travel. A train loaded with cavalrymen could cut him off, for the Mexican Northwestern tracks ran from El Paso to both Colonia Dublan and much farther south, to Chihuahua City. Villa could be caught in a vise if men could be deployed south and east of his logical escape route. One vital thing Pershing remembered from the Indian campaigns was that horsemen had to stay close to water for their animals. The Rio Santa Maria valley was Villa's only real choice if he fled in a southerly direction. But denied use of the railroad to cut him off, Pershing knew he would be forced to chase Villa from the rear, a much less desirable alternative. They would have to hunt Villa on his home turf. Almost all Chihuahuan citizens were Villa sympathizers; thus good information about his comings and goings would be hard to come by. The solution lay in securing reliable scouts and skillful trackers.

The best trackers in the world, Pershing believed, were Apache Indians. Peaceful Apaches had helped the army track down Geronimo. The general had already instructed his aide, Lieutenant Collins, to send for twenty of the most experienced Apache trackers from reservations in Arizona. In addition, he'd sent for Lemuel Spilsbury, a Mormon living in northern Chihuahua who knew the territory. Spilsbury had been asked to come to Fort Bliss immediately and to recommend others who could be employed as civilian scouts, men who knew the back roads of Chihuahua, men who could be trusted. Spilsbury was a reliable informant himself, but more scouts would be needed to guide the widely scattered patrols necessary to locate Villa in the vast Sierra Madre range. Spilsbury had been due at the fort hours before, and Pershing bemoaned the delay as he paced faster across his office floor with an eye to the windows, growing more impatient, hardly noticing the preparations taking place beyond the parade ground: trucks being loaded with supplies, wagons and mule-drawn caissons being readied for the order to march toward Columbus.

A knock at the door halted him near his desk. He recognized the soft quality of the rapping and bade the sergeant to enter.

The sergeant peered around the door cautiously at first, then came smartly to attention, snapping off a salute before he spoke. "A Mr. Lemuel Spilsbury to see you, sir."

John supposed everyone on his personal staff knew the dark mood he was in since the terrible fire. "Send him in," he said quietly.

A gangling fellow with ropy limbs and a prominent Adam's apple, dressed in an ill-fitted black suit layered with alkali chalk, entered the office. The men knew each other from previous meetings to discuss border unrest. Lem grinned, offering his hand. "Hello, General."

They shook. "Thanks for coming, Mr. Spilsbury," Pershing said, pointing to a chair opposite the desk. "Would you care for some refreshment? Iced tea or lemonade?"

"No thanks," Lem replied, settling into his seat.

The sergeant was dismissed. "You know why I asked you to come," Pershing began gravely, sitting down and folding his hands on the desktop. "I hope you can suggest a few names, men we can contact who will act as guides for the expedition."

Lem shrugged and made a feeble attempt to wipe some of the chalky dust from his coatsleeves. "A few, maybe. One in particular knows might' near every inch of Chihuahua good as a Mexican, if he'll come. His name's Will Johnson. He lives down in Laredo and makes a living buying Mexican cattle for Texas ranchers. I know for a fact Will buys steers now and then from Pancho Villa's brother. He'll know as much about Villa's habits as anybody on this side of the border. Trouble is, he don't cotton to authority all that much. But he might take a job as a guide for the army if the pay was right. It's been a dry year and the cattle business has been suffering."

"I'll send him a wire this afternoon," the general said. "We must have experienced scouts for this campaign. The locals won't be cooperative. Villa is something of a hero in Chihuahua, and we shouldn't expect his people to betray his whereabouts to us. Our arrival will be unpopular, to say the least. Give me a list of every man you can think of who knows the area well. I've appointed Lieutenant James Shannon as my chief of scouts because he speaks Apache. I've asked for twenty Apache Indians, to complement the men you suggest as guides who know Chihuahua. Major Jim Ryan of the Thirteenth Cavalry will serve as my intelligence officer and coordinate all information gathering." Pershing picked up a pen and scribbled Will Johnson's name at the top of a pad. "Who else besides this Will Johnson in Laredo?" he asked, preferring to get right down to business, for time was running short. With the passing of every hour, Villa was getting farther away.

"There's William Lunt," Lem went on, spelling the last name. "A cowboy from Arizona by the name of C. E. Tracy; he travels Chihuahua now and then for some cow outfit. J. B. Barker has been pretty far down south around Parral. He comes through Colonia Dublan from time to time."

Pershing continued writing down names until Lem had finished his suggestions. "I'll have each of them contacted immediately," he said, coming to his feet abruptly when Lem offered nothing more.

Lem got up slowly, frowning a little. "You might have to make a pretty good offer to interest Will Johnson, but he'd be the best man for the job. He knows plenty of folks down yonder who might tell him the truth about where Villa is hiding. Folks who know Will trust him. His father got him started early in the livestock business down in Mexico when Will was just a pup. His word, and his money, has always been good. He speaks Yaqui and Spanish like a native, and he knows most of those mountains like the back of his hand."

Pershing eyed Lem carefully. "You'll help us too, won't you? I can authorize payment for your services at once. One hundred and fifty dollars a month and all your expenses, beginning immediately."

Lem nodded somewhat sheepishly. "I can use the money. It's been a dry year all over Chihuahua and our crops won't make much unless it rains. Because of all the trouble, many of our people have left Mexico. Neither side will defend us. The Carrancistas take what they want from our fruit orchards and our goat herds without paying, and the Villistas treat us no better because we are Americans. Those of us who remain are praying the difficulties will end soon. If they don't, the rest of us will be forced to go elsewhere to continue farming."

"If we can capture Villa and round up his army, peace will come," Pershing replied, tearing the list of names off his notepad to give it to Lieutenant Collins. "With your assistance we can put a stop to the hostilities. I fully intend to crush Villa and his rebel band soundly, Mr. Spilsbury. All you have to do is show us where he is."

They shook again before the General showed Lem from the office. He handed the list of names to Sergeant Carter in the waiting room, with instructions to carry it to Lieutenant Collins without any delay. A terse note scribbled at the bottom instructed what the lieutenant was to do with the names.

Lem was going out of the building as a young soldier wearing a second lieutenant's bars hurried through the door. When the boyish lieutenant saw Pershing, he came to attention and snapped off a crisp salute.

"Could I have a moment, General?"

Pershing sighed heavily. "We already discussed your request for a transfer, Lieutenant Patton. Twice, in fact. I'll give it careful consideration, but not today. I have a thousand other things on my mind just now."

"I could help with some of the details, sir," the eager-voiced soldier replied quickly, pleading with his eyes while his demeanor remained steady, confident.

Refusing to be sidetracked even briefly from the all-important recruitment of experienced civilian guides, Pershing's countenance grew stern. "Come back tomorrow," he said, turning on his heels abruptly and heading back down the hallway to his office. It wasn't that he disliked the brash young lieutenant who kept on asking to be assigned to the general's personal staff; it was the man's persistence that annoyed him. Day after day, since the orders had come to go after Villa, George Patton had continued to request a transfer from the Eighth Cavalry to Headquarters Command, in any capacity.

Pershing closed his office door and forgot about Patton, turning to other details more pressing. He intended to march into Mexico no later than the fifteenth of the month. Entirely too much was at stake to allow any further delays. Villa, like Geronimo, was on the move continually now; and hampered by the lack of railroad access, the American forces must do likewise as quickly as possible if they meant to corral him.

Pershing sat in his creaking wooden swivel chair, facing one window without truly seeing what lay beyond it. Lem Spilsbury, a man who could be trusted, put a great deal of faith in this Will Johnson from Laredo. Turning from the window, Pershing made himself a note to ask Lieutenant Collins about Johnson's reply to the army's offer as soon as it was known. Everything hinged on having experienced guides at the head of his flying columns. Villa knew the terrain intimately and so must the men who led the American pursuit; it was a lesson the U.S. Cavalry had learned when they ultimately captured the wily human tiger, Geronimo.

Drumming his fingers on his desk, Pershing's thoughts drifted back to the fire and what it had taken from him, despite his wish not to think of it again when there was so much to be done. . . .

· 3 ·

When he got off the train at a siding near the gates to Fort Bliss hardly anyone noticed him. There was nothing remarkable about his appearance to attract attention—he had a stocky frame and average height despite unusually bowed legs, which were relatively common among cowboy types in the Southwest. He wore faded denims and runover cowboy boots needing polish as well as a flat-brimmed Stetson encircled by sweat stains, pulled low in the front to shield his eyes from the west Texas sun. He walked with an awkward gait due to his bowed legs, not quite a swagger, as though the absence of a horse between his knees restricted his mobility. He was twenty-six and a veteran of the Texas-Mexico border country, a native of the harsh desert surrounding Laredo in south Texas. His travels had taken him across most of northern Mexico and, in particular, the state of Chihuahua.

He was regarded as something of an expert on livestock, he supposed, and often served as a guide and interpreter for American cattle buyers who sought the rugged *corriente* cows of Mexico for their propensity to gain weight quickly on better grazing in more moderate climes. He spoke Spanish fluently without trace of an Anglo accent and two Indian dialects. He knew his way around the small villages in Chihuahua, and he knew the people, their customs and their ways. He had been summoned to Fort Bliss by Brigadier General John Joseph Pershing, upon recommendation by Lem Spilsbury, an old friend, to serve as guide for an expedition into the heart of the Chihuahuan desert.

His name was William Lee Johnson; he preferred to be called Will. As he walked to the gates of Fort Bliss shouldering his traveling gear, his deeply tanned face registered dislike for what he saw. He had little regard for military men, the senseless marching, the following of orders given by men who had more stripes on their shirtsleeves. Over a number of years, summing up the total of his experience with soldiers on either side of the border, he had come to the conclusion that armies were places of refuge for the helpless.

At a guardhouse beside the fort gates he was stopped by a young soldier, as was everyone else who sought entry without a uniform. Before saying a word he took a soiled telegram from his shirt pocket and handed it to the guard, resting his bedroll and war bag on the ground to wait for the wire to be read. Beyond the gates, squads of men marched back and forth across a dusty compound. Coughing, sputtering, chain-drive trucks sent clouds of yellow caliche dust skyward into gusty March winds as they moved slowly between rows of barracks and warehouses to the accompaniment of droning engines and creaking springs. Will also mistrusted internal combustion engines, preferring the dependability of a range-bred horse. In his experience automobiles stopped running at the most inopportune times, mostly on remote stretches of road where no one knew how to fix them. And now there were aeroplanes equipped with the same unreliable power source, and he'd be damned if he would ever ride in one. Horses and trains took him wherever he needed to go without once being stranded. A time or two he had watched the flight of an aeroplane, considering what it would be like to fall from the skies when the motor stopped, thus permanently erasing any curiosity he had about traveling in one.

"It says here you're to report to General Pershing at once," the guard said briskly, turning to point a finger in the right direction.

Will's expression remained flat. "I hardly ever do anything at once, soldier, but you can tell me where to go."

The guard's face showed brief irritation. He regarded Will's rumpled appearance with obvious disdain. "The big building at the center of the compound, Mr. Johnson. Show this wire at the front door and you'll be taken to General Pershing."

He took the telegram and folded it into his pocket. "Much

obliged," he muttered, picking up his gear, thinking about his saddle in the baggage car, wondering if the army could manage to lose it somewhere between the rail siding and the general's office.

He trudged slowly through the gates, pondering what this stint with the U.S. Army would be like. If he were any judge of events, no good would come of it. He was being hired to guide an expedition seeking Pancho Villa after the raid on Columbus, New Mexico, which Villa had supposedly led. The newspapers had been full of details and the outrage Americans felt when their border was violated and eighteen citizens killed by a brazen revolutionary leader. When Will had first heard about it, none of it made any sense. He had witnessed Villa's clever tactics for a number of years while negotiating cattle deals in Chihuahua, the raids by Villa's famed Dorados that always confounded Carranza's larger, better-equipped armies. Right from the start Will had found it hard to believe that a brilliant tactician like Villa would lead his undersized force right under the noses of a U.S. Army encampment outside Columbus to loot and plunder a small, impoverished New Mexico town. What was to be gained? Besides that, it was widely known across northern Mexico that the Ravel Brothers store at Columbus was smuggling guns to the Villistas, so why would Villa raid the same small town from which he was being supplied with badly needed arms?

Crossing the parade ground, he stopped to watch a squad of marching infantrymen pass before him. He shook his head when his gaze fell to the lockstep. "Looks like a bunch of toy soldiers," he muttered, his glance moving to the flat-brimmed campaign hats, olive-drab uniforms, the shouldered rifles.

The squad marched past, little swirls of caliche coming from their boots. Shouldering his bag, he continued toward the headquarters building, noting that the flag atop a pole at the center of the parade ground stood out straight. He climbed the steps to where a pair of guards flanked the doorway, taking the telegram from his pocket again. "I'm here to see General Pershing," he said tonelessly as one soldier took the message and opened it.

"He's in a meetin' right now," the guard said. "He'll be another half hour or so."

Will noticed a large, open-walled tent west of the parade ground where a few men idled around tables over bottles of beer. "I'll be over there cuttin' the dust from my throat," he said when the wire was handed back. "Kindly tell the general I'm here."

Without waiting for a reply, he went down the steps and headed for the tent. A blast of wind swept across the hardpan and he slitted his eyes to keep out the grit. He sauntered into the shade below the canvas roof, paying only passing attention to the khaki-clad men at the tables. Behind a makeshift bar, a pink-cheeked young soldier watched him approach.

"Gimme a beer," Will said, dropping his gear near his feet. A truck roared past the tent, sending a rolling cloud of caliche across the men at the tables. They hardly seemed to notice.

"That'll be ten cents," the barman said in a thin, tinny voice as he placed an icy brown bottle of Harper's on the warped plank between them.

Will tossed a dime on the bar and picked up the bottle, enjoying the feel of cold glass against his palm. He took a drink and felt the chilled liquid slide down his throat. "That's better," he said to himself.

He noticed the bartender staring at him. The boy smiled.

"Are you one of the scouts?" he asked. "Four of 'em got here yesterday. They was real Indians. Apaches, somebody said. I reckon you know Gen'l Pershing was the one who chased down ol' Geronimo."

"I didn't know that," Will replied. He was surprised to learn that some of the scouts Pershing had hired were Indians. It was, perhaps, an indication that Pershing had more sense than the average army officer. It wouldn't matter much, really. What would an Apache know about Mexico? If a few of the northern Yaquis could be persuaded to act as scouts, the campaign stood a better chance of success. The trouble would come from Villa sympathizers in Chihuahua, mostly impoverished *campesinos* who saw Villa as their champion, the man who sided with the poor. His good deeds—robbing rich land owners, giving some of the spoils to the needy—were widely known among the desperately poor across the northern Mexican states. Thus he had the support and fierce loyalty of most Mexican villagers in Chihuahua. Information as to his whereabouts would be hard to come by. False reports would be commonplace. If the army listened to them, the expedition would surely fail.

Will had a passing acquaintance with Villa, hardly more than the exchange of a few words and a handshake, some years earlier. Villa was an affable sort on the surface, but those who knew him well described another side, a vengeful, mistrustful man with a penchant for incredible violence toward his enemies or those whom he suspected of betraying him.

"You never did say if you was a scout," the barman said.

Will fixed him with a steely look. "No, I sure didn't," he replied dryly, hoisting the bottle to drink again.

He turned his back on the inquisitive bartender to stare blankly across the parade ground at big warehouses where dozens of trucks were being loaded by squads of uniformed men. Wind fluttered the tent roof above him as his thoughts wandered to the expedition. Fifty miles south of the border, the Sierra Madre Occidental rose to heights of ten thousand feet. Before they even reached the mountains, trucks would have a difficult time maneuvering the deep desert sands without bogging down. Climbing into the Sierra Madres would be next to impossible in a loaded truck, for there were few roads good enough for horse-drawn wagons. Automobiles would have the same problems. These were things he meant to discuss with the general.

If Villa, a superb horseman, was to be caught, it would have to be done with mounted cavalry. Will hoped General Pershing would understand the nature of the country. As a veteran of the Indian wars, he surely would know this. Geronimo would still be a free man if the army had pursued him in automobiles and trucks. Another enemy of the internal combustion engine was the unyielding heat of the Chihuahuan desert. Motors heated up and simply stopped running. Slowed down by overheated engines and repeated mechanical failure, Pershing would never get close to the elusive Villistas on horseback. The expedition would be doomed right from the start. If the U.S. Army meant to go after Villa riding motorized equipment, they needed mechanics more desperately than scouts.

Will downed the rest of his beer. Fort Bliss was a beehive of activity as it prepared for the expedition into Mexico. Down at the stables, perhaps thirty or forty horseshoers were nailing iron to trimmed hooves. Will thought about what the desert would do to the army's sleek, grain-fed horses. In only a matter of days the animals would be gaunt-flanked skeletons unless a string of feed wagons accompanied the march. There was precious little grazing in northern Chihuahua most any season, and *vaqueros* complained more loudly this year than ever that a drought was starving cattle in the arid regions.

American cattle buyers were staying away from purchasing weakened animals in Mexico, so Will had agreed to accept the army's offer of one hundred fifty dollars a month to help scout for the expedition. Cattle buyers wouldn't need his services until Mexico got some rain. As much as Will disliked the army, any army, he needed to make a pay day. Lemuel Spilsbury, a Mormon guide living in Mexico near Santo Domingo Ranch, had recommended Will to Pershing's chief of scouts. Thus the telegram had come, the message he carried in his pocket. He would be working for the U.S. Army until the cattle market improved or until the expedition to punish Villa ended.

A cavalry patrol trotted along the perimeter of the parade ground in orderly columns of two. Every trooper in the detail was black. Someone had told Will before boarding the train at Laredo that Pershing had earned the nickname "Black Jack" for having led a command comprised of Negro soldiers during the Indian campaigns. Will had little experience with black men, for they were as unwelcome in most of south Texas as they were in some other parts of the South, where whites still remembered the War between the States. Will's father had fought for the Confederacy, and Negroes were a subject Lee Johnson never discussed without bitter enmity creeping into his voice. And so, like many other white sons of the South, Will's feelings toward blacks could hardly be called impartial, even though he'd really never known a black man.

Three uniformed men walked out the front door of the headquarters building, donning their campaign hats, but a sudden gust of wind lifted one from a soldier's head and he gave chase. Will shouldered his bag and bedroll, as the meeting in the general's office was apparently over. Walking out into the sunshine, he squinted to keep out the glare, wondering what Brigadier General John Joseph Pershing would be like.

At the front door the guard waved him in. "Office at the back," he said. "The sergeant inside will show you."

Inside, he faced a desk at which a solemn-faced soldier was seated.

"I'm next to see the general," Will said.

"Says who?" the sergeant asked gruffly.

"I reckon the general himself," Will replied, removing the wire from his pocket again. "It says to report at once, so that oughta make me next, the way I see it."

The burly sergeant scowled at the telegram, then he stood up and walked around the desk. "Follow me," he said, his rigid spine reminding Will of a bed slat as he walked behind the sergeant down a narrow hallway.

When they came to a door at the end of the hall, the sergeant knocked gently, as though he'd been scolded for knocking too hard in the past.

"Enter," a muffled voice intoned.

Will was shown into a large room, its walls decorated with framed photographs of aeroplanes and various other military scenes. Will approached a big mahogany desk littered with paperwork. Behind the desk, a pair of deep gray eyes watched him carefully below a thinning shock of blond-gray hair. The man stood up to offer a handshake. "I am John Pershing," he said.

Will took the general's hand. "Will Johnson. I took the next train, as soon as I got your second wire about the pay."

"I received your answering telegram, Mr. Johnson. You come highly recommended by Lem Spilsbury. Please be seated. If all goes well, we intend to leave for Camp Furlong tomorrow morning, then directly into Chihuahua. I have orders from General Funston to proceed at once, just as soon as my command is adequately supplied."

There it is again, Will thought, the expression "at once."

He took a chair, thinking that he'd never seen an army that could accomplish anything "all at once." He made a brief study of the general's face. "If you aim to supply your men with those trucks I saw outside, you'd better be ready for trouble."

"Why is that?" Pershing asked, frowning slightly, adding crow's feet to the wrinkles around his eyes.

"They can't travel in deep sand, General. They'll bog down in the flats before we ever get to the mountains."

"You've had experience with motorized vehicles in the Chihuahuan desert, Mr. Johnson?"

"I've seen 'em stuck to the axles. Been asked to help pull them out with the horse I was ridin'. That sand is mighty deep in spots down where we're headed. I figure Villa will be down around Parral. He feels safer there. There's a white woman, a real pretty German gal by the name of Elisa Griensen, who lives there. Villa likes her, so I'm told. He trusts her. Some claim they suspect she works for the German government, but I doubt anybody knows for sure. That country down around Parral is some of the roughest in Mexico. Those trucks of yours ain't likely to cross the desert, an' if they do, they can't climb the mountains we'll have to cross. Hardly any roads to follow."

Pershing's full attention was fixed on Will now. "Do you know Villa personally?"

"We met a time or two. He don't trust *gringos*."

The general's gaze wandered. "I met him once. He came here with General Obregon. At the time he seemed agreeable enough, but that was a couple of years back. That's his picture over on the wall, the three of us posing at the bridge to Juarez."

Will did not turn around to view the photograph. "I know what he looks like, General. If he seemed agreeable, it's because that's what he wanted you to think."

Pershing's stare returned to Will's face. "The Jeffrey Quads will make it to Parral, Mr. Johnson. They have four-wheel drive. And if the others don't, we have engineers. We'll build roads if we have to. This command represents the most advanced mechanized army in the world. We'll have a squadron of JN-2 aeroplanes to gather intelligence for us. We're taking Vickers-Maxim howitzers with a range of five thousand yards. Villa's men are poorly armed, by any comparison. When we find them, we'll easily crush them. At present count, I'm taking eight thousand soldiers into Mexico to corral Villa, and our intelligence estimates give him no more than five hundred men. I expect this expedition to be short and decisive. Villa simply must be punished for attacking Columbus, and I fully expect to do it quickly."

"Findin' him is gonna be the problem," Will said, irritated by the general's attitude. He knew nothing about the terrain between the border and Parral, nothing about the rocky, unforgiving Sierra Madres where Villa would hide. "He intends to fight you like an Indian, I suppose because he's an Indian himself. If we get too close, he'll order his men to scatter in twos and threes. You try to track them all down to find him an' you'll be there for the rest of your life. They'll join up someplace else and start all over again. It ain't gonna be easy, findin' him on his home range where he knows the back trails."

"We have it on good authority that Pancho Villa is Mexican, not an Indian," Pershing insisted, his scowl deepening. "He was born in Chihuahua City to Mexican parents, where he used to run a small butcher shop. His father was a small-time bandit who also went by the name Pancho Villa."

Will wagged his head side to side. Hardly any of the army's information about Villa was accurate. "Your authorities, whoever they are, are dead wrong. I've negotiated the sale of thousands of head of *corriente* steers from his brother, Antonio. Villa's real name is Doroteo Arango. His mother was an Indian from the Tarahumara tribe, his father a part-blood Spaniard, part Indian. His Tarahumara blood is the reason he has curly reddish hair. He was born down in Durango, at a little village named Rio Grande. He's no kin to the old cow thief who called himself Pancho Villa. When the old cattle rustler died, Doroteo adopted his name, I reckon because he was stealin' cows himself right about then. His brother told me the story one time when I was down in Durango buyin' steers. The butcher shop in Chihuahua City was nothin' more than a place where stolen beef was sold. There aren't any brands on a skinned hindquarter.

"The problem's gonna be that Villa knows every back road and hidden canyon in the territory. He could hide right under your nose and you'd never find him. Most every poor farmer and goat herder in northern Mexico is willing to help him hide out, 'specially from a *gringo* army since nearly all of them have got no use for rich Americans. Villa is a champion for the poor, an' damn near everybody down there believes in him. He's smart. With eight thousand men, maybe even twice that number, we'll be lucky if we find him. That mountain range is one hell of a big place if you ain't never seen it."

Pershing stiffened a little, annoyed. "I've made arrangements for twenty Apache scouts. I'm familiar with Indian warfare, and Apaches are the best trackers on earth, in my opinion. I was with the campaign to find Geronimo. The Sierra Madre Occidental can't be any worse than the Dragoons."

Will shrugged. "Never been to the Dragoons, but a truck won't have an easy time of it tryin' to get to Parral. It's better'n five hundred miles from the border, an' I'd wager it's five hundred of the roughest miles anywhere. If I was you, I'd bring my own gasoline. If they've got any down there, they won't sell it to a *gringo* who's chasin' Pancho Villa."

"A full supply column will accompany us, Mr. Johnson. You have been employed to lead us to Villa, and that is all that's expected of you. Lemuel Spilsbury told my chief intelligence officer, Major Ryan, that you were the best possible man for the job. Spilsbury is an honest man, and we trust his judgment in these matters. Find Villa for us and we'll do the rest. Incidentally, the need for cavalry is not lost on me in guerrilla warfare. We will be well mounted."

Will said nothing about his opinions concerning the army's stable-fed horses. Of just as much concern as the lack of grazing, native Mexican horses had developed immunities to diseases common to livestock south of the border, diseases that could spread through the Americans' horses like a prairie fire. "I'll do the best I can, General," he said. "When will you be ready to leave for Parral?"

Pershing glanced out an office window. "We start for Camp Furlong tomorrow morning. Without any unforeseen delays, we will advance in two columns toward Ascencion the fifteenth of this month. I will lead a contingent departing from Culberson Ranch. The second column and the supply companies will leave Camp Furlong at approximately the same hour. We've wasted too much time already in my estimation, but my orders were slow to come."

Will nodded and stood up, mildly amused by something the general had said. "I'll meet you at Culberson Ranch in two days," he said. "Meantime, I'll nose around an' see what I can learn at Palomas. They oughta have my horse unloaded off that cattle car by now, and I need to see to him and my saddle."

"We will supply you with whatever spare saddle horses you need, Mr. Johnson," Pershing said, getting up to shake again. "We'll be taking almost six thousand animals."

Will took the general's hand. "No thanks, General. If it's all the same to you, I'll buy a couple of local horses. I'm kinda particular about the horseflesh I ride. Habit, I reckon."

Pershing's irritation showed. "Very well, Mr. Johnson. I can give you an army voucher to purchase extra horses. Report to Major James Ryan at Culberson Ranch the morning of the fourteenth."

With purchase vouchers in his shirt pocket, Will walked out of the building into blinding midafternoon sunlight, weighing what he knew now about the expedition and its commanding officer. Pershing, he judged, was in his mid fifties, old enough to be seasoned to adversity. But what the general did not understand was the nature of the undertaking. Nor did he know enough about the terrain where they were headed. What had amused Will earlier seemed even more amusing now: Pershing's mention of "unforeseen delays." Every inch of Chihuahua would present Pershing's mechanized army with unforeseen delays, of a kind no man could imagine unless he had seen them for himself.

Walking across the parade ground, Will shook his head. In the coming weeks, perhaps even months, the U.S. Army would learn a valuable lesson. The region they meant to navigate was unforgiving. Mistakes often cost men their lives. Pancho Villa knew the land intimately. In a dark corner of his brain, Will doubted that the expedition would ever find him. Among some of the *campesinos* in the mountain villages, there was the belief that Villa had supernatural powers that enabled him to simply vanish into thin air.

• 4 •

He brought himself back abruptly from a chilling recollection of the house at Presidio, the black hole in the roof of the bungalow where fire had consumed it before the flames could be put out. John J. Pershing had insisted upon seeing the house the moment he left Warren's bedside at the hospital, against the advice of friends and his sister, May. All the way to San Francisco he had wanted to know if anything could have been done to save his wife and daughters. Visiting the site proved nothing and merely left him with another painful memory to add to what doctors had told him: that Frances and the girls had died of smoke inhalation. Warren had somehow survived by crawling down a smoke-filled hallway, where one of the firemen found him.

Pershing forced his attention back to the desktop, to lists of equipment, assorted maps of Chihuahua showing the few roads of any consequence known to mapmakers of the Mexican state, lists of needed supplies that kept growing by the hour—requiring that he add more wagon companies to yet another list—a roll of regiments and companies available for the first thrust of the campaign. A general estimate of the number of horses and mules. Reports on the number and make of trucks on hand, with names like Locomobile, White, Jeffrey Quad, Packard, Velies, and Peerless. Parts lists and a guess as to the number of mechanics needed to keep them moving. Piles of notes concerning other details.

At times like this the task seemed overwhelming. Had it been left entirely up to him, he would have mounted every available cavalry unit and taken off after Villa with only light field packs at the same hour his orders arrived. But his orders contained more than a simple directive to capture Villa. Four detailed declarations as to the purpose and conduct of the expedition had come from President Woodrow Wilson along with the order to march, so that all field commanders clearly understood the exact nature of the role American forces would play in Mexico.

By direct order of the President, first, if any organized body of troops of the de facto government of the republic of Mexico were met, they were to be treated with courtesy. Second, neither by act, word, or attitude of any American soldier was this expedition to become or be given the appearance of being hostile to the republic, for it was only by the courtesy of the Mexican government that the expedition was allowed to pursue an aggressor upon the peace of a neighbor. Third, if for any reason the attitude of any organized body of troops of the de facto government of Mexico appeared menacing, commanders of American forces were authorized only to place themselves in proper situation for defense, and defend themselves only if actually attacked, but in no event would they attack or become the aggressor. Fourth, care must be taken to have in a state of readiness a means of rapid communication between the front and the general commanding the War Department, in the event that any evidence of misunderstanding on the part of officials, civilian or military, of the de facto government of Mexico as to the object or character of the expedition should arise. Any evidence of misunderstanding would be taken up with the government of Mexico through the Department of State.

Pershing privately disagreed with Wilson's foreign policy in almost every aspect, especially when it came to dealings with Mexico. American policy had two fundamental short-comings, in his view. President Wilson had never correctly gauged the aspirations of Mexican revolutionaries such as Villa, Carranza, Obregon, and Zapata, believing they acted out of greed and avarice. He never understood the wave of nationalism that motivated the average Mexican or the revolutionary leaders who surfaced to challenge the long-standing system of oppression in Mexico. To make matters worse, Wilson was continually making weak efforts to settle a civil war without a convincing threat of armed intervention. He made vague suggestions that America might wield a mighty sword, but he never unsheathed it, making America appear vacillating when it came to foreign affairs. Pershing often wondered if it were wise to interfere politically in the affairs of other nations unless America was willing to see it through with force, if necessary. Now Wilson had no real choice but to use force in the pursuit of Villa.

Yet the president's directives to his field commanders were typically riddled with cautionary restrictions that were sure to hamstring the expedition, and the War Department was insisting upon setting up cumbersome bases of operation along supply lines into Chihuahua, requiring the movement of tons of materiel across unknown territory. The campaign was beginning to take on the appearance of a huge field test for untried American equipment. Aeroplanes unproven in high altitudes for intelligence gathering in mountain terrain and trucks built for hauling freight over smooth roadbeds were to be employed in what everyone knew was rugged country, miles of mostly uncharted desert and then a mountain range with ten-thousand-foot elevations. Even the civilian guide, Will Johnson, who knew the Sierras, said they were attempting an impossible feat.

Pershing supposed it was inevitable that during his lifetime there would be a merging between the old and the new, as America rapidly became an industrialized nation. He had been schooled in the old ways, how to win wars with mounted cavalry, armed with saber and rifle, until experience taught him later that bigger and better guns oftimes outweighed clever strategy. While in the Philippines he'd quickly learned that the best way to rout guerrillas from their mountain strongholds was to blast them out with heavy artillery. But considering the task he was given—of transporting thousands of tons of war machinery over a mostly roadless wilderness—he would have preferred a return to proven methods. The option was not his, however. Chief of Staff Hugh Scott and others in the War Department wanted a fully complemented military campaign into the wilds of Chihuahua. Anything short of complete success would spell disaster for the expedition's field commander, John Pershing.

He scowled at a roll of regiments being prepared for the initial pursuit: the Seventh, Tenth, Eleventh, and Thirteenth Cavalry, besides men from the Sixth and Sixteenth Infantry and two batteries of artillery, along with engineers, field hospitals, and a detachment from the Signal Corps with battery-operated radios having a useful range of less than twenty-five miles. Then the First Aero Squadron, comprised of eight JN-2 aeroplanes with ninety-horsepower Curtiss engines, to fly reconnaissance—if they could get over the tops of the mountains, a fact some said was in doubt. America was far behind in the development of aeroplanes for military use. In France, both the Allies and the Central Powers had aeroplanes that could fire permanently mounted machine guns between rotations of the propeller. America had no such technology as yet. Pilots claimed the JN-2s, called Jennys, were scarcely airworthy, and they carried no firepower.

Again, Pershing was stricken with the notion that this campaign should be conducted from the back of a horse, although, with a mechanized army at his disposal, he deemed the idea somewhat romantic. Hadn't the guide, Johnson, also said that mounted cavalry was the wiser choice? At least they agreed on that subject.

He remembered the brief meeting with Will Johnson, finding a number of things about the man that irritated him. He seemed so damn sure of himself and his opinions, yet he was only twenty-six and couldn't possibly know as much about Mexico and Villa as he claimed. Or could he? Age was relative to a man's experience. One thing was certain: Whatever Johnson knew about remote parts of Chihuahua was significantly more than anyone on his staff at the moment. Until a more suitable alternative showed up, Pershing would have to rely on Will Johnson's savvy of the land.

Another man with a great deal of savvy when it came to horseback campaigns was due to arrive on the morrow. Colonel George A. Dodd of the Second Cavalry Brigade had been summoned by Pershing personally. George Dodd would replace James Irwin in command of the Seventh, at the front of one prong of Pershing's three-point attack plan into Chihuahua. Dodd was sixty-three, crusty, an old Indian fighter from the Pine Ridge days who continually chewed the stump of a cigar, but he was easily the most aggressive of the regimental commanders available. If anyone could ride Pancho Villa into the ground it was George Dodd. Putting Dodd on the proper trail was one of Pershing's top priorities. Perhaps the young guide from Laredo should be assigned to lead Dodd's men south. With a few Apaches, like old Es Ki Ben De, to read tracks, Dodd might stand the best chance of running Villa down from the rear.

Finding the trail Villa had taken south looked simple enough, for the Rio Santa Maria was the only watercourse shown on the maps. Unless there were others—Pershing should have asked Will Johnson about water in the Sierras during a dry year. Perhaps he knew of water holes and springs that would provide Villa with another route. The general made a mental note to ask when he saw Johnson at Culberson Ranch.

Gazing across the pile of paperwork before him, he ground his teeth silently. This wasn't his idea of generalship, being bound to a desk, besieged by a mountain of file folders and hastily scribbled notes. He found himself longing for nights spent under the stars, of which there would soon be plenty when the expedition was launched. Getting out in the open might help him forget about the fire, help ease the longing, soften the sting of so many pleasant memories about Frances and the girls. Seeing some action might lessen the hurting inside, make him think about it less.

A knock on the door awakened him from his trancelike state, and he straightened quickly in his chair. "Come in," he said, knowing it was Sergeant Carter by the knock.

"Some gentlemen from the press to see you, sir. A Mr. Floyd Gibbons of the *Chicago Tribune* and Mr. Frank Elser of *The New York Times.*"

"I don't want to see any reporters, Sergeant. I already told you I'm too busy for that now."

"Yes sir, but you also said the expedition needed automobiles, and both these gentlemen have offered the use of theirs in any way you see fit, just so long as they can accompany you into Chihuahua."

It was true, that the Dodge touring sedans had not arrived yet. He'd requested nine and been promptly told they were not all available at this time. Having the reporters along wouldn't be all that much trouble, and it would give him censorship over press releases coming from the front. Sighing, he put down his pen. "Tell them I'll see them in a few minutes," he said, taking a sheaf of notes and handing them to Carter. "See that those get to Lieutenant Collins right away, and tell him there will be more later."

"Yes sir," the sergeant replied. "And one more thing, sir. Second Lieutenant Patton has requested the first appointment with you tomorrow morning. Shall I give it to him?"

Pershing made a face. Patton was more persistent than a swarm of gnats. "I suppose so. Make it eight o'clock. The man's determined to worry me to death over a transfer. Give me five more minutes, Sergeant, then show the newspaper reporters in."

Pershing slumped in his chair again when the door closed. He had five minutes to decide if reporters would be allowed to join the expedition. With his military career riding on the outcome, it would be wise to have control over what they wrote about the campaign's successes and failures.

"Damn," he muttered under his breath, clamping his jaw in utter frustration when his glance happened to cross a photograph of Frances and the children he kept on his desk. He hadn't wanted to look at it now, but he could not put it away in a desk drawer as though they never existed.

Some weeks before he had promised himself he would shed no more tears for them. Despite that, his eyes watered briefly when he took his gaze from the family portrait. For a few minutes he stared out a window, allowing his agony to deepen, as he knew it must, before the scar across his soul would heal. Warren had been spared, he told himself, and he should take great comfort in that.

Footsteps sounded from the hallway. He assumed a posture befitting the leader of an important military operation, a stern face with which to greet the reporters, reminding himself that having good press in the weeks to come could prove to be a valuable asset, should for any reason his columns miss their objective. An unlikely prospect, that Villa would elude them completely, given the amount of preparation he was devoting to every conceivable detail.

• 5 •

Will found Poco in a cattle pen adjacent to the railroad siding. After a quick inspection of the gelding's legs, he was satisfied that the ride in the cattle car had not crippled his favorite trail horse. The sturdy *bayo* pony had carried him thousands of miles across Mexico without ever suffering so much as a limp, and Will trusted him. Unlike the cavalry's remount thoroughbred crosses, Poco was a descendant of the Steeldust line, horses bred for endurance and speed over short distances, toughness far beyond that of most saddle horses. They were more heavily muscled in the hindquarters, with a shorter croup and back, muscular gaskins and stifle joints that could withstand rough country. Poco had tiny foxlike ears and big, gentle eyes that bespoke intelligence. A nine-year-old, he was in the prime of his life.

Will entered the corral, dragging the cinch on his old Steiner saddle through the dust. He paused at Poco's head to scratch him behind an ear. "No more trains for a spell," he said quietly. "It saved you a hell of a lot of miles, and that general said he was in a hurry." He flung the blanket and saddle over the bay's withers and pulled the cinch. When his bedroll and war bag were tied in place, he slipped the bit in Poco's mouth and swung up. At the slight touch of a rein Poco whirled away from the fence and trotted out the corral gate, flicking his ears back and forth, snorting softly at the unfamiliar sights and smells around the army post. Will smiled unconsciously. Poco was a cowpony, unaccustomed to the noise of a city. He often shied when he encountered something he did not recognize, yet this trait, unwanted by some riders, was added value to men who rode wild, untamed country. Range-raised horses learned early that the scent of wolves and coyotes, rattlesnakes, cougars, and man-smell spelled danger. The man who broke a range horse found the job was never easy, but when the task was accomplished he owned an animal that would warn him when trouble lay ahead, for its senses were far keener than a man's.

Leaving Fort Bliss behind, he heeled Poco to a lope, headed for El Paso. John Abel, an old friend for many years, ran a livery not far from the international bridge. Abel would sell him the spare horses he needed and perhaps know more than most about Villa's favorite haunts. Abel was a veteran of the border, almost seventy years old by now, and he would know a great deal about what was really going on in Mexico.

Entering the outskirts of town, he rode past hundreds of windowless shacks where half-naked Mexican children watched him from shaded porches. Poco shied at clotheslines on either side of the road as gusts of wind flapped drying bedsheets and colorful garments hung from the lines. Burro carts and mule-drawn wagons labored along potholed sides streets and the main caliche road Will followed that would take him to the bridge crossing over to Juarez. Approaching the center of the business district, sleek carriages ferried the wealthy past adobe brick banks and stores. Main thoroughfares were crowded with traffic, and the city seemed alive with pedestrians. Among them, looking out of place in this predominantly Mexican border town, wandered American soldiers. Border cities had been heavily guarded since the beginning of the Mexican revolution, and El Paso, across the river from one of the worst trouble spots, had one of the largest contingents of American soldiers. Gunfire across the Rio Grande in Juarez was as common as guitar music. Stray bullets often flew over U.S. soil. Tensions had been rising along the border for several years now, and with Villa's raid on Columbus, anxieties were sure to be greater than ever.

Trotting Poco past the central plaza, Will swung west

down a side street to the El Paso livery. Before he pulled to a halt he spotted John Abel seated on a milking stool in the shade of an eave above the stable, whittling on a mesquite switch with his pocketknife.

"Howdy, John," Will said, climbing down from the saddle.

The old man tilted his head to see beyond his fallen hat brim, then he gave Will a toothless grin. "I'll declare, if it ain't Lee Johnson's boy. How've you been, Will? Drag up a bale of straw an' set fer a spell. What brings you so far west?"

Will sauntered over for a handshake, then to the barn, and leaned against the wall, resting a bootheel on a weathered plank, thumbing his hat back before he answered. "I've hired on to guide General Pershing through Chihuahua when he goes after Villa. We leave day after tomorrow, so the general says. There ain't been any cow business this spring. Too damn dry. It's a paycheck, I reckon."

Abel made a face. "It's a waste of goddamn money. Taxpayers' money, mine an' yours. They'd be better off chasin' butterflies with a sledgehammer. Have better luck too. You know it as well as anybody, Will. Villa's too smart to let 'em catch him. He's gonna be laughin' at you the whole time you're down there. If I was you, I'd take along some knittin' needles and plenty of yarn. You're liable to have more'n a hundred pair of socks before the army gives up and comes back."

"I can use the money," Will said, staring off at nothing in particular, thinking how right the old man probably was about the futility of Pershing's expedition. "My brother's had a hard year and he's got three kids to feed. I live on the place, so I feel sorta obligated. We're partners on those mother cows and their calves look like jackrabbits this spring, hardly as big as seed ticks. Won't be worth four dollars a head unless it rains. It's been so dry down south that no buyers are interested in *corrientes*. A government paycheck sounded mighty good to me."

Abel chuckled, wiping mesquite shavings from the legs of his faded denims. "It's like payin' yerself with your own taxes, if you ask me. But I understand hard times. Me an' your pa saw some mighty rough years back when we cowboyed together. Don't get me wrong. . . . I ain't faultin' you for takin' the job with the army. But you know as well as me they won't find Villa, not in a thousand years."

An overloaded truck rattled past the livery, weighted down with firewood. When John Abel saw the wood, he wagged his head and sighed. "This year they've cut down damn near every tree within a hundred miles to sell out at the fort. Won't be a goddamn shade tree left for a man to stand under. I got no use fer the army, which ain't no secret. Got my fill of it when I was a kid. Joined up with Hood when I was fifteen. Your pa was two years older, best I remember, when we went off to war."

"He didn't talk about it much," Will remembered.

The old man grunted. "Ain't many men like to talk 'bout misery." He gave Will a lingering stare. "How much do you know about that raid on Columbus?" he asked.

Will shrugged. "Just what I read in the newspapers."

Abel stopped his whittling and folded his pocketknife, then made another swipe with his hand to rid his lap of the shavings. "They claim it was Villa who led that raid," he began thoughtfully, his rheumy eyes watering a little as he continued. "But there's folks who know him who swear it wasn't him at-all that night. He was down in Parral when it happened, so they say. They say it was a bunch of Carrancistas who done it, carryin' papers to make it look like it was Villa's doings. There's some who claim that Carranza made a deal with the Germans to keep us busy chasin' Villa down in Mexico while the war is goin' on over in Europe. Carranza couldn't afford to declare outright war with us, so he made it look like Villa caused the trouble. President Carranza stands to gain both ways: . . . The American army gets rid of Villa for him, which he can't seem to manage with his own troops, an' he also gets a sweet deal with the Germans if they win the big war over yonder. A trade agreement, maybe. I know this feller from down in Mexico City who swears Carranza struck a deal with the German gov'ment. His sister is married to Carranza's cousin, and she overheard somethin' she wasn't supposed to hear."

"It could make sense," Will agreed, for he too had his doubts that a wily guerrilla fighter like Pancho Villa would have led such a small force into a direct confrontation with

American troops at Camp Furlong. Frontal attacks had never been Villa's style, not after his humbling defeat at Agua Prieta against well-entrenched Carrancistas a year earlier. "If Villa wanted weapons, all he needed was money. The Ravel brothers' store over at Columbus has been smugglin' him guns and ammunition for years, so why would he attack Columbus? There's at least a dozen banks north of the river that would have been easier to rob than the one at Columbus, probably with more money in 'em too. When I first heard about it, it didn't add up."

"It's a puzzlement," Abel said, "unless my *compadre* from Mexico City is right about the Germans and Carranza."

Will remembered the pretty German woman named Elisa Griensen who was said to be a close friend of Villa. Villa was a renowned womanizer. Could she be a spy for the German government, advising them of Villa's movements so that Carranza would know when to strike north of the border at a time when Villa would be blamed? Villa wouldn't be the first man to reveal secrets in the throes of lust. Perhaps it was a far-fetched theory, unless John Abel considered his source reliable. Then another thought occurred to Will: "If Villa didn't do it, why hasn't he denied it publicly? He always did like headlines. If he could prove he wasn't there and blame Carranza, why hasn't he done it? That might rally more support around him . . . win him more followers."

Abel's quick answer indicated he'd already considered the subject. "The Columbus raid made headlines all over the world. Folks who never heard of him before know his name now, an' some things about his cause, the reasons he's fightin' the gov'ment. It's my guess he's enjoyin' all the publicity, drawin' attention to himself. He'll win more followers this way, showin' he's brave enough to take on the big *gringo* army to the north with only a handful of men. *Campesinos* who hate rich Americans will cheer him for showin' so much courage. Some will join up with him to show their loyalty to the cause of the poor. Villa wins both ways, if he did it or if he wasn't there. Half the world knows about him, now an' he'll use that to his advantage. . . . Makes him look more powerful in Mexico, and elsewhere."

Will had to admit that everything Abel said made some sense. Villa was unpredictable, canny, a master of guerrilla tactics. The Constitutionalists under Venustiano Carranza could not defeat him no matter how many men they put in the field, and there were many other revolutionary factions to deal with. If Villa could be blamed for the Columbus raid, the U.S. Army was sure to send a punitive expedition like the one assembling now at Fort Bliss after him. If the Americans could capture Villa, it would remove a thorn from Carranza's side, even though an American invasion might infuriate many Mexican citizens. Carranza would have to be careful to appear to be straddling the fence in order to preserve national support if he was indeed behind the raid at Columbus. "I suppose your friend in Mexico City could be right. Either way, I don't figure we'll ever find Villa to learn the truth. He'll play cat and mouse with us all over Chihuahua. Probably have a good laugh when he sees all of General Pershing's trucks stuck in the desert, or hangin' off the side of those mountains on the way to Parral."

Abel shook his head knowingly, for he knew the Sierra Madres as well as Will from horse-buying excursions with Will's father back in wilder times. "Parral would be the best place to start lookin' fer him, only he's smart enough that he'll figure that too. He's got a thousand places where folks will hide him out. You're gonna have a job on your hands, Will, tryin' to find him. He won't be where you think he is, that's fer damn sure. But like you say, every man needs a payday when there's hungry mouths to feed. How's your brother, Raymond? Haven't seen him fer quite a spell."

"He's doin' okay. Rosa's gonna have another baby."

Abel chuckled, and there was a twinkle in his eye. "How come you never took a wife, Will? You always was the lady's man in the family."

Will looked down at his boots. "Never found a woman who could tolerate me bein' gone on cattle-buyin' trips for weeks at a time. Most females want a man who stays close to home."

Abel looked blankly at the horizon, lost in old memories, it would seem. "Your pa was a drifter. I used to josh him some about not bein' home long enough to plant seed in your ma when Raymond came along, like maybe it was like that time in the Bible when Mary come up with a child without no husband. Called it immaculate conception back then. Lee'd always get mad as hell when I was funnin' him about it. Your pa was a good cowman and he knew horses too, better'n most. You got that keen eye for livestock from your pa."

"It took some time," Will replied, remembering. "I bought a few snides now and then."

The old man laughed out loud. "I still get cheated every once in a while, son. You never get so smart in the horse-tradin' profession that another feller can't cheat your pants off if you get careless. A word of advice while you're down yonder in Mexico: Don't get careless around Villa. He'll kill you before you can blink if he thinks you're gettin' too close to him. If you know how to sleep with one eye open, I'd make it a regular habit in Chihuahua."

"I'll remember what you said. I came to see you because I need a couple of good horses that are wise to that country. I've got vouchers from the army to pay for 'em if you've got a couple I can use."

Abel was eyeing Poco while Will was talking. "I like the little cowpony you're ridin'. Deep through the heartgirth. He'll have plenty of bottom. Sound legs to boot. He'll cover them mountains without pullin' up lame. You've got your pa's eye fer horseflesh too, William Lee. I reckon I've got a pony or two that'll suit you in the corral out back. Come have a look. You can have the pick of the string."

Abel left his milking stool slowly, wincing as his knees straightened. He limped into the stable hallway, a limp Will didn't remember from the last time he'd seen the old man a couple of years ago.

In a wooden-plank corral behind the barn, Will counted nine horses and a small white pony less than twelve hands high at the withers. The pony would be a perfect first horse for his five-year-old nephew, Raymond Jr., Will's favorite among his brother's children. Junior, as he was called, followed Will all over the ranch when chores were done, calling out to Uncle Will to slow his steps until the boy could catch up. When Will was away on a cattle-buying trip, Junior asked about him almost daily until his return. In many ways it was like having a son without the full responsibility. Only to himself would Will admit to liking the closeness developing between them. "Is the white Yucatan pony gentle?" Will asked, examining the animal's legs for signs of old lameness. Judging by the sunken places above the pony's eyes it was carrying enough age, maybe fifteen years or so, to be well broken.

"Gentle as a lamb," Abel replied. "Solid broke too."

"It'd be for my nephew, Raymond's oldest boy."

"He'd fit the bill if the kid's old enough to hold reins."

"How much? He'd have to be cheap."

The old man frowned. "For Lee Johnson's grandson, even though he ain't here to know I done it, I'd take a bottle of good whiskey an' a handshake. Your pa done me a few favors. I reckon I owe him."

"Wouldn't seem right," Will protested, thinking about the look on Junior's face when he saw the pony. "I'd rather pay what he's worth."

"Take it or leave it," Abel said. "He's yours fer the whiskey, or he stays here."

Will chuckled. "It's done then. I'll tell the boy it's a gift from a friend of his grandpa." His gaze wandered to a blue roan gelding covered with brands on its flanks and shoulder. "The blue . . . is he sound on all four?"

"Sound as new money. Broke to the heart and the right kind fer the mountains. A six-year-old. Meskin-broke, so he's a little snorty to handle on the ground, but when you fork him he lowers his head and tends to business like he oughta. He'd be my pick of the bunch, him an' the sorrel yonder with the star in his forehead."

Will studied the sorrel a moment. A buckskin standing in a corner of the corral had more muscle in the right places. "I like the dun, if he's broke right."

Abel tried to hide the beginnings of a grin. "He'll pitch like hell on a cold mornin', but he's got more heart than most. I'll confess I was testin' you with the sorrel. Wanted to see if you was still sharp as you used to be. The sorrel's a stump-sucker, after you get him hot. Damn near pull a post out of the ground with his teeth. The sumbitch'll kick the pocket off your pants if you try to mount him careless. The dun's my second pick too. Take him an' the blue an' you won't be cussin' me whilst you're down in Chihuahua, 'cept on them cold mornin's I warned you about when you mount the dun. I'll take seventy-five apiece fer 'em. Was it anybody else, they'd cost a hundred."

Will took a voucher from his pocket. "I'll need halters so I can head an' tail them out to the post."

"Part of the trade, son," the old man replied, turning for the tack room inside the stable. "A cobbler don't sell boots without no heels on 'em. Horses have got to have halters."

Will cast a final glance at the white pony. "I'll be back in an hour or so with the whiskey. You'll have to hang on to the pony for me until I get back, whenever that'll be. I'll pay the board bill. I can't wait to see the boy's face when he sees the little horse and knows it's his. He'll light up like one of those electric lamps and smile like a possum eatin' a persimmon. Means I'll have to bring presents for Johnny and little Rosita too. I'm liable to need a wagon to haul 'em all home."

The old man looked over his shoulder as he hobbled through the barn. "You watch your ass down yonder, William Lee. Best you remember you ain't on no cow-buyin' trip this time. If Villa gets word you're leadin' the army after him, he'll send somebody to kill you if he can. You can take that guarantee to the bank. Don't trust nobody down there. Watch out fer a feller by the name of Fierro. I'd hate like hell to have to ship that white pony down to Laredo on the same railroad car carryin' yer coffin."

• 6 •

Doroteo watched each face carefully. Rudolfo Fierro stood behind him, powerful arms crossed over his chest with his back to the cantina wall, so he could keep an eye on the door and windows. Seated around the lamplit tables were some of Doroteo's closest associates, men who commanded divi-

sions of his army. Candelario Cervantes and Julio Cardenas
were there, along with others, all listening to him describe
the new opportunity he perceived in the future of the
revolution. They had come after midnight to the secret
meeting place in the tiny village of San Isabel, to hear their
leader's plan for the impending invasion by the American
army. To a man, each of them knew they would face
overwhelming odds and far superior weaponry when the
gringo soldiers entered Chihuahua. Doroteo had neither
denied nor taken responsibility for the Columbus raid
among this group of his officers, until now. He had decided
to let them wonder about it, certain in the knowledge that
the half dozen men who were with him that night and knew
the truth about where he had been would say nothing,
fearing for their lives if they went against his orders and told
anyone where he really was during the attack on Columbus.

"The people of Chihuahua will take up arms against
them!" he cried, shaking his fist and glaring around the
room. "Even the old men and the children will fight them
with grubbing hoes and hurl rocks at them when they come,
if they have no other weapons. No one will allow the great
Colossus to the north to intimidate them when these hated
Americans march across Mexican soil! Men will join us now
in numbers like never before. We must show them our
courage! The time has come for us to lead another attack
against Carranza at his weakest point. Thousands will join
us! The time has come to strike the Carrancistas when they
least expect it!"

Despite the fervor in his voice, he saw doubtful looks on
some important faces. Colonel Cervantes gazed around the
cantina to sample opinion, then he looked up at Doroteo.

"Where will you order this strike, *Jefe?*" he asked, sounding calm, only mildly interested.

Doroteo was prepared for the question. "At Guerrero.
The garrison there has machine guns, and guarded rooms
stocked with ammunition. The soldiers there have gotten
lazy. Many have not been paid for several months, and they
will have no heart for a fight. We will surprise them,
attacking just before dawn while they are still asleep in their
beds. Guerrero and San Isidro should fall easily into our
hands. We will seize their weapons and ammunition and

leave quickly, before the plodding Americans can get so far south. I do not expect the soldiers at Guerrero to put up much of a fight to hold either city. We take them by surprise, when neither the Carrancistas nor the Americans expect us to go on the offensive. They believe we are running for our lives now to hide in the mountains, until the Americans grow weary of searching for us."

Cervantes shrugged, looking around him for support. "You apparently did not expect much of a fight at Columbus, *Jefe*, and yet the reports say you lost almost two hundred men."

He had prepared for this objection as well, despite the fact that he truly knew very little about the battle. "We had so few weapons, while the *gringos* had many machine guns there. My men lacked battle experience, new recruits who were very young, and it was dark. Most were shot as they ran away from the fight. If only some of you had been there, *mi Dorados muy bravo,* things would have ended very differently that night. Someone, perhaps even one among you who is here now in this room, betrayed us to the *gringos.* They were expecting us when we got there, with the machine guns already in place to cut us down. They had been warned by a traitor among us, and I know his name, this Judas. When I confront him with his betrayal, I will kill him. He will die a slow, terrible death that is fitting for a traitor to our revolution."

A murmur spread softly through the cantina, whispers of concern for who the traitor might be. It amused Doroteo that he could arouse so much suspicion among them by claiming he had been betrayed at Columbus, explaining away the defeat so as not to appear foolhardy or lacking a good battle plan. Blaming someone as a traitor in their midst would make each of them more willing to attack Guerrero, thus demonstrating solid support for him as their leader rather than seeming reluctant, as a Judas might. He was counting on this strategy to convince them that a bold attack on the garrison at Guerrero was the best plan, at a time when the Americans and the *Federales* would think he was on the run with his tail between his legs, after taking a terrible whipping at the Columbus raid.

Only those few who knew the truth, perhaps just

Venustiano Carranza himself and one or two of his closest aides who actually performed the deception by posing as Villa's officers, carrying out Carranza's instructions while organizing the raid in Villa's name, might not be surprised when Guerrero was attacked. The secret would only be shared by a small handful of men on each side, and neither side would reveal it. If Doroteo could soundly crush the Guerrero garrison and capture the town and its weapons, attention around the world would be on the courageous revolutionaries led by Pancho Villa, who continued to fight for their beleaguered cause with the heart of a lion. Poor men from all over Mexico would abandon their fields and livestock to join the brave effort to overthrow Carrancista tyranny and an invasion by the much-despised *gringos,* who could be planning to permanently occupy Mexican soil.

General Julio Cardenas, who hailed from Namiquipa and knew the nearby garrison at Guerrero well, made a gesture, tenting his shoulders in a shrug. "It is true, *Jefe,* that there are many machine guns at Guerrero, but they could be used against us. If we attack them, it must be carefully planned in the utmost secrecy, and not in the presence of a traitor, who you say might even be in this room with us tonight. What will keep this same traitor from warning the *comandante* at Guerrero of our plans?"

Doroteo summoned his full height, squared his shoulders, then fixed the assemblage with a menacing stare. "Fear," he said evenly, passing his eyes over every man at the tables as he let a silence linger ominously. "Fear that I already know who he is and that I will cut out his heart." He gave the threat time to sink in, just in case there truly was an informant among them.

To avoid any hint of suspicion, not a soul stirred at any of the tables, nor did any man look askance when Doroteo's eyes fell on his face. In his heart, Doroteo believed the men gathered here were fiercely loyal to him, yet it always paid to be careful. As a precaution, at the last minute he would change some part of the battle plan, in case the Guerrero defenders knew the hour or from which direction the attack would begin.

"It would be a very brave thing indeed," Candelario agreed, "to attack the garrison instead of hiding from the

Americans. But even as slowly as the *gringo* soldiers will be crossing over the mountains, it leaves us precious little time to gather the experienced fighting men for a move against Guerrero. Some of our bravest Dorados are resting and hiding out at Rubio. Word can be sent to them quickly, and they can be trusted not to say anything about our plans."

Doroteo was forced to consider the actual amount of time they had to raise enough members of his widely scattered army for the march on Guerrero. The strike had to come quickly, in a week or less, if they were to be sure of pulling out with the spoils ahead of the advancing American columns. He looked at Candelario. "Ride to Rubio," he said, speaking gravely now that the decision had been reached. "Assemble as many men as you can and secure fresh horses. You will say only that we intend to be prepared for the American invasion when it comes, standing ready to defend our homeland from seizure and occupation. Let it be known that we will fight to the death to protect our farms and our herds from the greedy *gringos*. Remind the people of Rubio that it was the Americans who allowed Carranza to use their railroads against us, to carry troops to Agua Prieta across the United States where they waited for us, killing so many of our loyal followers with the help of *gringo* treachery. Send out a call for brave men who are not afraid of the invaders. Raise an army, and tell the people why we must fight the land-hungry *gringos*, so that our cornfields and farm animals can be spared for our children, and our childrens' children."

"*Viva* Villa!" someone shouted from the back of the room.

"*Viva la revolución!*" another man cried.

More shouts came from the tables. Some men stood up, shaking their fists in the air while voicing their avid support for the cause.

Inwardly, Doroteo smiled. His impassioned speech had worked wonders on the doubtful, those who harbored secret fears of the American invasion. Instead of retreating into the hills to hide until the *gringos* came, they were pledged to come out fighting, to strike a blow no one would expect at a well-supplied Carranza stronghold. He nodded to them and raised a hand for silence. "We will meet at Rubio in four days. Bring every weapon you can find, and good horses. Tell no one about our plan to attack Guerrero. Appeal to those who are afraid the Americans will take away everything they own, leaving them worse than beggars to prowl rubbish heaps for food."

Surrounded by a small group of his subordinates, Julio Cardenas was grinning as he listened to ideas for recruiting more men, and fervor for the raid began to swell infectiously throughout the cantina. Others filed out in twos and threes, talking among themselves. Each man who left the room nodded politely to Doroteo on his way out, until only Candelario, Julio, and Rudolfo Fierro remained.

Candelario paused near the door, his bushy eyebrows knitting with a trace of concern. "This traitor among us . . . who might he be?" he asked, keeping his voice low and sincere.

"Tell us, *Jefe,*" Julio urged in a whisper, glancing once to the darkened doorway leading to the street. "Give me the honor of killing him. If you know who he is, I will shoot him now, before he rides off to betray us again."

Thinking quickly that Julio and Candelario would feel better about the forthcoming raid if someone were sacrificed in their behalf as the Judas, he sought a name from among the men who were here tonight, someone whose life was unimportant to the future of the cause. He needed a scapegoat to satisfy two of his best field commanders. He remembered a face from Carrizal at the back of the room, and when the name came to him, he said quietly, "It is Jesus, I am sad to say."

"Jesus Torres?" Julio gasped, frowning in disbelief.

Doroteo shook his head, then he motioned to Rudolfo Fierro, who had been listening close by. "Take care of him now, Rudolfo," he said, feigning great reluctance, "before he rides away. Julio is right: It must be done tonight."

Rudolfo stepped outside, moving softly into the street on the balls of his feet, while men were mounting the horses tied to hitching rails along the darkened roadway.

Candelario was watching the door. "I cannot believe it was Jesus who betrayed us," he remarked sadly as, wagging his head from side to side, he briefly closing his eyes.

Julio said, "I never completely trusted him, perhaps. A quiet man, he said very little most of the time, though I hardly knew him."

"I too was surprised," Doroteo said, sounding grave while listening for the gunshot. "At first I could not believe it of Jesus." A soldier's life was about to be sacrificed for a good cause, he told himself. Many good men had died in the revolution for lesser reasons. It was important that Julio and Candelario believed the Judas in their midst had been unmasked: It would strengthen their belief in the success of the raid on Guerrero. The death of Jesus Torres was of no real consequence.

An explosion rocked San Isabel's main street, echoing off storefronts, followed by a scream. Horses snorted in alarm, and then startled voices asked, "What is happening? Who has been shot?"

Candelario had been the only one to flinch when the gun went off, something Doroteo took note of with disappointment, for it showed too much sensitivity, a weakness brave leaders could not afford in wartime. He had granted Candelario the rank of colonel, and because he had flinched over an execution, Doroteo would not ever promote him again.

Quiet returned to the street outside. Soft voices explained what had taken place, that the Butcher had been sent to claim the life of the traitor who betrayed *el León* to the Americans. Some exclaimed that it could not have been Jesus Torres, although this was said in hushed tones, not meant to be heard inside the cantina by *el León* himself.

Horses moved slowly away into the night, until there was absolute silence beyond the door. Julio nodded his agreement to the execution. "These things are necessary," he said stiffly, touching the brim of his sombrero in salute to Doroteo before he walked out to mount horse.

Candelario halted near the doorframe, looking at Doroteo before he departed. "Now the tongue of this Judas is silenced," he said. "I will gather my men at Rubio in four days, *Jefe*. We will defeat the garrison at Guerrero easily, striking swiftly in the hours before dawn, taking them by surprise, as you say we will. We need those weapons badly, to arm the new recruits who will most certainly come to join us when the Americans cross over the border." He touched his hat brim and walked out, leaving Doroteo to his thoughts.

A moment later Rudolfo appeared, his hands stained red with blood. "I took him into the alley," he said, wiping his palms on his pants legs. "He will die slowly, as you promised. I shot him in the belly, so he will bleed to death very slowly."

Doroteo's mind was elsewhere by now, the slaying forgotten. "Where is the woman?" he asked, fingering his mustache, arching his thick eyebrows into question marks.

"Come. I will show you. She waits for you eagerly, *Jefe,* in the hut behind the cantina. A candle burns in her window."

"Her name is Margarita," Doroteo said, reminding himself before he went to her, just in case he'd forgotten it with the passage of several months.

"Sí, Jefe," Rudolfo replied, leading the way around the side of the building, "and she is very beautiful."

They were all beautiful, he knew, for he would have them no other way. He followed Rudolfo to the back and saw a candle flickering in the window of a small adobe hut across the alley.

He crossed to the hut and tapped gently on its thin plank door. The door opened almost at once. There, standing in the dim light of the candle, a young woman stood with the front of her nightgown open, revealing most of her generous bare breasts where her gown was parted.

"My darling Margarita," he said gently, smiling. "Business has kept me away from you much too long."

The girl glanced past him to Rudolfo. "I heard shooting," she said, in a breathless, worried whisper. "I was afraid someone had tried to harm you, darling Francisco."

"It was nothing," he assured her, waving Rudolfo to the far side of the alley, where he could keep watch over the house until dawn. Bending slightly, he kissed Margarita's mouth, at the same time reaching for one of her breasts. When she felt his rough hand close over her nipple, she moaned with pleasure and pulled him inside, closing the door behind them.

Rudolfo settled on his rump against the back wall of the cantina. Taking off his sombrero, he rested his head on the cool adobe and watched the window of the hut until the candle was snuffed out. He sighed, remembering how the bullet had torn Jesus from his saddle, screaming, his hands clawing frantically for the hole in his belly before he struck the ground. It was good to kill a man before breakfast. Excitement still coursed through his veins. Tomorrow would be a good day.

In the light from the stars he examined the dried blood on his hands, flexing them, inhaling the coppery smell of death as one who scented delicious food. He smiled, content to watch over the hut until morning.

• 7 •

Inside the lamplit cantina, all was quiet. Among the few drinkers at the bar and around scattered tables, the mood was somber. Everyone in Palomas was aware of the military buildup at Camp Furlong and Culberson Ranch, for the movement of so many men and so much material would have been impossible to disguise. A pall of dust hung like fog north of the border as hundreds of trucks, horse-drawn wagons, and caissons for the howitzers assembled. Eight thousand men and six thousand animals added to the churning dust. Will had watched the activity from a distance for a time, after turning his spare mounts over to a sergeant in charge of the remuda. Staying as far away from the military encampment as possible, he'd ridden to the border gate below Columbus and shown his papers, then to Palomas for a quiet drink or two, perhaps some information.

Conversation in the cantina centered around the raid and the American army that would soon invade Chihuahua. Seated at a corner table, Will overheard most of what was being said. When his glass was empty, he would signal a girl behind the bar for more tequila and limes. She told him her name was Consuelo, when he asked the second time she filled his drink. Upon her third trip to his table, he spoke softly to her in Spanish. "The soldiers will come tomorrow."

She smiled. *"Sí. Los soldados Americanos."* Now she spoke a mixture of Spanish and English. "They look for *el León.* You are a stranger here, *verdad?"*

It was the truth, and he admitted to it. "I'm from Laredo, just passin' through. I heard about all the trouble." He put a silver dollar on the table. "Keep the change, Consuelo. I am no friend of the American *soldados,* so don't worry about me. I'm a cattle buyer from Laredo. Can I buy you a drink?"

The girl glanced over her shoulder, to a balding man serving drinks behind the bar. She was pretty, Will thought. Long black hair framed her smooth, oval face.

"I must ask Diego," she whispered. "He told me not to talk to you, because you are a *gringo. Los Americanos* will send spies to Palomas, Diego says, to ask questions about Pancho. A few of the *soldados* came yesterday, asking everyone where Pancho is hiding. They were *pendejos . . .* fools, thinking we would tell them about *el León del Norte.* No one in Palomas will tell them anything."

"Ask Diego if you can sit down so I can buy you a drink. I am a *vaquero,* not a soldier. All I want is the company of a pretty woman tonight. Tell Diego I'll leave three extra dollars on the table if you join me."

Consuleo's dark eyes hooded. "I am not a *puta, señor.* I do not sell my body."

"I only want a little company. Didn't mean any offense." Her slow smile returned. "Then I will ask Diego."

She walked to the bar, rounded hips swaying inside her thin cotton skirt. She spoke to the old man quietly. He looked at Will a moment, appraising him, then he nodded.

Consuelo brought a bottle of tequila and a clean glass over to the table. She sat beside him, pouring for him, then herself.

"My name is Will," he told her. "I buy cattle and horses in Chihuahua for a few American ranchers. This war is liable to ruin my cattle business. That, an' the fact that it's a real dry year down south."

"*Sí,* it is very dry," she agreed, taking a tentative sip of her drink after adding salt to a wedge of lime to mix with the tequila. Her eyes wandered across his face. "You are . . . *muy guapo* for a *gringo.* Is . . . 'handsome,' in English?"

"That's what it means," he said. "And you are very beautiful, *mi hita.* Maybe on my way back through I'll take you to Juarez. We'll have dinner at a nice place. Dance to some good music at a little cantina I know, if you like."

She was watching him intently now. "You no have a wife in Laredo?"

He wagged his head. "No wife. I guess I haven't found the right woman yet. If Pancho Villa doesn't shoot me while I'm down in Chihuahua lookin' for cows, I'd like to take you out to dinner over in Juarez. To tell the truth, I'm kinda worried about all this trouble, the raid on Columbus and all those soldiers on the other side of the fence. I could get killed if Pancho or some of his men show up around Casas Grandes or San Miguel. After what happened, they're liable to shoot every *gringo* they come across."

The girl looked around to see who was listening, then she lowered her voice. "You will not find them at Casas Grandes or San Miguel, *señor.* You will be safe."

Consuelo knew something. Will decided to press his luck. He dug three silver dollars from his pocket and put them on the tabletop. It was customary in Mexico to pay for valuable information. "I'd wanted to go a little further south to look for *corrientes.* Would I be in any danger if I went as far as Agua Caliente to look for steers?"

She looked at the money, then swept it from the table and dropped it down the front of her blouse. "There is no danger at Agua Caliente," she whispered.

She was telling him more than he bargained for. He took another dollar and placed it in her hand underneath the table. "If it is also dry around Agua Caliente, I may have to go as far as Parral to find the cattle I need."

She shook her head too quickly, glancing through her

eyelashes to see if Diego was watching her. "Do not go to Parral. It is very dry there," she whispered, so softly he had trouble hearing her clearly at first.

Culberson Ranch was a city of tents the morning of March 15 when Will arrived before dawn. By the time the sun came up, the tents would be taken down. Culberson Ranch was, as its name implied, nothing more than a cattle ranch commissary grown into a small border village over the years. Will was directed to General Pershing's tent by a perimeter guard. An aide to the general asked Will's name when he dismounted in front of the tent, but before the young lieutenant could summon Pershing the general came through the tent flap, drawn outside by voices as dawn grayed the eastern sky.

"Major Ryan has been looking for you, Mr. Johnson. You were expected yesterday," he said, mildly annoyed.

Will hooked his thumbs in the pockets of his denims. "I was doin' a little nosing around, General. I figured you wanted to know where to look for Villa. That's why you hired me, ain't it?"

"You should have reported to Major Ryan first. He's my chief intelligence officer. The information you gather is to be reported to him from now on. I'll have an aide show you to the major's tent."

Will was put off by the general's manner. "I'm not a soldier, General. Got no designs on becomin' one. I'll be happy to tell this Major Ryan what I found out, but I ain't gonna salute anybody or click my heels together or anything like that. I'll work for this army because I could use the money, but I won't join up with it. As far as reportin' to anybody goes, I reckon I can do it, if all it means is that I tell somebody what I found out."

Pershing had grown impatient during Will's lengthy explanation, and he let it show. "I understand that you're not a soldier, Mr. Johnson. You won't be asked to salute anyone. Lieutenant Collins will show you to Major Ryan's tent. That's all for now. We leave for Ascencion today, as soon as I've been in radio contact with the east column at Camp Furlong."

"No need to go to Ascencion, General," Will said, halting Pershing's return to his tent.

"And why is that?" the general asked.

"Because the men you're after ain't there. They made for San Miguel to get fresh horses and supplies right after the raid. By now, whoever pulled that raid is probably two or three hundred miles from Ascencion, boasting about how they burned down half of Columbus."

Pershing faced Will now, peering under his hat brim in the pale morning light. "What is the source of your information, Mr. Johnson?" he asked.

"A whore over at Palomas," Will replied.

The general's cheeks went taut, the muscles working furiously underneath his skin. "The word of a prostitute can hardly be considered reliable. Is there more?"

Will gave Pershing a half grin. "The word of a whore can be pretty damn reliable when it comes to Villa, General. He takes a shine to painted women, an' so do his top men. If it was Pancho Villa who led that raid on Columbus, then you'll probably find him down close to Parral, an' the odds are he's wakin' up with a whore this morning."

Pershing's scowl only deepened. "What do you mean, 'if' it was Pancho Villa? We have proof that those were Villa's men."

Will shifted his weight to the other foot, toeing the ground with his boot, avoiding the general's stare. "There's some who say otherwise, folks who oughta know. I asked around in El Paso an' Juarez. Some say Villa wasn't there, that it was Carranza's doing."

"Ridiculous!" Pershing snapped. "Why would Carranza's men attack an American military base? President Carranza has given us permission to go after Villa, in accordance with the joint treaty of 1880, although he has retracted some of his cooperation now. We can't use the Mexican railroads or go near any of the larger towns."

"Maybe the two are connected: the raid on Columbus and Carranza's permission to capture Villa."

"Your meaning isn't clear, Mr. Johnson. However, I don't have time to discuss politics or military strategy with you now. Report to Major Ryan and tell him what you learned.

It will be up to him to weigh its value. You were not employed to draw conclusions, simply to scout the way for us and locate Villa if you can."

The general turned on his heel and disappeared into his tent. Pershing's aide waited a moment, watching the tent flap.

"Come this way, Mr. Johnson," the lieutenant said a moment later, wheeling west to lead him through the maze of tents.

Near a banner identifying the Thirteenth Cavalry Regiment, the aide halted in front of one of the larger command tents. "Major Ryan, sir! Lieutenant Collins reporting with civilian scout Johnson!" he shouted.

The tent flap opened. A stocky soldier emerged, his lantern-jawed face turned to Will. The lieutenant snapped off a crisp salute, which the major acknowledged with a lazy imitation, never once taking his eyes off Will.

"So you're Will Johnson," he said, expressionless, dark eyes roaming up and down Will's frame. Lieutenant Collins turned sharply and hurried off.

Will offered his hand. The major took it slowly, still appraising Will carefully.

"Major James Ryan. Lem Spilsbury tells me you know Chihuahua better than any white man he knows. I hadn't expected you to be so young, frankly."

"I'm twenty-six," Will replied, dropping the major's hand. "I know most of that country reasonable well. Negotiated the sale of lots of cattle from those mountains."

"So I was told. You must have started in the cow business at an early age."

"I took some men from Fort Worth down there when I was fourteen, the first time I went alone. I used to go with my pa a lot, only he died that winter, the year I turned fourteen."

Ryan grunted, rubbing his chin. "We think Villa is now in hiding around Ascencion, although sources tell us he may have taken off cross-country toward Carrizal. We'll soon have some aeroplanes in the sky to do some reconnaissance. We should know in a day or two, after the Jennys fly over."

"He ain't either place, Major," Will said, preparing to tell

Consuelo's story a second time. "I asked around in El Paso an' Juarez, then down at Palomas. Most everybody agrees they made for the south. A woman told me they rode over to San Miguel, to pick up fresh horses and supplies, then they started toward Parral. They'll have plenty of time to get there. By the time this big army crawls through those mountains, they will most likely be headed someplace else. The locals will warn them that we're comin'. You hadn't asked me, but I'm gonna say so anyways. Those chain-drive trucks of yours won't make it across the desert. Sand will get in the chains, wear down the teeth, and the chains will fall off. Even if they do make it, they won't have a snowball's chance in hell of climbing the mountains, on account of there ain't any real roads. A few wagon tracks at best. The only way to catch up to them is with cavalry, in my opinion. I told General Pershing the same thing."

The major fixed Will with a piercing stare. "When your opinion is wanted, Johnson, I'll ask for it. We fully intend to pursue Villa with cavalry. However, cavalry detachments must be supplied. Trucks and horse-drawn wagons carry those supplies for our men and animals. Our field guns will decimate Villa's inferior weaponry. We have arranged for some Mescalero Apache scouts to join us. They are considered the best trackers anywhere. Some of them are here now. Others will follow. We will find Villa after we get down there and set up bases of operation. Your lack of confidence in army equipment and maneuverability is not warranted, Mr. Johnson. We know what we are doing, I can assure you. The trucks have been thoroughly tested. Our corps of engineers has been trained to overcome any obstacle."

Will was quickly tiring of the military attitude. Ryan was as bullheaded as the general about their trucks and the ease with which they planned to cross the desert and the Sierras. Trying to talk sense to a soldier, no matter what his rank, was proving to be a waste of time. Had it not been a dry year, with Raymond and his family needing the hundred fifty dollars a month to keep the ranch going, Will would have gladly told Major Ryan and the general what they could do with their money. "From here on out I'll remember to keep my opinions to myself, Major," he said with a shrug.

"If it's all the same to you, I'll bed down with those Apaches at night, when you show me where they are. Me an' the Indians oughta get along okay. That way my opinions won't get under your skin."

Ryan merely nodded, pursing his lips. His dislike for Will showed plainly on his face. A moment later, after considering something, he pointed to the southern edge of the camp. "Four of the Apaches built a fire close to the border fence. I don't remember any of their names just now. Find them and await any further orders. When General Pershing gives the order to pull out, I'll send someone for you. Scouts will ride three or four miles ahead of the column, reporting back every two hours about the terrain, or sooner, if you spot something that could mean trouble. We'll be relying on your judgment. Troops of the Seventh Cavalry will be at the head of the column, followed by the Tenth Cavalry and Battery B of the Sixth Field Artillery. In the event you encounter the enemy, men from the Seventh will be first to engage them. As to General Villa's whereabouts, we will only trust our own eyes and ears on this expedition. Intelligence gathering in Mexico will be up to us. Local sources probably can't be relied upon, since many will be Villa sympathizers. I will listen to anything you hear about Villa's location, but I alone will decide what General Pershing will be told."

"Suits me," Will answered quietly. He turned for his horse and mounted.

Ryan pointed to a group of open-walled tents north of camp where fires blazed, backgrounded by paling skies. "Those are the mess tents. If you're hungry . . ."

"No thanks, Major." He reined Poco south and heeled to a trot, glad to be away from Major Ryan, forcing his thoughts to the money he would make on the expedition, thus to be better able to endure what lay in store. His experience over the last few days only confirmed his belief that military men were incompetent fools. As yet, he had not met one here whom he felt could survive the Chihuahuan desert on his own. Maybe the trucks were necessary after all, so men like Major Ryan could haul feed for their horses and food for themselves, but such a cumbersome arrangement would never catch up to Villa.

He found the Apache campfire hundreds of yards from the last rows of army tents. Four men were seated around the flames. Long before Poco took him close to the fire, all four Apaches were watching him approach. He drew rein a short distance away and stepped down, ground-hitching the horse.

"I'm Will Johnson," he said. "I was hired as a civilian scout, same as you. If you've got no objections, I'd rather toss my bedroll here at night. I make no secret about it that I've got no use for soldiering."

One Indian laughed, a squat, muscular man with shoulder-length black hair. "Come to the fire. We have coffee, if you brought your own cup. I am called Loco Jim. This is Es Ki Ben De. He is named Nakay. Over there is Big Sharley."

"Howdy," Will said to the others. "I'll get my cup."

He took a tin cup from his war bag and ambled to the fire, leaving Poco to graze. Loco Jim stood up and took a fire-blackened pot from a rock beside the flames to pour for Will, giving him a passing glance.

"We don't like soldiers either," Loco Jim said, speaking near perfect English. He was in his thirties, Will guessed, too young to have been a truly wild Indian like Geronimo.

Big Sharley grunted. "They are stupid."

Will settled on his haunches to blow steam from the rim of his cup. "The ones I've met damn sure are. General Pershing is mostly okay, I reckon, but he's goin' about this all wrong, in my opinion."

"He is a white man," Es Ki Ben De said softly, palming his coffee for warmth. Much older than the others, his long hair showed streaks of gray. "They know nothing about fighting, but they are many, like locusts."

The Apache called Nakay said nothing, merely nodding. Loco Jim inclined his head toward the old man. "Es Ki Ben De fought the soldiers a long time ago. He still hates them. But like the rest of us, he needs their money."

"Same reason I'm here," Will remarked, carefully sipping scalding coffee. Somewhere in the encampment a bugle began to play, followed by a stirring in the tents, the whisper of cloth and faint mutterings. "We could be in Mexico a long time," he added, looking south. "The men we're after are smart, seasoned to this country. I doubt we'll ever find them unless they want us to . . . when they're ready to make a fight out of it."

"You know this place where we are going?" Big Sharley asked the question, watching Will across the flames.

"I know most of it pretty well. First there's the desert, which I don't figure the army's trucks can cross because the sand's so deep in places. Then there are the mountains, some ten thousand feet high. No roads to speak of. I told that Major Ryan it wouldn't work, trying to get trucks through. It made him mad when I told him."

Es Ki Ben De shook his head. "White soldier chief is loco. Loco Jim maybeso give his name to soldier chief."

The others laughed, although Will judged it wasn't genuine laughter, perhaps the result of nervousness.

Nakay leaned closer to the fire, obsidian eyes on Will's face. He looked to be the youngest of the four, wearing blue denims and a shirt made from flour sacking. "Do you know this loco Mexican bandit who calls himself General Pancho Villa?" he asked, as sounds from the army camp grew louder.

"Not exactly," Will replied. "Met him a time or two. I know his brother, Antonio, from cattle deals. I know enough about Pancho to keep my eyes peeled when I'm around him. Some say he's crazy. I know for a fact he's made a practice out of slaughtering his enemies. He's smart too."

"I never met a smart Mexican," Loco Jim observed.

"Villa isn't a Mexican. He's mostly Tarahumara Indian, by blood."

Es Ki Ben De nodded. "This why he fight hard. My spirit voice say this Pancho Villa no is Mexican. I tell Nakay, tell Big Sharley same thing."

Nakay was still reading Will's face. "Do you know where he is . . . where we will find him?"

Will swirled coffee around in his cup. "A woman told me that Villa is five hundred miles from here, at a place called Parral."

Loco Jim looked over his shoulder, watching the soldiers scurry about as the first rays of sunlight beamed above the horizon. "This army won't make it five hundred miles," he said thoughtfully. "Most of the soldiers are green. Too young. No experience being a soldier. The officers don't seem to know shit about dry country. When they marched the men over here from Columbus, some passed out in the heat. Many horses were limping, and so were some of the foot soldiers. Big Sharley and me were laughing so hard we thought our ribs would break. Only one day from their fort, and this big army has many sore feet."

"I've been predicting the same thing," Will said offhandedly, watching uniformed men head for the mess tents.

Es Ki Ben De tossed handfuls of dirt on the flames to smother them. "I find his tracks. But I no fight him. Maybeso look, see fight from far away. I no fight on side of loco soldiers." He spat loudly into the fire and got up, walking away from the firepit to attend to his tethered horse.

Loco Jim chuckled. "Ben still hates white men. He was with Geronimo for a time, until he was captured. He's like the rest of us, doing this because of the money. If his grandchildren weren't about to starve to death back at the reservation, he would not be here. General Pershing asked for Ben personally, because he knows the old man can read sign better than anybody. Ben didn't want to come."

"Pershing said there'd be twenty Apaches," Will remembered.

Loco Jim nodded once. "The others are coming. Some had to make arrangements for feeding their families."

"We could be down there for quite a spell," Will said, as the old Indian lifted one of the pony's hooves to inspect it near the border fence.

Big Sharley stood up, dusting off the seat of his pants. "That's okay by me," he said quietly, "just so long as nobody's shooting at us." He grinned, etching deeper lines beside his aquiline nose. Like the others, he had a broad, flat face the color of copper. Coal-black hair hung below his shoulders. He looked to be powerful, a little too fat, standing over six feet. "I'll come back home a rich man. Me and Loco can get drunk on the money before our women spend all of it."

Loco Jim and Nakay laughed. Still grinning, Big Sharley

looked toward the mess tents, flaring his nostrils. "I am hungry," he said, rubbing his belly. "Who wants to go with me to eat soldier food?"

"We'll all go," Loco Jim replied, standing up. He looked at Will. "They stare at us when we eat. No one will sit near us, like we have a bad smell."

Will got up, tossing out the last of his coffee. "I'd sure as hell rather eat with you than some stuffed shirt with stripes on his sleeve. I'll tag along, if you don't mind." He looked at the old Indian. "What about him?"

Big Sharley chuckled, shaking his head. "Ben won't eat the white man's food. He says it's poisoned, that they will try to kill us one of these days with a poisoned egg or something like that. Nakay told him the poison couldn't be any worse than the food they give us at the reservation."

Will tied Poco to the barbed wire and fell in beside the three Indians for the walk to the mess tents. He'd taken a liking to the Apaches immediately. If the expedition lasted for months, at least he would have some good company to share the misery, maybe a laugh or two when the ill-prepared army column broke down somewhere in Chihuahua.

A gust of March wind blasted through the sea of tents. Dust swirled as campaign hats were blown from the heads of young soldiers in the mess lines. Soon men were chasing their hats all over the campground. Big Sharley laughed.

· 8 ·

For the moment, Deputy Chief of Staff Tasker Bliss was not quite sure what to do with the information he received over the telephone. If true, it could have disastrous consequences. The punitive expedition was all but underway with President Wilson's reluctant blessings. Pershing was in place at Columbus, poised to strike deep into the heart of Chihuahua, having assembled more than eight thousand men and the necessary equipment and supplies. Wilson had finally been moved to take action against what Tasker believed was the most dangerous of all the rebellious factions in Mexico, the band under the command of Pancho Villa. Only now, there was this report that six men who had been captured following the Columbus raid by national guardsmen from El Paso were not Villistas.

They were being held in the El Paso county jail while awaiting transfer to a federal facility, somehow overlooked in the furor to form the punitive effort to go after Villa. The six had apparently tried to escape the fury of the battle at Columbus and fled the wrong direction in the dark, heading east instead of south along with the rest of the retreating raiders. A jailer in El Paso had recently taken note of the fact that a couple of the prisoners were wearing assorted bits and pieces of Mexican Army-issue uniform. When the men were questioned a few hours before by a bilingual El Paso county deputy sheriff, all six denied that Villa was present at Columbus. One, a frightened boy of seventeen, insisted they were not members of Villa's army at all but part-time regulars in the Mexican Army at Chihuahua City, rarely given any pay for their occasional soldiering. Three days

71

before the attack on Columbus they were summoned to the garrison, where they listened to orders that were said to have come directly from the lips of General Alvaro Obregon himself, calling for a forced march of the utmost secrecy to the American border. No other explanation was given, other than that they should be prepared for a fight. Just before the attack, they were handed written instructions, which they could not read in the dark. These, apparently, were the "papers" found on some of the dead raiders after the battle, proving the attack had been ordered by Pancho Villa. The boy remembered that during the fight some men were shouting *"Viva* Villa!" although he did not understand why. Under further questioning, he said none of the raiders were full-time *Federale* soldiers, that most were, like himself, members of small army garrisons who were seldom actually paid or given real military duties. Others were civilians.

What did it mean? Tasker wondered, as he gazed absently at the telephone by which the unexpected news had come. Was the boy telling the truth? Why would General Obregon order an attack on the United States with what amounted to part-time boy soldiers? Obregon must have known the strength of the American army at Camp Furlong, so why would he order a suicidal mission against it?

Or was this a ruse by Villa sympathizers, an attempt to delay the punitive expedition until things could be sorted out, giving Villa more time to hide in the wilds of Mexico? If the president had this information now it would be all the excuse he needed to cancel the expedition and order a return to his policy of watchful waiting. Wilson wouldn't send Pershing into Mexico until the boy's story was checked out thoroughly, and thus the entire effort by the War Department would be for naught. Villa would have plenty of time to make his escape while Wilson vacillated. Secretary of War Newton Baker would be furious, after so many hurried preparations had been made to assemble the American war machine on the Mexican border.

And what would Hugh Scott think? As chief of staff, he had as much invested in the expedition as anyone, and only today he'd boastfully predicted its early success under the capable leadership of John Pershing, a man who could follow orders and maintain discipline. But General Scott was also somewhat sympathetic toward Pancho Villa, for they had known each other almost since the revolution began, and Hugh liked Villa personally. From the very beginning he had expressed doubts that it was Villa's handiwork at Columbus. What would he think of this solitary report that Villa was not responsible? Would he put any faith in it when the expedition was literally poised to enter Mexico within the hour? There was no time to substantiate the story told by the Mexican boy.

Bliss stared at the telephone a while longer, debating with himself. If the press got wind of this the entire Wilson administration faced international embarrassment on a scale that could topple the Democratic party, turn Washington upside down, and end many military and political careers. It was a powder keg with a lit fuse sitting in a jail cell in Texas. Why had no one at the Columbus battle scene done a thorough check of the raiders' identities? Had everyone simply assumed it was Villa who'd led the attack because of a letter found on some of the bodies?

For months it had been rumored that Villa was close to the border, stirring up unrest, but reports of that kind were hard to substantiate. So many battles were raging all across Mexico that news of this type had become commonplace. Most attention in the War College had been on Europe and preparations for war with any one or all of the countries involved, even some that as yet still remained neutral. There had been extensive plans made for a fight with Germany. But in the hearts and minds of those who served under Woodrow Wilson, no one really expected we would go to war, for Wilson was determined to keep us out of it at all costs, frustrating the hell out of his military advisers with more watchful waiting.

So what was to be done about the tale told by the six men in the El Paso jail? Did he dare sit on it and do nothing? If the story leaked out, as it easily might with newspapermen as thick as flies converging on El Paso to cover Pershing's march, a trail of blame for keeping it quiet would lead straight to Tasker Bliss and he could count on an early retirement, his military career up in smoke. The chain of command required that he take the information directly to General Scott. But on the other hand, if he made some effort to verify the story first, he would be in a more defensible position later on. He could claim, justifiably, that he had not wanted to bother any of his superiors with hearsay, not until he could get to the bottom of it himself and know the truth of the matter. Taking the word of a few Mexican boys found wandering near the Columbus battle scene might be considered the mark of an incompetent leader. Common sense dictated that he make some sort of further inquiry, before alerting everyone in the War Department that Pershing's mission might be misguided, a very expensive manhunt looking for the wrong man.

He picked up the telephone and instructed the operator to put him through to the number he wrote on his desk blotter, with all due dispatch. Making a connection from Washington to El Paso took time, time enough for him to think about what he was doing. He could justify having the six prisoners moved to solitary confinement elsewhere, at least for now. His primary objective was to get them away from the swarms of reporters until they could be questioned at length by someone with expertise in very sensitive affairs. Getting at the truth, if this were indeed a clever ruse on the part of Villa, would require an expert at this type of cross-examination. According to the deputy, the men were young, and sooner or later a professional could break down their stories if this were all a fabrication masterminded by Villa to buy time.

Buying time was what Bliss told himself he was doing now, buying enough time for the expedition to get underway and move into the heart of Chihuahua, Villa's stronghold. With any luck and a well-planned strategy on Pershing's part, the campaign would be over before the six prisoners could be questioned by experts.

A distant voice at the end of the line spoke. Connections halfway across the country were always bad.

"Deputy Sheriff Salinas, please!" he shouted, holding the telephone close to his mouth. "This is Major General Tasker Bliss calling from Washington!"

A moment later he heard the familiar voice of Raul Salinas crackle in his ear.

"This is General Bliss. I want those six prisoners you told me about a short while ago put in solitary confinement immediately. I'm sending federal officers to pick them up as quickly as possible, so they can be questioned further. And another thing, Deputy Salinas: I'm asking that you keep everything confidential until we can check out their stories. Absolutely no leaks to the press. Do you understand?"

The deputy said he understood.

"Thank you." Bliss sighed, relieved to have the deputy's cooperation without any disagreement over who had jurisdiction in the matter. Bliss had been prepared to argue that it was very clearly a federal affair, since a U.S. Army military base had been attacked.

He cradled the telephone and leaned back in his chair to think about his next step. Without attracting the attention of anyone at the War Department, he had to get those men out of El Paso as quietly as he could. He began by making a list of the places they could be sequestered. The interrogations had to be a secret operation, and it would quite naturally be fraught with many delays, delays the Pershing expedition needed to close its powerful jaws around the brigand Pancho Villa.

• 9 •

It was an odd-looking group of men assembled around Major Ryan, all but one dressed in civilian attire. At ten that morning, the major had sent an aide to collect Will and the Apaches. Ryan made the introductions, reading names from a list through wire-rimmed spectacles. He mispronounced "Nakay" and "Es Ki Ben De" badly, then went on to introduce Will, a lanky cowboy named C. E. Tracy who hailed from southern Arizona, J. B. Barker, Bill Lunt, and soldier Bob Estes. Hands were shaken all around, none too enthusiastically by the Apaches, then the major began to pace back and forth while addressing the men, his hands clasped behind his back.

"We planned to pull out at noon; however, there has been a delay. The Carrancista general at Palomas has denied Colonel Lockett permission to enter Mexico with the east column, thus General Pershing has returned to Camp Furlong to wire General Funston in San Antonio for further orders. The east column may have a fight on its hands before traveling the first mile. We have been ordered to wait for General Pershing. When the order to move out is given, I want scouts moving ahead of us by no less than four miles." He looked at Will. "Since Mr. Johnson knows the territory, he will ride point. Reports concerning the terrain will be sent back to Corporal Estes, who will then bring them to me at the head of the column. Our destination is the Mormon settlement at Colonia Dublan, east of Casas Grandes. I want scouts flanking the road by at least two miles on either side. Anyone who sees anything unusual should report it to Corporal Estes at once. We will be in radio contact with the east column. If they run into any difficulties near Ascencion, we will swing east to reinforce them."

Will was hearing "at once" more than he cared to again. He supposed he could grow accustomed to it.

The major pointed to a gate in the barbed-wire fence. "Our situation is quite different here. The Mexican guards, it would seem, have wisely withdrawn. We may encounter Carranza forces on the road to Colonia Dublan. However, since none of them wear uniforms, it may be difficult to tell who they are. Should you run across a contingent of Mexican soldiers, they must be identified for us."

"That oughta be easy," the cowboy from Arizona said. "If they start shootin' at us, we'll know they're Villistas."

Everyone laughed. Everyone except the major. Ryan waited until the laughter died. "I expect you'll lose your sense of humor very soon, Mr. Tracy," the major said. "We've been warned that some of the Carrancista leaders don't want us in Mexico. It's quite possible that they will also shoot at us. We have orders to avoid the towns where Carranza forces are garrisoned. If we can, we are charged with preventing a confrontation with Carrancistas in the field. When any large group of Mexican soldiers is spotted, I want to know about it immediately."

Will glanced at the rapidly dismantling army camp. Mule-drawn wagons and strings of pack mules were being loaded with tents and field equipment. Eleven flatbed trucks with canvas-covered bows stood in a row. Three heavy cannons, howitzers, were being hitched to spans of harness horses. Five automobiles, open Dodges and a pair of Fords, waited empty to transport officers, Will supposed.

"Wait here for the order to move out." Ryan said. "We expect it to come at any minute, so don't wander off."

"Who's in charge of us while we're out scoutin' around?" J. B. Barker asked. He was older, close to forty, and by the tone of his voice he expected to be named the leader of this scout patrol.

The major's eyes passed over the group. "I suppose I'll put Will Johnson in charge for now. He knows the lay of the land, according to Lem Spilsbury. Spilsbury will join us at Colonia Dublan. When he does, he will be chief of scouts . . . unless the general deems otherwise."

Will raised his palms and shook his head. "I'd just as soon not be in charge of anything, Major. Givin' orders is somethin' I ain't too good at."

Ryan scowled. "Very well, then. Mr. Barker is in charge until further notice, but I want Mr. Johnson riding point at all times."

Barker seemed to stand a little straighter. "Understood, Major," he said, thumbs in his suspenders. He carried an older model Colt .44 on his right hip. Although he wore cowboy garb, he didn't look the part in Will's estimation. Tracy, on the other hand, reminded Will of an old-time bronc buster.

"That will be all, gentlemen," the major said, turning on his heel. He walked toward the pack train, shoulders thrown back as though he were marching in a parade.

J. B. Barker wasted no time assuming his authority. "Tie your horses to the fence, men. We'll wait by the gate for our instructions."

Loco Jim gave Will a sideways glance and a wry grin as they led their horses to fence posts. "Ben wants to scalp that major," he whispered. "Same goes for Barker. Ben said he would do it, if it wasn't for needing the money."

Will chuckled quietly. "I figure Barker will turn out to be an asshole before the day is over." He tied Poco to a cedar post and loosened the gelding's cinch. Like Es Ki Ben De, he was prepared to do plenty of distasteful things for the money, which included taking orders from anyone in charge, just so long as the order didn't threaten his life. A new private in the army made sixteen dollars a month, making a scout's pay seem sizable.

Nakay and Big Sharley came over. Es Ki Ben De shuffled off to roll a cigarette, his back to the stiff westerly wind. The Arizona cowboy, about the same age as Will by appearances, joined them after his horse was tied. Barker and the others formed a group away from the Indians, talking among themselves.

"You look like a man who knows his way around horses," Tracy said, addressing Will. He had a hawklike nose, ropy arms, and callused hands. When he smiled, his dark leathery face webbed with lines.

"I've spent my share of time on the hurricane deck of a cowpony," Will replied. "Been bucked off a few times too."

Tracy laughed. "I reckon we all have. After listenin' to that speech the major gave us, I believe I'd just as soon be bucked off as be in the army."

"Same goes for me. Takin' orders ain't my natural way of doin' things."

The cowboy's grin vanished. "The major said you know this country. How bad is it?"

Will leaned against a fence post, hanging a bootheel on the bottom wire. "The first fifty miles or so is desert, all sugar sand an' dry as popcorn. Then we come to the Sierras. Followin' the wagon trace south, some of those mountains are close to twelve thousand feet. After we cross Rio Casas Grandes, we come to El Valle, and that's where we start to climb. The river'll be shallow unless it rains before we get there. It's the climb that's gonna do us in. This early in the year it'll be cold as the dickens up there. . . . Probably snow some higher up. The general's trucks ain't likely to make some of those climbs. I'd hardly call it a road we follow, more like a pair of ruts. It's some of the roughest country

I've ever seen. The valleys will be pretty and green this time of year, but the mountains are the worst. The general's gonna have a bunch of crippled horses an' busted wagon axles, but a horse can make it through. I wouldn't give a plugged nickel for the trucks' chances, not where we're headed."

"Just where are we headed?" Tracy asked, looking southward across the fence.

"I was told Villa is in Parral. That's five hundred miles into Chihuahua, most of it straight up and down."

"I knew the money sounded too good," Tracy said.

The noon hour came and went. Thousands of soldiers, cavalry and infantrymen, were strung out in loose formation, awaiting the order to enter Mexico. Some of the trucks were started, two men working the hand cranks, then the engines were stopped. Horses and mules harnessed to wagons and caissons fidgeted and pawed the ground. The west column had been ready at noon. Will and the other scouts waited at the gate for orders from Major Ryan to proceed through the fence. No orders came.

Just before four o'clock, General Pershing and two aides arrived in an open automobile from Camp Furlong. Major Ryan conferred with the general briefly, then he walked along the waiting column toward the scouts.

"We won't pull out until midnight," he said. "Get some food from the mess wagons if you wish. The east column has moved forward at noon today and there have been no reported difficulties. Palomas is deserted: Everyone pulled out at the last minute. General Pershing has ordered that we wait twelve hours, to see if the east column runs into trouble at Ascencion."

"There won't be any trouble at Ascencion," Will said.

The major glared at Will. "We shall see," he said evenly, sounding for all the world like he hoped Will was wrong.

At twelve-thirty on the morning of March 16, General Pershing mounted his favorite cavalry horse in the dark to lead the west column into Mexico. Will and the other scouts took off at a gallop to cover four miles of scant roadway lying before the slow-moving army. The night had turned bitterly cold, the temperatures well below freezing, which only added to the misery of men and animals forced to wait since noon in formation. Will, ignoring Barker's position as lead scout, selected Loco Jim and Es Ki Ben De to ride point with him. The other scouts spread out on both sides of the wagon road to scout the flank as Major Ryan had instructed. The night was pitch dark and moonless, making for dangerous travel at a gallop across unfamiliar land until the scout patrol was in position.

When Will judged they were roughly four miles in front of the column, he slowed Poco to a walk, shivering inside his mackinaw. Loco Jim, huddled in a buckskin jacket, tried to keep his teeth from chattering. The old man rode his pinto pony clad only in a wool blanket and leather leggings as if he were somehow immune to the cold.

"The night is dark," Es Ki Ben De said, looking up at the stars. "Be good time for ambush by our enemies."

Will considered the possibility and said nothing. He had come to trust the information Consuelo gave him. Villa was at Parral by now, boasting about his exploits—even if they were not exploits of his own, as some felt. His men would entertain themselves with whores and tequila for a few days, knowing the Americans would be slowed by the rugged Sierras. Villa could appear confident, arrogant in the face of what many Mexicans called the colossus of the north, bragging about how he nipped its flank at Columbus. It would be good fodder for recruiting more loyal men, to claim a victory of sorts north of the border. Mexican people looked up to brave men—bullfighters were national celebrities—thus many young men would join a courageous fighting force like Villa's as a matter of honor. Villa's ranks would swell in the weeks and months to come unless the U.S. Army could strike a decisive blow against him very quickly.

Ten miles below the border, they came to a broad expanse of desert sand dotted with ocotillo and cactus where the wagon ruts spread out in many directions. Teamsters driving heavy freight wagons escaped bogging down here by avoiding each other's ruts. Poco hit the sand and began to labor, struggling through spots where the sand was deeper than his fetlocks. Frosty breath curled from the horse's muzzle as he began to tire. The Indians' ponies suffered similarly pulling through deep drifts. For a mile, then two, the three horses plowed through the sand bogs. No matter which direction Will chose, conditions were no better. Dodging the long, thorny arms of ocotillo and bristling prickly pear beds, their horses played out quickly. When there seemed to be no end to the bog, Will touched the reins.

"One of you better go back to warn Major Ryan about this sand," he said, listening to Poco gather wind. "I'll wager this is where the trucks get stuck, unless those drivers know what they're doin'."

"I'll go," Loco Jim said, wheeling his weary horse. Soft hoofbeats announced his departure across the drifts.

"I'm freezin'," Will said, searching his war bag for his gloves, groping through the contents by feel until he found them.

"It is cold," Es Ki Ben De agreed, his gaze sweeping the starlit desert around them. "Maybeso our enemies also be cold, no want fight here."

"I don't figure we'll find any of them this close to the border. Villa's a brave man, but he ain't plumb crazy."

Es Ki Ben De said nothing at first, still examining the land. Unexpectedly, Poco lifted his head, snorting softly as his ears pricked forward, a sure sign that the little horse sensed something to the southwest.

"Many eyes watch us now," Es Ki Ben De said quietly.

Will was suddenly alert, and he reached for the stock of the Winchester .30-.30 booted below a stirrup leather, his heartbeat quickening.

The old Indian chuckled softly. "Only the wolf," he said. "I count four. Maybeso coyotes. They no come close."

Will relaxed against the cantle of his saddle, wondering how Es Ki Ben De could see so well in the dark. "You had me spooked for a minute," he said, unable to find anything among the deeper shadows where the Indian and the horse were looking. "Let's keep moving, to see how far this sandy stretch runs."

They moved off at a walk, their horses still struggling through sand drifts. Ice had begun to form in Will's canteen, rattling softly with the motion of Poco's slow gait.

* * *

Dawn revealed a sight Will had fully expected to see. Sitting atop Poco on the crest of a low hill, he and the two Apaches saw dozens of wagons and five of the trucks spread out across the desert sands, hopelessly mired to the wheel hubs. Loco Jim brought back word of the bogged down column shortly before daylight. The three of them had ridden back in plenty of time to see Will's grim prediction come to pass. Men and animals swarmed around the stuck conveyances, fixing towropes. But when the wheels were finally freed, they only bogged down again a few yards farther south. The faint swell of angry voices lifted as a chorus from the desert floor, to the accompaniment of roaring engines and cracking bullwhips.

"The most modern mechanized army in the world, according to the general," Will said, shaking his head. Six of the trucks and several dozen wagons had made it safely across the deep sands to higher ground, where they sat in disarray, no longer in neat order the way they'd left Culberson Ranch. Clusters of infantrymen huddled around smoky camp fires to escape the numbing cold. Cavalrymen were scattered all over the desert, tying their horses to stalled trucks and wagons. Three mess tents had been erected on one of the hills where breakfast was being prepared during the unscheduled halt.

Loco Jim laughed. "So this is the army that catches the mighty Geronimo. The spirit of Geronimo is laughing now, seeing this from the spirit world."

Will looked over his shoulder at the surrounding hilly land, making sure it was empty. "If Pancho Villa could see it, he'd be having a good laugh too, I reckon." On the desert floor, black soldiers from the Tenth crowded around a wagon to lift it out of a sand bog. When the wheels came free, everyone gave a cheer. The teams of laboring mules went a short distance and stopped abruptly when the wagon suddenly mired again. "We could be here all day," Will added, watching three mounted soldiers strike a gallop toward the hilltop where he and the Indians watched the affair. "Yonder comes Major Ryan and a couple of his aides. He'll be steamin' mad by now."

The major and two lieutenants galloped lathered horses to

the top of the knob and drew rein in front of the scouts. By the look on Ryan's face, Will was right about his prediction.

"Why didn't you look for another way around this quagmire?" the major demanded hotly, staring holes through Will, his face beet red from the cold and seething anger, and perhaps a touch of embarrassment.

"There ain't another way," Will replied. "It's as simple as that."

Ryan ground his teeth together. "How much more of this shit lies ahead of us?"

"Thirty or forty miles, Major. But it ain't all sand like this. Some of it turns to rock near Casas Grandes."

Down below, a stuck Dodge automobile broke free amid rousing cheers from the men around it. The three soldiers looked back to see what had occasioned the noise.

"Have you found any tracks that could have been made by Villa's men?" Ryan asked, facing the scouts again.

"No," Loco Jim replied when Will had nothing to say. Es Ki Ben De shook his head.

Far to the north, the plodding mule train was just now catching up to the column, ushered along by a company of cold, weary soldiers. Overloaded mules refused to be pushed through deep sand, a discovery new recruits made during the frozen night when the pack train encountered drifts.

Frustrated, Major Ryan barely acknowledged the scouts' reply. "We should be out of this in an hour or two. Get something to eat and keep moving. I want to be informed when more of these sand beds await us."

Will shrugged. "Then I'd just as well go ahead and inform you now, Major. Just over these hills is another two- or three-mile stretch of the same sand. Then there's a few more hills like these before the sand starts again. Like I said, you can pretty well count on thirty miles of it, more or less. Some of it is worse than this, best I recall. Longer, an' deeper in spots."

"Sweet Jesus," Ryan muttered, making angry fists around his reins. "The east column will get to Colonia Dublan two days ahead of us at this rate, what with a twelve-hour head start."

"I doubt it," Will answered, remembering the road from

FRED BEAN

Palomas to the Mormon colony. "The sand's just as bad east of here. They'll be stuck just like us. Maybe worse, if that's possible."

"Jesus Christ!" the major snapped. "Lord help us if it takes us a week to get there. The general will be furious!"

"I wouldn't count on any help from the Lord," Will said dryly, enjoying Ryan's discomfort more than he should, perhaps. "Lots of men have tried to pray their way out of those sand traps over the years. Tried plenty of things an' none of them worked. We'll see the rotted hulls of abandoned wagons all the way to the mountains. Horses are about the only sure way to get across some of it," he added, resisting the urge to say he'd warned everyone beforehand.

A truck with a steaming radiator broke free of its sandy moor, lurching forward to a piece of harder ground propelled by a racing engine, sand and dust flying from its solid rubber tires. Whoops and yells from soldiers around it, assisting the rescue effort until the wheels found a purchase, rose like shrill notes from a choir of schoolboys in the frosty air.

The major said nothing more as he turned his horse. Flanked by the two shivering aides, Ryan urged his horse to a trot off the hilltop.

"It could take a week to go forty miles like this," Loco Jim observed without emotion.

Will recalled something John Abel had said about taking knitting needles and yarn. "The worst is still in front of us," he said, glancing to the mess tents, thinking of hot coffee to warm his insides. "When we hit those mountains you'll understand. I could use some coffee an' bacon." He touched Poco's ribs with his bootheels and led the way down the hill.

A radio operator confirmed what Will told the major. The east column was similarly mired in bottomless sand fifteen miles below Palomas. Colonel Lockett fired one of his civilian scouts, refusing to believe there was not a way around the sand fields. As Will and the two Apaches were securing breakfast, dozens of soldiers, men of every rank, approached to ask how much more of the sand lay ahead. Handed grim news to accompany their morning meal, most drifted away in a moody silence, preparing for the worst.

Will and the Apaches went off by themselves to eat. A tin

84

plate of half-cooked bacon and hardtack fried in bacon grease made for salty, almost tasteless chewing. But scalding coffee revived them some, as did the warmth of a rising sun. Will knew that in a couple of hours the desert heat would be merciless, draining men and animals of strength, causing motors to overheat, tempers to flare.

"We'll be lucky to make five or ten miles today," Will said ruefully. "I could be down here for the rest of my natural life at this rate."

Loco Jim nodded in understanding. "I'll quit before I stay here that long. As bad as I need the seventy-five dollars a month they are paying, I won't stay through the winter."

Will said nothing about the difference in pay, idly wondering why he was being paid more than the Indians. Perhaps it was the recommendation by Lem Spilsbury that carried so much weight, an extra seventy-five a month. He pondered the question himself, how long he would remain with a floundering army in the wilds of Chihuahua if the expedition lasted. Which it could, perhaps indefinitely, at its present rate. Halted ten miles below the border by sand beds, he wouldn't allow himself to think about what climbing the Sierra Madres would be like.

Tossing his empty plate aside, he sipped coffee while he watched General Pershing ride across the sands, seeing to the rescue operations himself. Will decided it wasn't entirely fair to be so hard on the general early in the campaign. No one could be expected to know how brutal the Chihuahuan deserts and mountains could be unless they'd seen it for themselves. Will made up his mind to give the general a chance before judging him as a leader of men. Pershing and his army would have plenty of chances to prove themselves under the worst possible conditions in the weeks to come.

• 10 •

Elisa rapped gently on the door three times. Off in the mountains north of Parral a coyote howled. The big *hacienda* was dark, for it was late, past midnight. She heard footsteps in the hallway, then a heavy bolt sliding back. A pale, bearded face peered cautiously through a crack in the door. The black muzzle of a pistol was aimed at her.

"Come in, *fraulein,*" a reedy voice said, then the gun disappeared and the door opened.

She glanced over her shoulder and stepped into a poorly lit terrazzo-tile hallway. A candle burned on a table beside a polished mahogany coat tree. She pulled off her jacket and hung it on a peg, glancing at her reflection briefly in the mirror, flipping a strand of hair away from her forehead. The man with the neatly trimmed Van Dyke beard watched her closely, placing the gun inside the pocket of his silk dressing robe. He closed and bolted the door without taking his eyes off her.

"What is wrong? Why did you come at this hour?" he asked, speaking thick English heavily accented by his native German.

"I have news, Herr Milnor. Francisco is planning an attack on Guerrero in five days. He is gathering as many soldiers as he can at a little village to the north called Rubio."

Rudolph Milnor summoned Elisa over to the candle, reading her face intently. "Let us go in the study," he whispered, after a look toward the kitchen where his housekeeper and a cook had small sleeping quarters in rooms off the back of the house. He trusted no one, not even the servants who had worked for him many years.

They entered a large room lined with bookshelves. Heavy drapes covered the windows. Elisa noticed a dank smell. Milnor put the candleholder on top of his recently waxed oak desk and sat down in a soft leatherbound chair behind it, tenting his slender fingers on a blotter littered with stacks of papers and coded telegrams. He watched Elisa the way a cat watches a mouse, mistrustful even of her despite their longstanding relationship.

"How do you know this?" he asked, certain of the answer. He already knew she had slept with the rebel chieftain three nights ago.

"He came to my house. He was there when word came of the attack on the United States. He reacted surprisingly. He was not upset by it. He ordered his bodyguards to keep their mouths shut about where he was that night. He intends to allow the Americans to blame him for it. Now he has gone north to Rubio, raising an army to strike Guerrero."

"Interesting, that Villa would react this way. Instead of running, he intends to attack. On the surface it would appear to be evidence of total insanity on his part, but as I think about it, I am not so sure it is insane. He means to use this incident to gather support for his cause. David spitting in the eye of two Goliaths, it would seem, both the Mexican Army and the Americans. Our agents in Washington recently informed the Imperial High Command of a sudden American army buildup on the Mexican border, as many as twenty thousand men backed by artillery and squadrons of aeroplanes. I expect they have begun marching into Chihuahua by now, looking for Villa," he said, sounding as though he knew very little about it.

"I should have telephoned you earlier," Elisa said quietly, avoiding Milnor's piercing blue eyes. "I knew how important it was that you knew of Francisco's plans."

Milnor's bushy eyebrows knitted. "I warned you never to use the telephone!" he snapped. "The operators can eavesdrop on any conversation! You must always deliver news to me personally!"

"That is why I am here now, Herr Milnor."

Milnor drummed his fingers impatiently on the desk without comment, then he said, "The Americans will send spies ahead of their columns to find out where Villa is hiding. If any of them show up around Parral, it is your duty to find out where they are going and how many American soldiers are being sent to Chihuahua. The spies may be cleverly disguised, so be wary of any Americans in the city. Make yourself . . . available to them and learn whatever you can, by whatever means necessary. Is my meaning perfectly clear, *fraulein?*"

"Quite clear," Elisa whispered, lowering her face to the floor. "I will do whatever it takes to find out what you want to know. Perhaps no American agents will come to Parral. . . ."

"They will come. American intelligence knows Villa is seen frequently around Parral. Your house is his favorite place to spend an evening while he is there."

She looked up at him then, and even in the soft candle-light her expression seemed harder than before. "I have always done as you asked, Herr Milnor."

He gave her a crooked smile. "And we both know why, don't we? Surely you have not forgotten why you are cooperating with my requests?"

"I have not forgotten," she replied hoarsely, eyes downcast again.

To signal their discussion had come to an end, Milnor stood up abruptly. "Make sure no one sees you leave the house. Never travel by the Santa Isabel road, not even at night."

"I understand."

"And keep me closely informed. I must know immediately if the Americans send spies ahead to Parral."

Before Elisa turned for the door she hesitated. "What about the attack Francisco plans at Guerrero?"

Milnor shrugged. "It means nothing to us. There are no German interests there, so let Villa fight Carranza over a few machine guns and ammunition. If he wins, he will create even more problems for Carranza and for the American expedition sent to punish him. If we could give him the guns ourselves it would serve our purposes. Under the circumstances, all we can give him now is money to buy them. At his core, he is nothing but an ignorant peasant, a common bandit who lacks the understanding he needs to command an army. Yet there are those in Berlin who feel he will be the ultimate victor in Mexico when this revolution finally ends. Should that unlikely event occur, we must have him as an ally. Thus we shall continue to buy his friendship, unless he makes a serious military mistake."

"He is very clever," Elisa said, as Milnor came around the desk to stand in front of her, blocking her escape from the room. She saw a different look in his eye now and she knew what would come next. She recoiled inwardly at the thought of it, the way she did each time he forced her to satisfy him.

"Take off your clothes," he demanded. "I want to look at your body."

"Of course, Herr Milnor," she whispered, reaching for the top button of her blouse, closing her eyes so as not to reveal any hint of the revulsion she felt toward him. She always tried to be careful to hide her real feelings. She had expected this might happen, had dreaded the possibility on the long ride out to the *hacienda,* and she had hoped to avoid it if she could, yet she dared not refuse him.

She opened the front of her shirt, watching his face through slitted eyelids. His gaze wandered over her bare breasts, her nipples.

"Take your pants off," he instructed. "Do it slowly. Make your hips wiggle, as though you are dancing. Imagine you are listening to beautiful orchestra music, *fraulein,* a slow waltz. Turn gracefully. Lift your arms over your head like a ballerina. Smile sweetly, and pretend you are very happy to be pleasing the audience at the Berlin ballet, wearing pink tights instead of hiding your womanhood in a man's work clothes."

She did as she was told, unfastening her denim riding pants, wriggling them down over her hips slowly, turning, lips frozen in a grotesque smile he barely noticed. His eyes roamed over her body when her pants fell to her ankles. She turned her back to him, gyrating. Spreading her arms, she let her blouse drop to the floor, then she raised her hands, pressing her palms together over her head. Only then, when he could not see her face, did she allow her expression to change, her eyes to alight with hatred.

He came up behind her and cupped her breasts in his clammy hands, squeezing them much too hard. She felt his erection touch her, parting her buttocks. His fingernails dug into the cleft of her bosom, clawing her skin, drawing a trace of blood, reminding her of the first time he took her so many years before, when she was not yet twelve years old. He had treated her roughly then, and as the years passed it had only grown worse. In many ways he was like Francisco in this regard, feeling that he had to hurt her in order to be truly satisfied, only he never slapped her face the way Francisco did.

She felt him enter her and she bent over to grab the edge of the desk, steadying herself when his short thrusts began inside her. Grunting like a pig, he clung to her nipples, stabbing his erection into her, his bony fingers trembling with growing excitement. She bit her lip, not from any real physical pain, waiting for his testicles to explode, silently praying it would end as quickly as it usually did. Long before she had learned to block out what was happening and the humiliation of it by directing her thoughts elsewhere, back to Germany and her short childhood before her mother and father died. When she remembered her parents and the few happy years she'd spent with them, she was able to lose herself in those memories without consciously thinking about the way she was being used by Herr Milnor.

A warm, wet feeling filled her, and she cried out the moment it happened, knowing how much it pleased him to hear her cries. "It hurts," she whimpered softly, thinking of the tulips in her mother's garden in springtime.

He gave one final thrust as the last of his seed was spent, then he sighed and backed away from her, releasing his iron grip on her breasts.

She waited a moment before turning around, listening to the soft rustle of fabric when he closed the front of his robe. She stared at the candle's small flame. Her eyes were dry, for she had stopped shedding tears over the way he used her when she was still in her early teens. In the beginning it had been quite painful when this man entered her. Now there was no pain attached to it at all, only humiliation.

She faced him, tiny drops of blood clinging to the tracks made by his fingernails across her bosom. He wasn't looking at her now.

"Get dressed," he snapped, walking around her to his desk. "I must send a wire to Berlin concerning Villa's plans to move on Guerrero. Herr Zimmermann should be advised immediately," he added, his mind apparently on other matters, even though Elisa was still naked, standing in the flickering candlelight.

She dressed while Milnor was scribbling a message on a slip of paper. He glanced up once when she was fully clothed and then he dismissed her with a wave.

"Make certain no one sees you leaving the house," he said again, before going back to his writing. "Inform me promptly if any Americans come to Parral, no matter who they are. We must keep Berlin informed of their movements and their intentions here, how long they mean to stay if Villa is not caught." He looked up now, his pen poised above the coded message he was preparing. "Should someone arrive who might be an American spy, seduce him and find out everything he knows." A humorless grin twisted his thin lips. "You are quite good at seduction, my child. Even I find your charms irresistible at times. Put them to good use in the service of your country. Never allow yourself to forget that you are *Deutsche.*"

Backing away from the desk, she shook her head. Her voice sounded strained when she replied softly, "I know who I am, Herr Milnor. I have not forgotten."

She left the study, walking quietly down the inky hallway to remove her jacket from the peg, hearing her own light footsteps on the tiles. She let herself out, stopping on the porch for a moment to listen to the night sounds around her and make sure no one was watching the house. It would not have surprised her to learn that Francisco was having someone follow her, although she had been very careful to study the hills behind her before she rode very far from her adobe east of Parral. Francisco had grown even more mistrustful lately, after his humbling defeat at Agua Prieta, where he'd lost almost half his army. He swore someone had betrayed him to the Carrancistas, and perhaps it was true, but he was beginning to show signs that he also suspected her of something, grilling her with endless questions about who she had seen since he visited her the last time. He had never been this suspicious or inquisitive. Something had changed. She hoped he didn't know about what went on during her meetings with Rudolph Milnor.

Her black mare stood quietly in front of the stable at the rear of the *hacienda* when she left the porch. Walking through the darkness, she felt sticky moisture trickle down her legs, wetting the crotch of her riding pants. She looked at the house, its pale adobe walls glowing in the light from the stars. Passing one curtained window of Milnor's study, she spat upon the adobe angrily and hurried toward her mare. Were it not for her brother back in Germany, she could easily have removed the Mauser from her saddlebags and returned to the house to kill the man who'd forced this feeling of shame upon her.

• 11 •

Exhausted soldiers lay everywhere beneath the stars, too tired to erect their tents despite a numbing chill, wrapped in thin blankets or huddled close to blazing campfires scattered over the flats where the column was again mired in bottomless sand. Pershing had never seen a desert that could change as dramatically as this: blistering heat during the day, then temperatures far below freezing only a few hours after dark. The scouts were reporting more of the same terrain ahead, some that could even be worse, if such a thing were possible. A sergeant riding up from the rear guard informed him only an hour before that the pack train had fallen many miles behind during the afternoon, when the mules grew weary and refused to be pushed. The men in charge of the mule train were freezing, due to the fact that no winter coats had been requisitioned by the Quartermaster Corps. All day men suffered in the heat, and at night they almost froze to death. Every man, animal, and machine in the column was covered with a layer of white alkali, causing some member of his staff to remark that the soldiers looked like "dough boys" rolled in baker's flour. The nickname stuck.

Tonight, barely thirty miles south of Culberson Ranch where the campaign had been launched with high expectations, they were mired again. Four trucks had to be abandoned today, either with broken drive chains, motors ruined by overheating, or a failed clutch for which no parts were available. Flat tires and broken rims had become so common over the previous three days that hardly anyone mentioned them now. Messengers from the Signal Corps reported that the east column under Lockett's command was similarly halted south of Palomas, in what Colonel Lockett ruefully described as dry quicksand. Lockett had summarily fired two more civilian guides and was now down to only one man who knew the area below Ascencion. Pershing had ordered a dispatch sent to Lockett, since every radio in the Signal Corps had suddenly failed to generate anything but static, informing the colonel that under no circumstances were any more scouts to be dismissed without a full inquiry. Lockett was blaming his guides for the sand traps, which made about as much sense as blaming Old Man Winter for the ice forming in the soldiers' canteens tonight.

The general stood in front of his tent a while longer, surveying the bleak scene around him of a military expedition with orders to proceed swiftly in pursuit of the enemy, run aground after only three short days in the field with the eyes of most Americans following its every movement, or lack thereof. Something had to be done quickly to stave off the appearances of a disaster in the making. A bit of daring action was desperately needed for newspaper headlines. The right leader for that sort of job had not arrived yet, delayed by red tape and missed train connections somewhere in Nebraska. When Colonel George Dodd finally got here he would assume command of the Seventh Cavalry, replacing Colonel James Erwin at the front of one prong of the advance. Dodd knew how to move cavalrymen over any type of terrain. If any man on earth could dog Villa's trail it was Dodd, for he understood old-fashioned hard riding and relentless pursuit as well as any soldier Pershing had ever known.

Pershing remembered campaigns with Dodd against the Sioux and Cheyenne. Dodd had an almost uncanny instinct for reading an Indian's mind, predicting which way they would go when it seemed no one else could, where to flank them, when to charge, and when to wait for the enemy to make the next move. Together, he and Dodd could plot Villa's most logical course and then plan a workable strategy to encircle him. And with Dodd at the head of a column of horseback soldiers, the cavalry would get there at the appointed hour even if hell were frozen solid.

Footsteps moving through the sand took Pershing's thoughts from Colonel Dodd's arrival. Lieutenant Patton stepped smartly to the front of the command tent and saluted, heels together as they should be, his back as straight as a ramrod, the very picture of parade-ground drill precision standing stiffly in the light from the general's campfire.

"Sir," Patton began, "with your permission I'll send some of the mechanics back to strip the abandoned trucks of usable parts. I've gone over the parts inventory kept by Major Madden, and it is woefully short, in my opinion. At the rate our motorized vehicles are failing in this sand, we will need every spare part we can get our hands on. The quartermaster should have foreseen this kind of difficulty, sir. The mechanics can remove all functional parts from the abandoned trucks before sunrise. I suggest that they be accompanied by armed guards, setting up a perimeter of defense around the vehicles until the mechanics are finished with their work."

Pershing couldn't help but agree, although it was a detail he had overlooked during the frustrating hours spent digging and pulling the rest of the vehicles and wagons from the sand bogs this afternoon. "Very thorough of you, Lieutenant, to examine Major Madden's inventory. I don't suppose it's entirely Madden's fault. Who could have foreseen this kind of endless quagmire?"

"The civilian scout named Johnson did, sir," Patton replied. "He also warns us that there is a considerable amount of the same terrain ahead of us tomorrow. I don't see how we'll ever get to Colonia Dublan like this. However, I do have a plan to speed our march when we get there, if you'd be willing to listen."

"I'll listen," the general said, rocking back on his heels a little to hear the rest of what Patton had to say. He had to admit that young George S. Patton, Jr., surpassed his senior aide, Lieutenant Collins, when it came to planning things. Patton had several mildly irritating qualities, not the least of which was his persistence when he set his mind to something he wanted, but he was a good soldier with a solid military mind, a West Pointer. He was tall and slender, a hard-looking man who had been with the Eighth Cavalry awaiting some action, and a promotion. He had almost driven Pershing over the brink begging for a transfer, literally camping at his doorstep until the request was granted. But Patton always followed orders to the letter, doing more than he was asked, and his suggestions bore the mark of wisdom beyond his years.

"It has to do with the trains, sir. We are ordered not to use the Mexican Northwestern Railway trains, but the written order makes no mention of a prohibition from using their tracks. If we requested a locomotive and cattle cars from El Paso to meet us at Colonia Dublan, we could send horses and cavalry over the Cumbre Pass and have Villa flanked at San Miguel, where reports say he went seeking fresh horses. I read the general orders very carefully, and they say nothing about using Mexican railroad tracks with our own locomotives."

It was a brilliant idea, employing the strategy Pershing wanted from the beginning, if the orders were as Patton stated. In truth, Pershing couldn't remember exactly what they said concerning the rails. "Are you quite sure the orders do not contain any wording to the effect that would prohibit us from using those tracks?"

"Absolutely certain of it, sir. I suppose the argument could be made in Washington that it might violate the spirit of the orders, but there is no specific mention of railroad tracks. By the time we asked Washington for a clarification, Villa could be in Brazil."

The general nodded and said, "Well put, Lieutenant. Wilson and Baker would argue about it for weeks. Wilson would call a full Cabinet meeting to discuss it in detail. Our commander-in-chief has a tendency to vacillate at important times. I am quite sure he gave the order to pursue Villa with great reluctance. If the general orders say nothing about railroad tracks, then by God we'll use them. This sand is all but unnavigable here. I'll prepare a dispatch for the Signal Corps immediately, requesting that the first available locomotive and cattle cars be rushed to Colonia Dublan. Good thinking on your part, Lieutenant. When I first learned we had been ordered not to use the Mexican Northwestern, I merely assumed it included the tracks. . . ."

"Should I sent the mechanics back to strip the disabled trucks, sir?" Patton asked.

"Yes, by all means. And make a note that I should add the shortage of parts to my field report concerning Major Madden's apparent failure to realize that my men needed winter coats. I wonder what else the major has overlooked. Let us hope he remembered the ammunition for our artillery."

"There is more than an adequate supply of shells for the Vickers cannons, sir. I took an inventory myself. We have enough to blast new roads through the mountains if we find we are unable to cross them, which may account for the way our heavy wagons and trucks bog down in the sand. I fear the extra weight will present added difficulty when we try to climb up the Sierras. The civilian Johnson says the roads are all but impassable for our motorized equipment."

Pershing scowled, remembering his first visit with Johnson at Fort Bliss. "This particular guide appears to know quite a bit more than any of the others about what we face here. Perhaps I should have listened more closely when he warned of problems."

"If a locomotive arrives in time, we might not have to deal with the mountains," Patton suggested. "With Villa flanked to the west, and a large force spread out to the east of him, we stand a good chance of netting him at San Miguel."

"If he's still there," Pershing said absently. "We may have wasted too much time already in this damn sand. Colonel Dodd was expected to arrive today. With Dodd leading the Seventh from the west over Cumbre Pass, we will have done everything we can to surround Villa where the reports say he went. Johnson doesn't think we'll find him at San Miguel, but we simply must try."

Patton frowned thoughtfully. "Johnson is rather an odd

duck at times. He seems to prefer the company of those Indians rather than his white counterparts. He avoids all contact with any of the Negro soldiers, yet he associates freely with the Apaches. Major Ryan has a rather low opinion of him, I gather, calling him insolent. The major does not completely trust Johnson's ideas about what Villa is up to or where he will go next. Major Ryan is counting on the aeroplanes to gather reliable reports as to Villa's whereabouts."

While Pershing had private doubts about the reliability of the Curtiss aircraft, he chose not to voice them until the JN-2s were in the skies above Mexico. The First Aero Squadron was due to fly in from El Paso tomorrow morning, led by Captain Benjamin Foulois. Foulois had the reputation of being able to fly a piano crate if it had wings, which was more or less what some younger pilots said about the Jennys during training exercises. "I've known men like Johnson," Pershing said, addressing Major Ryan's complaint. "I agree he wouldn't make a good soldier, but for the job at hand he is probably well equipped to find out what we need to know. Not everyone is cut out for a military career, Lieutenant. Johnson appears to be capable of leading us through this wasteland. He may seem odd, but he knows his way around the unsettled parts of Chihuahua, according to Lem Spilsbury, and I'm certain that is where Villa intends to take us on this merry chase we've undertaken."

"By the way, General, the two reporters are asking for permission to send stories for their newspapers back to El Paso with our couriers. I told them I'd take the matter up with you."

"Not until I've read what they have to say," Pershing said. "I made it plain from the beginning that I retained the right to censor what they wrote. That Gibbons from the *Chicago Tribune* is already complaining that he thinks we are lost, and I won't have him sending a story to that effect to the *Tribune*'s readers. I want to see what they've written about us before anything is sent back. Inform Gibbons and Elser that their reports are to be submitted to me."

Patton saluted crisply. "Yes sir."

Pershing returned the salute, then Patton turned on his heel and marched off into the night with his notepad tucked under his arm. More and more, the general found himself taking a liking to his brash young aide. Patton knew how to get things done.

Shivering in the increasing cold, he turned for his tent to prepare the request for a locomotive and cattle cars and get a few hours of badly needed sleep. He glanced up at the stars, thinking about Warren before he went to bed, promising himself he would get a note off to his son tomorrow morning. He had also neglected to make a single entry in his diary since leaving Culberson Ranch, and he made another promise to catch up tonight, even though he felt too tired to do so.

18 March:
We are hopelessly bogged down in sand. Making less than 10 miles per day. Recurring equipment failures. Lockett reports he is also stuck. Madden has shown his incompetence at the quartermaster's post by omitting any number of essential things. The men are nearly frozen to death without coats and complaining loudly. Morale is deteriorating rapidly and we must see some action soon. Dodd was scheduled to arrive today and did not make it. I long to see George again, although he will no doubt find the same frustrations I face now when he sees the mess we're in here. I am certain the 2 newsmen wish to hurry off the reports of our break-downs and delays to eager readers in the East, but I cannot allow it. We must appear to be proceeding according to plan, otherwise Wilson may have a change of heart and call the whole campaign off. Aero squadron due tomorrow and perhaps things will change for the better. I am lonely and tired tonight. I miss Warren, and I will miss dear Frances and the girls until my dying day. Bittersweet memories continue to haunt me, yet I must not let them interfere with my work. We must engage Villa soon and bring him to task, other-wise the hue and cry from the naysayers will fill the halls in Washington.

• 12 •

From a bluff overlooking Colonia Dublan, Will and the two Apaches were witness to what could only be called a minor miracle. Troops from the east column, strung out for half a mile to the northeast, came plodding from the desert to the outskirts of the village shortly after four o'clock in the afternoon. Colonia Dublan was a farming community nestled in a winding valley, home to a small American Mormon population running irrigation ditches through their fields from the Casas Grandes river. Like a pale green emerald in the midst of the desert, the farmers' crops thrived. Peach and plum trees were in bloom. To the south and west, towering peaks loomed, dark and forbidding, the beginnings of the Sierra Madre Occidental.

"The other column made it," Will observed. "Some of it, anyway."

Loco Jim studied their back trail. "Our boys are coming too," he said, shading his eyes from a blistering sun.

Will saw them, moving like ants across the distant horizon. "Appears the general figured out how to cross that sand. I'll ride down an' tell Lem Spilsbury that the soldiers will be here shortly."

Loco Jim turned his horse. "I will ride back to the corporal named Estes, to say the town is close." He kicked his bay gelding to a trot and rode toward the approaching soldiers.

Will and Es Ki Ben De urged their tired horses off the bluff, sending up a swirl of alkali powder. At a railroad depot down in the valley, a locomotive and six cattle cars sat quietly on a siding. Walking dusty roads of the tiny village, Mormon men wearing black flat-brimmed hats were gathering around the train. A Mormon mounted a gaunt-flanked sorrel and rode out to meet Will and the Apache. Will could tell by the way the man sat the horse it was Lem Spilsbury. Before reaching the bottom of the bluff they struck a lope. The three men came together on a plain north of the village and reined to a halt.

Lem smiled when he recognized Will. "Good to see you, my friend," he said, extending a hand and nodding politely to Es Ki Ben De. "I wondered if you would accept the army's offer."

"I couldn't turn it down," Will answered, thinking how much Lem had aged over the last couple of years. He had always been a raw-boned man, barbed-wire thin, not unlike the horse he rode. Life was hard in this part of Chihuahua for a farmer. The Mormons ran a few goats and cows in the mountains to supplement their crops, and Lem knew the land in this vicinity. "Has there been any sign of Villa?" he asked, guessing what the answer would be.

Lem pointed to the west. "I was told they swung wide of Casas Grandes to head for San Miguel de Babicora a few days ago to find fresh horses. A *vaquero* from San Miguel said they meant to ride southwest, into Sonora."

"Do you believe him?" Will asked, distracted by a troop of galloping cavalry heading into town from the northeast, the first to arrive from the east column, a detachment of less than forty men. The desert behind them was empty.

Lem appeared to be contemplating it. "It would be hard to say, truthfully. Villa is an unpredictable fellow. He may have told people they were going to Sonora to throw off any pursuit."

"That's the way I've got it figured," Will said, taking note of the alkali dust coating the soldiers' uniforms and their sweat-caked horses as they rode toward the spot where he conferred with Lem. "I heard he likes it down around Parral. He feels safer there, so I was told. And he has a girlfriend."

The cavalrymen arrived and drew to a halt, briefly surrounded by a choking cloud of dust, their horses panting. An officer at the front of the column spoke. "I'm looking for Lemuel Spilsbury."

"I'm Spilsbury," Lem replied, wheeling his horse to face the officer.

"Major Frank Tompkins of the Thirteenth Cavalry," he said, pulling off a glove to shake hands with Lem. He eyed Will and the Apache. "Colonel Lockett wanted to advise you that our column is down to a crawl in the midst of all that miserable sand. The colonel estimates that two more days will be required to navigate the desert, since we have most of the heavy supply wagons and ambulances, and those damnable trucks. Two of the Jeffrey Quads had to be abandoned. . . . The drive chains broke and engines were beyond repair. We had guides, only the damn fools led us squarely into the worst of the sand pits, and Colonel Lockett dismissed all but one and sent them back to El Paso. The colonel asks that you ride out to the column as soon as possible, to show us the way around the mire."

"There is no way around it," Lem replied, sounding almost apologetic. "The straightest course is by far the best choice, I'm afraid. Follow the wagon ruts as closely as you can."

The major wore an unhappy look. "I guessed as much. We been following what appears to be some sort of road." He gave Will another questioning stare. "Are you one of General Pershing's scouts?" He glanced at Es Ki Ben De. "We were told we would have Indian guides the rest of the way."

"We're with Pershing," Will replied. "The column is still a few miles from here. They should make it before nightfall. We had a shorter distance to travel, but the sand's just as bad by either route."

"How the hell did you make it?" Tompkins asked. "We've been stuck almost every mile since we left Palomas, thanks to those incompetent guides the colonel acquired."

"It isn't the guides' fault," Will declared. "Wagons and trucks are gonna sink if they're loaded too heavy for that road. Freighters who come that way know to travel light as they can. I tried to tell General Pershing and Major Ryan what would happen, only they both said their engineers could manage it."

"We have engineers," the major grumbled, looking away,

"only they didn't know beans about getting us out of the bogs." He looked past Will to the railroad station. "I see the El Paso Southwestern sent the train we requested. Colonel Lockett has conferred with General Pershing by wireless, after the Signal Corps got the damn things to work. The Southern Command at San Antonio agreed to President Carranza's condition that we wouldn't use Mexican trains to capture Villa. However, nothing was stipulated about using one of our own locomotives on their railroad tracks. Troops from the Seventh and the Tenth will board that train as soon as they can get here, bound for San Miguel to keep Villa from escaping to the southwest."

"It came a few hours ago," Lem said, "but the cattle cars are in bad shape and there is precious little fuel available to run the engine. It's an old woodburner. Repairs will have to be made before the cars can be used. There are holes in the flooring that will most certainly injure your horses."

"Damn!" Tompkins growled, lifting his reins. "I'll put my men to repairing them until General Pershing arrives. We'll have to hurry to make San Miguel before morning, if the distance shown on the maps is accurate. The cars must be serviceable by the time they get here."

"It's a waste of time," Will remarked. "Villa isn't in San Miguel now."

"You sound mighty sure of it," the major said, scowling and giving Will the once-over again.

"He's aiming for Parral. I'm sure he's there by now. They went through San Miguel to pick up fresh horses, but that was days ago."

"I've got my orders," Tompkins said. "Colonel Erwin is to take the Seventh Cavalry to a place named Galeana, then climb the mountains to San Miguel from the east. Colonel Brown, with a squadron from the Tenth, is to go by rail to El Rucio, cutting Villa off from the north. Major Evans is to continue by train to Cumbre Pass, sealing off the western escape route. We'll have them boxed in when the rest of the Seventh blocks Villa from the south. General Pershing reported by wireless that one of his scouts was given reliable information that Villa is enjoying a respite at San Miguel. I'm surprised you didn't know about it, being one of his scouts yourself."

Will pondered who might have given the general such useless information. Villa was much too clever to remain in one place so close to the American border. The news Pershing had been given was almost a week old, and yet an entire battle plan had been devised around it, another waste of valuable time. "I hadn't heard anything about Villa still bein' there," he told Tompkins. "Villa won't stay in one spot very long. You won't find him in San Miguel, I'm sure of that."

"You sound like a man who knows Villa's tactics," the major said, showing more interest in Will now.

"I've watched him operate over the past few years. It's been over a week since the Columbus raid. By now he's down around Parral, probably scattering his men for a while so they'll be harder to find . . . harder to corner."

"Interesting theory," Tompkins observed. "You may well be right. You given your views to the general?"

"I have," Will replied tiredly, "and to Major Ryan. Didn't seem to carry much weight with either one of them."

Tompkins swung his horse over to Will. "I didn't get your name. . . ."

"Will Johnson," he said, offering his hand, "and this is Es Ki Ben De, one of the Apaches from San Carlos."

The major shook hands with both of them, the Indian showing some reluctance to take a soldier's palm.

Lem said, "Will knows Chihuahua better than most Mexicans. He has traveled all over it buying livestock since he was a boy. If he thinks Pancho Villa is at Parral, that's where I'd look first. I agree it isn't likely that Pancho would still be at San Miguel."

Tompkins was frowning. "It isn't like the general to ignore reliable intelligence. I do, however, know Major Ryan. Perhaps he's listened to the wrong voices." He spoke of Ryan with a hint of contempt in his voice. "It isn't my decision," he added, after another look at the cattle cars. "Good day to you, gentlemen." He slapped alkali dust from his uniform sleeves and swung his horse for the depot.

"I suppose I should ride out to meet General Pershing," Lem said. "I'll inform him about the poor condition of the train and the shortage of firewood."

"We'll ride along with you, I reckon," Will said, wheeling

Poco north to be alongside Lem's sorrel. "We can catch up on things. It's been a while since we saw each other."

Lem's hollow cheeks broke into a grin, then his face fell. "Life has been hard for those of us who stayed here, Will. Only a few have been willing to run the risks. Villa's men tolerate us, for the most part, but they take whatever they want from our food stores. Carranza's soldiers are no better. This revolution has attracted all manner of evil men to both sides. Neither army will offer us any protection. It is only by the will of God that those of us who stayed are still alive. Carranza's men rob us and dishonor some of our women. . . ."

Will listened to the terrible sorrow in Lem's voice. The Mormons were gentle people, refusing to take up arms, not even to protect themselves. Although he could never understand a religion denouncing all forms of violence no matter what the reason, he genuinely liked Lem and his Mormon friends at Colonia Dublan.

"Maybe it ain't entirely God's will that's keepin' you alive," he said later. "There's this thing called luck. Lady Luck smiles on some folks and shits on some others. It's been my experience that luck runs in cycles, both the good and the bad. When a man's luck turns sour there ain't a damn thing he can do about it until it bottoms out. When things can't get any worse, your luck will improve some, most times. Hardly any other direction it can go."

Lem's expression did not change, making Will wonder if he'd been listening.

Pershing's west column was camped across a broad valley surrounding Colonia Dublan along a clear, spring-fed stream. Fires winked and flickered in the darkness. Bone-weary men huddled in wool blankets near the fires, while others slept away fatigue after the difficulties of the desert crossing. Work continued on the rotted wood of the cattle cars, the resounding clang of hammers, grinding saws, and the voices of tired, disgruntled soldiers working by lamplight echoing in the night. A detail had been dispatched to find fuel for the wood-burning locomotive. Abandoned corrals were torn down despite boisterous complaints from a few Mexican villagers, who were ignored by the army command. General Pershing, relying upon information gathered by J. B. Barker from a goat herder encountered in the hills, was determined to send troops from the Seventh and the Tenth to encircle San Miguel de Babicora. Will knew the information was worthless by now, if it had ever been the truth. They would form a circle around an empty mountain village after days of difficult travel, a waste of valuable time if the army wanted to capture the Columbus raiders, whoever they might have been.

There was a moment of silence in the command tent. General Pershing and Colonel Brown, a tall black officer from the Tenth, studied maps spread over a folding table below a kerosene lamp. Major Ryan, and Colonel James Erwin commanding the Seventh Cavalry, stood at Pershing's shoulder, also reading the maps. Will, Lem, and J. B. Barker were the only guides present at this hastily called meeting soon after the soldiers made camp.

The general aimed a blunt finger at a spot on one of the maps. "If we don't cut them off to the south they will probably flee to Madera, or even farther, to Agua Caliente. We must surround them quickly. As soon as the train is ready to travel, I want Second Squadron from the Tenth on its way to El Rucio. From there, Colonel Brown, you are to move due south to San Miguel. Major Evans with the First Squadron will continue by rail to Las Varas, thus effectively blocking Villa off to the south. We'll have him surrounded, if we can get there before he pulls out."

"You'll be several days too late," Will offered from a dark corner of the tent.

Heads turned quickly. Major Ryan spoke. "Mr. Barker has it on good authority that Villa is still in San Miguel. He talked to one of the locals this very afternoon while scouting in the hills."

Barker hitched his thumbs in his suspenders. "I feel the man I spoke with can be trusted. He told me Villa is giving his men a rest at San Miguel."

The general was watching Lem for his reaction. "What do you think of the report, Mr. Spilsbury?"

Lem rocked back on his heels momentarily. "I doubt that Villa would remain at San Miguel very long. It's too easily accessible by rail, and that would worry him. He's real good at knowing just when to clear out of a place. Will is probably right. Villa is long gone by now."

"But what about Barker's report?" Major Ryan demanded, showing more irritation than the occasion warranted.

When Lem said nothing, Will spoke up. "You can't trust most of what *campesinos* in Chihuahua tell you when it comes to Villa. He's a hero to them, a Robin Hood. They won't betray him. It's my guess that the story Barker heard today was false, meant to delay you."

Barker gave Will a withering stare. "I'm a pretty good judge of men, Johnson. I say the Mexican was telling the truth."

Pershing seemed undecided. "I don't see how we can completely ignore it. In any event, we'll have to wait here for Colonel Lockett and the supply train before moving south. We reached them by radio earlier. They're still bogged down in the sand, so he estimates two more days will be needed to get here." He turned to Lem. "Where do you think Villa will go, Mr. Spilsbury?"

"Probably down to Parral, like Will says. He didn't go through Agua Caliente, most likely, since there's a fairly good-sized garrison of Constitutionalists there. I'd be more inclined to believe he rode for Guerrero, maybe passing through Namiquipa, where Colonel Salas has only a small force loyal to Carranza. With five hundred men, Villa could overwhelm Salas and make off with his equipment. Colonel Salas has machine guns. We saw them when we drove our fall calves and goats to market."

Will added his thoughts. "Villa needs guns and ammunition. There's a big ammunition warehouse at Guerrero. A general by the name of Jose Cavazos commands the garrison. By now Villa knows we're following him and he'll want to be ready for us when he makes up his mind to turn and fight."

"I agree," Lem said, hands buried in his pants pockets. "He figures to run from you until he finds the right spot."

Major Ryan did not agree. "I still say we should trust the account Mr. Barker was given and surround San Miguel, General."

"Very well," Pershing said, sighing. He turned to Colonel

Erwin. "As soon as the men of the Seventh have a few hours of rest, strike out for Galeana. South of the village, swing to the southwest to ascend the mountains. When the train is ready, the Tenth Cavalry will depart for El Rubio and Cumbre Pass. The men will have to ride atop the cattle cars in order to carry enough horses. Major Evans will take First Squadron to Las Varas to patrol the southern escape route. If Villa is at San Miguel, we will have him surrounded. Each command will carry a radio pack to keep me informed, if the damn things will work. That will be all, gentlemen, unless there are questions."

The officers filed quietly out of the tent. Barker left with Major Ryan after giving Will a satisfied smirk, leaving Will and Lem alone with the general. A breath of cold night air came through the tent flap.

"With your permission, General," Will began, "I'd like to scout around up in the mountains near El Valle and Namiquipa. I've got a hunch that's where Villa's headed to find the guns and ammunition he needs. He'll be usin' up horses mighty fast too, and those mountain villages will have plenty of them. If I took along a few of the Apaches, we could cover a lot of territory."

Pershing was thinking. "Do you agree, Mr. Spilsbury?"

Lem nodded. "Will's got the right idea. Pancho won't be far from a supply of fresh horses."

The general slumped tiredly on a folding stool, staring at his boots. "Then take the men you need and proceed, Mr. Johnson. I want Mr. Spilsbury to remain here. Ask Colonel Brown of the Tenth to assign a pair of troopers to you, so they can be sent back with reports of what you find. Now, if you'll pardon me, gentlemen, I'm completely exhausted after a night without sleep and that miserable desert crossing."

"Good night, General," Lem said, edging for the tent flap.

"The Tenth Cavalry is a Negro outfit," Will said. "It might cause fewer problems in some of the villages if the messengers we had along weren't black. Mexicans don't take much of a shine to Negroes, usually, an' they dislike American soldiers in general."

Sudden anger flashed in Pershing's eyes when he looked up at Will. "Black soldiers are among the very best fighting men in the service of this country, Mr. Johnson!" he snapped. "I won't allow your prejudice to influence my decisions!"

"Beggin' your pardon, but it ain't my prejudice. It's the way most Mexicans feel toward Negroes."

"Frankly, I don't give a damn how they feel," Pershing replied tersely. "Take two men from the Tenth. I led Negro cavalrymen during the Indian wars and in the Philippines, and I can assure you there are no braver men on earth in the heat of battle."

Will shrugged and turned for the flap. "G'night, General," he muttered, following Lem into the chilly darkness.

• 13 •

On the morning of March 20, Will, Loco Jim, Es Ki Ben De, and two black privates from the Tenth Cavalry leading a pack mule loaded with provisions rode out of Colonia Dublan, the temperature just above freezing. Lem had worried that a freeze would ruin the Mormons' plum and peach crops, thus they set small fires between the rows of fruit trees and fed the flames scarce firewood needed for the locomotive. Private Calvin Fields, a green recruit from central Georgia, led the pack mule. Private James Washington hailed from Alabama. Neither was accustomed to bitter cold or a dry, desert terrain, nor had they ever seen mountains. With the dim outlines of the Sierra Madres in sight along the southern horizon, they rode toward Galeana, where only the night before the Seventh Cavalry under Colonel Erwin, almost seven hundred men, had advanced along the same road to branch off for San Miguel de Babicora. The sandy roadway was covered with horse tracks and droppings.

PANCHO AND BLACK JACK

"More dry country," Loco Jim observed, sweeping rolling hills and shallow gullies with a passing glance. Scrub mesquite trees dotted the hillsides. Chaparral and cactus grew everywhere. Brittle agave plants lay like dried starfish between scattered bunches of yellowed grass parched from lack of rainfall. Tumbleweed rolled across the wagon ruts, driven by irregular gusts of cold wind, to collect in bunches in shallow ditches or in tangled underbrush.

"Driest country I ever seen," Private Washington agreed.

Es Ki Ben De grunted, slitting his eyes when wind blew dust across the road. "San Carlos Reservation is more dry," he said. "Too dry. My people starve."

With the lush valley around the Mormon settlement behind them, the land had become desert again. Will recalled most every mile of the road ahead, the steep climbs below El Valle, the last farming village for many miles. They would cross Rio Santa Maria north of Galeana—water would be scarce, if mountain streams had dried up during the drought gripping the countryside. He knew the location of a few springs at some higher elevations that would keep their horses alive. A danger greater than thirst was the prospect of running into Carranza forces, now that word of an American invasion to capture Villa had spread. Will knew the U.S. Army had almost as much to fear from some undisciplined Carrancistas who resented American intervention on Mexican soil.

Mexican newspapers in Juarez had been full of denouncements regarding the Pershing expedition. Some of Carranza's generals promised no cooperation with the invaders, even hinting at direct confrontation if the Americans tried to occupy any Mexican towns. Will had been ready to make a stronger case against having the two uniformed soldiers accompany them on the scouting trip, until the general got mad over the remark about Negroes. Now there was a risk that trouble might arise in one of the villages, either by men loyal to Carranza or those who supported Villa, when they spotted American soldiers. Few Mexicans of either persuasion were likely to cooperate with them or offer any accurate information; thus it would simply be a reconnaissance mission. The ride to Namiquipa would take a day and a half, perhaps two. An equal amount of time was needed to return to the united east and west columns at Colonia Dublan before they pulled out. There was little time to spare, inquiring as to Villa's whereabouts.

At midmorning they rode to the outskirts of Galeana, after making the shallow crossing over Rio Santa Maria and following the road beside the river to the village. Passing adobe huts and a row of stores and smaller shops, Will sensed an angry mood among the citizens when they saw the two soldiers. Horse tracks left by the Seventh Cavalry covered the roadbed through Galeana, explaining the hostile looks everyone gave them. Seven hundred heavily armed American soldiers had ridden through their peaceful village a few hours earlier, arousing fears of U.S. occupation.

"They don't like us," Loco Jim remarked.

Will knew it was pointless to ask for any information about Villa here. He kicked Poco to a trot and held a steady gait until Galeana was well behind them.

On the road to El Valle they rode broken land, steepening foothills leading to the first peaks in the Sierras. They passed a few overloaded burro carts, a *vaquero* now and then. Entering the sleepy village nestled at the mouth of the fertile Santa Maria valley, townspeople stopped to stare at them, in particular the two black soldiers. Will knew an older *caballero* here, a man who sometimes sold him young horses. Riding through El Valle at a trot, he led the way south to a small adobe house near the southern edge of town where Arturo Gomez lived. Judging by the sun, Arturo would be there, taking his *siesta*. When they rode up to the adobe Will examined the horses in corrals behind the house, the natural thing for a horseman to do at a place like this. A barking dog soon brought Arturo to his doorway. He saw the soldiers first and halted on the front porch uneasily, then he recognized Will and appeared to relax a little.

"Buenos días, compadre," he said, running a palm across his thinning hair as he glanced at the soldiers again. He was dressed in soiled leather leggings and a shapeless cotton shirt.

"Buenos días, Arturo," Will said warmly, stepping down from the saddle. "Might need a few horses in a week or so. From the looks of what you've got in the pens back yonder, you've got some colts I may be able to use."

"Sí, my *americano* friend. I have good *caballos* to sell, and the price will be very cheap." His gaze returned to the pair of cavalrymen. "Do you work for *los soldados americanos* now?"

"After a fashion," he replied, walking closer to the porch so Arturo could hear him when he lowered his voice. "The army has hired me to help them locate Pancho Villa. I'm only acting as a guide through the mountains."

"Mi sabe," Arturo whispered, eyes flickering from the soldiers to Will's face. *"El León* was here only two days ago," he continued. "He called everyone together, asking for men who would join him. Forty men became part of his army. Others who would not join him were taken prisoner. They took many horses with them."

"Which way did they ride?" Will asked softly.

Arturo crossed himself quickly before he answered, making sure no one else could hear him when he spoke. "They rode for Namiquipa, staying in the valley most of the night. At Namiquipa they found many Carranza *soldados.* Only this morning, my cousin from Namiquipa came to tell me about the big fight there. *El León* defeated *los Carrancistas* easily, taking all their horses and guns, sending them running into the mountains. Now he has many more guns and bullets, and fresh *caballos.* He is even more dangerous, *compadre."*

"Did your cousin know which way they went, or where they were going?"

The Mexican cowboy swallowed, hesitating, as though his next words were very difficult to say. "They rode over the mountains, to the little village of Rubio. My cousin told me *el León* plans to attack the Carrancistas at Guerrero in only a few days, but you must tell no one where you learned of this."

Will looked southeast at the imposing rocky peaks between El Valle and Rubio, a distance of perhaps seventy or eighty miles. He remembered Rubio from cattle-buying excursions, a tiny hamlet of no particular consequence, and wondered why Villa would go there. Guerrero was almost due west of Rubio on the Rio Papigochic, across the towering Continental Divide. Crossing the Divide at this time of year, men would encounter icy winds and snow, a difficult journey even for experienced men who knew the climb. More puzzling, there were large garrisons of Carranza forces at Guerrero and San Isidro, just across the river valley. Was Villa now looking for a major battle with Carranza?

"Muchas gracias," Will said. "Maybe in a few days we'll be back to buy some horses." He slipped Arturo a few silver dollars and turned to mount Poco, taking note of the fact that a handful of villagers had come to the edge of El Valle to stare at them.

"Buena suerte," Arturo said quietly, wishing him good luck and pocketing the money hurriedly.

As Will was swinging over the saddle, a gunshot rang out from somewhere in the village. Private Washington lurched forward, reaching for the pommel of his McClellan saddle. A plug of skin erupted from his right cheek amid the crack of splintering bone. Blood flew from the hole in his face as he fell off his frightened horse. The gelding lunged forward, toppling Washington to the ground beneath its hooves. Private Fields made a grab for his holstered .45 automatic an instant later, letting go of his horse's reins. His chestnut, shying from the explosion, swung him out of the saddle before he could right himself. He fell, landing on his back with a loud grunt, while both unarmed Apaches turned their horses away and heeled them to a run. Will ducked down and drew his Winchester, bringing it to his shoulder as quickly as he could, reining Poco around to face the echo of the gun blast. A woman at the edge of town screamed. Arturo shouted, *"Madre!"* and disappeared inside his house. Will settled his horse, trying to find the source of the shot as villagers ran in every direction. He saw no one carrying a gun.

Private Fields scrambled to a crouch, sweeping his pistol barrel back and forth in a trembling hand. "Who shootin' at us?" he cried. Then Private Washington groaned. Both riderless horses galloped off, trailing their reins.

"Nobody's there," Will answered tightly. "Nobody with a gun that I can see."

Fields lowered his automatic and turned to Washington when all the villagers had fled. He knelt beside his fallen companion, making a face when he saw a spreading pool of blood on the ground around Washington's head. The wounded soldier's limbs began to shake violently. When Will was satisfied that no one was there to shoot at them again, he swung down quickly from Poco's back.

"Let's turn him over," Will suggested, taking Washington's shoulder to pull him over gently. The two Apaches had halted their horses a hundred yards from the house, and now they rode back toward the adobe cautiously at a walk.

Will's stomach knotted when he saw the soldier's wound. A dark bullet hole behind Washington's left ear seeped more blood on the ground, but it was the exit hole high on the private's right cheek that told the fatal story. Flinty bone fragments still clung to a ragged tear in his skin. Blood pulsed from the hole with each beat of his heart. "Go fetch his horse," Will said thickly as Private Fields started to cry. "We'll try to get him back to the column. They've got doctors there. . . ."

"He ain't gon' make it, is he?" Fields sobbed, looking at Will with tears in his eyes.

"Looks like the bullet went through his brain. We'll do all we can. There won't be any doctors here, so gettin' him back to the column is his only chance."

"I jus' know he gon' die." Fields wept. "We wasn't doin' nothin' to them. Askin' questions is all we was doin' here."

Will turned his gaze toward the Mexican village. "Feelings are runnin' mighty high around here. I tried to warn the general not to send soldier boys along with us, but he wouldn't listen."

Increasingly violent death throes gripped Washington. His eyes were glazing over. He stared up at the sun blankly, legs and arms shaking, while the crimson stain around his head grew larger, turning milky when it mixed with alkali dust, smelling faintly of copper. Fields took one of the dying soldier's hands and held it in his own for a time, then he dried his tears with his shirtsleeve and stood up to go for the loose horses.

Will's shadow fell over Private Washington's face. "Hang on, Mr. Washington," he said, doubting that the soldier could hear him now. "We'll take you to the closest doctor." He bent down and tied his bandanna around the private's head, hoping to stem the flow of blood. Washington's breathing was shallow, nostrils flaring irregularly. A moment later he seemed to awaken from his trance. His eyes focused on Will.

"Hurts," he whispered. "Tell my momma . . . Jimmy loves her."

Bloody spittle formed on his lips as he was speaking. His skin was turning gray. Will touched his shoulder. "I'll ask Private Fields to write your ma, tellin' her how brave you are, how good a soldier you are. Just try to hang on until we get back to the column. They've got plenty of doctors. They'll have you fixed up in no time."

"Feel . . . sleepy. Can I . . . have . . . some water?"

Will wheeled around to get his canteen from the saddlehorn. By the time he got back, Private James Washington was dead.

Es Ki Ben De was looking down at the soldier from the back of his pony. "He begins walk to spirit world now," he said.

Loco Jim was watching the village. "The man who killed him is a coward, like a dog who only kills young sheep."

Will listened to the dead man's bladder drain into his olive-green pants, remembering the roar of the rifle shot. "Whoever killed him used a large-bore gun, judging by the size of that hole. He never had a chance. The slug went plumb through his brain. Damn the luck. We'd better get started back. I found out what I needed to know from Arturo. We'll swing wide around the village, stayin' out of rifle range, just in case the same *hombre* aims to try again."

"Good idea," Loco Jim agreed, as Private Fields walked up leading the horses. Fields looked down at his friend. "He dead, ain't he?" the private asked in a faraway voice.

Will nodded. Arturo crept out on his porch just then, with an eye toward town. *"El soldado es muerte?"* he asked softly.

"Yeah," Will replied, sounding tired. "He's dead, shot plumb through the head. Any idea who would do it?"

Arturo wagged his head. "There are so many who hate the *gringo soldados, señor*. You are my friend, so I ask you, *por favor*, please leave my house *muy pronto*. Some will think I have betrayed *el León*, and perhaps they will kill me also."

"We'll be on our way," Will said, turning to Fields. "Help me tie him over his horse."

The dead soldier's body was hoisted and tied to the McClellan saddle. Blood still dripped from the private's gaping wound, forming coppery circles in the dust below a stirrup that shone brightly, like new pennies in the sunlight. Will knew he and the scouts were returning to General Pershing with the first casualty of the expedition. With a touch of nausea churning his stomach, he mounted Poco and reined west, around El Valle.

There was just one bit of news he could bring to the general's attention: He now knew where Villa meant to strike, and where he had been only two days earlier. If Pershing and Major Ryan would listen to him, the army could move cavalry to the city of Guerrero quickly, perhaps just in time to engage the elusive Lion of the North and crush him decisively before he ordered his men to scatter and hide in the mountains, where no one would ever find them.

They had no more than begun a circle around the town when a distant gunshot cracked in El Valle, followed by two more sharp reports, then the sizzle of airborne lead passed above their heads. Will dug his heels into Poco's sides and yelled, "Ride like hell! Don't shoot back!" Thundering hooves drowned out something Private Fields said as they galloped farther west to be out of rifle range. A quarter mile farther into the desert, Will slowed his horse to a trot, then a walk. Panting horses gathered wind in the following silence, until Loco Jim spoke.

"What was that about?" he asked, looking back.

Squinting in the sun's fierce glare to make sure no one was coming after them, Will replied, "I reckon they're tellin' us how they feel about havin' American soldiers in their village."

Private Fields, leading the horse carrying the dead soldier, pointed to a group of Mexicans swarming around the forgotten pack mule. "We left our food," he said, as dozens of eager hands took down the packs and started to empty them not far from Arturo's house. The mule had run off when the shot killed Private Washington, and Will had forgotten about the pack animal.

"It's too late now," Will said, swinging Poco north to intersect with the wagon trace back to Galeana. "We could all get killed over some bacon and coffee and a mule if we try to go back after it. I'll explain it to the major. A mule ain't worth but four or five dollars anyway."

Pushing through the dark, unwilling to risk a fire in what he knew now was hostile territory, Will debated the choice he'd made to work for the army. Something about the black soldier's death touched him in a way he'd be hard pressed to define. Will was no stranger to violence and death. The region around Laredo, on both sides of the Rio Grande, was home to some of the most violent, blood-thirsty men on earth. The last of the old-time gunfighters, wanted by the law in Texas and half a dozen other states, occupied many of the cantinas in Nuevo Laredo, only a stone's throw from the border. Now and then, perhaps merely from boredom or too much tequila, they killed each other in grisly duels that were mostly ignored by Mexican officials, as if to say good riddance to men of their ilk. Rival Mexican bandits often shot it out with each other in squabbles over territory or stolen booty.

At the age of six, while accompanying his father on a cattle-buying trip, Will had witnessed his first killing at Sabinas Hidalgo, and there had been many similar scenes since, many bullet-riddled corpses lying in pools of drying blood in Mexico and Texas. Violence was a way of life where he grew up, yet there was something about Private James Washington's death—perhaps the role Will had played in his demise as leader of the scouting expedition—that was like a burr under a saddle blanket on a green-broke colt. Riding through the darkness chilled by bitterly cold winds sweeping across the desert, with the soldier's death on his conscience, he began to wonder why he had agreed to the army's offer. The bullet that ended Washington's life could have just as easily ended his own. A change in the whim of Lady Luck could have robbed him of the happiness he enjoyed at his brother's ranch, the closeness he felt toward Raymond and his family, the contentment that was his with the life he had there. He would have been denied the joy of giving Junior the reins to the white pony, seeing his cherubic face light up with happiness when he learned that the little horse belonged to him.

Was it worth a hundred and fifty dollars a month to risk losing all that was dear to him? The question echoed back and forth in his mind as the miles passed beneath Poco's hooves. He had always known that he was never cut out to be a soldier, and although he was not a soldier now, the result could be the same if bad luck sent a stray bullet his way. "I oughta quit this outfit," he muttered, lips numb from the cold. "There's easier ways to make money."

"Stealing white man's horses easier," Es Ki Ben De said.

"They'd put you in jail," Loco Jim warned, then he chuckled softly.

Will hadn't known the Apaches were listening. "I guess I was thinkin' about the dead soldier," he said, shivering, turning up the collar on his mackinaw. "That bullet could have been meant for any one of us. Maybe it ain't very patriotic, but I'm not ready to die for this army. I'd feel different if I knew somebody was tryin' to take what belonged to me back in Texas."

Es Ki Ben De edged his pony closer to Will. "Maybeso you make war with Pancho if he burn your lodge, like at Columbus."

"I suppose that'd be reason enough," Will agreed, wishing he hadn't made the remark about quitting out loud. It wasn't the sort of thing he wanted to talk about just now. Honestly, he wasn't quite sure how he felt about things. He couldn't shake a feeling of guilt for his part in Washington's death. Logic told him it wasn't really his fault, but the feeling was there just the same.

"None of us wants to die," Loco Jim said, teeth chattering, head bent into the chill wind. "It was easy for an Apache to decide to take the army's money. Our children are hungry and cold. The winter will be long. Money will buy food and warm clothes. For this, I will try to outrun the bullets."

A faint sound, hard to hear because of the wind, reached Will's ears from the rear. He looked over his shoulder, scanning the darkness until he recognized it, a voice. Slowing Poco, he waited for Private Fields, listening to soft words the soldier was mumbling.

"The Lord is my shepherd. I shall not want. He leadeth me beside green pastures. . . ."

"You okay?" he asked when Fields rode alongside him.

The private nodded. "Jus' prayin' for Jimmy's soul," he said, sniffling, rubbing tears from his eyes with a trembling forearm. "Sayin' the only prayers I know by heart."

Only then did Will notice that Fields was not wearing a jacket. "Where's your coat?" he asked. Shivering spasms gripped the soldier's limbs, and his teeth chattered.

"Ain't got one. My blanket was on the mule," Fields replied quietly. "I'm cold, but I ain't dead like Jimmy is. I'll make it all right."

Will reached behind his saddle, unfastening saddle strings around his bedroll. He shook the blanket out and leaned over to drape it around the private's shoulders. "Take this," he said, shivering himself despite his heavy wool mackinaw and gloves. "I've got an extra flannel shirt in my bag, if you want it."

"This'll be fine," Fields said, tucking the blanket underneath his chin, shuddering once. "I'm mighty grateful, Mr. Johnson."

"My name's Will," he said, touching Poco's ribs to ride back to the front, tilting his hat into the wind to shield his face.

Later he looked up at the stars, wondering if the prayers offered by Private Calvin Fields had found an audience in the heavens above them. Had he known any prayers himself he might have considered sending them along in Jimmy Washington's behalf, and perhaps a word or two concerning his own fate. But the offspring of Lee Johnson had never been inside a church. It wasn't that he didn't believe in such things, really. At times he had pondered it: the existence of God, life after death, and so forth. From birth he had been denied the opportunity to learn about it from a bona fide preacher, and now that he was full grown he lacked the courage to enter a church for the first time alone. Thus he remained uncommitted more or less, wondering if any of it could hold even a grain of truth.

• 14 •

Colonel George Dodd gave the situation a quick study as he was being shown to Pershing's command headquarters. Gaunt, whip-cord lean, a thin gray mustache on his lip, he seemed to wear a perpetually sour expression. Even in the darkness he noticed uncharacteristic disarray, chaos, and he could sense frustration among the men gathered around scattered campfires, hearing only fragments of their gripes and complaints. There was no semblance of order here. This wasn't like Pershing, to allow his command to grow lax. Chewing the stub of his unlit cigar, Dodd considered Pershing's dilemma, that of finding a rogue bandit in his own back yard with no personal knowledge of the bandit's countryside. And he was burdened with all manner of equipment that would slow him down in this miserable sand. Dodd spoke to the aide escorting him between the field tents. "I'll bet Black Jack is pissed off, having to drag all this goddamn equipment along."

The aide, who'd introduced himself as Lieutenant Patton when Dodd arrived, replied, "Do you mean General Pershing, sir?"

"That's what they used to call him at West Point when the cadets tried to get his goat, back when he was an instructor of tactics there. They nicknamed him 'Nigger Jack' because he used to command an all-black outfit during the Indian troubles out west. He was always telling his snotnose cadets at West Point how good his buffalo soldiers were when it came to discipline. Later on, they softened the monicker to 'Black Jack.' John's a good soldier, but he wasn't very popular as a teacher. If you ask me, most West Pointers are a bunch of pampered sissies."

"I graduated from West Point, sir," the aide said, lengthening his strides, "and with all due respect, Colonel, I do not consider myself a pampered sissie."

Dodd fell silent. No point in giving the lieutenant any more history lessons. West Pointers believed they knew everything anyway. The army did pamper most of them. John Pershing was one notable exception, although his training at West Point had given him the chance to meet some of the right people early on, like Nelson Miles, who'd favored Pershing when promotions came around. It hadn't hurt Pershing's cause when he married a senator's daughter while Senator Warren was chairman of the Senate Military Affairs Committee. He then quickly leapfrogged all the way from captain to brigadier over the heads of hundreds of senior officers. Dodd secretly held to the belief that it had been Teddy Roosevelt's doing. At the War Department Pershing's rapid promotion was credited to his courageous service in the Philippines.

Dodd had fond memories of Pershing when they served at Fort Assiniboine in Montana Territory, rounding up a band of renegade Crees causing trouble along the Canadian border. John was tough, smart, brave under fire. He had balls, and balls were what it took to fight the Indian wars back then. Dodd felt no resentment when the other man was promoted. Pershing had earned whatever he got through competent leadership. Marrying a powerful senator's daughter really had nothing to do with the fact that he deserved a brigadier's rank.

And just when it seemed Pershing had everything—a beautiful family and an almost certain future high up in the War Department in Washington—there had been the awful fire at Presidio. Dodd had sent his condolences to El Paso as soon as he learned of it. He wondered how much it had changed Pershing. Hell, it would change any man, even a man with big balls like Black Jack. It had come as a surprise when, so soon after the disaster, Pershing was given command of this campaign in Mexico. Fred Funston was probably steaming over it, since he would have been the more natural choice. Dodd had been glad to get the message from Pershing ordering him to join the hunt for this Pancho Villa character. It had begun to look like America meant to stay out of the war in Europe at all costs, leaving fighting men like Dodd with little to do but read about the stalemate in the trenches in newspapers. An expedition into the wilds of Mexico was just what he needed to get the old juices flowing again.

He saw a banner above the command tent fluttering in a cold night wind long before they got there. A lantern burned inside the tent despite the late hour. The aide announced their arrival, and a moment later the tent flap parted. But the man who peered out didn't look like the soldier Dodd remembered.

"George!" Pershing exclaimed warmly, extending a hand with a grin. "I've been wondering what delayed you."

Dodd did not bother with proper military protocol requiring a salute. He shook hands with Pershing and took the cigar from his mouth. "Good to see you again, General," he said. "Sorry I'm late, but I had one hell of a time finally gettin' here. Those goddamn Washington desk jockeys screwed everything up like they always do—the wrong train schedules, the works. They're all idiots, if you ask me. It'll be good to be around someone who knows which is his left foot."

"Come inside," Pershing said, holding the flap open. "We have a thousand things to talk about." He looked at Patton and added, "That will be all, Lieutenant. Have someone from the mess bring us a pot of coffee."

"Whiskey sounds better on a cold night," Dodd offered as he stepped into the tent.

"Bring a bottle of whiskey," the general added, noticing how much stronger the wind seemed now.

"I'll bring it myself," Patton replied. "By the way, sir, the repairs on the cattle cars are almost finished. I expect the train will be underway in a couple of hours."

Pershing nodded and turned around. He looked at Dodd and let the flap fall shut behind him.

Dodd examined his old friend's face in the lamplight. "I wanted to start off by saying in person how sorry I was to learn about the fire, John. How awful it must have been for you."

Pershing took a seat on his cot and pointed to a canvas stool. "I can't say I'll ever get over it, not entirely. I suppose

I should be thankful that Warren was spared, which I truly am. But I miss Frances terribly. And the girls . . ." His eyes fell to the tent floor.

Pershing looked haggard, thinner, considerably older, more salt and pepper in his hair and mustache. Although he had tried to sound cheerful when Dodd arrived, he seemed tired. Maybe his appearance suffered in the harsh glare from the lantern, but his voice betrayed how he really felt. Perhaps it had been the trials of the desert crossing. Logically, it had to be the burden of his recent devastating loss. "Tell me about Villa," he began, changing the subject. "Any word as to where he is now?"

"Conflicting reports," Pershing replied. "One of my guides found out he was in a place called San Miguel—he heard it from a local shepherd. Another scout insists he is headed south to the city of Parral. San Miguel is closer. In order to make sure we haven't bypassed him, I'm sending cavalry to surround the village. It's the only way to be certain he isn't there. It wouldn't be the logical place to find him, not so close to the border. Maybe that's the best reason of all to look for him there."

"Expect the unexpected, Johnny. If it makes the most sense to go south, I'd start checking every inch of ground to the north. Remember how those miserable little Crees kept doubling back on us? Just when we were sure they were headed one way, they'd turn around and go the other. The first rule of Indian fighting is to count on finding them spread out all over the place. They won't stay together. Little bunches will pop up here and there, but you won't find them concentrated until they're ready to go after the things they need most. In this case I suspect that'll be horses and ammunition. Wherever they can get bullets and more horses is the most likely place Villa will turn up."

Pershing sighed, gazing off into space as though remembering something. "That is precisely what one of our civilian guides has been saying, but it means Villa must go south to find any sizable amount of ammunition, which contradicts what the other guide was told about Villa being at San Miguel, giving his men a rest."

"The smart ones don't rest," Dodd declared. "Geronimo hardly ever slept a wink, and neither did Crazy Horse. If

Villa is as smart as everyone thinks, he won't be sitting on his fat ass some place. He'll be moving as fast as he can toward the easiest place to resupply himself."

"He has to stay close to water," Pershing said. "You've seen what this desert looks like. It means he has to stay close to the Santa Maria river, if we can believe these maps."

"Not necessarily, not if he's real savvy. He may know where to find hidden springs in what appears to be the most illogical place. That was a big part of Geronimo's secret: He knew the territory, every little water hole, every nook and cranny where a man could hide. Finding Pancho Villa will require someone with the same knowledge of this area, somebody who knows the trails as well as a mountain goat, and where the water is. A river on a map is too logical. Johnny my boy, if Villa has any sense at all, he'll know that's where we'll look for him in a desert."

"You're right, of course," Pershing said. "I suppose my instincts have been telling me all along to listen to the young civilian guide, Will Johnson. He's the one who keeps telling us to head south toward Parral, that Villa won't be at San Miguel any longer."

"Where's Johnson now?" Dodd asked, edging forward on his stool. "I'd like to talk to him."

"He went south this morning with a couple of Apaches to see what they could find. Major Ryan said he didn't expect them back for a day or two. I sent James Erwin and most of the Seventh in the same direction a few hours earlier, with orders to turn west when they could, completing a circle around San Miguel as soon as the Tenth reaches the other side by train."

"With your permission, at first light I'd like a fast horse and a couple of men who know how to ride. If I can catch Erwin before he turns, I could take half his command and strike out for Parral, where the scout thinks Villa is going."

Pershing nodded his assent. A hint of a smile curled his lips. "I'd planned to put you in command of the Seventh as soon as you got here, Georgie. I need experienced men to finish this campaign successfully, and fast. We've already been given a dose of what this treacherous sand can do to our columns. Lockett is still bogged down in it somewhere east of here with more than half of our supplies. Things ought to improve tomorrow, when the First Aero Squadron arrives. With aeroplanes we can gather meaningful intelligence."

Dodd frowned. "I've been told the damn things can't fly higher than a pissant's bootlaces. Our country has fallen way behind in the development of aircraft meant for warfare. Over in France, both sides have got machine guns mounted on aeroplanes, according to what Tasker Bliss told me last fall, and bombs big enough to blow the hell out of deep gun emplacements. Some of 'em can even shoot through the propeller! It's all our Jennys can do to get a pilot's ass off the ground, Tasker says, and Congress won't give the War Department enough money to get manufacturers like Curtiss to develop anything better for us. Hugh Scott is howling mad over it, and so is Secretary Baker, but Wilson refuses to budge on the war issue and Congress has free rein to concentrate on some of the finer arts of pork barreling. Until enough crooked politicians get interested in building aeroplanes, the United States Army is all but grounded."

"So I've heard," Pershing said, sitting with his shoulders rounded. "Wilson is the stumbling block. He wants to keep us out of the war at any cost. And the illustrious William Jennings Bryan sides with Wilson on keeping the peace."

George chuckled softly. "Makes it hard on a couple of old war horses like us, don't it? We spent half our lives training for action, and we're ordered to sit while there's a real fight to be won. Hell, Johnny, I'm sixty-three and I haven't got that many years left. A bunch of pantywaists up in Washington are keeping men like you and me from the battlefield. I'll confess I was damn glad to get orders to report down here. You give me some men and good horses, and a man who knows this part of Mexico, and I'll find this renegade bastard for you before a cat can lick its ass. That's a promise. I'll give Pancho Villa the worst whipping he ever dreamed of and hand him to you on a silver platter."

For only the second time since they greeted each other, Pershing smiled. "That's the spirit, George. I knew I could count on you in a campaign like this. I'll assign Will Johnson and some of the Apaches to you as soon as he gets back. In the meantime I'll prepare orders to Erwin, giving you half his cavalry and a machine-gun unit, to push south for Parral.

When Colonel Lockett finally gets here, I'll send Major Tompkins with part of the Thirteenth to reinforce you from the rear. We'll close the net around San Miguel, and if we come up with nothing we'll move on further south, combing every square mile of northern Chihuahua until we join forces with you somewhere between here and Parral."

Footsteps neared the tent: the arrival of their coffee and whiskey. Pershing got up slowly and pulled the tent flap back just as Lieutenant Patton got there with a tray of glasses, cups, a coffeepot, and a bottle of Kentucky bourbon from the officers' mess.

"Sorry I was delayed, sir," Patton apologized as he ducked inside, a flush in his cheeks from the icy wind. "The train to Cumbre Pass is loading now, but there is still a shortage of wood for the locomotive." He placed the tray on a folding table. "I told the engineer to proceed at once despite the shortage. They can forage for firewood along the way. Colonel Brown didn't like it much. He said his men were complaining of the cold, having to ride on top of the cattle cars. I informed him the order came directly from you, sir, and that was enough to silence him."

"Thank you, Lieutenant. Get some rest. You've done quite enough for today."

Patton saluted and left the tent, his heels grinding in the gravel. When the footsteps faded, Pershing said, "That boy has the makings of a good officer. It seems there have been a thousand small details to attend to, and he sees to them all."

Dodd kept his opinions of West Pointers to himself, taking a glass to pour a generous whiskey while rolling the sodden stump of his cigar to the other cheek. "Too bad there's no chance for good officers to prove themselves in battle these days. Hell fire, we're sittin' on our American asses while the rest of the world builds better aeroplanes, bigger guns and bombs, and even those goddamn U-boats are better than anything we can send out to sea. Tasker says the Hun submarines might enable Germany to conquer the whole goddamn world."

Pershing poured himself coffee and sat back down, slumped on his cot with a grim look on his face. "The Kaiser knows he can't win a trench war on land with a submarine, George. I've been studying our intelligence reports, and the

U-boats are slow, with small crews. The British Admiralty says they are sinkable. If every one of the Central Powers starts building them, they'll be more of a problem for the Allies. Austria-Hungary has the shipbuilders. Turkey doesn't have the steel mills yet. Neither does Bulgaria. But it could become a thorn in the side of England, France, and Russia if the seas are full of submarines, even as slow as they are. Surely no one has forgotten the *Lusitania*. Imagine, over a thousand people lost, almost a third of them women and children."

Dodd heard the sorrow in Pershing's voice when he talked about dead women and children. He tried to think of something to take his mind off the tragedy. "We're a nation gone soft around the middle. We elect men like Woodrow Wilson to lead our country, and it makes us look like weaklings. But here's a chance to show the rest of America and the whole goddamn world what we'll do if somebody screws around with us. When we catch up to this cocky little Mexican bastard and trim his feathers real good, it'll send a message heard 'round the world that we're no pushovers. If we can find him, I promise you I'll deliver a good pounding to Mr. Villa and his followers. All I want is the authority to go after him any way I see fit. Don't ask me to haul a bunch of goddamn delivery trucks all over Mexico to get the job done. My men will travel light, like we did in the old days. Ride hard and sleep in the saddle if we have to. You can keep your howitzers and all the rest of that War Department crap. Just give me good men, good horses, and a handful of those machine guns. I'll do the rest."

He tipped back his glass and emptied it in one gulp, letting out a satisfied sigh when he felt the whiskey burn.

Again, Pershing grinned. "I knew I could count on you, George. I'll give you everything you've asked for, but you must promise me that you'll abide by Wilson's agreement to avoid the bigger cities and all use of Mexican trains. We can't give Wilson a reason to call this thing off over some international incident that violates the treaty with Mexico. Other than that, I'm giving you the authority to pursue Villa by any means you choose. Help me find him. The sooner the better, for both of us."

Dodd bit down on his cigar and poured more whiskey. He

eyed the amber fluid before tossing it back. "He's as good as caught right now, Johnny. Wherever the bastard is hiding, he's about to be discovered and introduced to an old-fashioned ass kickin' from a man who knows how to kick ass."

• 15 •

They were coming to him like lost children, one at a time, or in twos and threes, from mountain villages all over Chihuahua. Young and old, some brave and some fearful, they came to join his army, carrying what little they had: a change of clothes, spare sandals, usually a machete, sometimes an ancient gun. Word was spreading, as he knew it would, of his recent valor across the border against the Americans, stirring a spirit of nationalism in the hearts of men who worked the land, men who had been robbed of their birthright by rich landowners and devious politicians. More often, those who came to him were simple peasant farmers who had no hope of owning farms, who worked for small shares of another man's crop and lived in poverty, while big landowners grew fatter and richer. Doroteo knew these humble people for he'd been born to them, and only by the whim of fate and sheer determination had he been able to rise above his lowly beginnings.

He turned to Ramon Salas. They were seated in the shade of a ramada in the hills above Rubio, watching new arrivals creep out of the forest to cautiously approach the designated gathering place in a valley west of the village. "So few have weapons," he said, thinking ahead to the battle for arms stored at Guerrero. "The guns we captured at Namiquipa will not be enough. We must have more horses, many more good horses. . . ."

Candelario and Julio were in the mountains now with gold taken from the American mining company at Cusi, buying strong young horses and recruiting more men.

"The ones who come have so little," Ramon observed, squinting in the sun's glare, watching men leading starving burros and a few rawboned horses into the valley, where hungry animals were being given corn to strengthen them for the climb over the peaks after sunset. "But they have very brave hearts, *Jefe*. They will fight to the death if you ask it of them."

Hearing this stirred something in Doroteo's breast, a deep feeling of immeasurable pride. "These are my people. I ask for their courage on their own behalf, not for selfish reasons. They must be made to understand this, that I do not seek any personal glory or material gain, only to lead them to what is rightfully theirs." He smiled, for as he stated these reasons for having assumed leadership of this just cause, he liked the sound of it. They were things he must add to his speeches in order to persuade the doubtful, those who were afraid. Asking for their courage on their own behalf might be something a simple man could understand, something that appealed to those who longed to control their own destiny rather than spend a lifetime in servitude. "All they need is courage," he added. "I will provide them with guns and horses, and a good battle plan to defeat Carranza's soldiers."

At moments like this, Doroteo felt as though he had the innermost counsel of *Dios* Himself to implement his plan. Surely God was speaking to him in a voice only his spirit could hear, directing him to the right spot at just the right time with divine wisdom, which would enable him to defeat the forces of *el Diablo* in the person of Venustiano Carranza. Sometimes he was almost certain he could hear the voice of God whispering to him, urging him onward, warning him when to go into hiding or that a traitor was in their midst. Surely these strong feelings, if they were not truly the voice of God, were given to him by the spirit of *Dios*. How else would he have been able to win so many one-sided battles? What other reason could there be for knowing things he could not possibly have known otherwise? A few times, it felt like some unseen force was guiding him. He had been chosen, he believed today, to act as God's mighty swift sword to bring the land back to the poor people of Mexico, and then serve as their benevolent president until he chose to retire, leaving a hand-picked successor.

"I must confide in you, Ramon," he said gravely, as if he were about to reveal some deep secret, knowing that Ramon would swear an oath of secrecy, then hasten to tell everyone what he learned. One of Ramon's greatest virtues was that he was stupid and did little thinking on his own. "But you must promise to keep this between us. I only tell you this because you are my friend and my trusted associate."

Ramon watched him with dark, dull eyes. "I swear to tell no one, *Jefe*," he promised.

Doroteo looked around them, finding only the girl, Isabela, preparing his lunch, and Rudolfo Fierro, who was always there. "Last night I had a vision," he said, almost whispering. "And I heard the voice of *Dios*. He commanded me to take my faithful men over the mountains to Guerrero, where He assured me the evil men of Venustiano would be caught unprepared. *Dios* has promised us a victory, Ramon. I saw Him standing in my bedroom with my own two eyes, while the girl was asleep. He spoke to me in a voice as real as your own, telling me what we must do."

"You saw God?" Ramon exclaimed, blinking once.

Doroteo held a finger to his lips. "Yes, my friend, I saw Him and I heard His voice. Our victory at Guerrero is assured."

"But *Jefe*," Ramon protested, trying to keep his voice low, "you must tell the others! They should be told the hand of God will protect us from harm during the battle. Everyone, even the old men and the young boys, will fight much harder, knowing God is protecting them from Carrancista bullets."

Prepared for this, Doroteo wagged his head. "I do not wish to make this a holy war, Ramon, for I fear our enemies might use this against us. Venustiano gives generously to the Church, and the priests are very powerful men. If I say God has spoken to me, to tell us He is on our side, Carranza might ask the priests to say otherwise. Rich men who support the Church with money may do likewise, and we must always remember that the rich are our enemies, for they have taken the land from our people long ago by treachery and deception. It is better to say nothing about my vision publicly, yet there is great comfort in knowing that *Dios,* in His infinite wisdom, has chosen us to succeed in this struggle. He knows what is in our hearts, Ramon. We cannot deceive Him. Neither can the black-hearted Venustiano."

Ramon nodded, then he got up slowly, casting a wavering glance over groups of men in the valley preparing for the march over the mountains. "I will keep your secret, *Jefe,"* he said, hitching up his gunbelt and leaving the shade of the ramada in a careless amble, as though without purpose.

Doroteo watched him walk away, smiling only to himself now. Before nightfall, Ramon would have told everyone about the vision, and men all over the valley would believe they were undertaking a mission blessed by God.

He turned to Isabela. "Come here, woman!" he said, beckoning to her. "Show me what is hidden underneath your dress. It was dark last night, and I could not see how beautiful you are without your clothes."

The girl's face paled. She looked at Rudolfo, then at the men scattered over hillsides around them. "Everyone will see me," she gasped, clutching the buttons on her blouse as though his eyes alone could undress her. "Come to the hut, Francisco! Please!"

His gaze roamed down the front of her skirt, remembering her passionate cries in the dark. She was a pretty peasant girl, but not beautiful. Not like the others. Rudolfo had assured him she was the prettiest girl in Rubio, and so he had agreed to take her to bed, needing a woman after the dashing victory at Namiquipa, where he and his men routed the unsuspecting Carrancistas, taking all their weapons and horses, even forcing some of them—the ones they did not kill—at gunpoint to join the other side. It was good to bed a woman after a tiring battle. Somehow it made a victory more complete.

"Go to the hut!" he commanded. "Take off your clothes. I will be there in a moment."

She wheeled away from the small fire where she was

preparing tortillas and hurried toward an adobe hidden in the trees behind the ramada. Doroteo examined her slender ankles, then the sway of her hips. He pushed himself out of a sagging bullhide chair and looked across the valley, seeing men prepare themselves for the difficult march over the Divide. He hoped Julio and Candelario were able to find the horses they needed. Before dawn tomorrow Guerrero would fall and its rich stores of machine guns and bullets would be theirs, along with hundreds of horses. No one would expect this bold strike. Venustiano would soon feel the teeth of the Lion again, growing stronger than ever before.

"I must satisfy the woman," he told Rudolfo, plodding away from the ramada as if he carried the weight of the world on his shoulders.

Rudolfo leaned against a post at one corner of the thatched roof, thinking about tomorrow's fight. Like those of some wild creature in the forest, his nostrils flared, seeking a familiar smell, although he knew it was too soon to scent the blood that would be shed at Guerrero before sunrise.

The door of the hut slammed shut. A moment later, there was a scream. When he heard it, Rudolfo grinned. *El Jefe* knew how to treat a woman.

Numbed by the bitter predawn cold, men exhausted by a brutal, night-long climb over the Sierras spread out soundlessly among the dark adobes of San Isidro. Across the starlit valley in Guerrero, another contingent of soldiers entered the slumbering village quietly, surrounding the military garrison as dogs began to bark at the intruders. Here and there a lantern came to life behind a window, and still no shots were fired. Everyone was sound asleep at four o'clock in the morning.

From the Guerrero cemetery, Pancho Villa watched his soldiers move into position through his field glasses. All seemed to be going well. Behind him, thirty men, including seven former Carrancistas who'd been pressed into service after the fall of Namiquipa, readied their guns for the forthcoming fight.

Among the seven unwilling volunteers was eighteen-year-old Hector Lopez, a skinny boy who had been an apprentice blacksmith in Namiquipa until Pancho Villa sacked and looted his home town. Hector pulled back the bolt on the very old .44 caliber Springfield rifle he had been given and thumbed one large lead bullet into the firing chamber. Like the other soldiers around him, he aimed his gun for Guerrero. To his right loomed the distinctive shadow of General Villa, calmly sitting his horse at the front of the men waiting in the cemetery. Hector sighted down his rifle barrel, both hands sweating despite the chill. The muzzle of his rifle wavered, moving slightly to one side, unnoticed by the other anxious men on either side of him.

A muffled shout sounded from somewhere in Guerrero, followed immediately by the heavy clap of a gun. Then gunshots exploded from every direction and the air above the cemetery was suddenly full of speeding lead.

Villa started his horse forward, leading his soldiers toward the town, where winking muzzle flashes accompanied the thunder of hundreds of guns. People were screaming, awakened in their beds by unending volleys of loud gunfire. Barking dogs and nickering horses added to the deafening noise swelling from the valley floor. Villa's horse began to prance, held in check by a strong pull on the bit. Shadowy figures raced back and forth along the village streets between stabbing fingers of bright yellow flame. Window panes and lantern globes shattered. The shooting grew even more intense until a single gunshot had no identity, the moment Hector Lopez had been waiting for.

A lead slug entered Villa's right leg opposite the knee joint, exiting through his shinbone four inches below his kneecap. He toppled from his horse and crashed to the ground below the left stirrup of Ramon Salas, shrieking in pain.

Ramon saw the general fall, then he looked up at the sky as he jumped from his saddle to rescue *el León,* wondering what could explain what had just taken place. How could God's promise to their brave leader have been broken? What had happened to the prophecy revealed in *el Jefe's* vision?

Soldiers charged from the graveyard, firing into the town,

racing past Ramon, where he knelt beside Villa near the cemetery fence. It was as though no one noticed the general had fallen. Then one more mounted soldier rode up to the spot and halted his horse, gazing down. Ramon recognized Rudolfo Fierro's fearsome countenance even in the dark. Rudolfo listened to Villa's pain-ridden cries a moment before he spoke.

"I saw who shot him," Rudolfo snarled, then he spurred his horse forward to a lunging gallop, riding up behind a slender young man on a trotting burro. Rudolfo aimed a pistol for the back of the boy's head and fired, instantly killing Hector Lopez as he was joining the attack on the village.

Ramon saw what happened and shook his head in disbelief. Had *el Jefe* truly been shot from behind by one of his own men?

The rattle of guns continued, coming from both ends of the valley now as Julio Cardenas began the attack against San Isidro. Ramon bent down to gather the general into his arms.

The youth gave his name as Modesto Nevares, although because of the searing pain in his leg, Doroteo was scarcely listening. He applied potassium permanganate gingerly to his gaping wound with a piece of cotton, unwilling to trust anyone else with the sensitive task. His leg was shattered, and when he moved it at all he was almost rendered unconscious. Julio and Candelario stood in the room watching him dab potassium solution on the tear in his skin, after giving their reports of the victory. The garrison at Guerrero had fallen, but not without cost. Carranza general Jose Cavazos offered fierce resistance, and many brave followers of Doroteo were slain or wounded. For the moment, distracted by his own wound, Doroteo paid little attention to what Julio and Candelario said about the fight. He was far more interested in what the boy, Modesto Nevares, had to say.

"I know a way through the mountains," Modesto said, replying to Doroteo's question, "a very old road used long ago by burro trains when the ancient padres carried gold to

Mexico City. With a buggy pulled by two good horses, I can take you to Parral in less than a week, General. Hardly anyone knows about this road, perhaps only a few Yaquis."

Doroteo began to wrap his leg with strips of bedsheet, adding four splints to hold the mangled bone in place. Sweat beaded on his forehead, and at times he cried out softly until the job was finished. He looked at Rudolfo. "Find a hack and two gentle horses. Make sure the hack has springs for the axles." He turned to Modesto. "You will drive the hack. I will pay you well for taking me safely to Parral. I only pray that the road is smooth. I must see a doctor very soon."

Modesto bowed and followed Rudolfo Fierro out of the adobe where the meeting took place. Rudolfo turned for the livery. Modesto hurried home to pack his few belongings and say goodbye to his mother.

Doroteo addressed Julio and Candelario, his face twisted in pain. "Allow the men to rest here for one day. Take everything, every horse, every gun, and as much food as you can carry. Pay the men in gold and tell them to return home, going by different routes. Take the machine guns to Rancho San Miguelito and store them in the secret cave. For now, with the Americans coming, we will scatter to the four winds and let them try to find us a few at a time. I will be in Parral, if the boy can get me there in time, before the poisons spread from my wound. You can send word to me through the German woman. . . . She will know where I am. If I am still alive."

• 16 •

Major Ryan dispatched a burial detachment with Private Washington's body to a hillside cemetery outside Colonia Dublan the morning Will gave his report. "It's a casualty of war, Mr. Johnson, an unfortunate thing," the major said.

Will gazed absently toward the northeast. Elements of the east column were still straggling in. The Apaches were at the mess tents and Private Fields had gone with the body for burial to say a final goodbye to his friend. "I reckon so, Major," he said, simply to avoid an argument with Ryan over the senselessness of sending uniformed men along with a scout detail.

Major Ryan was watching him closely. "Tell me again about the intelligence you gathered on Villa. How well do you know the source?"

"Real well. I've known Arturo for years. My pa bought horses from him. I believe he's tellin' the truth."

"It doesn't fit with what the other scouts have learned," Ryan said, neither thoughtful nor belligerent now. "General Pershing believed so strongly in the reports of Villa being at San Miguel that he sent Colonel Dodd to lead Colonel Erwin's Seventh Cavalry for the attack. Colonel Dodd is an experienced Indian fighter, and the general wanted him to get there first; then if Villa is not found, Dodd is to take half of the command directly toward Parral."

"Villa ain't *at* San Miguel," Will said, growing tired of the major's refusal to listen to the news he'd brought back about Villa's raid planned for Guerrero.

Ryan scowled. "I'll tell the general what you found out," he said, making a half turn as though he meant to leave at

135

once. A noise in the sky halted him, the drone of an engine. An aeroplane appeared above the valley from the south and dipped downward rather suddenly.

Will watched the contraption swoop down and make a bumpy landing in a vacant field east of the irrigation ditch. When it came to a halt the motor coughed and died, its propeller still spinning briefly. A pair of cavalrymen galloped toward the Jenny at full speed, reining to a stop a few yards from the pilot, who had jumped from the open cockpit. A conference was held, then one soldier helped the pilot up behind his saddle and took off for the army camp at a lope.

"Wonder what the hurry is," Will said.

Major Ryan had already started off to intercept the horse and riders. "That's Lieutenant Dargue, back with reconnaissance from San Miguel. In a moment we'll know whose information was correct, Mr. Johnson: yours, or Mr. Barker's."

Weary after the ride without rest to reach Dublan, Will still forced his legs to carry him down to the meeting between the pilot and Major Ryan. He wanted to see the look on Ryan's face when the major learned Villa was not at San Miguel. He followed from a distance, until the horse bearing the pilot came to a halt in front of Ryan. Lieutenant Dargue jumped down and saluted. From the largest tent in the encampment, Will saw General Pershing striding quickly toward the meeting with Ryan and Dargue.

"Sir," the pilot began, "those damn things aren't meant to fly in these mountains. I can barely get it high enough to miss the lowest peaks, and it isn't stable in those changing valley winds."

"What did you find out, Lieutenant?" Ryan demanded, dismissing the pilot's complaint quickly with a wave.

"The revolutionaries were not at San Miguel. I landed on a road where I spotted the Seventh Cavalry, and they were already on their way south, away from the town by twenty miles or more. I reported to Colonel Erwin as you instructed. The colonel said a Carranza informant told him that Villa and his men were bound for the south of Chihuahua, possibly to Guerrero. I was running low on fuel, Major, so I didn't try to fly over and substantiate the report. I also had some trouble with my propeller. The wood is peeling apart, and I doubt this JN-2 will ever fly again without a replacement."

"Report that sort of problem to Captain Foulois," Ryan said impatiently. "What else did Colonel Erwin have to say?"

The pilot noticed General Pershing's arrival and wheeled around to salute him.

"Go on, Lieutenant," Pershing said. "Finish what you were telling Major Ryan."

"Colonel Erwin found out that part of the train carrying the Tenth Cavalry overturned, sir, before they reached San Miguel. Some men were hurt and several horses had to be destroyed. As I reported, Colonel Erwin found no revolutionaries nearby. He said to inform you that he is on his way south with all dispatch and he intends to engage Villa's army wherever he finds them. He requests all possible reinforcements be sent at once."

Major Ryan was slow to look at Will. He did, and then he faced the general. "Mr. Johnson's scout detail returned earlier this morning with some information, General, that Villa was at Rubio, planning an attack on Guerrero."

"Why wasn't I told immediately?" Pershing asked. His cheeks held a splash of color.

"The other scouts brought back differing reports," Ryan replied, his tone a little softer now.

The general regarded Will a moment. "It would appear Lem Spilsbury was right about you, Mr. Johnson, when he told us you were the best man for the job down here. How soon do you think Villa will strike at Guerrero?"

"I'd only be guessing, General. I was told he went to Rubio with forty new recruits from Namiquipa the day before yesterday. There was a fight there with some of Carranza's men. He'll have to cross the Continental Divide to get to Guerrero, same as your Seventh Cavalry will. Crossin' over is tricky any time of year; it could still be snowin' up there now and the wind will be like ice. Some of the passes are eleven thousand feet."

"If anyone can do it, George Dodd can," Pershing said,

eyes still fixed on Will. "Colonel Dodd was late to arrive. I sent him south to take command of half of the Seventh Cavalry. I know you and your Apaches are tired, Mr. Johnson, but as soon as you are sufficiently rested and supplied with fresh horses, I want you to find Colonel Dodd and the Seventh. Perhaps you can guide them over the Divide and help the colonel plan the engagement at Guerrero."

Will rested his weight on the other foot, hooking his thumbs in his pockets. "The real trouble's liable to come from the Carranza garrison at San Isidro, just across the valley from Guerrero. It could go either way, which side they take. The *Federale* commander at Guerrero is General Jose Cavazos, and some say he has political aspirations himself. He had machine guns and cannons last time I was there. If Villa gets there first, Cavazos will give him all the fight he wants. But if this Colonel Dodd shows up, Cavazos is just as likely to fire on our soldiers. You gotta understand that President Carranza has what I'd call real loose control over his armies. They do what the president wants when it suits them. Sometimes. General Cavazos will do whatever he thinks will give him the most glory in the eyes of the people in his district. Killin' American soldiers, if he claimed to know they meant to occupy Guerrero and San Isidro, might be just the ticket to get him elected president, if Carranza falls."

"I know Mexican politics gets complicated," Pershing said, "but surely General Cavazos won't attack an American military column. President Carranza has given us permission to go after Villa, so long as we limit pursuit and avoid any major cities."

Will shrugged. "A man who tries to make a livin' predicting what Mexican officials will do will starve to death, General. I figure they do whatever suits them unless they're bein' watched real close by somebody higher up."

"Colonel Dodd must be warned, then. We've lost all radio contact with the Seventh. As soon as you and your Apaches are rested and able to travel, find them and inform Dodd of what you told me. If you need an armed escort, Major Ryan will supply you with whatever troops you need. Show

George Dodd the best way over the Divide and he'll do the rest. He's a veteran. He'll know what to do."

"I'd just as soon go without an escort, if it's all the same to you."

Pershing nodded. "As soon as the rest of Colonel Lockett's column arrives, we'll be right behind you, setting up bases of operation along the road. They may not be necessary, however, if Colonel Dodd reaches Guerrero in time. I told General Funston at Southern Command I expected this would be a short campaign. With a bit of luck, it could be over even sooner than I hoped."

Perhaps due to fatigue, or indifference, Will said something that he knew would draw Pershing's ire. "I wouldn't count on it, General. At the rate this army is movin', Villa could be down in Mexico City before Guerrero is surrounded. Mounted cavalry is the only way to catch him, and your soldiers are gonna have to learn to live off the land the way he does. Villa don't have any pack mules or wagons to slow him down. He rides his horses into the ground and trades for fresh mounts at the next village. You'll never catch him like this, waitin' for wagons and trucks and mule trains so your men and horses can eat regular and sleep in warm tents."

The general's gray mustache twitched. His eyes were like ice. "I already know you have a low opinion of the manner in which the military operates, Mr. Johnson." He cleared his throat and stiffened his knees. "I have no doubts now that you are something of an authority on this region and its people. However, it is quite obvious that you know nothing about the movement of men and materiel across a battlefield. Pancho Villa may be elusive and clever, perhaps an expert on his type of guerrilla warfare in this terrain, but let me assure you that he will ultimately be defeated by sound military strategy. History has known many other warriors of his kind, yet they have always met with defeat in the end when proven military principles were employed. You are entitled to your opinion, of course, but our methods of operation will not change because of them. I'm quite familiar with guerrilla tactics. I took part in the final campaigns to quell the last Sioux uprising in Nebraska. I was in Cuba on San Juan Hill, and I fought the Moros in the Philippines quite successfully. The United States Army will not change its methods of field operation because of a troublesome Mexican border bandit. We will find him, and when we do, we will crush him soundly."

Will was watching the pilot explain something to a soldier wearing captain's bars, pointing to the aeroplane. "Maybe you will, General," he said tonelessly, too tired at the moment to care about it either way. Nothing would change Pershing's mind anyway. "I'll take the two Apaches and some spare horses and food. If we change mounts on the fly and eat in the saddle, we stand a good chance of catchin' up to the Seventh. I'll ask that pilot if they were on the road to Bachiniva. That'd be the most sensible way to get through those mountains below San Miguel."

"We will contact Colonel Brown by radio if we can," Pershing said. "His squadron from the Tenth will be sent south to reinforce Colonel Dodd. Major Tompkins is somewhere to the west with men from the Thirteenth Cavalry. He will be directed to Guerrero as well."

Will shook his head, then sauntered off on trail-weary legs, numbed by lack of sleep and a night-long ride through icy winds, to ask the pilot where the Seventh Cavalry was. He wondered if he and the Apaches could catch any sleep in the saddle along the way.

Once, he glanced over his shoulder. General Pershing and Major Ryan were watching him, talking, and he was sure he was the topic of their conversation.

After only two short hours of sleep below a peach tree in full bloom near Lem Spilsbury's house, Will and the two Apaches rode out of Colonia Dublan at a gallop, leading spare horses. It was the middle of the afternoon, almost three o'clock. Will rode the branded blue roan, leading the dun that John Abel warned would pitch on cold mornings. Poco rested with the army's big remuda. Supplied with bacon, hardtack, and coffee, they left the encampment as more of the wagons and trucks from the east column rolled slowly into the valley from the desert, having taken seven days to cross barely fifty miles.

Racing toward Galeana at a pace that quickly sapped their mounts, they changed saddles hurriedly at the crossing over the Rio Santa Maria and rode on through the village before sunset. Will was satisfied with both horses he'd bought from John Abel, preferring the dun's longer strides but the roan's temperament. Neither gelding was a match for Poco's endurance or quick speed, but they were seasoned to dry, rough country. Loco Jim and Es Ki Ben De had chosen well from the army's saddle stock, and their horses were able to keep up, although they tired more rapidly than the two mustang crosses. Pushing so hard, there was little time or opportunity for conversation among the men, for the rumble of galloping hooves made words difficult to hear. As night fell, the twisting road to El Valle darkened, and with the dark came more of the bitter cold they had endured the night before.

Just before ten, following the familiar road coursing along the Santa Maria valley, they encountered the lights of El Valle and once again swung wide of the town. Changing horses south of Arturo's adobe, they moved on at a steady lope, unnoticed by the villagers, chewing brittle, tasteless hardtack. Dark mountains rose into the night sky on either side of the wagon trail. Cold wind whipped their horses' manes and tails, lashing the mens' faces when a gallop only increased the velocity of the chill night air. To keep his mind occupied, Will counted the days since the ill-fated expedition left Culberson Ranch. It was now the night of March 28.

The hour was well past midnight when they galloped through Las Cruces, awakening sleeping dogs in a tiny village that was little more than a collection of adobes nestled along the edge of the road leading south. The surrounding mountains were even higher now to the east and west, looming black and forbidding against a background of twinkling stars. A few hours away was Namiquipa, where Villa had recruited more volunteers and found fresh horses. Below Namiquipa was San Geronimo, then the small town of Bachiniva, which was due west of Rubio. Bachiniva lay in a direct line between Rubio and Guerrero, a logical place for Villa to pass through on his way to attack the garrison. But to the west, blocking Villa's path, the Continental Divide would test horseflesh and men to the limit. Villa knew the easiest climbs, the hidden passes, the shortest route. Will tried to remember the cow trails he'd ridden in that part of the Sierras, hoping he could avoid a costly mistake.

Dawn came slowly to the Santa Maria valley, a slight paling to the east behind towering peaks, then gradually more light brightened the steep western mountain slopes, revealing thick stands of pine, juniper, oak, and cedar. Some were impassable, the trees so close together no horseman could navigate between them and much too steep for a horse to climb. But in places, hidden by pine branches and undergrowth, slender trails wound to the tops, twisting over narrow passes, dropping almost straight down to ribbonlike, tree-choked valleys and occasional mountain streams. Craggy rock peaks marking the Continental Divide stood farther west, some reaching twelve thousand feet, where barren slopes above the tree line were lashed by brutally cold winds and occasional snow flurries. In summer, the Sierra Madre Occidental offered unrivaled beauty for infrequent travelers who braved its most remote reaches. But from late October until the last part of April, its challenges and temperature extremes were too much for all but the most hardy.

Will called a halt to boil coffee when they were a few miles below Namiquipa. Namiquipa was a hotbed of revolutionary activity in Chihuahua, and he had wisely chosen to ride around it without stopping to ask about Villa or Colonel Dodd and his cavalry. One of Villa's favorite generals, Candelario Cervantes, was a native of Namiquipa, and asking questions about Villa there would have been a waste of time. Since dawn the roadbed had revealed hundreds of hoofprints heading south, which was all the proof Will needed that they were moving closer to Dodd and the Seventh Cavalry. But as easily as Will and the Apaches read the horse sign, so would local Villa sympathizers. By now Villa would know that a large contingent of American soldiers was closing in from the north. Will wondered if the news would prompt Villa to change his plans for the raid at Guerrero.

Inside a circle of stones, hidden in a grove of tall pines, they boiled a small pot of coffee and warmed their hands above the flames. As the sun rose higher, the chill lessened in the thin mountain air, but after their night-long push to reach the cavalry column, all three men were still numb from the cold winds. Will listened to the crackle of burning pine cones and needles, inhaling the sweet smell mingling with the scent of coffee.

"I am made of ice," Es Ki Ben De said stoically, not a complaint, merely an observation.

"Me too," Loco Jim stammered, his chin quivering as he rubbed his palms over the fire.

"I'm afraid it's gonna get a lot colder," Will said, with a glance up the mountain behind them. "When we start up the Divide you'll know what bein' cold is really like."

The old Apache grunted, looking through the tree trunks to see across the broad river valley beyond. "In my time I have been very cold," he said. "I am no stranger to winter. I will be cold again for seventy-five dollars. Stay all winter if they pay me." He turned south, following the road with his eyes. "We very close to the soldiers now. Droppings are fresh, maybeso only a few hours. These soldiers different. Ride hard. Fast. No stop for rest like others."

Will had been thinking the same thing, for they had not found blackened fire ashes where the Seventh had stopped to rest and warm themselves anywhere along the road. "Maybe this Colonel Dodd understands what we're up against," he offered, although in his heart he doubted that any American soldier truly understood the nature of the undertaking here in Chihuahua.

The coffeepot bubbled softly, giving off delicious smells. Using his Bowie knife, Loco Jim cut strips of salt pork and affixed them to a pointed stick, then held them above the flames until they dripped fat that spit when it fell on the coals. The horses grazed on meager grass below the pine limbs. When the coffee and bacon were ready, the men ate in silence, wolfing down the hot meat and scalding liquid like starved pups.

The fire was smothered as the sun was rising above the mountains. They changed saddles, and when Will's dun gelding felt the cinch, it bowed its back a little. Es Ki Ben De was watching when Will caught the left cheek of the bridle to mount, preparing for the animal to buck when it felt his weight in the saddle.

"Maybeso yellow horse will buck," the Apache warned, a wry grin deepening the wrinkles in his cheeks.

"I was told he'd pitch on a cold mornin'," Will replied, fitting his boot into the stirrup. "Some of the best horses I ever owned had a little hump in their back when it was chilly."

He swung a leg over the dun and was ready when the gelding lunged, crow-hopping a few times, fighting the steady pull of the bit when Will sawed back on the reins. As quickly as it had begun, the bucking stopped, then the horse lowered its head and snorted softly through its muzzle, standing hipshot, resting a rear leg.

Es Ki Ben De laughed. "For a white man you know many things," he said.

Will glanced over his shoulder and grinned, watching the old man swing effortlessly over his saddle without using the stirrup to mount. "I don't figure the color of a man's skin has much to do with it. I reckon it's the road he takes in this life that gives him experience. There's probably a thousand things I don't know a damn thing about, but my pa saw to it that I learned enough about horses to get by reasonable well." He tied the roan's lead rope to his saddlehorn and heeled the dun out of the trees, checking the wagon road for traffic before he swung south, urging his horse to a short lope.

They passed through San Geronimo before noon, following even fresher horse sign along the road. Mexican villagers stared at them from shaded porches as Will and the Apaches galloped among the adobes, chased by barking village dogs. Only twenty miles lay between them and Bachiniva. Then the terrible climb over the Divide would begin, if they could find the Seventh Cavalry in time to show them the easiest way. It was evident that word of the American cavalry column had spread through the mountain villages, for there was no traffic on the road. The usual donkey carts and burro trains avoided it. No *vaqueros* rode the mountainsides, no goat herders showed themselves in the meadows, and it was as if everyone was staying out of sight to await the clash of opposing armies. Even the winds had died, as though Mother Nature were holding her breath until the shooting started.

Their horses labored as the road rose and fell. Like the mountain air, time seemed frozen as they drew nearer to Bachiniva.

• 17 •

Firelight danced among the pines and cedars like hundreds of fireflies at the base of the ridge behind him. Will scanned the snowy slopes to the west and turned his horse to ride back to the bottom of the ravine where the Seventh was thawing out, some boiling coffee while others rubbed down shivering horses with blankets. Will guessed they were camped roughly five or six miles from the eastern edge of the valley where San Isidro and Guerrero lay. They found Colonel Dodd and his men just before sundown and then began the arduous climb over the Continental Divide in the dark. Encountering snow flurries as soon as they hit higher elevations, it had been hard on men and horses. The snowstorm had ended when they reached lower altitudes, and here the ground was only covered by an inch or two of powdery flakes. Freezing winds still swept across the slopes, but now deep forests blocked some of the cold gusts. Building fires had been a risk if Villa sent scouts to watch his back trail, yet the condition the soldiers were in left no choice but to allow the men to warm themselves. Judging by the stars, it was near five in the morning. As soon as the column could travel, despite more rough, rocky terrain ahead to reach the bluffs above Guerrero, the Seventh Cavalry should arrive shortly after dawn.

Will rode into camp and swung down at the fire where Colonel Dodd awaited his report about the land ahead of them. Dodd gave an aide instructions while Will was tying off his horse. A steaming cup of coffee was given to him by a pink-cheeked young corporal when he reached the warmth of the flames.

"Five or six miles farther," he said, taking a tiny sip of scalding liquid that burned his tongue. "It's rough going on this side of the valley. Easier to the north and south."

"The map shows deep canyons to the west," Dodd said, screwing his face into a thoughtful frown as he bit down on a soggy cigar butt. "If I sent a detail around to the west armed with machine guns, they could cut Villa off from escaping through the canyons."

"I reckon that'd work, but I ain't a military man," Will replied, recalling the rocky canyons west of the Rio Papigochic. "There's a railroad line along the east side of the valley, just behind San Isidro. Your men could follow the rails from both directions, north and south, to get to Guerrero. That way you'd have him corraled."

The colonel gazed blankly at the dark outline of the western horizon. "Then we'll make it in time to surround him. I can almost taste sweet victory. An officer with battlefield experience develops a sixth sense for these things, Mr. Johnson." He looked at Will. "And we have you to thank for it. Without your help getting over the mountains so quickly, we might have missed our moment of glory."

Will drank more of the wonderfully warm coffee, feeling his insides glow pleasantly. He had taken a liking to George Dodd almost at once, but Dodd seemed too optimistic about success when they got to Guerrero. "I wouldn't count on that glory just yet, Colonel. If you find Pancho Villa at Guerrero, you've still got the job of whipping his army. There's been plenty of proof over the years that he knows how to fight. He's defeated Carranza's armies all over this part of Mexico, then he up an' disappears like he's some sort of ghost."

Dodd smiled, without real mirth. "There are no such

things as ghosts. Men are mortal. Some are more skillful at military tactics than others, but when soldiers of equal skill engage Villa's men, he will be overwhelmed by superior firepower and an iron will equal to his own. Lead us to him, Mr. Johnson, and I'll prove this is no idle boast. We're gonna kick his ass."

A few at a time, fires were extinguished when the order to form ranks was given. Cavalrymen moved about in the dark, saddling horses. Four troops were assembled, dividing the men under separate command, each troop containing men from the machine-gun unit armed with Benets and clips of ammunition. Colonel Dodd rode down the column, giving orders to the troop commanders, the approach they would undertake to reach the valley. A hush spread through the men as word came that they were about to meet the enemy.

The columns moved off, riding quietly through the powdery snow.

Following the Mexican Northwest Railroad tracks from the south, Will was out in front of Colonel Dodd's troop by half a mile when he saw a *vaquero* riding toward him on a rawboned bay pony. Will worried that the rider was a Villista sentry and reached for the stock of his Winchester, until he saw that the Mexican cowboy was unarmed. The sun had risen, but it was still behind the mountains as the two men came together. Es Ki Ben De and Loco Jim had ridden with other troops to scout for them; thus Will was alone. The young *vaquero* grinned when he halted in front of Will, then his face grew dark and serious.

"Cuidado," he said, turning to look back in the direction of Guerrero. "It would not be wise for a *gringo* to go to Guerrero now. *El León del Norte* has taken over the village. General Cavazos and his *soldados* were driven from San Isidro yesterday. Many *soldados* on both sides are dead. General Pancho Villa himself has been mortally wounded. *Los Villistas* are celebrating their victory even now, drinking tequila, using our women. Do not go there if you value your life."

Only then did the boy notice the dust from Colonel Dodd's column rising above the trees east of the railroad tracks. "Who comes behind you, *señor?*" he asked, eyes narrowing in alarm.

"The American army," Will replied, glancing over his shoulder. "If I was you I'd keep ridin'. There's gonna be one hell of a fight here pretty soon."

"Gracias, señor," the *vaquero* whispered, crossing himself quickly. He swung his pony and kicked to a lope, riding southwest to avoid the oncoming soldiers.

Will wheeled his dun around and struck a gallop back to the column. When the colonel saw Will's haste, he seemed worried. Before the dun slid to a halt, Will began telling Dodd what he had learned from the *vaquero*.

"Villa hit Guerrero yesterday. His men routed the Carrancistas and they scattered. Villa was wounded, maybe seriously, according to the cowboy who told me about it. Villa's army is still there, gettin' drunk and celebratin' their big victory. The village is around the next bend, less than a mile."

Colonel Dodd looked up at the brightening sky. "We'll charge them now," he said, sounding eager to begin the battle. "It's still early. Maybe we can catch them with their pants down. The other detachments will hear our gunfire and rush to placements. Surely there has been enough time for E Troop and I Troop to circle the valley. Tommy Tompkins should have had enough time to get C Troop in position by now." He turned back in the saddle. "Captain Shaw, give the order to draw carbines and spread the troop into attack formation. When I give the order, charge the town. Shoot every son of a bitch wearing a sombrero or carrying a gun."

Captain Shaw saluted quickly and wheeled his horse. Will rode off, seeking a piece of high ground where he could watch the forthcoming battle from a safe distance.

He wondered about Villa's wound. Could an unlucky bullet have ended the life of northern Mexico's great hero, the Lion of the North? Perhaps Doroteo Arango's luck had finally run out.

Turning to the southwest, Will urged the dun up a forested slope, climbing higher at a steady trot, winding his way through deep pines until at last he had a view of the broad valley where San Isidro and Guerrero lay. Riding to the edge of the trees, he watched sunlight beam across the peaceful scene below. From a distance, the valley floor seemed quiet and serene. Both villages appeared to be asleep. Then the rattle of armaments and the deep rumble of hooves arose from the south. Colonel Dodd's cavalry, spread out in battle lines, charged along the railroad tracks, fanning out to cross the shallow San Isidro river. A detachment rode along the Rio Papagochic, rifle barrels glistening in the early sun. Suddenly, to the east, a staccato of rifle shots blasted from the foothills behind the village of San Isidro. C Troop, commanded by Lieutenant Colonel Tommy Tompkins, opened fire when they saw Colonel Dodd's all-out charge. E Troop, descending the western slopes behind Guerrero, halted and started shooting into the town randomly at targets Will could not see among the adobes. Moments later, guns popped and cracked from the north, abruptly ending the silence there. In less than half a minute the valley became a killing field, guns roaring from all sides.

In both villages men scurried from adobe buildings, returning fire in scattered bursts, dashing for horses stabled in tiny pole corrals, some collapsing before they ran more than a few steps. Stuttering machine-gun fire opened up from the men of E Troop behind Guerrero. Galloping horsemen among Dodd's advancing cavalry tumbled from their saddles when riflemen opened up in San Isidro. Wounded horses fell, crashing to the ground, spilling riders into the churning dust. A cavalryman, galloping his mount across the shallows of the Rio San Isidro, was toppled from the saddle and splashed headfirst into the chilly waters with a cry of pain when his horse stumbled. His dying sorrel fell on its side, pinning him among the rocks along the river bank.

Minutes later, in San Isidro, a large group of sombreroed riders swirled away from one of the corrals, angling southeast toward an offshoot canyon. Will noticed a flag bearer among them carrying a large Mexican national banner. American soldiers on that side of the valley apparently thought they were witnessing the exodus of a large unit of Carranza cavalry, and the shooting stopped to let the

Mexican soldiers escape the slaughter of Villista revolutionaries. Soon more than a hundred mounted men galloped past the machine-gun placements atop the canyon walls. Although the incident was taking place on the far side of the valley, Will saw it clearly. He shook his head, certain that the Mexican flag had allowed some of Villa's men to flee the battle unharmed. The Villistas would have seen to it that no Carranza soldiers were left alive after yesterday's fight.

Murderous volleys of machine-gun fire opened up from the bluffs west of Guerrero. Men were cut down as they ran for cover between the adobes. Frightened horses milled about in corrals all over the village when the sputter of automatic fire grew to a chorus of exploding shells. Sometimes in twos and threes, men raced for safety from the hail of bullets toward the center of Guerrero, dodging into open doorways, ducking down behind every form of shelter until the Benets fell silent to reload.

From the north, cavalrymen charged both villages, Springfield rifles popping in the distance. Colonel Dodd's troopers, bending low over their horses' necks, fired again and again as their mounts galloped across the valley floor from the south. Answering fire from San Isidro became sporadic. Villa's men, the few remaining there who had not been able to reach their horses, fell back toward the tiny central plaza, shooting less often now, hoping only to save their lives. As the fighting continued, more and more bodies lay in the dusty streets of Guerrero and San Isidro. The death toll was mounting rapidly. Despite an empty stomach, Will felt his belly churning. He wanted to turn away, yet something held him there, watching the grisly scene unfold from the edge of the pine forest, safe from the speeding bullets screaming back and forth below the slope.

More gunfire erupted in Guerrero. Tiny wisps of blue gunsmoke came from dark windows and shadowy doorways. Defending Villistas shot back at the muzzle flashes from Benets high on the western bluffs. In the streets of the village men were rushing back and forth, seeking better firing positions, until some were suddenly dropped by a hail of lead. Minutes dragged by as the valley swelled with the noise of battle.

A cluster of mounted Villistas galloped from the hallway of a wooden stable on the south side of Guerrero. They rode southwest, spurring their horses relentlessly, whipping the animals' rumps with their reins. Some of Colonel Dodd's cavalry swerved to pursue them toward the mouth of a winding arroyo leading from the valley, but their tiring horses were no match for fresher mounts. The Villistas fled, outdistancing Dodd's men quickly, and were soon lost in the rocks. Before the American cavalrymen reached the mouth of the arroyo their horses were finished, down to a trot or a shuffling walk, with heads lowered, flanks heaving for wind.

San Isidro was the first to fall as Colonel Dodd led his soldiers into the village. Wounded Mexicans limped into the streets with their arms held high in surrender. Troopers from C Company entered the town from the north, finding no resistance. Across the river in Guerrero, scattered pockets of fighting continued a few minutes more until most of the shooting stopped. Along the bluffs, high atop the canyon walls, gradually the machine guns fell silent.

Not until then did Will realize that his palms were wet, clamped around his reins in a viselike grip. His jaw muscles ached from gritting his teeth. He had no idea how long the battle had lasted, nor did it matter. Everywhere he looked he saw dead bodies, wounded men, and crippled horses. From a distance, it appeared American casualties were light. Both villages had been unprepared for the attack, taken by surprise perhaps, Will guessed, due to Villa's reportedly mortal wound. Without the leadership of Villa, his army quickly succumbed to the Americans.

"I've seen dyin' before," he told himself quietly. The dun's ears flicked back at the sound of his voice.

Off to the southwest, a handful of Dodd's cavalry prodded limping, exhausted horses into the mouth of the arroyo. Some held automatic pistols, their supply of rifle ammunition gone. Now and then a single gunshot echoed from Guerrero as the last of the Villistas offered token resistance.

In San Isidro a badly wounded man crawled to the edge of an adobe hut, leaving a red smear in his wake across the pale roadway. The American trooper who was pinned beneath his dead horse at the river's edge tried vainly to pull his leg from beneath the animal's carcass, his plight going unnoticed by any of his fellow soldiers, despite weakening pleas for help issued too far from the village to be heard.

"I oughta give him a hand." Will sighed, heeling his horse down the mountainside when it appeared the shooting had stopped completely around San Isidro. "Nobody can hear the poor bastard way out there. . . ."

He rode the dun down to the valley floor and struck a trot toward the river. A blue haze hung above the valley now, rising slowly on currents of air, filling his nostrils with the scent of burnt gunpowder. At the edge of the river he dismounted quickly, seeing the pain in the young soldier's eyes as he waded into the shallows. The boy, barely old enough to shave, was shivering. Tears flooded his cheeks. Will took the saddle forks and lifted with all his strength, allowing the trooper to pull his leg free.

"Jesus . . . thanks," the soldier cried softly, when Will helped him to stand.

A distant gunshot made both of them flinch as they struggled out of the river.

"Can you walk?" Will asked.

The soldier tested his leg. "I think so. Thanks again." He glanced to the village. "Is it over?"

"Most of it, I reckon."

Another lone shot cracked in Guerrero, then a burst of automatic-pistol fire. An eerie silence followed, until they could both hear cries from the wounded coming from San Isidro.

"It's the worst thing I ever saw," the boy said softly, as though he feared someone else might hear the admission. "It's not the same . . . training on a rifle range, shooting at paper targets. They don't tell us what it's like to kill another man, even if they are only Mexicans. We don't have any Mexicans back in Ohio. . . ."

Will let go of the soldier's arm. "I'd better find Colonel Dodd. If you can walk to the village, maybe somebody'll find you a horse."

"I'm grateful for what you did, mister."

Will shrugged off the remark and mounted his horse as a

renewed wave of nausea gripped his stomach. When he reined for the village, wails from the streets seemed louder than before.

A single thought preoccupied him as he rode into San Isidro at a walk: Where was Villa? Was he lying fatally wounded in one of the adobes? Was he dead? Or had he simply vanished? as the legends among *campesino* farmers claimed he could. Had he been among the men who rode out of Guerrero carrying the Mexican flag? Colonel Dodd insisted there were no such things as ghosts, yet some inner voice spoke to Will on the ride through the outskirts of San Isidro, telling him that they would not find Villa here today. It had been too easy when the villages fell. Down in his gut, Will was certain Villa had eluded them.

He found Colonel Dodd at the plaza, giving instructions to a large group of mounted soldiers.

"Search every goddamn house, every building. Line all the prisoners up in the middle of this town square under guard, and pay particular attention to anyone who resembles Pancho Villa. Our scout was informed that Villa may be wounded. I want him brought here the minute he is found. Send a detail to see to our wounded while I ride over to Guerrero."

Two officers saluted and began shouting orders to the rest of the men, dividing them into squads for a search of the village. The colonel wheeled his horse just as Will rode up to the plaza.

"Ride with me across the river to Guerrero," Dodd said, heeling his winded horse toward a side street. "It appears we have things under control here. Above all else we must find Villa, so I can make a present of him to Black Jack when we ride back to join the main column."

"I wouldn't count on the fact that he's here, Colonel. I saw nearly a hundred men ride out of Guerrero while all the shootin' was goin' on. One of them was carryin' a Mexican flag and your soldiers let them pass, figurin' they were *Federales,* I reckon."

The colonel whirled around in his saddle, astonished. "You saw this?" he asked. "We allowed some of the bastards to escape?"

"I'm afraid so. The flag fooled everybody, only common sense should have told them that there weren't any Carrancistas here now."

"Damn," Colonel Dodd snapped, glaring across the broad open expanse between the villages. "There's the folly of leading inexperienced soldiers, Mr. Johnson. Which way did they ride when they got away?"

"East, up that canyon yonder," Will replied, pointing over his shoulder. "Another small bunch made it up that arroyo to the west of Guerrero. Some of your men tried to follow them, only their horses were spent by the time they got there."

Dodd was scowling. "Maybe Villa wasn't with either group," he muttered. "For now, we'll hope for the best until both towns have been thoroughly searched. As you observed, our horses have nothing left in them. Pursuit is out of the question until our mounts are rested."

They came to the river and rode across. Will studied the buildings around Guerrero, watching Colonel Dodd's troopers move back and forth, assembling only a tiny handful of prisoners here and there. He wondered how many casualties both sides would have when a final tally was taken. Judging by appearances, American casualties would be few, while the other side had suffered a large number of dead and wounded.

"If you want, I'll ask around about Villa," he said a moment later. "The locals will know what happened to him, where he went if he ain't still here."

Urging his horse to a trot away from the river, Dodd gave Will a quizzical look. "You sound like you think he got away."

"It's just a feelin'. Maybe I'm wrong."

The colonel swept the battleground with a lingering stare before he answered. "Do as you wish, Mr. Johnson. You seem to have a special knack for knowing what to do in this part of the world, so ask your questions of the villagers. Report back to me if you find out anything."

Glancing up at the sun, Will guessed the time at ten o'clock and swung his horse toward the southern edge of Guerrero, leaving the colonel to his duties. The closer they came to the village, the more certain Will became that they would soon learn of Pancho Villa's miraculous escape from this valley, where the smell of death hung like a pall above the homes of simple farmers and goat herders caught between battling armies. After witnessing the carnage here today, Will knew he wanted no part of this war. As badly as he needed the army's money, there were some things for which the price simply came too high.

The little girl's name was Conchita. Her tattered cotton dress, faded from too many washings, barely covered her slender brown legs. Braided hair hung almost to her waist, and when he questioned her, she toyed with a pigtail and would not look at him, although she answered him in Spanish readily enough and appeared to be telling the truth. The girl's mother stood in the shadow of their hut, listening to Conchita tell Will what she had seen.

"They loaded him in a wagon. His wound was very painful and he cried out. Modesto Nevares helped them lift him into the back of the wagon. Modesto told me that a bullet had gone all the way through General Villa's leg. It was right here, *señor,*" she said, pointing to a spot behind her right knee. "The bone was broken. Modesto saw it sticking through his skin. They put wooden splints on his leg and then Modesto was selected to drive the team. He told his mother that they were taking the general to Parral until his wound could heal. Modesto's mother was crying when they left. She worries that she will never see him again."

Will digested the information carefully while reading the girl's face. Due to her apparent innocence and her tender years, he believed her. "How many men rode with Villa when he left Guerrero?"

"Many, *señor.* I counted more than one hundred."

The number fit what Will knew about Villa, who always traveled with a huge escort, fearing for his own safety. "When did they leave?"

She hesitated, as though she had trouble remembering. "It was after midnight."

It came as no surprise to learn Villa had escaped, but his wound did sound serious; a shattered shinbone, judging by the spot the girl indicated. "Which way did they go?" he asked carefully, seeking the most valuable piece of information.

Conchita pointed south. "Through the mountains, *señor*. It was the reason Modesto was chosen to drive the brave general's wagon, because he knew a road through the mountains where no one would find them on the way to Parral."

He nodded, then tipped his hat to the girl's mother. "I am grateful for what you have told me," he said, still speaking Spanish, for Conchita knew no English at all. She spoke with a trace of Yaqui dialect, and looking at her broad cheekbones, he was sure she was part Yaqui.

Turning away from the hut, he looked south into the mountains. Villa was on his way to Parral, traveling the back roads. No one would find him. The U.S. Army would try to track him down, but it would be an impossible task in the empty regions where he would lead them. Will knew the country almost as well as local *vaqueros*. Hundreds of square miles of steep mountains and twisting canyons lay between Guerrero and Parral. Remembering them, he shook his head and stepped aboard his horse.

Colonel Dodd needed to be told the bad news. Once again, as he had a number of times in the past, Pancho Villa had slipped from the grasp of his enemies, just in the nick of time. Maybe there were no such things as ghosts, but Villa came just about as close to behaving like one as any mortal man could.

• 18 •

"Villa is gone, Colonel," Will said, glancing up at the noonday sun. "He left around midnight with an escort of about a hundred men. A bullet broke his shinbone. Somebody put splints on it an' then they loaded him in a buggy. Accordin' to what I was told, the wound was mighty painful. They headed across those mountains to the south, makin' for Parral."

Dodd examined the southern Sierras briefly, his face showing the toll of their difficult march to reach the valley. "If you can find his tracks, we'll go after him as soon as the men and horses are rested."

Will was almost too tired to think. "It ain't likely we'll find him in those peaks, Colonel. He has a local guide who knows the mountain back roads. There's a thousand places to hide down yonder, places we could never look even if you had every soldier in the United States Army. Villa will order his men to scatter, if he hasn't already. He'll find a place to hide until his leg gets well, an' it's my guess he'll do it close to Parral, where he has lots of friends. There's a German girl down there. Her name's Elisa Griensen. Villa is known to associate with her. If it was me doin' the lookin' I'd head down to Parral, maybe keep an eye on her house. One of Villa's men is liable to show up, askin' the woman to help with Villa's wound."

"A splendid idea," Dodd said, stroking his chin. "In the absence of further orders from General Pershing, since our radio pack isn't working, I'll send you ahead to Parral to watch the German woman's house. You seem to know more about Villa than anyone else on the general's staff."

Will had been deliberating a decision to quit the scouting

job after watching the battle from the mountainside. In his heart he wanted no more of the killing, but if all he had to do was keep an eye on Elisa Griensen for a while and report back if he saw anything unusual, that was different. "I reckon I could do that. To tell the truth, Colonel, I was fixin' to resign from this outfit and head home. I need the money, but watchin' men kill each other ain't exactly what I had in mind when I took this job. But if all you want from me is information I can gather about Villa, I suppose I'll stay on for a spell. Never was cut out to be a soldier in the first place."

"I understand," Dodd replied. "See if you can find Villa's tracks for us. I'm sending couriers back to General Pershing with a report of what happened here. After giving my men a day of rest, we'll head south, if you can locate the trail Villa took. In the morning, take the shortest route to Parral and keep an eye on the Griensen woman. Report back to Major Ryan if you find out anything concerning Villa's whereabouts."

Will merely nodded and trudged away from the plaza leading his spare horse. Although he figured it was a waste of time looking for buggy tracks south of Guerrero, he would do it at the colonel's request. He found that he genuinely liked George Dodd. Curious, that he met a military man he liked. Dodd wasn't like the other officers on this expedition. He showed common sense and seemed to understand what he was up against in Mexico.

Chewing a sandwich of bacon and hardtack, he rode away from Guerrero an hour later, flanked by the two Apaches. It was most likely a futile attempt, but they would look for tracks until it got too dark to see. Trotting his horse into the foothills, he remembered pretty Elisa Griensen, her green eyes and long blond hair. He'd met her a few years back while buying cattle from her brother-in-law, Pedro Alvarado. Pedro had always been an ardent Villa supporter, and some of his enthusiasm had been infectious. It was more than a whispered rumor that Elisa liked Villa in a number of ways. Locals often talked about the times Villa had been seen at the German girl's house outside Parral.

If Villa made it to Parral, Will guessed he would try to contact her. He needed medical attention, and Elisa might be willing to provide it. Besides that, watching the house would get Will away from the army for a spell, a much more promising way to spend time earning his money for scouting. And Elisa was not hard to look at, either. Will could pass off his presence there as one of his regular cattle-buying trips into Chihuahua. Talking to her would be a pleasant change from army routine.

He found he was looking forward to the ride to Parral as they ascended the first mountain slope to look for buggy tracks. Anything to get away from the army for a time and the memory of bullet-riddled bodies, the thunder of guns, cries from so many wounded. War wasn't the sort of thing Will understood.

An hour after dark they returned to Guerrero. Just before sundown, Es Ki Ben De had located the hoofprints of many horses leading southeast. The colonel was pleased. At first light, the two Apaches would lead the Seventh Cavalry down the tracks while Will made for Parral by well-traveled roads.

After a meager supper of beans and bacon, the three scouts found a vacant adobe at the edge of Guerrero and spread their blankets on the smooth earthen floor. No sooner had Will rested his head on his saddle, he drifted off to sleep, dreaming of the German woman's beautiful face.

"It is good to see you again," she said, bowing slightly as she stood in the doorway of her adobe house. "Pedro wonders why you had not come this year."

"Too dry," he told her, doffing his hat. Outside a low adobe wall around her yard, his horse stamped a hoof at a fly and swished its tail. "Not many orders for *corrientes* this spring, on account of everybody knows they'll be too thin."

A gust of warm wind rustled leaves in oak trees surrounding the house, sweeping a stray lock of blond hair across her smooth tan cheeks. She flipped the hair aside carelessly with the back of her hand, still smiling the way she had when she first came to the door to answer his knock. "Please come in," she said in thickly accented English. "I have lemonade. Tequila also, if you prefer it."

"I was on my way out to Pedro's to ask about steers. No need to go to any trouble. Just thought I'd pay a social call along the way."

Her smile only widened. "I am glad you came. It is a long ride out to the *rancho.* Come in *und* have some refreshment. I made *pan dulce* this morning. Have some while it is still warm."

He grinned and pulled off his hat again to enter the house. "Much obliged, Elisa. I couldn't turn down an invitation like that, could I?" He walked into the front room, noticing several leatherbound chairs and polished tables, the scent of *candelilla* wax and a hint of perfume. Exhausted after a hard two-day ride with little sleep to reach Parral, the insides of his legs chafed from too many hours in the saddle, he slumped into one of the chairs and dropped his hat on the floor as Elisa went into the kitchen. He had watched the house for a couple of hours and had seen no one come in or out. With luck, he might have beaten Villa and his escort to Parral.

Elisa returned carrying a tray of sweetbreads and a pitcher of lemonade. When he looked at her, somehow she seemed even prettier than he remembered. She smiled and placed the tray on a coffee table before him, then she self-consciously spread wrinkles from the front of her soft cotton skirt and poured lemonade into two glasses. She gave him one of the sugar-coated rolls and a glass of lemonade. Gentle breezes passing through open windows around the room tousled her hair.

"Pedro will be glad to see you," she said, sitting across from him, crossing one long, shapely leg over the other. "He is worried that his yearlings are too thin for American buyers this year."

"That's the reason I'm late. Hardly any orders. I almost decided not to come at all, what with all this trouble brewin' down here."

"You heard about the killings at Columbus?" she asked.

He thought he detected something guarded about the tone she used. "I heard about it. Eighteen Americans killed, accordin' to what the newspapers said."

Her sparkling green eyes narrowed. *"Und* what about the brave men who died with Francisco? More than a hundred, we are told."

She called Villa by his first name. "I don't recall readin'

how many of Villa's men were killed," he replied with a note of apology. "I don't pay much attention to politics."

His remark caused her to visibly stiffen. "How can you ignore so many lost lives? It is not only politics."

"Maybe it'd be better if I said I didn't take sides."

A fire smoldered behind her eyes, then it cooled quickly as she collected herself. "The revolution drags on. Some say it will continue for many years, until President Venustiano Carranza retires, or until he is killed. There are always whispers of plots to assassinate him. His own men conspire against him."

He took a sip of lemonade, then a bite of *pan dulce*. "This is good. You're a wonderful cook." He was suddenly conscious of his appearance while she was staring at him. His clothes were rumpled, and he needed a bath and a shave, a haircut, some rose-hair tonic. "Sorry 'bout the way I look. It's a long ride down here," he added, grinning to hide his embarrassment, hoping she wouldn't give him too much notice. It did, however, seem she was paying closer attention to his face, more than usual.

"You are welcome to use the bathtub," she said. "I can boil some water. I have soap."

"Thanks. Maybe I'll take you up on that after the ride out to Pedro's to look at his steers."

She drank daintily from her glass, nibbled on the edge of a roll, listening to the *chicharras* in the trees. "If you do not mind, I will ride out with you. It is a warm day, *und* my mare needs the exercise."

"Don't mind at all," he replied, feeling his heartbeat quicken a little. "It'd be foolish to object to havin' the company of a pretty girl."

He thought he noticed a trace of color rise in her face, and she turned her head slightly, perhaps to hide it. "I will change into my riding breeches. It will only take a moment." She put down her glass and got up, walking to the bedroom door, bare feet padding across wooden floorboards. She closed the door gently behind her, then he heard a drawer open.

He turned his gaze to a window, idly watching the curtains flutter in the breeze. So far, the meeting with Elisa had gone smoothly. She gave no indication that she suspected his motives for being in Parral. Judging by her relaxed manner, she didn't know about Villa's wound or the fall of Guerrero. If she knew about the Pershing expedition into Mexico, she made no mention of it yet. Thinking about her, he wondered if she could truly be a spy for the German government, as it was rumored about her. She seemed much too young and innocent for that sort of intrigue. He had only a limited understanding of such international dealings, having grown up in a tiny part of the world that seemed so far removed from places like Europe and elsewhere around the globe. In school, what time he spent inside a classroom, he had often daydreamed through studies of world history, geography, and the like. Those subjects had little to do with the struggle he and his family underwent to make a living in south Texas. He had dropped out of school in the seventh grade, bored with things, needed by his father at the ranch to help with cattle chores.

Thus, lacking knowledge of international workings beyond the border difficulties with Mexico, how could he judge whether or not the German girl was a spy? On the surface, she appeared to be no different from thousands of other immigrants settled in Mexico. A dozen different nationalities were represented in small colonies all over Mexican states. Why would anyone suppose they were spies for another government? The rumors about Elisa were probably only idle gossip.

A gust of wind swept through open windows on the west side of the house, stiffening curtains, fluttering the hems of lace doilies on the arms of chairs. The bedroom door opened with a muted click, pushed a few inches away from the door jamb on silent hinges. He glanced that way, distracted from his ruminations by the sound.

He saw Elisa standing naked before a bedroom window, her back turned to the door, slipping out of her blouse, her skirt around her ankles on the floor. He caught his breath and watched her, completely fascinated by the beauty of her rounded hips and slender waist, the delicate curve of her thighs and calves. She turned to a four-poster bed without noticing him, revealing the gentle swell of one breast outlined by sunlight from the window. A rosy pink nipple stood erect, twisted into a tiny knot. He knew it was ungentlemanly to be staring at her, yet he was unable to take his gaze away. Skin tanned lightly by the sun held his rapt attention. A light tingling sensation went down his arms, spreading to his fingertips, and now his heart was laboring beneath his shirt. His mouth went dry watching the girl put on a man's workshirt, button it, the shirttail barely concealing her buttocks. Then slowly, as if someone whispered to her that he was watching from the other room, her head turned.

She looked at him and he was suddenly embarrassed, his cheeks turning hot, although he did not look away immediately, still fascinated by what he saw.

"Sorry," he muttered, looking away now. "The wind blew the door open. Didn't mean to stare, but I reckon I couldn't help myself, seein' as you're such a pretty lady."

He heard soft footsteps. Elisa came into the front room, her legs still bare, carrying a pair of denim pants over the crook of an arm. He glanced up at her when she stopped beside his chair. The beginnings of a playful grin lifted the corners of her mouth.

"It is all right if you look at me," she said softly, "only I will be the one to choose the time and place. I am no longer a foolish little girl, Will Johnson. I am a woman. When I was a girl back in Furstenburg, my mother taught me it was wrong for a woman to show her body to a man. My mother died when I was very young, my father only a year later. I was forced to learn many new things, different things. A man took me and my sister to Cuba, then to Mexico, and I learned what a young woman must do in order to survive on her own. Those were hard lessons for a girl, but I learned them. I am not an old-fashioned girl any longer."

Right at first, he didn't know what to say. Elisa kept standing there, bare legs tempting his eyes to stray downward, yet he couldn't take his gaze from her remarkable face. "I reckon we both had a hard upbringin'," he said thickly, his throat a little tighter than usual. "My pa died when I was fourteen. Ma died when I was six, so I understand hard lessons. Pa was gone most of the time down in Mexico. He took me with him as soon as I was old enough to lend a hand with the cattle. It's fair to say I never did have many old-fashioned notions about the way life is supposed to be." He cleared his throat when it became clotted. "I couldn't help starin' at you, Elisa. You're a very beautiful woman. It was just my good luck when that wind blew the door open, I suppose."

She laughed, webbing soft lines into the skin around her mouth, revealing rows of even, white teeth. She took her pants and stepped into each leg slowly without taking her eyes from his, wriggling them over her hips as though she heard a lazy melody. "Give me time to saddle my mare," she whispered, still smiling playfully. Then she turned and walked into the kitchen. Moments later, a rear door slammed shut.

He was outside, tightening the cinch on his saddle, when Elisa rode around from the stable at the back of the house on a black pacing mare. She sat perfectly straight aboard the horse's back with the poise of an experienced equestrian, heels down, her hands in the proper place on the reins, pants stuffed into the tops of knee-high black riding boots. Her house sat on a hilltop above Parral where winds blew continually, and when a gust caught her yellow hair it swept her locks around her face, framing it briefly until she shook her head.

He mounted the blue roan, leaving the dun tied to a tree limb on a long rope so it could graze. As he was settling into the saddle, he noticed a 9mm Mauser automatic pistol tucked into Elisa's waistband.

"Do you figure we'll need the gun?" he asked, bringing the roan around to head for Pedro's ranch.

"These are dangerous times," she said, glancing to the hills around them. As if she had no more to say on the subject, she heeled her mare to a lope toward a range of mountains to the east of Parral.

He caught up to her and settled his horse to the same gait, taking sideways glances in her direction when he could. She rode her mare expertly, almost effortlessly, without bouncing in the seat of her saddle. He admired the way she handled a horse, and he said so. "You sit a horse like you were born in the saddle."

She chuckled, yet her attention seemed drawn to the trees

on the steepening hillsides around them. Did she suspect they were being watched?

"You seem a little edgy," he added. "Any reason to expect trouble on the way to Pedro's place?"

For a time she didn't answer him, watching the pine and juniper forests. "There is always a reason to expect trouble in Chihuahua," she replied, unconsciously touching the butt of her pistol.

Pedro Alvarado's *rancho* lay at the bottom of a steep valley three hours east of Parral. Old cattle trails criss-crossed the route they took, but they saw no one and passed no houses along the way. Parral was one of the largest cities in the southern part of Chihuahua, a major trading center for livestock and farm produce, home to twenty thousand citizens who, for the most part, were known to be Villa sympathizers. Carranza forces held a garrison there, yet soldiers loyal to the president seldom ventured far from the encampment. Will avoided the city of Parral itself as much as he could, for anti-American sentiment ran high among the villagers.

Pedro greeted him with a smile when they stepped down from the saddle in front of his rambling adobe. Chickens pecked around the yard, and Pedro scattered them when he left the porch to shake hands with Will. He had gained some weight since the year before, a paunch hanging over the gunbelt he wore around his waist.

"*Buenos días*, Will," he said, offering his palm. "I did not think you would come this year. *Dios!* It has been the driest year in all my memory, and *las vacas* are *muy* hungry for grass."

Will's eyes strayed to Pedro's gun. "I don't have many orders this year, *compadre*. Everybody up north knows it's been dry down here. I'm only looking around, so I can tell my best customers what's available, in case they're interested."

"I understand," Pedro said sadly, wagging his head. He paid no attention to Elisa, as though Will had ridden alone. "Come inside. We will talk, then I show you *las vacas*. But please remember, my *Tejano* friend, the cows will be very thin."

It amused Will, as they walked to the front steps, that Pedro, out of respect for his visitor, spoke to him in English. A mixture, if the truth were told, for there were many English words he did not know. They entered the house and were met by a chubby blond woman, Elisa's younger sister, pregnant with her fifth child. Will took off his hat and bowed politely. "How are you, Christina?"

"Quite well, Mr. Johnson," she replied, as always speaking with less of the German accent than her sister. Once she could have been called pretty. "Can I get you something to drink?"

He was distracted and didn't answer Christina right away, thinking how unusual it was that both Pedro and his wife seemed to be ignoring Elisa completely. Something must have happened between the sisters, and between Pedro and Elisa. He wondered if it could have anything to do with Doroteo Arango.

• 19 •

General Pershing had been listening patiently for almost an hour to Captain Benjamin Foulois describe what was happening to the aeroplanes. Foulois was the most experienced pilot the army had. He was a spare man, a pipe-smoking, dedicated soldier who believed in the future of air power. But the aeroplanes the army had commissioned from Glenn Curtiss were notoriously unstable, and it seemed that no matter how they were modified, they flew no better. Of the eight JN-2s comprising the First Aero Squadron, only five managed to fly from Columbus to Casas Grandes without crashing or running out of fuel. Foulois was explaining what needed to be done in order to provide aerial reconnaissance for the columns pushing south. New propellers, more powerful engines, and a larger tail surface were required to get the Jennys over even the lowest foothills leading into the Sierras.

"Carberry and Gorrell are still unaccounted for," Foulois said. "Mounted search parties are looking for them now. Dargue's propeller is warped and the entire aeroplane vibrates so badly that it will surely kill him if he takes off again without a replacement. Only Kilner and Willis and myself have flyable craft. We'll do whatever we can to look for any sign of troop movement. However, we can't fly over those mountains."

Pershing sighed, watching the arrival of three new Dodge automobiles from the desert, a part of the shipment he'd requested while at Fort Bliss. "First the radios fail, and now you tell me we have no trustworthy aircraft," he said bitterly. "Only three of your aeroplanes can fly, and even they are suspect."

"We can achieve very little in the way of altitude," Foulois explained, "and God help us if there is any wind or rough air. Two of my men may be dead, or at best walking away from a crash site somewhere in the desert. We got separated in the dark last night and they could have been forced down almost anywhere."

Pershing was reminded of his conversation with George Dodd only two nights before. George wanted nothing to do with the army's best machinery, only good horses and hard-riding men, his lone concession to a new age being the willingness to take along a few of the French machine guns. In many respects George had his full sympathies, for as things were now, the main body of the expedition was more or less stranded at Colonia Dublan, repairing truck motors and tires, broken wagon wheels and axles, seeing to the care of tired horses and mules and footsore men after traveling a scant fifty miles into Mexico. At this rate Villa could tap-dance across southern Chihuahua without ever worrying about any difficulties from the U.S. Army trailing along behind him. The American effort to punish him for the atrocities at Columbus would make a mockery of any threat of American intervention on foreign soil unless something dramatic could be accomplished very soon. Much now depended on George Dodd reaching Guerrero in time, since the rush to encircle San Miguel had been for naught, only creating further delays, until Colonel Brown could return with men injured in the train derailment, for treatment at a field hospital. Perhaps the reputation of the entire nation rested on Dodd's shoulders, and lacking any air reconnaissance or radio communication, Pershing had no way of finding out about Dodd's success or failure.

"Do what you can," he told Captain Foulois. "If the damn things were not airworthy in the first place, I wonder why the War Department ordered them down here."

Foulois shook his head, chewing his pipestem. "More aeroplanes crash every day in France than we have in this entire squadron, General, and apparently no one considered the need for spare parts. I can't risk the lives of my men. If I may say so, sir, it's a reflection of the congressional attitude toward flying in general. The Huns spent twenty-eight million on military aviation last year, and Russia at least twelve million, while the War Department can only beg half a million dollars from Congress for American air combat readiness. It's an embarrassment."

"It tends to show our overall willingness to engage in combat, I'm afraid," Pershing replied, his thoughts still miles away with the men of the Seventh. "We have the shortsightedness of our peace-loving president to thank for it. See if you can get one or two of your planes in flying shape and send them south along the road to Guerrero. I'm traveling in one of these new automobiles down the same road, in hopes that by one means or another, we can learn what has happened to the Seventh Cavalry. If both these methods should fail, we may resort to carrier pigeons. That would make Congress and the president happy. Pigeons are inexpensive, and at least we could lay claim to controlling the skies here."

Lieutenant Collins drove one of the Dodge touring cars over to the command tent and got out. Pershing had already decided what would be done with the automobile. This open-top vehicle was to become his mobile headquarters. As his aide was hurrying over to give his report concerning the arrival of the Dodges, the general met him halfway to inspect the one Collins had driven, leaving Captain Foulois so abruptly that he'd forgotten to dismiss him.

"Fill it with gasoline," Pershing said. "We're driving down to San Geronimo this afternoon."

A commotion behind him made him turn around. Frank Elser and Floyd Gibbons came trotting toward the row of new Dodges with notepads in their hands.

"Are we going someplace?" Elser asked, out of breath. "Has something finally happened?"

The reporters had begun to get under Pershing's skin, although he needed their cooperation now more than ever. "I'm heading toward Guerrero, where Villa is suspected of launching an attack. We haven't heard anything from our advance column and the pilots are having difficulties with the wind, so I intend to find out for myself what is going on." He addressed Lieutenant Collins again: "Load enough supplies for a few days and assign a guard detail to the other two automobiles."

"Shall I bring a field radio, sir?" Collins inquired, "so you can stay in touch with base operations here?"

He was tempted to say it would be a waste of time, then he thought better of it while newsmen were present and agreed to the radio by way of a silent nod.

"We'll tag along," Gibbons offered. "Maybe at last we'll get to report some real action we can send to our editors."

Frank Elser had not been fooled by a story about the wind. "The only thing wrong with those aeroplanes is that they can't fly at all, wind or no wind," he said, mopping his brow with a handkerchief. "Glenn Curtiss has gotten rich selling the War Department the equivalent of a horseshoer's anvil with wings and a propeller. I've been watching them land—if that's what you wish to call it—and I say men with enough nerve to go up in one of those things ought to be recommended for a congressional medal or a Silver Star. I can piss higher than they can fly."

Pershing turned away before Elser finished, striding toward his tent to pack his trunk for the drive. It was pointless to argue the obvious with Elser and Gibbons, since they had been a witness to almost every crash landing the Jennys performed while arriving at Colonia Dublan.

* * *

The road, if it could be called that, wound and twisted up and down through a maze of box canyons and increasingly rugged mountainsides, climbing steadily. The general sat beside Lieutenant Patton in the passenger seat, watching Patton furiously work the steering wheel and the gear lever to avoid obstacles in the way. The air grew colder, and to the south a bank of dark clouds hung over the peaks, promising either rain or snow. Jostling along at the rear were the remaining pair of Dodges, containing six infantrymen, and Elser and Gibbons driving a Ford Model-T. Frequent stops were soon necessary to refill steaming radiators or repair many punctured tires. As they drove past Mexican farmers in rare cultivated fields along the way, people stared at the procession, but no one spoke to them or waved a friendly greeting. Even as they raced through El Valle to continue the climb into higher parts of the Sierras when there was no sign of the Seventh Cavalry, local citizens avoided them and often turned their backs on the string of automobiles.

During each stop a corpsman tried in vain to reach the Seventh by radio. The battery-operated field pack generated nothing but static. Patton paced back and forth during every delay, only adding to the growing strain on Pershing's nerves. Nothing seemed to be going right. Both newsmen became keenly aware of his increasing agitation. Gibbons continually asked more questions concerning the report of a possible raid by the Villistas on Guerrero and what the army meant to do about it, while Elser kept up a diatribe about the failure of American aeroplanes to prove their worth, wanting to know if Pershing would report their many shortcomings to the War Department in his next dispatch to Washington.

There was a reprieve of sorts for the First Aero Squadron, when shortly before five o'clock a motor was heard in the skies. A lone Jenny appeared from the north, flying along the bottom of a winding valley below the roadway. Frank Elser made verbal note of the fact that the string of automobiles had achieved greater altitude than the JN-2, as he peered over the lip of the road to watch the aeroplane fly past the mountain during yet another halt to repair a flat tire.

Pershing looked south, toward San Geronimo and Guerrero, hoping George had fared better than he at preserving America's military dignity.

Two messengers from the Seventh riding winded horses met the procession of automobiles just before dusk. Corporal Lyle Hood gave his report directly to Pershing, trying not to omit any important details.

"Pancho Villa attacked Guerrero before we could get there, sir. He captured the cache of arms and killed or drove off the *Federales* the day before we arrived. Colonel Dodd followed the advice of one of the civilian scouts and turned off the main road to ride over the Continental Divide on a cow trail. We got to Guerrero the next morning and charged the town in time to catch Villa's men resting. We captured or killed almost two hundred of them, but more than a hundred got away by carrying a false flag of the Mexican republic past our machine-gun emplacements, and Colonel Tompkins thought they were friendly forces."

"What about Villa?" Pershing asked sternly, for it seemed from the beginning that this entire war was being waged against only one man.

"He escaped, General," Hood replied, "but it is reported that he was badly wounded, a bullet through his leg. Our scout interrogated some of the local villagers and found out that Villa is making his way toward Parral in a wagon. Colonel Dodd said to inform you that he is following Villa's tracks into the mountains as soon as the wounded were attended to."

"How heavy are our casualties?" the general asked, dreading the answer.

"Only five wounded, sir, and just one seriously. At last count, fifty-six Villistas are known dead and scores of them are badly wounded."

"What a relief," Pershing said, as Elser and Gibbons scribbled furiously in their notepads. "Colonel Dodd is to be commended for conducting a successful strategic maneuver under most trying conditions. We have dealt Villa a severe blow, and with luck and good weather, we will continue to hound him until he is caught."

Corporal Hood grinned somewhat sheepishly. "The colonel said to tell you . . ." he paused for a moment ". . . that we kicked their asses real good, sir, and that he personally guarantees he will have Pancho Villa by the balls before the week is out, if our horses can withstand another punishing ride."

"I knew George could do it," Pershing said quietly, as if he spoke to himself. Even though Villa had gotten away, events had finally taken a turn in the right direction. "I intend to ask President Wilson to nominate him for a Silver Star."

"We've got to get our reports to the border without delay," Gibbons said excitedly. "The entire country will be so happy to read about our smashing success. Americans will have a new hero in Colonel George A. Dodd. Imagine what this story will look like in bold headlines!"

Darkness was spreading quickly over the mountains. Pershing made a hurried decision. "We'll push on to San Geronimo for the night. You can write your reports there, and tomorrow morning I will send my aide back in one of the automobiles, carrying your dispatches, along with my report to General Funston about the Guerrero engagement. Remember to show me what you've written concerning the battle." He eyed Frank Elser ruefully. "Be sure you omit any mention of our displeasure over the performance of the aero squadron, Mr. Elser. While I may share your feelings that the Jennys are not airworthy, the general public should not be informed of it until the proper time."

"And when might that be, General?" Elser asked. "After the last pilot has been killed?"

30 March
George has saved the day. I have just completed a glowing report of his victory at Guerrero. The news will be greeted with great enthusiasm in Washington. Problems have been stacking up at an unbelievable pace. Prior to today's wonderful revelation I was fully prepared to be replaced by the War Department at any given moment. As far as I know, nothing has leaked out from the press regarding our recurring failures here. Should the American public become aware of our many

shortcomings in the field, it is more than doubtful that we would ever join the Allies at the European front. George was successful by employing time-proven methods of warfare, although it may be unfair to compare what is happening in France to this unique situation. The terrain here is our worst enemy thus far. I freely admit I have never seen any place its equal in roughness or severity.

It may well be a black omen that Villa escaped our clutches. I wonder if we will ever find him now. Should he go into hiding for any length of time it will look bad for us. Until I saw this region I would not have believed it possible that he could elude us forever, but now I must face such a possibility honestly. We could be here for an indefinite period unless George is able to track the wounded lion to his lair.

I find I must keep a tight rein on the two newsmen. Elser seeks every opportunity to report our failings to the press. Gibbons is somewhat more pliable in most regards, yet I am not deceived into believing either will not attempt to sneak an unfavorable story away from the front to their publishers. All along I have believed Leonard Wood will quickly succeed me in command here if prompt results are not achieved. Unless Villa himself is caught soon the public perception will be that I have failed. I have no doubt whatsoever that Secretary Baker will summon us home if this is the case. It is a common mistake when it is believed Baker wanted this expedition in the first place. The Secretary is an avowed pacifist. Hugh Scott is the driving force behind us and he cannot bring the hounds to bay by himself. Public opinion is essential to our continued stay in Mexico, thus I must not allow any unfavorable stories to come from the front. All must appear to be going well if we hope to stir feelings of patriotism in American hearts.

I wrote a long letter to Warren and May, telling them how much I miss them. I believed it would be beneficial to my state of mind to spend nights under the stars, however I still feel disquieted and the change in my surroundings has yet to accomplish what I hoped it might in this regard. Dreams of the fire still haunt me at night and I wonder if they will ever cease.

Tomorrow, if all goes well, we will continue to push southward in hopes of establishing a base of operation at Satevo, which is more or less the geographic center of the area where we expect to find Villa. I am mentally prepared for a long campaign as of this writing and sincerely hope Washington is similarly equal to the task. If I am successful here my chances greatly improve to assume command of an American expeditionary force in Europe. In a most recent newspaper account of the war it appears the British blockade will surely collapse under attack by the U-boats, then the Central Powers may well blockade Great Britain and bring to an end all American profit-taking from sales to the Grand Alliance which, I believe, keeps Wilson from bringing us into the war. I often wonder why Wilson made the concession to Hugh Scott, putting a Republican in charge of this expedition. Quite possibly it was suggested to Wilson that whoever came here was ultimately doomed to fall flat on his face in total disgrace.

He closed his diary and put it aside, glancing at the envelope he'd addressed to his sister, May. Thinking about Warren, he wondered if he would ever forget about the fire, what it had cost him, how much it had changed him.

• 20 •

Deputy Chief of Staff Tasker Bliss took the message, read it, and left his office quickly to find General Scott. A breath of life had been pumped into the punitive expedition in the nick of time. For two days and nights, Bliss had been feeling close kinship with a circus high-wire performer, balancing without a net at dizzying heights where a misstep was sure to be fatal. Certain disaster awaited him if everything was not carefully calculated from here on. Ever since Major Lawson had called to report his initial findings, after interrogating the six Mexican prisoners taken from the El Paso County Jail, Bliss had known he was up to his neck in hungry alligators. Frank Lawson had said he was sure the young men were telling the truth, that they were not Pancho Villa's men after all. Frank had questioned each of them in private, and their stories matched.

Not one of the men had ever met Villa personally or served in his militia. They were part-time soldiers in the Mexican Army, and at the time of the raid on Columbus they believed they were acting on orders from General Alvaro Obregon, a Carranza ally and a newly appointed district military governor for the de facto ruler of the republic. It was the worst possible news that the punitive expedition had been launched based on incomplete information.

What puzzled Bliss most of all was why Villa was accepting blame for something he didn't do. Villa had allowed the American army to mobilize for a manhunt, its sole purpose being to destroy him, without uttering so much as a whimper of protest. Was Villa completely mad? Or was there some sinister means behind his apparent insanity that Bliss did not presently comprehend?

One thing was painfully clear, as Bliss hurried down the hallway to Hugh Scott's office with a copy of Pershing's field report about the battle at Guerrero: The Mexican prisoners must be kept silent. If word leaked out that the United States had knowingly, abeit belatedly, thrown most of its military might into a campaign to capture or kill an innocent man, heads would roll in the War Department. Bliss's own head would be among the first to be offered on the chopping block, for it was he who had been sitting on information that would shed light on the grim truth about Columbus. Everyone involved in the decision to launch the so-called punitive expedition would be looking for the highest window from which to jump. A national scandal of the grandest proportions could only be averted by making sure the young Mexicans never talked to anyone else about how they'd wound up in a Texas jail.

Frank Lawson was an intelligence specialist. He would have some ideas about how and where to dispose of—if that was the best word for it—the six prisoners. They spoke no English, which was turning out to be a blessing. Awaiting further instructions from Washington, Lawson had them locked away in the basement of a vacant building at Fort Sam Houston in San Antonio under heavy guard, where they could not possibly talk to anyone. As things stood now, only he and Bliss, and the deputy in El Paso, knew the truth about them and what had happened at Columbus. If the Mexicans disappeared and Deputy Salinas could be made to understand how valuable his silence truly was, perhaps in the form of a comfortable federal job pushing paperwork across a desk, a lid could be put on the affair once and for all. Now that hostilities had begun in Mexico between American soldiers and Villa's revolutionary army, there was no turning back.

What remained unanswered was who had actually been behind the attack on Columbus, and with what purpose in mind. Why would General Obregon initiate an attack against an ally? The report from Pershing also contained one bit of hopeful news. Villa had been wounded, and although he had temporarily escaped, his wound was said to be serious. If Bliss had any luck at all, Villa would bleed to death before he had a change of heart and started denying any involvement with the bungled raid on Columbus. It was about the only way Bliss could think of for many high-level American military officers—including himself—and a few civilian leaders, to survive this fiasco untainted.

He entered the chief of staff's waiting room and walked past the general's aide without waiting to be announced. Hugh Scott sat behind his desk, dawdling over a stack of papers, peering through wire-rimmed glasses with his usual squint, which some often mistook for a frown. Scott was going blind, wary of cataract surgery necessary to rectify his failing vision: In private he maintained the belief that no army surgeons were competent to operate on his eyes, but going to a civilian doctor might make the medical corps look bad.

"Pershing has engaged Villa at Guerrero," Bliss said, with what he hoped was a sufficiently solemn tone. He halted in front of the general's expansive desk and glanced down at the report to begin reading it. "The Mexican force was thoroughly routed. Our casualties were light, only five wounded, while casualties on the other side were quite high. More than fifty known dead and more than a hundred wounded. Pancho Villa was taken down during the action, however as of this hour he is still at large. His wound is reported to be mortal, and Pershing does not believe he will get far."

"Bully for old Black Jack!" Scott exclaimed, slamming a fist on top of his desk. "I knew all along he was the right man for this mission. This should silence his critics, especially Funston. Just this morning Freddy called to complain loudly that Pershing was accomplishing next to nothing and appeared to be stranded in the midst of the Mexican desert." Scott lowered his voice. "It's the last thing we needed, having Pershing languish in a sand dune while everyone is watching. The president has been making regular inquiries, at least twice daily, as to any news from Pershing. Wilson is looking for any excuse to call off the expedition, and he is being cheered on in that regard by both secretaries. By surrounding himself with pacifists, he is assured of hearing nothing but dire forecasts over any type of military action we take. Thank God Pershing moved quickly, before Secretary Baker could convince Wilson to pull us back. Baker has been mewing in the president's ear like a motherless kitten, so I've been told. I've heard reports Baker has threatened to resign over it."

"I know a score of men who would wish him Godspeed," Bliss said. "I'm not sure which is worse, having Baker as our secretary of war, or Robert Lansing running the State Department. Baker shares Wilson's belief that war is out of date in this century, being too uncivilized. It has seemed from the very beginning that the essence of nonsense was appointing someone like Baker to the top post in a department where a plan for warfare might need to be devised. It's absolutely ludicrous."

"Some have called him our secretary of peace," Scott agreed softly. "It would appear good old Black Jack has nipped further vacillating in the bud, for the time being. With banner headlines all over the country announcing that Villa has been given a dose of his own medicine by Pershing's vengeful saber, Americans will hail a return to justice. The people have had enough of Wilson's watchful waiting. I've grown weary of seeing cartoons depicting panty-waist sissies in American military uniforms. Under the best possible circumstances Pershing will capture Villa alive and bring him back to stand public trial for his war crimes before the eyes of the entire nation."

"Villa would certainly deny culpability for what took place at Columbus, if that should eventuate," Bliss warned, thinking how terribly things could go awry if Scott got his wish. Idly, Bliss wondered what it was like to be burned at the stake.

"It's far too late for that," Scott cautioned. "He waited much too long to start protesting his innocence. No one in his right mind would believe him so late in the game."

Some might, Bliss worried, if they knew about the statements being made by six Mexican soldiers captured at Columbus. Pershing's moment of glory would turn into the Great American Nightmare in newspaper headlines across the country. Any man who admitted to being a Democrat after this debacle could scarcely count on winning election to a dogcatcher's post. Of paramount importance now was making sure the Mexican prisoners at Fort Sam Houston vanished as completely as the white rabbit in Harry Blackstone's top hat.

"Pershing has deployed every available man to go after Villa into the wilds. He says it is only a matter of time before they find him."

"Keep me fully informed," Scott said, removing his spectacles to wipe the lenses on his shirt front, as if cleaning them could somehow reduce his visual impairment. "Send Black Jack our most hearty congratulations. Tell him to keep up the good work. I have little doubt his quick success was greatly enhanced by the use of air reconnaissance. Modern battlefield equipment easily brought the cocky Mr. Villa to his old-fashioned knees. I'll personally recommend Captain Foulois for a Silver Star if Pershing hasn't thought to do so already. Congress will be more pliable now when it comes to appropriating money for our aero squadrons."

"I'm sure they will have a much clearer understanding of the wartime role of aviation," he replied. "I'll keep you posted of any further developments from Pershing."

Bliss was not thinking about congressional appropriations as he wheeled and went briskly out of General Scott's office. A more pressing matter needed his immediate attention, a monster with six heads lurking in the background, a dragon Major Frank Lawson must slay before loose tongues started wagging. The prisoners had to be dealt with, a deputy sheriff in El Paso quieted. Time was of the essence, for if Villa were captured alive he would surely protest his innocence of the Columbus crimes in order to save his neck. Unsubstantiated by the prisoners' corroboration, his cries would go unheeded all the way to the gallows, as Scott had correctly predicted they would. But only if a chorus of six Spanish-speaking voices did not accompany Villa's denial.

On his way to the telephone, Bliss remembered an old saying used frequently by his father: Luck is quite often an acceptable substitute for good intellect. If a man is lucky, shit will suffice for brains.

He could not count on being lucky in this instance. He had to make absolutely sure nothing was left to chance.

• 21 •

The tour through Pedro's cow pastures was what Will had expected, viewing hundreds of thin *corriente* yearlings wandering in search of scant grass. Pedro talked about the absence of rain, poor beef markets, and the hope that next year he could begin a new breeding program, introducing Hereford bulls to his herds of longhorn mother cows. Elisa stayed back at the ranch and Will supposed it was to visit with her sister, despite the fact that a strain showed between the sisters when Will and Elisa had ridden up. Neither Christina nor Pedro said much to her, it had seemed to him.

It was dusk by the time he and Pedro made it back to the ranch. Pedro offered supper as they were riding back through the mountain meadows. After turning their horses into a corral, they walked to the rear of the house. As they approached the back door, Will heard angry voices speaking in German.

"Women," Pedro said, wagging his head. "They argue over nothing. I am glad I do not understand their language."

When the women heard boots on the back steps they fell silent. Entering through the kitchen, Will noticed a hot flush in Elisa's cheeks. Wonderful smells filled the room, the scent of chilis and fried meat, and a sweet smell he couldn't identify.

Pedro sauntered over to his wife. "Why are you always yelling when Elisa comes to the house? We have a guest today."

Christina gave Elisa a look through her eyelashes. "We will talk about it later," she said, lowering her voice. "Supper is ready. Come to the table."

Will was shown to a dining-room table laden with bowls

and platters, beefsteak and refried beans, tortillas and hot sauce, corn and squash seasoned with cilantro, dishes of egg custard covered with caramel syrup called *flan*. "It smells delicious," he said, taking a chair beside Elisa.

Pedro smiled. "My wife is a good cook. Who could have guessed that a woman who spoke *Aleman* could learn to cook the best Mexican dishes in all of Parral?"

"I don't suppose it makes much difference what language a woman speaks," Will replied, taking some *carne asada*, then passing the platter of steak.

Some of the color had drained from Elisa's cheeks. She took some beef and began to eat quietly, head bowed above her plate. Will wondered what the argument between the sisters had been about as he folded a tortilla around a spoonful of beans. What had come between them?

He was wolfing down mouthfuls of food when hoofbeats pounded up to the front of the house. Pedro frowned and got up from the table. Elisa and Christina shared meaningful looks. Boots clumped across the porch as Pedro was opening the door. Through an open doorway, Will glimpsed a man in a dust-caked sombrero. Just as the *vaquero* was about to speak, he saw Will and held his tongue.

"It is all right," Pedro said quietly in Spanish. "You may speak in front of him, for he is an old friend."

"But he is an American," the *vaquero* replied in soft Spanish. Criss-crossed bandoliers heavy with cartridges caught the lamplight across his chest; a gunbelt was tied around his waist.

"He is a friend," Pedro said again. "Now tell me why you have come."

The *vaquero* spoke very softly now, giving Will nervous looks. "The American army has come into Mexico. Many thousands of soldiers. They struck at Guerrero only three days ago, taking us by surprise. A great many were killed. *El jefe* has been wounded. We are hiding in the hills. Someone must bring a doctor at once."

Elisa jumped from her chair and hurried into the front room, leaving Will and Christina alone at the table. Elisa ushered the *vaquero* outside, where Will could not hear any more of what was being said.

"Who is *el jefe?*" Will asked, pretending not to know.

Christina closed her eyes briefly. "Francisco Villa. My sister knows him and so does Pedro. Pedro is loyal to Villa's cause, providing his men with horses and beef whenever he can. It is not possible to live in Chihuahua without being involved in this revolution. The Constitutionalists support Carranza, the others favor Villa. I try to remain silent when my husband does business with them. I say nothing."

"What does Elisa have to do with it?" he asked, pressing her for more. "She left the table so quickly. . . ."

Christina leaned forward, making sure they were alone. The muted sound of voices came from the front porch. "My sister is a fool!" she whispered sharply. "She risks her life for a man who cares nothing for her! A man who will kill her if she makes a mistake!"

Will wondered what made Christina think Villa had no feelings for Elisa. Villa had many women, but Elisa was rumored to be one of his favorites. "Somebody told me last year that your sister was Villa's special girlfriend. If that's true, why would her life be in danger?"

The question put Christina on edge even more. She glanced through the doorway again. "It is not Francisco I worry about," she replied, saying it so softly he had trouble hearing it.

He was about to frame another question when Pedro and Elisa came into the house. Elisa hurried to the dining room and spoke to Will.

"I must leave," she said, gathering a bundle of tortillas and strips of meat in a linen napkin. "A friend has been hurt and I must do everything I can for him."

"You are welcome to stay here tonight," Pedro said to Will, his face dark with concern, as though preoccupied with other matters. He watched Elisa prepare the food. "I am sorry for the interruption of our meal, *compadre,* and I hope you will understand."

Will risked a quick look at Christina, judging her reaction to the sudden turn of events. "It's no problem, Pedro, but my spare horse is tied in front of Elisa's house and I'll have to tend to it. I'm obliged for the supper—it was delicious, but I'd better head back to see to my horse."

"I understand," Pedro said, as Elisa folded the napkin around the food.

"You are welcome to stay at my house tonight," Elisa told him, turning from the table, then hesitating a moment. "You can stable your horses in the barn. I must go now. I am sorry, Will, to leave like this, but I must help a sick friend." She hurried across the front room and went out, banging the door shut behind her.

Will noticed that Pedro and Christina were looking at each other, communicating without words. "I'd best be goin' now," he said, pushing his chair back. He stood up, trying to read Pedro's expression. "Mind if I ask what all the trouble is about?" He felt he knew Pedro well enough to ask without arousing suspicion.

Pedro's gaze flickered to Will. He swallowed, seemed a little uncertain for a moment. "An American invasion of Mexico has begun," he said gravely. "General Villa has warned everyone that this would happen. They came to Guerrero, a thousand *soldados,* slaughtering many innocent women and children, even horses and cattle. General Villa's brave men tried to stop the Americans, but he was badly outnumbered. Carlos, the man who came tonight, was with the general at Guerrero. He saw the terrible executions of the children and their mothers. In the battle, General Villa was badly wounded leading his men against the cruel American *soldados.* Carlos said it was a horrible sight, and it left the general weeping."

Pedro's version of events was badly distorted, yet Will couldn't admit he knew the truth: that Villa had been shot by Carranzas the day before—not by the American army— nor were there any women and children slaughtered by Colonel Dodd's men. "It sounds like all hell's gonna break loose, Pedro. My cattle buyers won't be interested in buyin' cows down here with all this trouble bein' stirred up. Chihuahua's gonna be a dangerous place for any *Americano* now, and I reckon that includes me."

Pedro nodded, a sad expression crossing his face. "It could be very dangerous for you, *compadre,"* he agreed.

The sound of Elisa's galloping horse passed the house and faded off into the night.

"I'd better be goin' now." Will sighed, moving around the table to shake hands with Pedro. He bowed to Christina, puzzling briefly over what she'd meant by the remark she'd made earlier, that Villa was not the man Elisa should fear. Who had she been talking about? "Thanks for the dinner, ma'am."

Pedro followed him to the back door, then out to the corral while he bridled and saddled his horse. No words were said until Will was ready to leave.

"I am sorry, *compadre,*" Pedro said, "that we will do no business together this year. Perhaps in the fall it will rain."

Will swung up and gathered his reins. "Maybe sooner. If it don't, I'll be back next spring. *Adios, amigo.* I hope things go well for you." He tipped his hat and rode off into the darkness, guided by a handful of twinkling stars, knowing he had lied to his friend Pedro in omitting any mention of his role as scout for the U.S. Army. Then his thoughts drifted to Elisa, and to the curious remark her sister had made. It was plain he had been right with his first guess, that Villa would seek aid from Elisa as soon as he made it to Parral. Right now Villa would be hiding somewhere in the mountains close by, waiting for the girl to bring him medical help and food. Pershing's army needed this bit of information as quickly as Will could ride north. If he left Elisa's house at dawn, he could carry the news to Pershing in only a matter of days. Yet the most difficult task would remain: locating Villa's hideout. Was it better to wait, perhaps try to trick Elisa into telling him exactly where Villa was hiding?

Trotting his horse through the night, listening to the distant call of coyotes in the mountains, he considered the wisdom of remaining at Elisa's on the off chance she might tell him where Villa was hiding. Should that fail, he might be able to follow her from a distance the next time she took food or medicine to his hiding place. The mountains around Parral were as vast and empty as the rest of Chihuahua. Knowing where Villa meant to stay until he recovered from his wounds would help the American army greatly.

He thought about Elisa, remembering the glimpse he'd gotten of her naked body in the bedroom, her forthright admission that she was not an old-fashioned girl. It was a delightful notion, the idea that he might share her bed, learn the pleasures of her soft skin against his, make love to her. She was certainly one of the most beautiful women he had ever seen.

Lost in blissful dreams, he rode toward Parral, until a stark reality awakened him. A recollection of the Mauser Elisa carried in her waistband ended his reverie, making him wonder if she would kill him, should she find out he meant to betray her trust.

It was after midnight when he reached the dark house and put his horses away for the night. He went in and spread his blanket on a leather sofa in the front room and promptly dropped off to sleep.

A sound awakened him, a soft stirring in the darkness. He opened his eyes but did not move his head, listening. Footsteps crossed the floor, drawing nearer. He remained frozen underneath the blanket, holding his breath, trying to see a shape in the inky shadows around the room. A figure, a mere outline, came to the sofa and halted a few feet away. Then, in the faint light from the stars coming through the windows, he saw the glint of metal and he knew instinctively it was a gun barrel. Without knowing who was in the room, his heart stopped beating altogether and he was suddenly wide awake. Was Elisa about to kill him? Or was the shadow one of Villa's men, sent to stop the treacherous American who scouted the way for Pershing's army to Guerrero? He remembered what John Abel had said, that Villa would send someone to kill him if he felt someone was helping the Americans get too close. Will quickly judged his chances of making a dive for the gun before a bullet took his life.

Before he had time to gather himself for the lunge he needed to make to seize the gun, the dark figure turned away slowly and walked to the bedroom door on soundless feet. Will let out the breath he was holding as quietly as he could, noticing a tiny tremor in his fingers. A match was struck beyond the bedroom doorway, the flare of igniting sulphur flickering brightly at first, casting dancing shadows on the wall. The wick of an oil lamp glowed yellow, the scrape of glass echoing softly when the globe was lowered, then the faint scent of coal-oil smoke. He calmed himself, watching Elisa place her automatic pistol on a night table beside the bed.

With the door still standing open, she began unbuttoning her shirt, her back turned to him. She let it fall from her sloping shoulders, caught it before it went to the floor and tossed it on the mattress, revealing a side view of bare breasts as she unfastened her denims. Once, before she wriggled the pants off her hips, she glanced to the opening between them and he thought he detected a faint smile on her face, although the half dark in the bedroom made it impossible to be sure. The pants fell to her ankles, and even in the pale light he could make out the swirl of hair at the tops of her slightly muscular thighs. She stepped away from the denims and bent to pick them up, her ripe breasts swaying gently in the lamplight. When the garment lay beside her shirt she turned, facing the bedroom door. Through slitted eyelids he watched her trace a fingertip through her pubic mound, doing it slowly, rhythmically a few more times, until she moved toward the lamp. Then there was darkness.

She carried another pail of steaming water to the big cast-iron bathtub where he sat, surrounded by soap bubbles, scraping whisker stubble from his chin with the freshly honed straight razor he carried in his war bag. She poured more hot water into the tub, careful to avoid his bare legs. Dawn paled the sky above the back porch where he took his bath. He had undressed outside in chilly morning air, shivering, covered with goose flesh until he lowered himself into the wonderfully warm tub with a bar of scented soap. He could smell spicy *chorizo* sausage cooking in the kitchen.

She spoke to him in Spanish, and he thought it odd.

"The eggs and sausages are almost ready. I will bring you a towel when you are finished." Then, as if she suddenly remembered she was speaking to an American, she spoke English. "I am boiling your clothes on the stove. I will hang them out to dry before I leave for the city."

"I probably oughta be goin' back this mornin'," he told her, feeling his way across his chin, using the razor without a mirror. "I'm much obliged for your hospitality, Elisa. Wish I could tell Pedro my customers would buy some of his steers, but with all the trouble over the Columbus raid, nobody's gonna risk investing in Mexican steers, hoping to get them to the border. Besides that, his cattle are awful thin."

She put down the pail and rested her hands on her hips. This morning she wore pants and a shirt made from flour sacking cloth that was open at the top, showing off just enough of the cleft of her bosom where she neglected the buttons. Her hair was freshly brushed, falling carelessly across her shoulders as if by design. Unconsciously she turned her gaze to the slopes east of Parral. "There will be a terrible war in Mexico very soon," she said. "It has just begun. The American army is marching toward Parral. No one will be safe. Pedro *und* my sister could lose all their cows to the invading Americans after they take over the town."

Wishing to change the subject, so as not to reveal how much he knew about Pershing's advance, he asked, "How was your injured friend last night?"

She looked at him, perhaps a bit too quickly. For a time she regarded him silently, chewing her bottom lip. "He was wounded in a battle with the Americans. A bone in his leg is broken *und* there is swelling. I rode to Parral last night to summon a doctor. His leg is very painful."

Her brother-in-law would tell her that Will knew the wounded man was Pancho Villa. "Pedro told me that it is Villa after you rode off. I don't stick my nose into politics, so don't worry."

She still watched him with a hint of suspicion. "Soon he will be well enough to continue the fight against the government. Now the Americans come to hunt him down, but they will never find him. He has many allies across Mexico. Thousands of poor people believe in him *und* his cause. They will help him. Even with the powerful Americans against him, he will not be defeated. He has, as the people say, the heart of a lion."

Cupping water in his hands, he washed the soap off his face and rinsed his hair, appearing to give little thought to Villa's troubles. "There's no doubt he's a hero to the *campesinos* around here. I've had a lot of dealings with his brother, Antonio, and I met him a few times some years back. Most everybody is on his side against Carranza, only the part that don't figure is why he would attack Columbus.

The Ravel brothers have been sellin' him guns and ammunition for years, so they say. Can't figure why he'd draw attention to Columbus. Some folks don't think it was Villa who led that raid, folks who oughta know. Maybe Villa was framed. Somebody who wanted it to look like Villa did it, maybe even Carranza himself."

When he glanced up at Elisa, rubbing water from his face, he noticed a sudden change in her expression. Those same deep green eyes that could hold so much allure were now darker, almost black with some inner fire he couldn't explain.

"Here is a towel," she said, handing him a strip of thin cotton cloth. "The sausages will burn if I don't turn them."

She wheeled abruptly and walked into the house, leaving him more bewildered than ever. He had expected her to echo Villa's claim to the Columbus raid, a claim he apparently wanted, since he had made no effort to deny it. Elisa's silence said more, her obvious anger unexpected. If she supported Villa's bloody feud with the government in Mexico City, then why did she react so strangely when she heard that some doubted Villa's role in the attack? It made no sense. Unless what he saw in her eyes was not anger at all. Could it have been fear?

He shook his head and stood up, covering his genitals with a corner of the towel until he was sure the girl couldn't see him from the kitchen window. Drying off, he contemplated Elisa's curious reaction a moment more, then he decided it made no real difference. He had been hired to scout the way for Pershing's punitive expedition into Chihuahua, not to conduct an investigation into reasons why the U.S. Army had been sent here. What mattered most, he kept reminding himself, was the pay, money he and Raymond desperately needed to keep the ranch in Webb County going through a terrible drought.

Reaching for his clean pants, he thought about the look he would see on Raymond Junior's face when the boy saw the white Yucatan pony. Will still remembered his first horse, a mouse-colored *grullo* mustang colt his pa had given him, unbroken. Breaking the colt to a saddle had given Will a lifelong education in the temperament of both horses and men. His father's patience, and the unyielding wild nature of a range-bred mustang, pitted man against animal in a contest of iron wills. After being kicked, pawed, and bucked off a number of times early in the struggle, Will was made to understand the wisdom of patience and the advantage a smaller, upright creature had when employing the know-how acquired by a much larger and more efficient brain.

He walked into the kitchen. A plate loaded with eggs and sausages awaited him at the table. Elisa turned from the stove to hand him a cup of coffee. Their eyes met, and he was sure he saw something behind hers, something new.

"You're worried about Villa, aren't you?" he asked.

She averted her gaze and whispered, "Yes. Not only for his wound, but because the Americans will follow him. If they find him, they will execute him for the killings at Columbus. His men are gone into the hills, frightened by the American army coming to Parral, *und* now there is no one to help him. Last night he was in terrible pain, yet he was still very angry, cursing the men who helped him escape *und* treat his wound. He believes someone has betrayed him to the Americans. No one knew he was going to Guerrero—only the men he trusted, *und* now he suspects one of them is a traitor. He even accuses the five loyal followers who are with him now, the men who saved his life. Even when he is able to sleep, he keeps a loaded pistol in each hand."

Sipping coffee, he watched her face. "He trusts you, don't he?"

The question evoked that same darkening in her pupils he'd seen earlier. She stared at him a moment. "Perhaps it would be best if you go now, as soon as you have eaten your breakfast. Francisco may have some of his men watching my house. If he is told I have an American staying here, he may think I was the one who betrayed him to the American soldiers."

"But I'm not a soldier," he protested. "Plenty of people in Parral know me from cattle-buying trips. Pedro can vouch for me, that I'm not a spy for the U.S. Army."

She seemed uncertain, glancing to a kitchen window. "Please go," she said urgently, as if she suddenly realized how it might look to one of Villa's men if he were seen here.

"I am sorry, but I must ask you to leave at once. It has nothing to do with you, Will. I like you very much. You are a very handsome man, but it could mean trouble for me . . . for both of us if you remain."

"I understand." He grinned and touched her arm. "And you are a very special lady. I wish circumstances could be different. I'd like to get to know you better, if you'd permit it."

She returned his smile briefly, then she stood on her toes and kissed him lightly on the mouth. "Perhaps another time," she said, resting a fingertip against his cheek. "Now eat. I will put your wet clothes in a burlap bag. Be careful on your way back to Texas. After what happened at Guerrero, there are many who will hate all Americans, even those who are not soldiers. I ask one small favor. Please say nothing about Francisco to the American army. If they learn where he is, that he is wounded, they will look even harder for him here."

Her kiss left him tingling all over. "There's a way you can buy my silence," he joked. "If you kissed me again, I'd probably forget everything else that happened while I was down here. I'd be thinkin' about you all the way back home, instead of what I overheard last night."

She continued to stare at him a while longer, tilting her head slightly, looking deeply into his eyes. Then she slowly took his coffee cup and placed it on the table. "Come," she whispered, a throaty sound, taking his hand.

• 22 •

Shafts of early morning sunlight passed through lacy white curtains, creating dancing patterns of gold across the bedsheets when gentle breezes rustled the thin fabric hanging over the windows. He lay between her muscular thighs, spent, catching his breath with the scent of her hair filling his nostrils, listening to the sharp whistles of jays in the trees outside, the softer whisper of air flowing from her parted lips close to his ear. Despite a slight chill remaining in the room after sunrise, their skin was damp, dewy, clinging together. Her arms were still curled around his neck, her fingers entwined in his hair. A quiet moan of pure pleasure arose in her throat when he stirred inside her.

He lifted his head and brushed his lips across hers, only the gentlest of touches, searching the depths of her emerald eyes. She gave him a slow smile, then she planted her mouth against his hungrily and moaned again, louder now, tightening her legs around him. She began with a tentative thrust of her abdomen, a slow rotation when he was deeper inside her. Her fingers tightened in the locks of his untrimmed hair, pulling his lips hard against her teeth, her nostrils flaring when her breathing grew faster. He met her thrusts with his own, arching his spine in concert with her quickening movements atop the mattress, lost in the ecstasy of the moment. Her arms fell from his neck, and she released her fierce grip on his hair, then her fingernails dug into the muscles of his shoulders, moving down his back in short, trembling bursts of passion. Coming together, damp skin rubbing back and forth where their bodies were joined, the tempo of their lovemaking increased. Suddenly she tore her lips away from his and began to cry out with each thrust, cries that became louder as her passion mounted. Bedsprings squeaked. Her legs and arms trembled, muscles turning to iron. Her soft breasts were flattened against his chest, rosy nipples twisted, glistening with sweat that was his and her own.

At the peak of her ecstasy she went rigid underneath him, and for a moment it was as though she had turned to granite. Frozen fingers impaled the skin of his back and held him fiercely, yet he continued to drive deeper inside her until a wave of pleasure spread from his groin. Shaking, gasping for breath, his legs stiffened while his seed flowed into her. He groaned, gritting his teeth until the sensation lessened, then he collapsed on top of her and closed his eyes, listening to the beat of his heart and the woman's breathless pants. Her limbs went slack. Tiny beads of perspiration clung to her forehead, her cheeks, the soft skin of her neck. He could feel the drumbeat of her heart against his ribs, the rapid rise and fall of her chest, the gentle caress of air flowing from her mouth and nose across his face.

For a time they lay there, arms and legs entwined, until their breathing slowed, listening to the birds, the fluttering of new spring leaves on tree branches tossed by the wind outside the bedroom windows. Filmy curtains lifted, then dropped to windowsills lifelessly between swirling gusts. Minutes passed and she did not stir, the urgency she voiced earlier to get him away from the house forgotten for the moment.

Elisa kissed his neck and began to stroke his hair gently with her fingertips. "I wish you could stay with me," she said, her voice trailing off.

He raised his head, then kissed the tip of her nose. "I'd like that. I've never been . . . with a woman like you before," he whispered.

"Will you come back when all this is over?"

He grinned, and nodded once. "Sure I will. But thinkin' about you, the time is liable to pass mighty slow until then. If I could, I'd like to stay here for quite a spell."

Her eyes clouded. "It is much too dangerous. Things will only get worse. Francisco believes that the American army will occupy all of Chihuahua until he is caught, or until he can escape *und* raise another army to drive them away."

"There are too many of them," he said. "They have better weapons, machine guns, aeroplanes, big cannons. Villa can't win against them. If he's smart he'll go into hiding someplace else and stay there."

Elisa moved her head on the pillow. "But he must win, for the sake of all the poor who believe in him. The government takes everything from them, *und* they have nothing without the help of Francisco."

"He can't whip the Mexican Army and the Americans too. The job's too big. Nobody's backing him. He can't buy better weapons or feed his men without money."

It seemed she was about to say something, then she changed her mind. "Please go now. *Und* remember your promise to forget what Pedro and I told you about Francisco." She kissed his lips and smiled sweetly. "Do come back, Will Johnson. I want to see you again when the fighting is over."

He rolled over and swung his legs off the bed, searching the floor for his pants after a last lingering look at Elisa's naked body, skin still slightly damp after their frenzied lovemaking.

"You might do me one small favor," she said, pulling the sheet over the tops of her milky breasts, then reaching out to touch his forearm. "If you encounter the Americans on your way north, they will ask you if you have heard where Francisco has gone into hiding. If you told them he has ridden to Durango, or perhaps to Sonora, they might believe you."

He felt a twinge of conscience while slipping on his jeans. "I suppose I could say somebody told me that," he said, keeping his face from her. He put on his shirt and boots, then his hat. As he was turning around, Elisa left the bed wrapped in the sheet and came over to him. She stood on her tiptoes and kissed him.

"I would be very grateful," she said quietly, gently, with a hint of promise. "I would always remember that you did me this small favor, *und* it would help the cause Pedro and I believe in so strongly. The revolution means nothing to the

Americans, but to the poor people of Mexico, it means everything. It is their only chance to be free of the poverty *und* oppression Venustiano Carranza forces upon them."

Her sentiments seemed genuine enough, although it surprised him that a woman, especially an immigrant in a foreign land, felt so strongly about a political struggle here. "If they ask me what I've heard about Villa, I'll say a woman in Parral told me he went to Durango to raise another army. It'll be the truth."

Elisa appeared to be satisfied. Gathering the front of the sheet to partially hide her nakedness, she gave him a smile.

He was lying on his stomach, hidden by tall grass on a hill overlooking Elisa's house, when he saw a distant rider coming from Parral. It was midafternoon, and the hours watching her adobe had seemed long. His horses were hobbled in a swale, well out of sight from the path leading to Elisa's. He watched the man ride closer, noting how careful he was to avoid being seen, halting every now and then to make sure he was alone. He was a small man, with a Van Dyke beard, dressed in a brown suitcoat and a derby, hardly the sort of visitor Will expected to see at Elisa's place. He rode up to the low adobe wall on a prancing, dappled-gray Arabian horse, an expensive animal uncommon in this impoverished area of Mexico. Was this a friend or supporter of Villa? He certainly didn't look the part.

The newcomer stepped down. Elisa came out on the porch, looking around at the hills, her glance sweeping over the spot where Will was hiding. Sunlight reflected off the Mauser tucked in her waistband. Her visitor was talking, but the distance was much too great for Will to overhear what was said. For several minutes they spoke to each other. All the while they both seemed uneasy, watching their surroundings. The gray horse pawed the ground nervously, flicking its ears back and forth.

Will saw the man reach into his coat pocket and take out an envelope. He gave it to Elisa and she peered into it briefly, then she shook her head and tucked it into the top of her blouse.

"I wonder what it is," Will whispered. "It'd help to know who he is. . . ." He watched the stranger take off his derby to run a hand through a windblown shock of graying hair. The man had come from the direction of Parral. Perhaps if Will asked in the right places, someone would know him there.

Moments later the man mounted. He gave the hills another careful look, then he wheeled the Arabian and galloped off to the east, riding back toward Parral.

Elisa went back in the house. "She'll wait until dark," he told himself, "so nobody can follow her when she rides to Villa's hideout. Whatever's in that envelope has somethin' to do with Villa."

Inching backward, he crawled off the hilltop and came to a crouch to return to the horses. Finding out who the man in the brown derby was would require caution. A *gringo* asking questions around Parral, since word of the fall of Guerrero had surely reached the city by now, would be risky. With the American army marching southward, fears would run high that the soldiers meant to occupy the town.

Mounting the dun, he led the roan down a twisting gulley at a trot, gazing toward the valley where Parral sat at the foot of the towering Sierras. Tonight he meant to follow Elisa if he could, to Villa's hideout. Supplied with that information, and perhaps with the identity of the bearded stranger who came to Elisa's house with the envelope, he could inform Major Ryan and General Pershing of everything he'd learned. In a way he felt badly about his intention to betray Elisa, until he told himself that he was here for just one reason; to earn the money the army was paying him. Still, the voice of his conscience nagged at him on the ride down to Parral, and no matter how hard he tried, he could not completely silence it.

Near the outskirts of the city he turned north, toward the house of a horse dealer he saw infrequently on cattle-buying trips. The old man had been an acquaintance of his father's in the early years of Will's visits buying livestock in Chihuahua. Called "Benito" due to his diminutive stature, little Ben Sanchez would know, if nothing else, who owned the unusual Arabian horse. Horses were his business.

He approached Benito's livestock pens at a walk, taking note of the poor condition the horses and mules were in, their ribs and hip bones jutting through thin hides. A spotted dog began to bark angrily before he drew rein in front of a small, windowless adobe hut beside the corrals. A shadow came to the doorway of the hut. Benito, looking shriveled with age, peered out at Will from the shade below the brim of a shapeless straw sombrero.

"Buenos días, Señor Sanchez," he said, casting a look across the dealer's offering in the sunlit pens. "I'm Will Johnson, the youngest son of Lee Johnson from Laredo."

"Sí. I remember you," Benito said, coming from the doorway on deeply bowed legs, a straw stuck between toothless gums. "Do you wish to buy *caballos, amigo?"*

Will nodded and said, "Maybe one or two, but they must be fat and strong to cover the mountains when we drive *las vacas corrientes* back to Texas."

The old man spread his gnarled palms helplessly. "I have no fat horses. There is no corn, no grass."

"It's sure as hell dry around here," Will agreed, knowing what must be done to get the information he wanted. "I would pay a few *pesos* to find out about a particular horse I saw today. If the owner would sell him, I'd pay a good price." Reaching into a pocket, he took out a silver dollar and held it so the sun made it shine. "This horse is a fine dappled gray. Arabian stock, if I ain't missin' my guess. The man who rode him had a beard an' he wore a derby hat."

"I know this horse," Benito said, eyeing the coin wistfully. "It is, as you say, *un* Arabian. The owner is *un muy rico Alemán.* He has *mucho dinero.* If he would sell this horse, the price would be very high."

"What's the owner's name?" Will asked. He tossed the coin to Benito. "Give me directions to his house, or his place of business, so I can ride over an' talk to him."

The old man pocketed the money quickly. "His name is Rudolph Milnor. There are some who say he works for the government *de Alemania,* but no one knows this for certain. He speaks to almost no one in Parral. He lives in a big *hacienda* east of the road to Santa Cruz. He has lived here for many years, and still no one truly knows how he has come to be such a rich man. Long ago, he came here with two very small girls from across the big ocean, perhaps his daughters, only they had different names than his own. One is the wife of Pedro Alvarado now. The other lives alone in the hills west of Parral, a woman of bad reputation."

"A bad reputation?" he asked. "Why's that?"

Benito gave him a toothless grin. "She is a *puta, señor,* a woman with a heart of stone. She has feelings for only one man, the great general himself, Pancho Villa. The general comes to her bed in the dark of night. He gives her money, good horses, and fine clothing, then he rides to the houses of many other young women, laughing, making jokes about all his *mujeres.*"

Will's mind was racing and he wasn't really listening to the rest of what Benito said. The man in the derby was Rudolph Milnor, possibly an agent for the German government, according to Benito. More surprising, he was the man Elisa mentioned when she told the story of her flight from Germany to Cuba, then Mexico, with Christina. Did this add further credibility to the rumors that Elisa was herself a German spy, perhaps helping Milnor gather information about the Mexican revolution? And was Milnor the same man Christina felt Elisa should fear? A man who might kill her for reasons Christina didn't explain?

The information Benito gave him only complicated matters, and they were things Will didn't fully understand. *"Muchas gracias, Señor Sanchez,"* he said. "I'll ride out to Rudolph Milnor's house an' ask about the dappled gray." He looked toward Parral as a late-day sun slanted over the mountaintops into the city, where clouds of dust arose from busy streets. Hardly anyone had seen him ride to Benito's place. He touched the brim of his hat and reined away from the hut to again swing wide of the town.

Once more his conscience troubled him on the ride back to the hills above Elisa's adobe. He had never known another woman capable of so much passion, so much tenderness. He found he could ignore the fact that she was Doroteo Arango's whore, nor did he care about her reasons for selling herself. . . . Unless there was more to Elisa than he knew, her connection to a man suspected of being a German agent. If she were involved in spying for the German government somehow, pretending to be an ally of Villa while gathering information about the revolution for Rudolph Milnor and the Germans, it might change the way he felt about her. Was she only pretending to have affection for him, using him for her own purposes? Could she be cold-hearted enough to make love to a man merely to have him deceive the U.S. Army? Did Elisa already suspect, even know, that he was a scout for the Pershing expedition?

It's all guesswork, he decided, arriving at the swale where he'd hidden the horses earlier. Swinging down, he tried not to think about it any longer. He was being paid to find Villa for the army, and if he could, he would follow Elisa tonight without worrying about the right or the wrong of it. A small ranch back in Webb County, Texas, depended upon him for its survival. Raymond, Rosa, and three small kids needed money for food, clothing, and cow feed.

A dark shadow galloped away from the house around midnight, the black mare carrying a rider dressed in dark clothing, heading southwest. He waited a moment more and then swung in the saddle, leaving his dun hobbled in the ravine. He knew he had to stay very close, so as not to lose her in the darkness. Urging the roan to a slow lope, he rode around the side of the hill cautiously, keeping gentle pressure on the reins.

Demonstrating her cleverness, she stayed among the trees, moving through inky forests, only rarely crossing any open ground where he could see her easily in the starlight. Staying back about a quarter mile, he lost sight of her often and had to slow his horse until he saw her again in a clearing, or galloping over a barren hilltop. Yet her direction remained unerringly southwest, almost a straight line toward the faraway shapes of the Sierras below Parral.

Soon the roan began to tire. Hills steepened near the base of the mountain range. Pine and juniper forests deepened as he rode to higher elevations. Surrounded by trees now, he lost all trace of Elisa in the forest shadows and slowed his horse to a trot. Villa would have sentries posted near his hiding place to warn him of anyone's approach. A tiny voice inside Will's head told him that he'd gone far enough, riding blind the way he was.

He slowed the horse to a walk, approaching a dark ridge lined with juniper and cedar. The roan bowed its neck and then snorted softly, a warning to any experienced horseman that some unfamiliar scent lay beyond the trees. Will touched the reins and sat quietly in the saddle when the gelding halted, listening to night sounds, the call of an owl higher up the slopes, a night hawk's shrill hunting cry farther away. He noticed the roan's ears prick forward, the animal's head turned slightly to the north, pointing toward the direction in which it sensed something it did not recognize. Was it only Elisa's mare? Or something far more ominous—a Villista sentry?

He edged his horse away from the shadow below a pine tree when it seemed the gelding had begun to relax underneath him. The roan had only taken a few steps when a terrific explosion thundered from the forested ridge, accompanied by a stabbing finger of pale white light near the trunk of a tree. Something struck Will's right foot, a powerful blow that almost knocked the roan over on its side. The horse whickered, wheeling on its haunches, lunging away from the noise as Will was clawing for the saddlehorn to steady himself. Gathering speed, increasing the length of its strides, the roan galloped down the side of the ridge, dodging and darting between the junipers and pines in an all-out run, grunting oddly through its muzzle with each movement of its powerful hindquarters. At the same time a white-hot pain raced up Will's leg, growing, spreading from his foot to his knee in ever-increasing waves.

"I've been shot!" he groaned, clinging to the saddlehorn as his horse bounded down the slope. Flashing pinpoints of light surrounded him, clouding his vision, making the trees seem only a blur when he passed through them. His stomach knotted. Bitter bile arose in his throat. The strange sounds his horse made grew louder and its strides began to falter until it was stumbling, trying to keep its forefeet from buckling. Something warm filled Will's right boot, and he knew it was blood. The pain grew worse, almost unbearable, threatening to rob him of consciousness. He felt himself swaying in the saddle. Struggling to remain upright, hands clasping the horn with a mighty grip, he rode a few yards more through a maze of tree limbs slapping his face and chest. Then his horse tumbled forward, grunting loudly when it crashed to the ground on its chest.

He somehow managed to remain in the saddle when the roan fell. Wind whistling through its nostrils, the gelding tried in vain to struggle to its feet, legs thrashing. Will knew now that the bullet at close range had passed through his ankle, mortally wounding the game little horse until bloodloss weakened it and it collapsed, unable to take another step. Attempting to clear his addled brain, shaking his head back and forth, he reached for the stock of the Winchester rifle booted to the pommel of his saddle. Whoever fired the shot would be searching for his victim now, and time was precious.

The coppery scent of blood grew stronger as he drew the gun and took his war bag from the saddlehorn. The roan's struggling became feeble efforts to rise, and he wished with all his heart that he could end its misery with a bullet to the brain, but the gunshot would draw his attacker to the spot before Will could crawl into the forest and hide. He slowly took his right boot from the stirrup and was almost rendered unconscious when a sharp stab of pain jolted through him. He knew he could not walk, and even crawling with a damaged ankle would require a tremendous effort.

The roan rolled over on its side, panting, suddenly leaving Will without support for his bad leg. He slumped to the ground on his rump, unable to brace for the fall, his mind reeling with dizzying pain. Valuable seconds passed until he could clear his head sufficiently to turn over on his belly, clutching the rifle in one hand, the drawstring on his war bag in the other. He felt broken bone grinding in his ankle when he moved. Blood filled his boot, and a cold sweat dampened his skin. He started to crawl, inching painfully across a bed of pine needles. As though it came from far away, he heard the blue mustang nicker softly and he knew the animal was dying, yet he put it out of his mind and forced his limbs to move. His heart was beating wildly. Arms and legs trembling, almost blinded by shooting pains, he crawled away slowly into the black forest, dragging his rifle and gear as best he could.

He heard voices off in the distance. When he paused to catch his breath and listen, he heard someone shout, "*¿Donde está?*" in Spanish.

A softer voice, a woman speaking English, cried, "I can't see him. Find him! He must not get away!"

Leaving a trail of blood that could be followed easily after sunrise, he snaked his way around thickening tree trunks while on the brink of unconsciousness, a single thought forcing him to put forth greater effort: Elisa Griensen knew she had been followed, and by whom, and with the aid of a Villista sentry she would hunt him down; and when they found him, they would kill him.

• 23 •

Her heart was racing as she ran through the woods. By the sound, she knew the bullet had found its mark. Gripping the Mauser, she dashed ahead of Ramon, listening to hooves rumble down the mountainside in front of them. Someone, or some thing, grunted as soon as she fired. The slug had struck either the horse or its rider, of that she was quite sure, even though the shot had been a difficult one in the dark.

Dark pines loomed in front of her, making it harder to see movement among the shadows. Gasping for breath, she ran harder, with her pistol covering the trees ahead, cursing her stupidity for having trusted the handsome *gringo*, believing he would ride north to give the Americans a false report about Francisco's retreat to Sonora. She had believed him when he'd said he was going back to Texas, and now she was paying for her carelessness. Her own life hung in the balance, for if Francisco did not kill her for allowing the *gringo* to follow her, then Herr Milnor would perform the execution for having bungled her assignment. She had been told to watch for Americans coming to Parral, yet because she knew this man, she'd foolishly believed him when he told her he was only looking for cows at Pedro's. He had outsmarted her, a fact Herr Milnor would be quick to point out if she lived long enough to tell him about what had happened tonight. But it was Francisco she feared most. Experience reminded her that it was not without justification. On nothing more than an impulse Francisco might shoot her, or cut her throat and watch her bleed to death without showing so much as a trace of emotion or regret. She knew him too well for that. His women were only to satisfy his lust—he cared nothing for any of them, least of all her, for she was a foreigner, the blond whore who slept with him and gave him money from another government to fuel the revolution. She was only intended to be used, and then he would cast her aside when he no longer needed her or any German money, or when she grew too old and wrinkled, not young and pretty enough to appeal to his sexual urges.

Her boots thumped softly over fallen pine needles while she picked her way among the trees and her breath came in short, whistling gasps. Her sides began to ache from exertion. Off to the left she could hear Ramon running, his spurs clanking like small chimes. Still there was no sign of Will Johnson ahead of them, and hoofbeats continued to drum down the slope. If her bullet struck the horse it had no effect on it yet. Wounded deer often ran for miles before they collapsed and died.

"Ramon!" she cried, stumbling to a halt. "Keep after him! I am going back for my horse!"

"Sí, señora," Ramon shouted, crashing through tree limbs.

Elisa whirled around, furious with herself, and desperately afraid for her life. Francisco would have heard the gunshot from the cave, and he would send the Butcher to find out what was going on. It was quite possible that Rudolfo had been given orders to kill whoever approached the hideout in the dark. Now she had to search the night very carefully for Rudolfo's shadow, to keep from walking blindly into an ambush set by Francisco's personal executioner.

If only she had been more careful to make sure she wasn't being followed . . .

• 24 •

Doroteo's leg was turning black. The end of everything was not far away unless there was a miracle. The doctor was an old man who knew almost nothing, little more than the *curanderos* who treated superstitious Yaquis with amulets made of garlic and herb remedies no one understood, which only worked if you believed in the magic of the *curandero*. Poison was spreading from the wound. His mind often wandered now, and he simply could not tolerate any more pain. Alternately he sweated, then shivered, until he felt so cold that he was willing to lie across the fire burning in the pit beside him and allow the flames to consume him rather than freeze to death. A miracle was the only thing that could possibly save him, yet it seemed God had forsaken him in his hour of greatest need. Where was the voice that sometimes advised him in important matters? Since the traitor's bullet struck him from behind there had been only silence, silence and unending agony. What had he done to deserve the vengeful wrath of *Dios?* Why had Almighty God abandoned him now when the people of Mexico needed him to rise up and lead them?

He had done his best to live a good life. He did not drink alcohol, or smoke. He gave liberally to the poor, he was always kind to children, and he contributed to the Church a portion of whatever he took from the rich *patrones.* No one could call him selfish. He always gave lavish gifts to his women: silk dresses and gold, jewelry, expensive shoes. He was good to his most loyal followers and only called for the execution of those who meant to betray him and the revolution. When people were hungry, he made sure they were given food. Surely *Dios* would balance these things against a few minor wrongs he might have committed when he was younger.

Rudolfo was seated across the firepit, watching him like a faithful dog, his hard face made even more fierce by poor light from the flames. The cave smelled dank, like mold, and it was so terribly cold. Diego sat near the entrance with his rifle across his lap, looking out into the night. Ramon was standing guard outside. Doroteo clutched two pistols underneath a threadbare blanket covering him, a matched pair of plated .45 Colt revolvers, comforted by having them in his hands. He had an abiding mistrust for all American and German automatic pistols, for one had jammed on him during the battle for Celaya and he'd thrown it down in disgust, forevermore to be fonder of the reliable mechanism in older-style revolvers. Yet the wisdom of owning machine guns was never lost on him, for he had seen the destruction they were capable of at Agua Prieta and in a dozen more battles, where his men had been cut down like harvested wheat by their murderous volleys. In the past he had attempted to employ the big howitzer cannons in a number of raids, but they were always too slow and cumbersome to move into the right positions, or when a need arose to fall back quickly for another strike at the enemy's flank. Moving rapidly to a weak spot was the key to winning battles when he and his men were outnumbered; however the cannons could not move quickly enough to be useful. They were designed to fortify a particular place, and until they could be changed in some manner to move more speedily, they were nothing more than a burden to cavalrymen, like plodding columns of foot soldiers.

Fever wracked his body now, and there were times when he grew delirious, alternately calling out for Luz and his children, then his mother, Maria. But when he was lucid he did all he could to remain quiet, to preserve his image of *corazón*, for it was not beneficial to let the others know he lacked heart during difficult times. All Mexican men prided themselves on being *macho*. Doroteo's *machismo* was legendary, the subject of folk ballads and poems written about him, and even at the brink of death he would do nothing to seem unmanly to his soldiers. As best he could he stifled his cries of suffering, and only when his mind was beyond his control did he beg for his wife or mother helplessly.

"Bring the doctor again," he moaned, looking over at Rudolfo. "I need morphine . . . something."

"The doctor is dead, *Jefe,*" Rudolfo replied quietly. "You told me to kill him when the medicine did nothing to stop the pain in your leg. I took him down the mountain and shot him in the head. We hid his body in some rocks. There is more of the medicine, *Jefe,* but the old doctor is buried under many rocks where he would not stink in this small cave."

He remembered now, although he had not truly meant for Rudolfo to kill the old man, even though the medicines did not work. "Yes, I did tell you to kill him. Someone must bring me another doctor. And better medicines this time."

"Blame the woman," Rudolfo said. "She brought the old man here—" A noise interrupted him, and he whirled around, startled, to the mouth of the cavern. Diego jumped to his feet at the same time, leveling his rifle at the entrance.

"What was that?" Doroteo asked, barely able to lift his head to listen to the sound.

"A gun," Rudolfo whispered hoarsely, creeping forward on his hands and knees to peer out into the night. "Cover the fire. I will see who it is." He pulled a pistol from inside his coat and disappeared through the opening without making a sound.

"Have . . . they found me?" Doroteo asked feebly, his brain awash with fever. He tried to move the blanket aside so he could sit up and aim his guns toward the mouth of the cave. His surroundings looked fuzzy, indistinct. Diego threw handfuls of dirt over the flames, and suddenly it was too dark to see at all. "Where are they?" he gasped, trying to clear both his thoughts and his vision at once.

Diego crouched near the opening again. "Who can say where they are, *Jefe,* for we only heard a single gunshot. The Butcher and Ramon will find them. We must be patient. And very quiet."

Doroteo fell back on his makeshift bed. "They have found me," he said, sighing heavily. "Another Judas has betrayed me, showing our hiding place to the American soldiers. It can only be the German woman. She is the only one who knows where we are. Tell Rudolfo to kill her immediately, Diego. As soon as Rudolfo comes back, tell him to shoot the blond woman. . . . I have forgotten her name just now because my leg hurts so badly. Have him shoot her and cut off her head. He must bring her head to me, to prove she is no longer able to show the Americans where we are."

Diego glanced over his shoulder. "But she is so beautiful, *Jefe*. She is the most beautiful woman in all of Chihuahua. Her hair is like gold, and she has the face of the Blessed Virgin. Why would you have the Butcher kill such a pretty girl when there are no others as beautiful as she?"

He considered what Diego had told him. "Maybe you are right to say that this woman should be spared. At least it could wait for a better time. Rudolfo could kill her later, after we have proof she is the one who betrayed us."

"There was only one shot," Diego added thoughtfully, "so I do not believe the soldiers are coming now. Leave it to Rudolfo. He will find out who made the noise."

Doroteo closed his eyes when another wave of fresh pain shot through him. "My leg is very painful," he said with a groan, wagging his head from side to side, tears beginning on his cheeks. "Never in all my life has anything hurt me like this. Why is there no medicine that will help me?"

Diego shrugged, still looking outside. "The old ways are better, *Jefe*. Medicine in a bottle can never be as good as a healing potion prepared by *las brujas*. The juice of a certain mushroom and the pulp of the peyote will make you well again."

Like most mountain people in Chihuahua, Diego believed in witches and magic spells. Doroteo, however, knew there was no magic that would end his terrible pain. Let Diego believe in the old ways if he wished, but what Doroteo wanted was a good doctor and some powerful medicine.

"Someone comes," Diego whispered, cocking his rifle very quietly.

Footsteps approached the cavern, the crunching of tiny rocks underneath shoe leather. Closing one eye, Doroteo aimed a pistol at a patch of night sky beyond the cave opening.

"It is Rudolfo," Diego announced, lowering his gun, "and

the woman." He lit a match and held it to a tuft of dry leaves and grass that he brought to the firepit, then fed kindling to rapidly building flames.

Elisa was first to enter the cave, followed closely by Fierro the Butcher, with his pistol against the small of her back. Doroteo saw fear in her eyes as she approached the fire, and he was sure there was something else behind her expression.

"I was followed," she said in Spanish, kneeling beside him. Her hand reached for his forearm, and she touched him gently. "An American from Texas tricked me, for he was a friend to Pedro and my sister for many years and I trusted him. I saw him following me and I shot him before he came close to the cave. I heard the bullet strike him. There was another sound, a groan. His horse carried him down the mountain, but together, Ramon and I will find him and make sure he is dead. Ramon is looking for him now."

Doroteo looked past the woman to Rudolfo. "There are no American soldiers?" he asked softly, resting his gun across his stomach when his arm became too weak to hold it steady.

"Only the woman," Fierro answered, holding Elisa's Mauser at his side, one of his Colt automatics in the other hand aimed at the back of her head. He questioned Doroteo only with his eyes, asking if the girl was to be shot.

Diego was looking at Elisa with hunger on his face, a slight grin, and at the same time a suggestion of anguish. Knowing she was Doroteo's woman was making him suffer.

It was this desire Doroteo saw in Diego's eyes that made up his mind, and she was indeed a beautiful girl other men lusted for. Her life would be spared because of her rare beauty and natural blond hair, unusual among women found anywhere in Mexico. She enhanced his image as a ladies' man. Possessing Elisa only added to his reputation as the Don Juan of Chihuahua and Durango. "I believe you," he said benevolently, signaling for Rudolfo to put his gun away. "Who is this American?"

Despite her attempt to hide it, relief flooded Elisa's face. "His name is Will Johnson. He told me he was in Parral to look at cows for some American cattle buyers."

Doroteo grunted, glancing briefly at Rudolfo again. "And

now we know the truth, my darling Elisa. He is a spy for the American army, a Judas! Did you question him about where they are now? Where they intend to search for me?"

She shook her head. "He fooled me completely, Francisco. I did not believe this man could be an American agent. He is only a cowboy, a man I knew from before, a friend to Pedro and Christina for many years."

Pain brought a grimace to Doroteo's face suddenly, yet he did his best to put it aside for now and spoke to Rudolfo. "Find the American. Make sure he is dead." His gaze slowly returned to Elisa. "Show Rudolfo where you shot him, then ride to Parral and bring back another doctor. Be sure no one follows you this time, my darling, or I will ask Rudolfo to cut off your head!"

• 25 •

He passed out more than once, never knowing how long he remained unconscious, until he slowly awakened again with his face buried in pine needles. Instinct told him to keep crawling, no matter how weak he became. Searing pain throbbed in his ankle, and when he moved too quickly it was as if someone held a hot poker to his leg. Fighting to stay conscious, he forced himself onward on his belly, pushing the rifle forward a few inches at a time, then dragging his heavy war bag a similar distance before pulling his pain-wracked body over the cold ground. His breath came in frosty bursts in the chill night air, curling from his frozen nostrils in tiny clouds. Several times, when he bumped his ankle over a rough spot, he cried out softly and closed his eyes, fighting back a stream of tears.

It was some comfort when, looking over his shoulder, he no longer heard the voices behind him. He'd lost all track of time. Had he been crawling an hour? Two? Or only a few minutes that seemed much longer in his pain-ridden state? Now and then he caught brief glimpses of stars above his head, when he crawled across a small opening in the trees. In rare moments of clear-headedness he knew he had to stop and stem the flow of blood from his wound. His boot made a squishing sound when he moved his foot, and his entire lower leg felt wet.

He reached a tree trunk and managed to sit up without too much pain, resting a moment, catching his breath, leaning his head back against the pine with his eyes closed. Later, he felt the top of his boot gingerly, wincing when a finger found a big bullet hole in the leather. It would have required a large-bore gun to make a hole like that, he reasoned, and for the slug to pass through his ankle with enough force to kill his horse.

Rummaging blind through his gear, he found his pocket-knife and a spare shirt for a bandage. It would be too painful to take off his boot, so he sliced the leather upper carefully until he could feel his gaping wound. Almost passing out, a fingertip touched shattered bone fragments at the edge of the jagged exit hole in his skin. His ankle was ruined, and it was unlikely he would ever walk again without the assistance of a cane, if the bone healed at all. Working slowly, he cut strips of cloth and tied them around his leg to stanch the flow of blood. Tying the knots made him wince, bringing more tears to his eyes. He then wrapped several layers of cloth around the wounds, as much for support as anything else. When he was finished he rested again, head lolled against the tree, breathing deeply.

Gradually, his mind cleared. He knew he had to get as far away from his dead horse as possible before morning. Villa's men would find the roan, if they hadn't already, then follow the trail of blood through the trees to track him down. His dun gelding was many miles away in the ravine. How could he travel so far with a bad leg? One thing was certain: He must try to walk if he could, hobble with the aid of a stick or his rifle, to cover more ground before daybreak. It was the only chance he had of staying alive.

Summoning all his strength, he gripped the stock of the Winchester and used it to make it to his knees. He waited for a wave of nausea to pass, then struggled to his feet, leaning on the rifle butt, trembling with weakness and fatigue while shutting his mind to the pain and dizziness threatening to send him back to the ground. When he could stand without weaving back and forth, he bent down and took some salt pork and hardtack from his bag, for the added weight of his gear would be too much for him in his weakened condition. He added a handful of cartridges to a pocket of his mackinaw and briefly considered what else he might need, before he tried to walk. Using the rifle as a crutch, ignoring the grinding of broken bones and flashes of renewed pain in his ankle, he took the first hesitant step, then another.

Never in his life had anything approached the level of pain he suffered now. Hobbling, groaning softly now and then, he leaned on the buttplate of the Winchester, his face and body drenched in a cold sweat, to take the next step. And the next. To keep his mind occupied he thought of Texas, the ranch above Laredo, his brother and family. He imagined Junior, riding the white pony across pastures with a broad grin on his lightly freckled face. All these things awaited Will north of the Rio Grande. All he had to do was get there.

Keeping to the trees where shadows were deepest, he struggled downhill at a snail's pace, pausing now and then to catch his breath and listen closely for sounds of pursuit.

A tinkling bell awakened him. He slowly raised his head to find its source, blinking. The sun had started to rise behind the eastern hills. Some time before dawn he had collapsed from sheer exhaustion beside a thicket of scrub cedar and passed out. He had been following a dim trail out of the mountains for what seemed endless hours, hobbling painfully with his rifle for a crutch, shivering from the cold. Now, at daybreak, he feared he was too weak to go any farther. But with the sunrise, the trail of blood he left behind would be easier to follow.

Peering between short, gnarled cedar trunks, he spotted a Mexican boy riding a burro behind a herd of Spanish goats moving slowly up the trail. The boy's attention was on his goats, and for the present he paid no attention to what lay ahead, riding with his head lowered so that his face was hidden beneath his straw sombrero. If it stayed on the trail the burro would pass just a few feet from Will's hiding place. Slowly, he pulled the Winchester alongside him and rested the stock against his shoulder. He needed the burro to escape Villa's men, and if necessary he would take the animal at gunpoint.

A lead goat, the nanny wearing the bell, sensed his presence in the cedars and shied away, leading the other goats wide of the thicket. The boy swung his burro and shouted, *"¡Ándele!"* at the herd, forcing the animals back on the path. The white nanny made a wide circle around the spot where Will lay, trotting past him, leading the others higher up the hill. The boy came at the rear, paying no heed to the trees as he rode to the edge of the thicket.

"¡Alto!" Will commanded, cocking his rifle, aiming for the boy's chest.

"Madre," the boy cried, halting the burro, throwing up his hands to show he had no weapon.

"Get down," Will said in Spanish. "I will not harm you if you do as I say. My foot is broken. I must have your burro to get to my horse and find a doctor."

The boy dropped to the ground. "You have no need of the gun, *señor,* for I will gladly help you." He came over cautiously and looked down at Will's bandage-wrapped boot. "Come. I will help you climb up on the donkey. My name is Juan Morales. Our house is just over the hill. My mother will prepare a poultice of cactus for your foot, only please, *señor* . . . do not point the gun at my face any longer. I will help you."

"Sorry," Will muttered in English, lowering his rifle at once. "I couldn't take the chance that you wouldn't stop to help me."

"You . . . are . . . *un Americano,"* Juan said, examining Will's face more closely, "but you speak *Español* like *un Mexicano."* Coming a step closer, he reached down to take Will's arm.

With Juan's help he was able to stand, although his head was swimming. Juan led the burro over and pushed Will by the seat of his pants over the animal's withers. Pulling his injured leg over the burro's rump very slowly, Will was then astraddle its back.

"Hold on to the mane, *señor,*" Juan said, leading the burro in a turn to go back down the mountain.

Clutching the rifle to his chest, Will glanced over his shoulder, to the mountains from which he had come. Morning sun brightened the slopes. Somewhere in the trees a search party was combing the forests, following a trail of crimson across the forest floor, closing in on him.

The boy hurried the burro all he could down a winding path descending the foothills, tugging the animal's bridle, pulling continually to keep it in a fast walk. Will clung to the burro's back, slumped over its withers, shivering in the cold while trying to ignore the pain in his leg worsened by the burro's gait. The trail wound around clumps of brush, dropping into shallow arroyos, then up sloping cutbacks lined with more trees and brush. In places they crossed open meadows. A slow mile passed underneath the burro's hooves, then another across more of the same land as the sun rose higher, warming the hills.

Rounding a bend in an arroyo, they came upon a small adobe on the crest of the dry streambed. "*¡Mama!*" Juan shouted, pulling harder on the burro's reins.

A woman in a white cotton dress came to the doorway of the hut, shading her eyes from the sun to watch them approach.

"*¿Quién es?*" she called out when Juan could hear her.

Will answered for the boy as they came to the house, speaking Spanish. "I am hurt, *señora.* Someone shot me. My ankle is broken. Your son brought me here."

Juan halted the burro. The woman's eyes were on the rifle Will carried in the crook of his arm.

"I mean you no harm," he said gently, to reassure her. "The bullet also killed my horse. I used my gun for a walking stick to get away before they found me."

Juan's mother still regarded him with suspicion. "Who shot you, *señor?* Did you see who it was?"

"It was too dark. I was riding up the mountains when I heard the shot and felt something strike my leg."

"You are American," she said, frowning a little. "Are you with the soldiers that are coming from the north?"

He decided quickly that it was best to hide the truth. "I am a cattle buyer from Texas, *señora*. As you can see by the way I am dressed, I am not a soldier."

"Everyone is talking about how the American soldiers are coming to kill everyone in Chihuahua because of what General Villa did across the border," she said, making no move to leave the doorway of her house or offer him assistance.

A wave of dizziness made him reel momentarily on the burro's back. He dropped the rifle and held the animal's scant mane with both hands to keep from falling. When the Winchester clattered to the ground Juan picked it up quickly, balancing it in the palm of his hand.

"The stranger will not hurt us, Mama," the boy said. "I told him you would make a poultice of cactus for his wound. You can see how much he is bleeding."

"I can pay you for your help," Will said weakly. "I have a spare horse hobbled in a ravine not too far from here. I'll pay the boy to go get the horse for me, then I'll be on my way."

The woman seemed uncertain at first, then she looked at the surrounding brushland. "We will help you, *señor,*" she said in a quiet voice, "but we do not want your money, even though we are very poor. My husband is away in Parral selling our kid goats to the markets. Help him down, Juanito, then take the machete and cut some cactus as soon as he is resting on the bed. I will boil some water."

Juan leaned Will's rifle against the side of the house, then he assisted him gently to the ground. With his right arm wrapped around the boy's neck, he was able to hobble slowly into the hut without losing consciousness.

He was helped to a cornshuck mattress covered with homespun cloth. As he was lowering his head, his surroundings suddenly went black and it felt as if he were being carried away like a feather on a gust of wind.

Something wet filled his mouth. He swallowed and opened his eyes. Liquid fire went down his throat and he coughed when it took his breath away. "What was that?" he asked feebly. The fire crept slowly down to his stomach.

"Mescal," the Mexican woman replied, holding a bottle of golden liquor near his mouth. "Drink more. It will help with the pain."

He drank again of the distilled agave juice, recognizing it now. He saw the boy standing near his mother's shoulder. "My horse. You must go find it and bring it here," he said, feeling dull pain awaken in his ankle.

Juan nodded. "Tell me where it is, *señor.*"

"I hobbled it in a ravine north of the house belonging to *Señora* Elisa Griensen. Do you know where she lives?"

The boy and his mother exchanged meaningful looks.

"He knows," the woman said gravely. "The German woman is a friend to General Villa. Everyone in Parral knows her."

Will beckoned the boy closer. "Do not let anyone see you when you come with the horse. Stay out of sight. Whoever shot me may be watching, to see if I come back for it."

"I understand, *señor,*" Juan said. "I will be very careful." He turned away from the bed and hurried out the door, his sandals making a soft sound on the hardpan outside.

Will looked down at his foot. A fresh bandage surrounded his ankle, oozing a pale green substance. "Thank you for the poultice, *señora,*" he said, resting his head again. "How long was I asleep?"

"Several hours. It is noon. Many bones are broken in your ankle. You must see a doctor soon."

"I will, as soon as the boy comes with my spare horse."

She offered him more mescal and he drank it, then he remembered his rifle. "Where is my gun? If the men who shot me come, I must be ready for them."

Her head turned to a corner of the hut. "There," she said, pointing to the Winchester resting near a window.

A sudden chill made him shiver, although the sunlit room was warm.

"The fever has begun," the woman whispered, frowning. "You must go to a doctor very soon or I fear you will lose your leg."

Looking blankly at the thatched ceiling, he wondered if the boy would make it back with his dun without being discovered by one of Villa's men, or Elisa. He knew he couldn't ride to Parral for medical attention, for any number of Villa sympathizers might notice him and send word to Villa's henchmen. He had to make it back to General Pershing's column somehow, despite the pain of a long ride to reach a surgeon with the army medical corps.

Dully, he remembered hearing a woman's voice after the bullet struck him. Elisa had ordered one of Villa's sentries to find him in the dark forest. Had she known the identity of the man who followed her? Did she mean to make sure he was dead?

She would recognize his blue roan horse when they found it at daybreak and then she would know the truth, that he had meant to betray her all along. If he lived to return to Chihuahua after the border troubles ended, he would never again share her company or know the sweet passion of her lovemaking.

"I am making some soup," Juan's mother said. She turned away from the bed and shuffled over to a badly rusted iron stove, leaving him to his thoughts.

He closed his eyes.

Later, he ate a few spoonfuls of salty chicken broth and drank more mescal until his brain grew fuzzy. Glancing out a paneless window of the hut, he wondered what was keeping Juan with the horse. Resting his head on the pillow, he listened to the soft buzzing of flies inside the house while the woman was making flour tortillas. Without realizing it, a moment later he drifted off into a light, uncomfortable sleep.

Someone touched his arm. He bolted upright on the bed with his heart racing. The Mexican woman held a finger to her lips to silence him.

"A man comes," she whispered, pointing to the window. "He follows the tracks made by the burro."

Moving his face to the edge of the opening, he peered out cautiously, squinting when bright sun hurt his eyes. Riding along the bottom of the dry wash, less than fifty yards from the house, a bearded Mexican wearing a drooping felt sombrero came slowly toward the front of the hut. Twin cartridge belts crossed his chest. The butt of a rifle rested on his thigh, its barrel glinting in the glare of a setting sun. He was watching the door and windows carefully, keeping his bay in a collected walk.

"My gun!" Will hissed, clenching his teeth as he swung his bad leg off the mattress. He pushed himself up, using the adobe wall for support until the woman hurried over with his Winchester.

He hobbled the few steps to the edge of the doorway with a grimace twisting his features, pain shooting up his leg. The woman hurried to the back of the single room and knelt on the floor, cupping her hands over her ears as though she was sure there would be shooting. Listening to the soft grinding of shod hooves moving up the side of the wash, Will pulled the rifle hammer back with a shaky thumb, judging the distance by sound. The horse moved closer. There could be no doubt this was one of Villa's men, searching the lowlands for the man he'd missed in the dark. The burro's tracks told him what had happened when the trail of blood stopped. The tracks led to the hut, and he knew he had his quarry cornered now.

I'll have just one chance, Will thought. He had never killed a man, although he had been a witness to death many times.

The horse stopped suddenly. A silence lingered, only the buzzing of flies near the stove. Then he heard a metallic click, the loading mechanism of a rifle being cocked outside the hut.

Taking a deep breath, Will gripped his rifle in sweaty hands and swung around the doorframe, bringing the Winchester up to his shoulder, almost falling when his bad leg gave way under his weight. He brought his sights to bear on the chest of the man aboard the bay. Behind him, Juan's mother whimpered softly in the half second before his gun went off.

The Winchester kicked and spat flame, slamming into his shoulder with an ear-splitting blast and knocking him back a step. The Mexican's horse shied, wheeling away from the explosion on its hind legs, snorting, eyes walled white with fear. The roar of the gunshot filled the small room, echoing off dried mud walls. The rider slumped forward and dropped his gun as he clawed for his chest. A stream of red squirted from a hole in his back when his horse whirled to flee the noise. The bay lunged, toppling the Mexican over its croup, his sombrero fluttering crazily in midair above him. Blood splattered over the bay's flanks before the rider tumbled toward the ground. The horse jumped down the bank of the dry stream, loose reins flying, while the Mexican landed hard on the flat of his back, grunting when the air rushed from his lungs. His sombrero fell with a soft plop beside him.

Will steadied himself against the doorframe and lowered his rifle, the acrid scent of burnt gunpowder assailing his nose. He let out the breath he was holding. Twenty yards away, lying in a spreading pool of blood, the Mexican stirred, one shaky bootheel digging a furrow in the caliche with a spur. In the back of the hut, the woman started to cry.

Will took his eyes off the dying man to speak to her. "It is over, *señora*. The man who shot me last night will be dead soon."

"¡Dios!" She whimpered, rubbing her eyes, then she quickly crossed herself and got up from the dirt floor.

Will's attention returned to the Villista when a thought drew his gaze to the galloping bay racing down the arroyo. The horse had a saddle. He turned back to the woman again. "If you can catch his horse for me, I will leave and there will be no more trouble here. I am grateful for what you have done. If you will do this one small favor for me, I can ride to a doctor."

She hurried around him out the door, but when she saw the man spreadeagled in front of the hut, she clasped her hands over her face and started to cry again.

"Please hurry, *señora*," he pleaded. "There may be more of them close by, and the sound of the gun will bring them here."

She took off in an awkward run without answering him, the hem of her dress flying behind her. Farther down the arroyo, the bay slowed to a trot, then a walk, lowering its head to graze.

Using the rifle for a walking stick, Will hobbled from the hut to the man he'd shot, beginning a silent argument inside his head. There had been no choice, really, to shoot him or allow himself to be killed or taken prisoner. But when he stared down at the bearded face, the sightless black eyes looking blankly up at the sun, the bloody hole through the Mexican's ribs and the red stain spread over the ground, something recoiled inside him. He knew he would carry this terrible scene in his memory until the day he died, and he wished with all his heart things could have ended otherwise.

• 26 •

The little town of Tomochic was quiet. Barely a dozen old adobe buildings sat beside a peaceful river in a narrow valley. Colonel Dodd was on the summit of a rocky hill overlooking the village, observing things carefully through field glasses. Only the day before, after a forced march along the far side of the Sierras, he led his exhausted men into Yoquivo, where he learned that two hundred Villistas under the command of Candelario Cervantes had recently left there bound for Tomochic. Loco Jim and Es Ki Ben De had unerringly followed horse tracks and the impressions made by buggy wheels to Yoquivo and now Tomochic. It was quite likely that Cervantes was also bound for Tomochic to join Villa, since Villa's tracks from Guerrero led them here.

Tomochic was said to be mostly Tarahumara Indians and of no strategic importance to Villa, but today a large force of Villistas was present. The high elevation had been hard on Dodd's men and their animals, making him rethink his plan to strike suddenly the minute the enemy was encountered. The town was at least nine thousand feet into the Sierras. His men were poorly fed, weary after a punishing march. He had driven them relentlessly, mindful of his pledge to Black Jack that he would have Villa by the balls in a week or less. Scanning the river valley through his binoculars a second time, he decided the opportunity was too good to waste. The Villistas' horses were grazing far downstream in a loose herd. "Their mounts will be easy to drive off," he said under his breath, returning the glasses to a leather case.

Captain Leslie Shaw stood beside Dodd awaiting orders, his unshaven face red from too much sun and raw wind. "It would appear we caught them napping, Colonel."

Dodd set his rugged chin. "Then let's wake the bastards up," he growled. "If you know how to pray, Captain, say a word or two in our behalf that Pancho Villa is down there with them. I gave Pershing my word that I'd hand him Villa on a silver platter before the week was out. Unless we capture or kill him here today, you and everyone else in this outfit can count on marching until your feet are too sore to pull on your boots, or until we find the dirty son of a bitch."

"I'll pray as hard as I can," the captain replied sincerely, looking down at his feet. "The men are very tired and somewhat dispirited. We could all use a rest."

Dodd wheeled around, glaring at Shaw. " 'Dispirited,' you say?" he bellowed, losing control of his temper. "I'm not even sure I know what that means, exactly, but you can have it tattooed across your ass that I won't tolerate sissies or weaklings in my command! Pass that word along to the men you think are dispirited in this column. Those who believe they would rather have a rest than follow marching orders may do so in the guard house as soon as we get back to the states. Inform them of this at once, Captain Shaw!"

"Sorry, sir," Shaw mumbled. "I was only saying morale is a little bit low after so much hardship. . . ."

Dodd aimed a baleful stare down the back of the hilltop where men from the Seventh stood beside their tired horses. "Those boys don't know a goddamn thing about hardship," he snapped. "I'm old enough to be a grandfather to damn near every one of them, and I can still ride all day and fight all night if I have to. Fuck a pretty young woman or two after that, and drink a fifth of rye whiskey in the meantime. Being a soldier in my outfit means you obey orders without complaining like some willy-nilly die-in-bed aristocrat. This is war, in case nobody told you. I'm gonna catch that bastard Villa if it takes every inch of shoe leather and every ounce of guts in the Seventh Cavalry. I want that understood by every man wearing a U.S. Army uniform at the bottom of this hill!"

"I'm really very sorry that I mentioned it, sir. I assure you it won't happen again."

The Colonel regained his composure somewhat, but he would not take a softer stance. "Send C Troop to surround the horse herd. I want Sergeant Rogers to lead E Troop to those eastern ridges to set up machine guns. He is to begin raking the village with sustained fire as soon as we mount the cavalry charge. Lieutenant Hickman will take his men across the river first, and I will lead a charge from the northwest. In no event shall anyone from this town be allowed to pass under a Mexican flag, the way they did at Guerrero. I want every son of a bitch in that village to surrender to us or they will be shot. Advise the men to spare no gunpowder, and under no circumstances allow any survivors to escape. Mr. Villa got away from me once, but by God he shall not do it again. Move the men out, Captain. Surround the village."

Shaw hurried down the hill, trying not to limp in spite of blisters on his feet. To save the horses, Colonel Dodd had given the order that their mounts would be led most of the way from Yoquivo to Tomochic. Men had walked all morning up and down a twisting road leading to higher elevations, and like everyone else, Shaw's blisters were bleeding and his socks were spongy with fresh blood.

Dodd gave the river valley a final examination, satisfied with his battle plan. Most of his anger had subsided by now. It rubbed him raw that men less than half his age were complaining about a forced march. Hell, he could have walked circles around them if he'd cared to really show them up. Men were softer than they used to be when he was growing up. At sixty-three he would have bet his army pension he could outmarch, outfight, and most likely outfuck every man in the Seventh. He knew damn well and good he could outdrink them too.

Turning from the hilltop, he strode purposefully down the slope to his horse as Shaw was repeating his orders to the men. Troops broke away from the column to go where Dodd wanted them. Sergeant Paul Rogers led his machine-gun troop to the east down a winding gully choked with brush. Lieutenant Horace Hickman directed his cavalry troop around the hill toward a ridge cloaked in tall pines. Dodd climbed aboard his sorrel gelding and rode to the front of I Troop to take them to the valley floor, where they would begin the attack from the north. Even the long march from Yoquivo had done nothing to dampen his excitement, with the prospects of a pitched battle looming before sundown.

This was what he had been needing for several years, a final chance to demonstrate his fighting prowess and leadership. The big brass in Washington had continually overlooked him for promotions, in private saying he was a relic from the past, too old to adapt to modern methods and too hardheaded to change if he could. This campaign would prove otherwise. He intended to capture Pancho Villa almost singlehanded and hand him over to John Pershing like a stuffed pheasant under glass. Those bigwigs at the War Department already knew about his victory at Guerrero, and he was about to add to his list of accomplishments by blowing the hell out of Colonel Candelario Cervantes and his revolutionary force, perhaps bagging Villa in the process. He glanced at his pocket watch as he led his troopers behind the bluffs above Tomochic. It was four-thirty in the afternoon, leaving plenty of daylight to kick some Mexican ass.

Turning north, he kept to thicker pine and oak forests as much as he could, weaving his way toward the river while staying out of sight from the village. When they came to a steeply sloping embankment above the shallow river where the trees ended, he signaled a halt and drew his .45 automatic, checking his belt for extra clips before ordering the charge. Looking behind him, he saw solemn-faced soldiers fanning out into the woods carrying Springfields. He preferred a pistol for close-quarters fighting and used his rifle only when necessary. It was better to see the whites of a man's eyes in any engagement, he believed.

He directed his attention to Tomochic now, feeling the blood race through his veins. Slitting his eyelids unconsciously to adopt a fierce expression befitting a soldier riding into battle, he shouted the order, "Charge!" Driving his heels into the red horse's sides, he swayed in the saddle when his gelding lunged away from the tree line. Knees clamped below the forks of his McClellan saddle, he rode down to the water and started across, listening to the shouts of cavalrymen around him. Splashing hooves thundered through the river, showering riders with spray. Then they struck dry land and pounded over a grassy plain half a mile from the northwestern edge of town, the rumble of moving horses like the beat of a hundred kettle drums suddenly flowing across the peaceful valley.

From rocky ridges to the east, machine gunners under the direction of Sergeant Rogers opened up, and now the stutter of gunfire from the Benets rose above the drumming hoofbeats. Dodd hunkered down in the saddle, leaning over his horse's neck with his pistol aimed at Tomochic. In the town, dozens of men came running from doorways of ancient adobes carrying rifles. Machine guns sprayed the buildings with lead, immediately instilling fear in the Villistas who came outside to face the hail of bullets. Dust spewed from adobe walls and caliche roads where the Benets raked back and forth. Men toppled, some kicking and screaming while holding their wounds. Others merely collapsed instantly, dead before they fell. Machine guns were taking a deadly toll from the ridges before Dodd or any of Hickman's troopers got within range. The Colonel witnessed the efficacy of his battle plan with more than a little satisfaction. A difficult forced march and a suprise attack from all sides were paying off handsomely, even better than he'd dared hope.

From the south, Lieutenant Hickman rode at the front of his charging cavalry beside the river, effectively cutting off the Villistas' escape route in that direction. Steep cliffs of forbidding barren rock blocked a westward retreat unless Villa's men were part mountain goat. Dodd was pleased. A net was soon to be dropped around Candelario Cervantes, and hopefully the catch would include a bonus, in the person of the self-styled general Pancho Villa.

Exploding guns popped and cracked on all sides as Colonel Dodd spurred his horse up a gradual incline to a low hill just north of town. The lighter chatter of rifles was dimmed by the heavy roar of thundering Benets from the ridges. Villistas were being mowed down wherever they fled by blistering machine-gun fire. Answering shots from

Tomochic were few and widely scattered, as the Mexicans took flight in every direction.

A saddler by the name of Ralph Ray reached the hilltop first and was instantaneously knocked from the saddle by a bullet in the head. Blood shot from the young soldier's skull just below the brim of his campaign hat. He fell and tumbled through lush spring grass behind his horse like a rag doll, arms flapping without life at his sides, legs bent unnaturally, shattered by the fall. The back of his head had been blown away by a Remington rifle slug at close range. Dodd saw the Villista who fired the shot rise up from his hiding place behind an empty burro cart just as Private Ray went to the ground.

Aiming carefully, making slight corrections for the jarring gallop of his horse, he fired at the Mexican, emptying his cartridge clip amid the heavy recoil and a clapping series of explosions he directed at the man behind the cart. Bullets riddled the wagon's wood sides and the spoke of one wheel, a final pair of molten slugs entering the torso of the Villista rifleman just below his breastbone. He was torn from his feet and thrown backward, flinging his rifle in the air before he fell out of sight behind the cart. Dodd was ejecting the empty clip and replacing it with another when he felt the horse between his knees shudder.

His sorrel went down, crashing to the ground on its chest with a mighty grunt as Dodd went flying from the saddle. He braced for the fall and landed on his belly in front of the horse in a slithering broadslide through tall grass, blinded briefly when dirt went into his eyes. He held fast to the butt of his gun and finally slid to a halt. For an instant he could not breathe, his lungs refusing to take in any air no matter how desperately he sought it through his nose and mouth. He had not heard any bones being broken when he fell, and despite a serious lack of oxygen, he scrambled to his feet to get back into the fray before the fight was over.

Crossing the river, Private Oliver Bonshee screamed and fell off his horse when a bullet struck him in the belly. He dropped his Springfield to clutch his abdomen just as he landed among the rocks along the riverbank. Riding at the rear of Horace Hickman's frontal charge toward Tomochic, Private Thomas Henry yelled and caught his leg, then he spilled from the saddle and went spinning to the ground, shrieking in agony with a bullet through his right thigh. Trooper August Hanna saw his fellow soldier fall and swung his horse for Private Henry. A second later, the bay gelding Hanna rode collapsed in a heap between his legs, floundering, whickering, a gaping wound in its windpipe casting a fountain of crimson spray over the grass in front of it during a fierce but brief struggle to regain its feet. Finally the horse fell over from exhaustion and blood loss, leaving August Hanna afoot in a direct line of fire from the village.

Hanna ignored the bullets speeding around him to make a dash for Private Henry, ducking and weaving back and forth to make a difficult target of himself until he reached the wounded soldier. Scooping Henry into his arms, he threw him over his shoulder and staggered toward the river.

Colonel Dodd, having gotten his wind back, now turned his automatic on the doorway of a church at the edge of Tomochic where two riflemen fired steadily at the cavalry charge. Steadying the Colt, he triggered off seven fast rounds and knelt quickly to reload again, watching the door from the corner of his eye to see what effect his bullets had. A man dressed in leather leggings and a white shirt leaned away from the doorframe oddly, as though he couldn't quite see what was going on from inside the building, until a dark red stain spread down his shirtfront. His knees gave way and he fell on his rump against the adobe wall, then his head lolled to one side and he finally went still, slumped against the church, his eyes wide open.

With a freshly loaded clip rammed into his .45, Dodd sought a new target in the melee while remaining on one knee, sweeping the gun muzzle back and forth in widening arcs, unable to find anything to shoot at. Guns cracked around him as mounted troopers charged back and forth, firing into Tomochic. Then, out of range to the west of town, he saw a sight that made him jump to his feet in alarm even though the air was full of lead. Scaling impossible cliffs behind the village, dozens of Villistas were fleeing the battle, and more were quickly joining them.

So much noise surrounded him that it was useless to shout an order directing his men to fire up at the cliffs. Apparently none of the machine gunners noticed the swelling exodus of men behind Tomochic. For a time he stared helplessly at the escaping Villistas, until Major Edwin Winans from C Troop came riding up, leading a saddled horse.

"I saw your horse go down!" Winans shouted, handing Dodd the reins, ducking relexively when a flying slug came too close. "I got here as quickly as I could!"

The Colonel swung aboard the nervous brown gelding with an eye to the retreating enemy. "Ride over to Sergeant Rogers and have him direct his gunners to shoot up there!" he cried, pointing to the west.

The major wheeled his horse away and galloped for the river as quickly as he could, leaving Dodd cursing silently with his face to the craggy cliffs. More and more Mexicans were scaling the sheer rock walls, turning a splendid victory into a rather meaningless skirmish, it now seemed. He could not have been made to believe men could climb out of this valley there, not until he saw it for himself. The Villistas crawled up the rocks like so many scurrying lizards, a superhuman feat by any estimation.

It was after dawn the following day before George Dodd penned his report to General Pershing. Thirty-four Villistas were dead as a result of the attack on Tomochic. Twenty-five wounded had been captured. Colonel Cervantes and most of his force had melted away into the night as soon as darkness came. At daybreak, a few Tarahumaras came through the trees to rob the dead of clothing and small weapons. The Indians were such a pitiful lot that Dodd allowed them to scavenge unmolested.

The Seventh Cavalry lost two men, Saddler Ralph Ray and Private Oliver Bonshee, whom they buried in the village cemetery. Eight men were wounded, Private Thomas Henry being the most serious.

It was learned from a captive Villista that Pancho Villa had not been at Tomochic. Colonel Candelario Cervantes had escaped with most of his revolutionary force intact. Dodd prepared the grim news for Pershing and signed it with his usual flair, adding a note that the Seventh would push on toward Parral, where, it was now believed, Villa was in hiding. He bade the courier farewell and began making plans for yet another forced march beginning at noon, without having any idea that the day was Easter Sunday. All that mattered now was saving face with his superiors and, most important of all, making good his promise to John Pershing, even though a week had already run out. *John would understand,* he said to himself. *He knew how difficult this Godawful terrain could be.*

• 27 •

The cavalrymen assembled at Bachiniva were eager to be the first to plunge into the Cusi District of Chihuahua, where the most recent intelligence reports indicated Villa had fled. Parral was the logical place to look for him first, everyone agreed. General Pershing summoned commanders from every available company to a meeting where he would decide which troops to send ahead. Present was Major Frank Tompkins of the Thirteenth, who led a small provisional squad comprised of two troops of cavalry mounted on fresh horses recently driven down from Culberson Ranch. Tompkins was itching to get into the fight somewhere after learning that his brother had been at Guerrero with George Dodd, where he'd distinguished himself leading a valiant charge into the teeth of enemy resistance covering Colonel Cervantes's retreat. Major Robert Howze, commanding the Eleventh, was equally impatient to see some action, his troops poised for a swift march along the base of the Sierras to the east. Word had come that Dodd's Seventh was at this hour dashing south. Colonel W. C. Brown's black Tenth was still somewhere close to Agua Caliente, complaining of bad weather and inhospitable citizens along the way. The General felt keen disappointment over Brown's poor showing thus far, for he had privately hoped for a much better performance from the buffalo soldiers.

Thus Pershing had to choose between Howze's larger Eleventh Cavalry and Tompkins's force mounted on better horses. "With the utmost expediency in mind, gentlemen," he began, "I am dispatching the Thirteenth to Parral. I have no doubts that George Dodd is burning up every available roadway to get there himself from the west." He eyed Frank Tompkins carefully before continuing, ignoring a look of dismay on Howze's face. "I now feel that the initial reports we had from one of our guides was accurate. Villa has gone to the mountains near Parral where he has friends. A Carranza general by the name of Luis Herrera visited my camp at San Geronimo and he insists Villa is dead, that he is buried in a cave south of Guerrero, which he claims he can take us to if we wish to recover the body. Frankly, I don't think the man knows what he's talking about. Until we learn otherwise from sources we trust, we will assume Villa is very much alive, making for Parral, if he is not indeed already there.

"The Thirteenth will proceed at once to the city and begin a thorough search of the surrounding mountains. I expect Dodd will arrive there shortly. The Thirteenth will be reinforced by Major Howze and Colonel Brown, if Brown can somehow manage to get the Tenth moving again. I will lead Headquarters Company to Satevo, where we will establish a forward command post and direct further operations in the south. Supply routes will be maintained between Satevo and the border. I asked Southern Command for authorization to offer a reward for Villa's capture, and last night I was informed that General Funston has asked the adjutant general for fifty thousand dollars to be paid for the delivery of Pancho Villa into the hands of American troops. It may be the only way to elicit any meaningful information from his countrymen. However, until such authorization is handed down from Washington, we must undertake this search without counting on any local cooperation. I fear that unless we find him quickly, while his mobility is restricted by a wound, he will slip away to a neighboring Mexican state and disappear completely."

Tompkins nodded his assent. "We can be ready to pull out

within the hour, General, although we are dismally short in the number of mules we need to carry provisions."

"Get what you need from the Eleventh, Major," Pershing said, without looking at Howze. "Press ahead at full speed. If George happens to get there first he will be seriously undermanned for any full-scale search of the countryside. A word of warning . . . Herrera was quite obdurate about our intrusion into this district. Be wary of the local militia at Parral. Herrera demanded to know how long we intended to stay, what our troop strength presently is, and how much farther south we mean to go. I suspect we may encounter some resistance from Carranza leadership if we appear to be violating any tenets of the accord with Mexico City. Parral is a major city, and the treaty states we must avoid them."

Tompkins frowned. "What happens if we learn that Villa has ensconced himself in the village square, General? What shall we do?"

Pershing pursed his lips a moment. "We must cross that bridge when and if we come to it, Major. If Villa is so brazen as to set up shop in the village marketplace, I'll be sorely tempted to disobey orders for the first time in my career. Until then, let us hope fate will not tempt me. I believe Villa is much too clever to lounge in plain sight as you suggest he might. It is far more likely he has hidden in some remote region, and our task will be to ferret him out. Scour the countryside, Major. Leave no stone unturned. Inform the Carrancista officials at Parral of our mission, but say as little as possible about how we mean to accomplish it."

Tompkins saluted and turned on his heels, marching off to assemble his men. Pershing watched him depart with a certain amount of satisfaction, although the choice between the Thirteenth and the Eleventh had not been easy. Howze was a good tactician, but his column was slowed by materiel. Tompkins would get to Parral in less time, and time was clearly of the essence now.

Major Howze cleared his throat, awakening Pershing to the fact that he was still there.

"What are my orders, General?" Howze asked, disappointment keen in his voice.

Pershing looked down the road toward Satevo. "Press on for Parral as quickly as you can, Major, while searching the countryside for any sign of Villista activity. Close off any possible escape route to the east. If Colonel Brown can finally manage to get his ass in gear, Villa will be effectively cut off to the west. Lockett is bringing the main column from the north. If those blasted radios would work, I could inform George he's needed along the southern perimeter."

Frank Elser, jotting down the results of the meeting while seated beside Floyd Gibbons on the fender of his Ford, halted his pen and stood up. "Almost nothing this army owns has worked so far, General. Your aeroplanes crash with what has become rather routine predictability. Your radios pick up only static, and we have left a trail of broken vehicles along this road that can only serve as a tragic monument to a most serious lack of American mechanical ingenuity. What shall I tell my readers that might explain so many dismal equipment failures?"

Elser had picked the wrong moment to remind General Pershing of the army's mechanical shortcomings. He aimed a baleful look at the reporter and clasped his hands firmly behind his back. "It is entirely possible, Mr. Elser, that you won't be telling your readers anything regarding this expedition from now on, unless you are able to bridle your wagging tongue. I've grown exceedingly weary of hearing your assessments of what has gone wrong up to this point, and I fear readers of *The New York Times* will find news of this campaign almost nonexistent on its pages until you and I have arrived at an understanding. I am painfully aware that we have experienced some equipment difficulties, and I do not need to have anyone remind me of them. This is a wartime military maneuver, and as such all information regarding our comings and goings must be kept secret. As you will recall, I have absolute censorship over your dispatches, and unless you wish to have blank columns appear below your byline in *The Times* you will find a way to keep from irritating me further with your observations about our failings."

Lieutenant Patton needed no urging to take charge when Pershing's displeasure with Elser surfaced. From the start he had shown a dislike for the two reporters, and the General's outburst only served to fuel Patton's revulsion for the press. He strode forward to come between the newsmen and

Pershing, jutting his chin purposefully. "That will be all, gentlemen!" Patton snapped. "The two of you are excused!"

"Now hold on a minute," Elser protested, looking Patton in the eye.

"No, *YOU* hold on a minute!" Patton bellowed, cords standing out in his neck. "You have been dismissed!"

"I'm not a soldier," Elser said. "I don't have to take orders from you."

The lieutenant's cheeks were purple with rage before Pershing intervened. "That's enough," he said, touching Patton's shoulder. He directed his next remark to Elser and Gibbons. "While my aide has expressed my sentiments with unnecessary clarity, it is pointless to go on with this ranting and raving. Get back in your automobile, and we will drive to Satevo as quickly as possible. A continuation of this discussion is a waste of time. However, until further notice I won't allow any dispatches to be sent back with the couriers until we've reached an accord."

"You can't do that," Elser insisted, wiping alkali from his coat sleeves. "You cannot censor us entirely. The public has a right to know what is going on down here."

Pershing stared into Elser's eyes. "The public's right to know is outweighed by a military need for absolute secrecy, Mr. Elser. No more of your dispatches will be sent from the front until I have given my approval."

"This isn't a front," Elser said, looking to Gibbons for moral support. "This is a disaster, and the American people have a right to know how their tax dollars have been spent. Nothing this army owns works the way it should. Even a renowned pilot like Captain Foulois is deathly afraid of our aircraft. The aero squadron might as well be flying kites! Your radios are useless, and your trucks keep breaking down. This smacks of corruption at the War Department, General. Seems the army has purchased all manner of equipment from dishonest manufacturers who must have known it would not perform satisfactorily. Bribery could be involved. Secret payments made under the table, perhaps. An investigation should be conducted to see who looked the other way while this fraud was going on, and at what cost to American taxpayers."

"It's too widespread," Gibbons agreed. "Someone must

have known at the War Department that they were buying crap."

Patton looked as if he were about to burst at the seams, yet he held his tongue with Pershing's hand resting on his shoulder. For a moment, the General considered his answer to the charges carefully. An uneasy glance passed between Elser and Gibbons.

"If corruption exists, it must be proven before anything substantive can be done about it," he finally said. "Workmanship that fails under extreme conditions is not necessarily a fraud. At the present, halfway across Mexico, little profit can be realized by creating a stink over our mechanical troubles, and it might lead our enemies to conclude that we are vulnerable. An attack against our unprotected columns could be the cost if we let it be known in your newspapers that some of our equipment is suspect. You will print nothing that might encourage Villa or anyone else who stands against us that we have a weakness. You have my final word on the matter, gentlemen. Now return to your automobile, or you will be left standing beside this road to fend for yourselves."

Nonplussed, Elser opened his mouth to say more, which only served to further provoke Pershing, and he lost his temper completely. "I said, get in the car!" he snarled, lips drawn across his teeth, aiming a finger at the Ford.

Gibbons caught Elser's arm. "I'll drive," he said quietly, pulling the still reluctant Elser away.

Major Howze, witnessing the exchange without saying a word until then, watched Patton raise the holster flap on his .45 as though he meant to shoot Elser. "Now, now, Lieutenant, let's not have a misunderstanding turn into a bloodbath. I hate newspapermen myself, but not enough to kill one."

The general saw Patton's hand close around the butt of his automatic. "That will not be necessary, Lieutenant," he said evenly, as his anger cooled somewhat. "Get our automobile started and we'll be underway. No reporters will be shot on this expedition unless the order comes from me."

As Elser was being assisted into the passenger seat of the Ford by his comrade he saw Patton reaching for his gun. Then Patton wheeled around in response to the general's instructions and, still fuming, stalked angrily toward the Dodge sedan. "That man is out of control," Elser told Gibbons in a hushed voice. "I swear he looked like he was going to shoot me."

Pershing overheard the remark and let it pass. Walking slowly to the front of the line of automobiles with Major Howze, glancing across troops from the Thirteenth assembling for the push toward Parral, he thought about what Elser had said. Surely Patton hadn't actually meant to draw his gun and fire.

"Your young aide is quite a hothead," Howze observed. "He won't go very far in this man's army without discipline."

"Well, he's very thorough. He may be a bit strong-willed at times, but overall, I'd call him a good soldier."

Howze shook his head, watching Patton crank the motor of the automobile. "For a moment there it looked like he was completely beyond reason."

In private, Pershing had a similar concern over his own outburst moments earlier. He had lost control when Elser pointed out how many things were going awry under his command. His anger could only be an admission that he knew Elser was right to suppose that corruption might exist in the War Department. What else would explain why so many things did not function properly? Did he dare suggest such a thing to Hugh Scott in his next report? It would only focus more scrutiny on the campaign in Washington if he started blowing warning whistles. With the expedition in a state of chaos, and Villa still on the loose, it would be tantamount to tossing raw meat to hungry lions.

He climbed into the rear seat of the Dodge after dismissing Major Howze, settling back for a long drive in the heat. Columns of mounted cavalry were forming as the automobile sputtered off.

10 April
We have reached Satevo. No word from George. Frank
Tompkins is expected to hit Parral tomorrow, and
everything may ride on the outcome. We simply must
not fail to find Villa, or I fear I will be removed from

this command almost immediately.' So many break-downs are occurring that even Patton cannot keep track of them all. Patton has shown a dangerous tendency to ignore discipline in favor of emotion, and unless he learns to exert more self-control his career will surely end early and on a sour note. He is at heart a good soldier, but I notice there are times when he appears to view military discipline as unnecessary baggage, and his temper can be worse than mine when provoked. I intend to speak with him about this at the first opportunity.

I miss Warren so very much. I have written to him and to May this evening and sent the letters with my dispatch to Funston telling him of our arrival here. The couriers have been instructed not to carry any dispatches from the newsmen until further notice. I will not have them sending negative reports to their readers at this crucial point in the campaign. If word of our repeated failures and ineptitudes were to leak out now I can be assured of being replaced by Leonard Wood forthwith despite his game leg. My hopes lie with George Dodd and Frank Tompkins now. Unless Villa is caught soon I will be coming home in disgrace, of that I am quite sure.

May God be with George and Frank Tompkins. They seem to be the only natural leaders I have in my command.

• 28 •

The woman handed him a bundle of tortillas, concern lines showing around her eyes. He gripped the wooden horn of the big Mexican roping saddle, both feet fitted in *tapadero* stirrups, beads of sweat dripping from his forehead. Without her help he could not have made it up to the bay's back.

"Go with God," she said, giving him his rifle.

He nodded, his brain awash with dizziness. He had taken the dead man's pistol and the bottle of mescal. With tortillas he could survive the ride to the army column if only he could stay in the saddle. He put the warm bread inside his shirt and then dug into a pocket for the last two silver dollars he had. "One is for you, the other for the boy. Tell him he can keep the buckskin horse. I owe both of you my life."

He clucked to the bay and swung away from the hut with the setting sun to his back. He meant to ride well to the east of Parral, missing Elisa's house by several miles, thus staying out of sight from travelers until it got dark. Keeping the bay in a slow walk, he reined into the arroyo to stay off the skyline as best he could, gritting his teeth when even the slow gait of the horse worsened the throbbing in his ankle. Resting his Winchester across the pommel of his saddle, he took the mescal from his coat pocket and drank deeply, making a face when the fiery liquid scalded his throat. He drank again, of necessity not thirst, and settled against the cantle for a long, painful ride.

Following the dry arroyo eastward, he wound his way a few miles wide of the distant valley in which Parral sat before turning north, heeding the voice of his conscience. Since leaving the hut he had worried about the boy, and in spite of the fact that he was in no shape to help Juan if someone had been watching the dun for Will's return, he rode toward Elisa's house now. Juan should have returned with the horse long ago. Something had gone wrong, and he owed it to the boy to investigate and do whatever he could. He'd said nothing about his concerns to the boy's mother, not wanting to worry her. But it was clear too much time had passed since Juan had left to fetch the dun. Had one of Villa's men discovered the horse, hiding close by until someone came for it? Could Elisa have been waiting there to surprise the boy, even now holding him at gunpoint until he told her where he had taken the *gringo* with the wounded leg?

He found his answer a short time later, guiding the rawboned bay between a group of gently rolling hills as dusk purpled the land around him. He saw a slender figure in the distance leading a horse over the crest of a bald knob. Grimacing with the added pain of it, he sent the bay into a shuffling trot and rode for the hilltop as quickly as he could.

When Juan saw him he tried to run away, leading the dun at a trot toward a thicket of brush at the bottom of the knob. The boy didn't recognize Will nor the bay horse, knowing nothing of the grisly killing that had taken place in front of his house. Just before Juan reached the bushes, Will called out to him.

"Juan! Juan!"

Hearing his name, the boy stumbled to a halt to watch the rider approach, still wary, eyeing the thicket now and then with the dun in tow. Then his coppery face broke into a grin and he waved as Will rode up and hauled back on the reins.

"Where did you find the bay horse, *señor?*"

Will noticed the boy's torn cotton pants and a bloody spot on his left cheek. "What happened to you?" he asked, ignoring Juan's question for the moment.

Juan pointed to the dun. "This horse does not like me," he said. "When I tried to get on his back, he bucked for all he was worth. He threw me many times. My pants have a hole in them now and my mama will scold me until papa comes home to give me a whipping for ruining my clothes."

Despite the boy's sincere worries over his pants, Will gave him what might pass for a grin. "I was afraid something worse had happened to you. One of Villa's men came to your house and I had no choice but to kill him. If you will change the saddle to the dun's back, I will give you this bay as a present. The bay is gentle. You will have to help me down."

Juan's eyes rounded with surprise. "You would make me a gift of the horse?" he asked, not quite believing it. Then his face grew dark. "But *señor,* with a bad leg, this terrible horse will throw you off and your pain will only be worse!"

Will was midway through swinging his right leg over the bay's rump when Juan rushed to his aid. "I know how to ride the dun," he said, easing himself to the ground with the boy's help. "Now change the saddle, and you should hurry so your mother will not worry."

Juan began with the cinch as Will rested, leaning against the bay's withers, sipping mescal to silence the flashes of pain in his ankle. He could tell by the tight feeling inside the bandage that the swelling had gotten worse. When the boy had the saddle on his dun, he slipped off the bay's bridle and hobbled over, using the rifle for a crutch, and put the bit in the dun's mouth, leading the bay by its mane.

"Help me up," he said, when everything was ready. "Then hand me this gun."

"Be careful, *señor,*" Juan pleaded. "This horse is very mean to ride."

With a tight rein and a push from Juan, Will swung over the dun's back. The horse stood quietly, head lowered.

Juan stepped back in amazement. "You have magic with wild horses," he whispered, awe in his thin, reedy voice.

It ain't magic, Will said to himself, *just an understanding between me an' this yellow bastard that I ain't in the mood for any foolishness today.* He leaned down and took the rifle, looking Juan in the eye. "Thanks," he said in Spanish, "I owe you my life. Maybe some day I can repay you proper. For now, keep the bay horse an' the silver dollar I gave your mother. *Adios, compadre.*"

He reined the gelding north and headed into the deepening twilight at a walk, buttoning his mackinaw around his throat to keep out the colder night air. Down deep, he knew it wasn't the cold making him shiver. Fever was spreading from his festering wound. Time was growing short.

Pershing's column was somewhere to the north on the road to Parral, an unknown number of miles away. Will's life depended upon staying in the saddle until he found the army doctors. The way he felt now, the odds against him were long.

To keep his strength up he took a tortilla from the bundle inside his shirt and chewed it methodically, washing it down with small swallows of mescal. Riding the hills east of Elisa's adobe as dusk turned to night, he remembered the woman, her soft sighs of pleasure, the wonderful moments he spent in her bed. Thinking of her now, he faced the truth: After what had happened last night she would never allow him to come near her again.

"I should have ridden back to the column yesterday," he said quietly as, his tongue loosened by liquor, he began talking to himself in the lonely darkness. "Nobody'd have known the difference."

He had to consider what life would be like with a useless leg or no leg at all. If his ankle couldn't be repaired, or should gangrene set in before he found an army surgeon, the result could be amputation. All because he'd taken a job too seriously, going a step further than he had to when he tried to follow the woman to Villa's hiding place. If only he'd left well enough alone.

The lights of Parral fell away behind him. Plodding along with his shoulders rounded, he drank sparingly from the bottle and angled northwest to strike the road running to Agua Caliente. Pershing's army would be coming south by that route, the only possible way to get heavy wagons and trucks from Colonia Dublan to Parral through the Sierras. Colonel Dodd's men were trekking in the same general direction by back roads, guided by the Apaches following Villa's tracks from Guerrero. Before the middle of April rolled around this part of Chihuahua would be crawling with American soldiers. If Villa stayed close to Parral he would have to be very clever to avoid being caught.

But what did it matter now? Will's employment as a scout for the army was finished, ended by a bullet in the dark. He hadn't yet earned a month's pay, and already his stint with the expedition was over. What could be worse, he might be a cripple for the rest of his life.

There was, however, one small consolation: The bullet could have just as easily killed him.

A quarter of an hour later he encountered the wagon road to the village of Santa Cruz, remembering what Benito had said about the big *hacienda* on this road where Rudolph Milnor lived. As he was crossing the wagon trace he looked south, toward Parral, where he saw a pale white adobe wall surrounding a magnificent house on the side of a mountain less than a mile away. "That must be the German's place." Teeth chattering, he halted the dun briefly to study the wall, the two-story mansion and its red-tile roof illuminated by the stars.

His leg was throbbing, yet he paused to wonder if Elisa had ridden out here to tell Milnor what had happened on the mountain last night. Too, the remark Christina made about Milnor still puzzled him. Why should Elisa fear for her life around the German? What was her connection to him? It made little sense. And what was in the envelope Milnor gave her? Was it money to finance a new army for Villa? Will couldn't figure why the German government cared one way or another about Villa's revolution in Mexico, until he remembered something John Abel had said about the Germans seeking a trade agreement or something like that. Although Will did not understand world politics, almost everyone knew there was a big war going on in Europe. America wasn't involved, and President Wilson intended to leave it that way, according to the newspapers. What did Germany have to gain from an alliance with a border bandit like Pancho Villa? Or was there more than Will could guess about Rudolph Milnor's involvement in Mexican politics, an involvement that included Elisa in some way?

Tiny lights behind the windows at Milnor's *hacienda* beckoned in the night. Behind those windows lay some of the answers. Were it not for his bad leg, Will might have investigated. But not now, not with a foot so badly swollen it felt as though his skin would burst. Any delay in reaching the services of a doctor was out of the question, filled with too much risk.

He urged the dun across dim wagon ruts and sighted along the horizon. His chills were growing worse. Before midnight, riding the high mountain road toward Agua Caliente, the temperature would drop below freezing, and his suffering would surely be worsened by the cold.

It could hardly be called a village. After crossing the Rio Conchos he came to a place known as San Jose del Sitio, barely a dozen adobes where goat herders lived and a single store closed for the night. Dogs started barking when he rode in, his body wracked by increasingly violent chills. He sat resolutely in the saddle with no thought to stopping here, rocking with the dun's slow gait, hunkered down inside his coat with both hands shoved deeply in his pockets to keep them warm. He'd consumed the last of the mescal over an hour before and tossed the bottle away, his mind dulled by pain and fever rather than any effect from the distilled spirits.

A man carrying a lantern came out on the front porch of his hut to see what had alarmed the village dogs. He peered up at Will as the dun walked by and said, *"Buenas noches, señor."*

"Buenas noches," Will replied, reaching for the reins to stop his horse. In Spanish he continued, "Could I trouble you for something warm to drink? Coffee, perhaps? I have injured my leg and I must ride all night to reach a doctor."

The Mexican stepped off his porch to have a closer look at Will's face in the lantern light. *"Gringo,"* he said with obvious dislike. He wagged his head from side to side and turned away abruptly. *"Váyase,"* he added, snuffing out the wick, blanketing the road in darkness. He closed the door to his hut with more force than necessary. Then there was silence.

Gently heeling his horse forward with his left foot, Will rode through San Jose del Sitio toward more of the same silhouetted mountains. The people of Chihuahua knew of Pershing's advance and Villa's defeat at Guerrero. Americans expecting hospitality here would soon find out how strongly Mexicans could believe in a revolutionary cause.

Fatigue tugged his eyelids on the ride from the village. He started to doubt his ability to reach the army column. He had to somehow remain in the saddle long enough to find them.

The road climbed and fell, twisting along switchbacks. A layer of frost clung to the grasses growing beside the wagon ruts, sparkling in the starlight. Will's face was numb from the cold. His head reeled, and when he was capable of clear thought he was certain that he could go no further. His muscles had begun to cramp from too many hours frozen in the saddle, and yet he knew that if he got down from the horse he lacked the strength to climb back up on his own. He couldn't continue, and he could not stop. Silently cursing his bad luck, he guided the dun over a starlit ridge and suddenly awakened from his trancelike state when he caught a glimpse of twinkling campfires at the bottom of a sloping bend in the trail. In the back of his foggy brain was a warning that the fires might belong to some of Villa's scattered men, but in his present condition, almost frozen to death and slipping closer to unconsciousness, he made for the distant flames as quickly as he could without caring who awaited him there.

When the sounds of his horse reached the fires, a voice cried out, "Who goes there?"

Hearing English, he was immediately flooded with relief. He tried to form a reply, only to find that his lips were frozen stiff, and he could only manage weak, unintelligible sounds. "Help . . . me!" he finally croaked, aiming for the closest campfire in a half-blind daze.

Shadows ran toward him, men carrying rifles. He slumped over the saddlehorn just as a uniformed soldier caught the dun's bridle.

"Help me," he said thickly, choking on phlegm and tears. "My ankle is broken. I'm a scout for . . . the army."

He heard voices and could not understand them as he was being helped from the saddle by gentle hands. The sky above him started to swim crazily. Trees in the forest surrounding the fires tilted at impossible angles, then everything went black.

"I'm Major Frank Tompkins," a bearded face said. "Tommy's my brother. He was with you when the Seventh took Guerrero. We heard all about it from the courier Colonel Dodd sent back. I'm commanding a company of the Thirteenth Cavalry. You were lucky to find us, Johnson.

Can't remember ever seeing an ankle shot up so bad. It's a goddamn miracle you could sit a horse. We gave you some laudanum for the pain. I'm afraid it's the best we can do for now."

A fuzzy glow dulled Will's consciousness, but the pain was less. "I was tracking Villa on orders from Colonel Dodd," he said, tongue thickened by the medicine. "He's hiding out in the mountains southwest of Parral. I trailed a woman who knew Villa an' got shot by one of Villa's lookouts."

"We were told Villa may be dead," Tompkins said. "The *comandante* of the Federal garrison at Agua Caliente said Villa bled to death from his wound the day after Guerrero fell. An informant told him Villa was buried in a cave and offered to take him to the grave. General Pershing is sending us to look for Villa near Parral. No one believes the story that Villa is dead."

"It's a lie," Will said. "That's what Villa wants everyone to think, so he'll have time to raise another army without havin' the hounds nipping at his heels. Villa is alive. The German woman took him food and brought him a doctor. His soldiers are scattered all over Chihuahua, waitin' for him to call them back together again. The woman told me herself that Villa has gone into hiding where he feels safe. He's popular with the *campesinos* around Parral, an' they won't betray him."

"A German woman? What does she have to do with it?" Tompkins asked.

Will was too tired to tell all of it. He wagged his head. "It's a long story, Major. Mostly speculation. Some claim she's a spy for the German government. Villa likes her, trusts her. . . ." His eyelids fluttered momentarily, and then he slipped toward a blanket of fog closing in on him and felt nothing.

Hot coffee and bacon revived him some, although the laudanum, slowing his reflexes, made chewing and swallowing difficult. He had been propped against a tree trunk near a roaring fire when a cook had awakened him with food. Major Tompkins was seated next to him as the sky paled with sunrise.

"You look a little better this morning," the major said, "a bit more color in your face."

"The medicine helps. Still hurts like hell."

"I'm sending you back with an escort. They'll try to keep you as comfortable as possible. Most of the medical corps is with the main column outside Bachiniva. General Pershing deployed Major Howze's Eleventh Cavalry to the east and Dodd, as you know, is west of us, pushing toward Parral. I'm taking the Thirteenth by the shortest route. The Federal commander at San Borja, Major Castanada, insisted that while Villa was dead, the bulk of his men were camped close to Parral."

"Villa is very much alive," Will said, feeling warm with the coffee in his belly. "At least that's what the German woman told me. I followed her into the mountains southwest of Parral, maybe five or six miles, where I got ambushed."

Tompkins nodded thoughtfully. "That's good information, more than we had. According to the maps, Parral isn't far."

"A day's hard ride. Wish I could show you the spot where I caught that bullet, Major, 'cause I know it was real close to Villa's hideout. Looks like this job is over for me now, an' I sure as hell could have used the money."

"You'll be compensated, Johnson. Explain everything to General Pershing and he'll see to it that you don't go home with empty pockets. I'd call this special circumstances, and so will the general. You've given us valuable information. There are some on the general's staff who are arguing that we should go home, now that Villa is reported to be dead."

"He ain't dead. A bullet broke his leg just below the knee, and a girl who saw it said Villa was in a lot of pain. But he's seen a doctor by now, the one the woman guided from Parral the other night. It may take a spell before he can ride, but I sure wouldn't count him out of it just yet. He'll raise some more men when his leg is better, an' then I 'spect he'll be up to his old tricks again."

"I'd like to be the one to find him," Tompkins said, his gaze falling to the embers in the fire for a time. "Nobody knew what Mexico was really like."

"I tried to tell 'em," Will remembered, "the general

himself and Major Ryan, before they ever crossed the border."

"Off the record, Ryan is an idiot. Pershing is a good man, dedicated to his men, a good soldier. He's doing the best he can under very trying circumstances."

"He ain't real good at listenin' to advice," Will said. "He offered to pay me a hundred a month to track down Villa, but when I told him he couldn't do it from the seat of an automobile or a truck, he wouldn't listen. Said Villa wouldn't stand a chance against him. From the looks of things, by now the general oughta be ready to admit he was wrong. Villa stands more than just a chance, if you ask me. I saw a feller by the name of Rudolph Milnor hand the German woman an envelope to give to Villa. I figure it was money to finance another big army, maybe. Milnor is a German too, an' word is he works for the German government. I've been tryin' to figure why Germany would help Villa in the first place."

"We've had intelligence reports that the German High Command is actively trying to form an alliance with Carranza. What you saw is interesting, if this Rudolph Milnor is actually a German spy. Our sources, according to General Pershing, have been led to believe that Germany is backing Carranza. Be sure to inform the general of what you witnessed, and what you heard about the German being a government agent. It might be an important bit of news to relay to Washington."

"I'll mention it to him," Will said, doubting the general or anyone on his staff would really listen.

All across the encampment, men were crawling out of sleeping blankets. Others were already at the picket lines, saddling horses. Will thought about the forthcoming ride to Bachiniva, over a hundred miles to the north. A hundred long, rugged miles through the mountains with a busted ankle.

"If I showed you a map of the area around Parral," Tompkins began, "could you point to the spot where you were wounded?"

"Pretty close, I reckon. Within a mile or two. But I imagine that by now, Villa is someplace else. He knows I got away an' that'll force him to move."

"I suppose you're right." The major sighed, getting up and dusting off the seat of his pants. "Show me anyway. I'll be back with the map shortly. We'll be pulling out in less than an hour. I'm sending four men back with you. One will be carrying a bottle of laudanum, as much as you'll need."

"I'm mighty grateful, Major. That stuff makes me feel like I'm half asleep, but it sure as hell helps deaden this leg."

Tompkins halted a few feet from the fire and turned back to look at Will's ankle. "You'll be a lucky man indeed if the surgeons can save your leg, Johnson. An injury like that needed medical attention right away."

"There wasn't any," Will replied dully, hoping the major was wrong about the possibility of amputation.

"By the way, Johnson, just what was that smelly green pulp you put inside the bandage?" A clean bandage had been wrapped around Will's ankle last night while he was unconscious.

Will smiled a little, remembering Juan's mother. "Some prickly-pear cactus. Mexicans make a poultice out of it. It's an old-time remedy."

The major frowned. "It doesn't appear to have done much good."

He strode off to find his maps before Will could tell him that cactus poultice worked well in drawing poisons out of the wounds of injured horses and cattle. But then what would some soldier know about folk medicine? When there were no doctors or veterinarians close at hand, men did what their forefathers had done for injuries, using whatever they had to keep a wound from festering. Will's pa had used just such a remedy dozens of times successfully, out of necessity, It was, however, a waste of time explaining necessity to a soldier, although Tompkins did seem like a decent officer, a man who would listen. Maybe, if he got lucky, Tompkins would find Villa before he recovered sufficiently to go on the run again.

• 29 •

Elisa felt a chill despite the warmth of a spring evening. The look in Rudolph Milnor's eyes awakened the terror she had known since her childhood, since he first brought her to Mexico. Her fear of Francisco Villa was quite different, for while he was dangerous and unpredictable he still desired her, where Milnor was calculating, unyielding, untouched by emotion. The flat look on his face was unlike anything she had ever seen in him before.

"The Americans are very close to Parral. Some will arrive tomorrow, only a small force," he said, his voice like a new rasp across iron. "Someone should inform General Ismael Lozano that his city is about to be invaded. If his concern can be aroused, he might make a show of force against the Americans. If the citizens of Parral were up in arms over the possibility of an American invasion, it might create an incident here, some shooting, perhaps. Another problem for the American government . . . another delay. The High Command asks for more time. The war in the trenches goes badly and the French will not be budged. The British naval blockade is starving our people. If a conflict in Mexico seems imminent, America will not be so quick to join the Allies overseas with the potential for a war with Mexico growing." Milnor's eyes narrowed. "How serious is Villa's injury?"

"His leg has turned black and he appears to be in endless pain. He ordered the old doctor executed when his medicines did not help. Fierro shot him. This morning, I took Dr. Fuentes to another cave where Francisco is hiding now. Unless he can give Francisco something to end his suffering soon, Fierro will be ordered to kill him as well."

"Then Villa is too badly wounded to harass the Americans when they come," Milnor said darkly. "Someone else must do it. Go to the Federal garrison and ask to speak to Lozano. Tell him you have a message of grave importance. Use your . . . considerable charms to convince Lozano that a show of strength against these Americans will make him a hero. He has political ambitions. This will appeal to him, to his vanity." He leaned closer to her, and now she could smell garlic and beer on his breath. "Make sure you are convincing, Fraulein." He reached for the buttons at the top of her blouse, opening one, then one more, until her cleavage showed. "Why, you are trembling, my dear," he added, a cruel grin twisting his mouth. "You have nothing to fear. Unless you fail to convince Lozano . . ."

"I will be convincing, Herr Milnor," she whispered, feeling a bony hand cup one of her breasts.

She hurried away from the garrison after midnight with her fingers clutching the front of her blouse where Ismael had torn it off. A sticky wetness stained the seat of her riding pants. Tears rolled silently down her cheeks while she was mounting the black mare. When she rode through Parral, the city was asleep. Tomorrow, because of what she had done at the garrison tonight, the quiet would come to a sudden end when the American cavalry arrived. Ismael had been easy to manipulate.

Her final instructions from Milnor had been the most puzzling, difficult to understand. She was told to come to town after sunrise wearing a white dress. Underneath her skirt, she was to conceal her Mauser. If General Lozano blocked the Americans' path with his *Federales,* then why would she need to bring a gun?

More than a hundred mounted soldiers waited in front of the garrison *oficina,* their uniforms and hats, their underfed horses coated with alkali dust. It was noon. Crowds had formed to watch the Americans enter the city. Rumors of an impending invasion spread quickly through clusters of worried people lining dusty streets leading to the center of town. All forms of commerce had come to a halt. An uneasy quiet gripped Parral, an ominous calm. Everyone's attention was on the meeting taking place inside the building between General Lozano and the tall American commander. General Lozano had made a public promise this morning that the Americans would be ordered to leave Parral as soon as they arrived. The column of heavily armed cavalrymen was surrounded by unfriendly faces on all sides. More and more people came from every corner of town to watch what was going on, until the side streets became almost impassable, choked with curious citizens.

Elisa saw Rudolph Milnor ride to the rear of a group of men who were watching the proceedings from the porch of a cantina south of the town square. His gray stud pranced impatiently, fighting the bit as Milnor paused to speak to some of the onlookers. Elisa could feel tensions growing. A few whispered voices could be heard in the crowd, asking about the arrival of the foreigners. Would houses and farms be seized? Would the Americans loot their stores?

A shout went up on the far side of the plaza. Milnor stood in his stirrups, crying, "*¡Todos! ¡Ahora! ¡Viva Mexico!*"

A murmur in the crowd became a swell of angry voices. Men raised their fists, shouting, "*¡Viva Mexico!*"

American cavalrymen began reaching for their carbines. A few exchanged nervous looks. This was the moment Elisa had been told to wait for. Lifting the hem of her soft white skirt, she took her Mauser from a holster she wore underneath her dress and let it hang by her side, hiding it in a fold of the material as Milnor further incited the mob in front of the cantina.

"Who's that son of a bitch with the beard doin' all that yelling?" a soldier in olive green asked, trying to settle his fidgeting horse.

More angry yells echoed across the square, and now men were pushing and shoving toward the column of soldiers. Elisa came down the steps of the *mercado* porch where she had been awaiting Milnor's signal, moving along with the crowd, still holding the pistol in a fold of her skirt. Men jostled her, pushing her to one side, trying to get closer to the plaza.

General Lozano and the American commander came outside when the commotion in front of the office grew louder. Lozano raised his arms, hoping to silence the crowd.

Some of his *Federales* hurried from the compound armed with rifles, but the shouting only grew worse. The American officer swung up on his horse, then he drew his .45 pistol. His cavalrymen broke ranks, turning their horses around, looking for a way to escape the crush of the oncoming angry crowd.

A shot rang out. The clap of exploding gunpowder thundered from the south, and everyone started to run. Women screamed and frightened children shrieked. Horses bounded to a gallop in the middle of the street when soldiers began a hasty retreat away from the center of Parral. Another gun cracked. Rumbling hooves drummed over the roadway, kicking up a boiling curtain of dust. An American took aim and fired into the crowd as his horse lunged past the *mercado* where Elisa was trying to avoid being trampled by terrified men and women rushing away from the gunfire.

More guns sprang to life, the chatter of pistols and the heavier pounding of rifles. Bullets whined through the air, the singsong of flying lead difficult to hear above the noise and confusion of the Americans' headlong dash out of town. Elisa stepped to one side of the throng and raised her Mauser, firing twice before she cried, *"¡Vayanse, gringos bastardos!"* as loudly as she could. The sharp report from her pistol made men stop and look at her. *"¡Andale!"* she yelled, pointing the muzzle toward the Americans, *"a sus caballos!"*

She took off in a run, lifting the hem of her skirt to reach her own mare as dozens of citizens mounted their horses and mules to give chase on the heels of the fleeing cavalrymen. Before she could climb aboard her horse she caught a brief glimpse of Milnor charging through the crowd on his dappled gray with a pistol in his fist. Elisa swung her black around and clamped her feet into the mare's sides, paying no heed to her bare legs when her skirt went above her knees over the saddle. The mare struck a gallop into the dust cloud rising up behind the retreating soldiers, and for a moment she was riding blind. Then she saw Milnor bending over his stallion's neck, leading a group of horsemen racing down the dust-choked street, the clatter of shod hooves and the bang of gunfire making such a din that no single noise stood out from the swell.

The Americans swung north at the edge of town, firing over their shoulders sporadically. Elisa heeled her black through the mob of riders giving chase, dodging slower animals, reining back and forth to keep Milnor in sight. A brown mule galloping just in front of her mare went down suddenly with the distant crack of a rifle. Legs flailing, the big mule flipped over on top of its rider, and there was a muffled scream when the man was crushed. A staccato of answering gunfire erupted from a group of townspeople who saw the mule fall. At the rear of the retreating soldiers a cavalryman dropped his rifle and swayed in the saddle, clutching his left arm and losing his hat to the wind.

Leading the dash to escape Parral, a group of twenty men rode hard for the mouth of a ravine overlooked by two brushy hills, driving spurs into their horses' ribs relentlessly. A soldier on a streaking sorrel reached the arroyo ahead of the others and sent his horse bounding down the embankment. More riders spilled over the lip of the ravine following the sorrel. Another bunch of men swung wide to reach the top of a hill and disappeared into the brush. A moment later, guns crackled from the hilltop, muzzle flashes winking back and forth from small openings in the bushes. And through this hail of sizzling lead, mounted citizens of Parral charged after the invaders with rifles and pistols blazing. Riding cautiously near the back of the enraged mob, Rudolph Milnor continued to shout encouragement to the pursuers while firing a pistol over his head. Elisa watched him as she urged her black mare through thickening dust. Out of nowhere, she suddenly awakened to an opportunity that could set her free of his sinister grip forever.

Angling her mare away from the main body of riders, she kept Milnor in sight when he made a turn toward a low adobe wall near the outskirts of town. He galloped his Arabian stud to a corner of the wall and reined to a halt, then jumped down to be out of the line of fire from the arroyo and hilltops as the thud of big-bore rifles opened up from the Americans' positions. A Yaqui boy on a sleek pinto pony riding along the same adobe fence was torn from his saddle by a shot from the lip of the ravine. An old musket flew from his hands before he went tumbling to earth, a fist-sized hole in the back of his cotton shirt sending blood showering across the parched ground where he fell. Elisa turned the black sharply and headed for an opening in the wall with bullets flying all around her. A slug struck the top of the fence, ricocheting off in a shower of dust only an instant before her horse raced to safety.

The mare bounded to a sliding stop as she was swinging down. Milnor glanced over his shoulder, then he raised his head above the top of the wall, aiming his automatic pistol at the arroyo. Elisa trotted up behind him, leading her winded horse just as the German's gun exploded three times in rapid succession.

"Shoot at them!" he snapped, without taking his gaze from the raging battle beyond the wall.

"Yes, Herr Milnor," she answered softly, edging closer with the Mauser. "I had planned to do just that." Looking around quickly to be sure no one saw her, she placed the muzzle of her gun against the base of his spine.

Milnor's head turned slightly when he felt something nudge his back. Their eyes met, and in that fraction of a second she knew he understood what she was about to do.

"Schluss der Depesche," she hissed—the way he ended every dispatch to his German superiors—clenching her teeth so tightly that when she said it the words ran together. As she pulled the trigger she saw a kaleidoscope of events flash before her eyes, beginning with the first time he forced her onto a mattress in the stinking hold of the cargo vessel that brought them across the Atlantic. Tiny Christina had been asleep beside her. She had tried not to awaken her sister, even though she suffered the most agonizing pain when Milnor thrust himself inside her.

The Mauser spat lead, slamming into her palm, making a noise that was dimmed by the battle sounds. Something popped like a piece of green wood. Milnor stiffened, his body driven into the adobe wall by the force of the bullet, pinioned there for an instant before his shoulders sagged. Crimson spray splattered across the front of Elisa's white dress, her hand and wrist, and the pistol. The pungent smell of gunsmoke assailed her nose, until a gust of wind passed along the wall, drawing it away. The black mare snorted, neck bowed, frightened by the explosion.

She stepped back when Milnor slumped to his knees as though he was praying at the base of the adobe fence. The flesh of his back lay open where the bullet had cracked his spine. Blood pooled underneath him. He groaned. His pistol fell into the puddle of red steadily growing below his belly. Muscles trembling, he bent over with his hands clasped to his stomach.

"You deserve to die slowly," she spat in German, feeling a rush of emotion, a strange mix of excitement and fear. "I want you to remember the little girl you hurt one night, lying in a bed of rotting fish in a ship's hold crossing the sea. Remember that night, Herr Milnor. The girl wanted desperately to scream, but she would not awaken her sister. Think of that night while you are dying. No one will hear your screams now. No one will ever know why you were found like this. . . . No one but you and I, Herr Milnor. Only the two of us know the reason why your life was ended. Remember that you are a German—this is what you told me when I did the terrible things you asked me to do for the sake of our motherland. Tell yourself that you are dying for Germany, for the Reichstag. Perhaps then you will suffer less."

She whirled away from the wall when a flood of hot tears obscured her vision, to lead her horse from the scene of the battle with the American invaders. What did she care now if the *gringo* soldiers lived or died? It was no longer a matter for her concern. She was free.

• 30 •

Rudolfo Fierro held a pistol in the mouth of Dr. Felix Fuentes while waiting for Doroteo to make up his mind. A fist holding a lock of the physician's hair kept him from backing away from the gun.

"I cannot tell," Doroteo said weakly. "It still hurts so badly. Give me more of the morphine."

Rudolfo arched one bushy eyebrow so that it moved like an inchworm on his sloping forehead. "Give him more," he growled, pulling the gun barrel slowly from the doctor's trembling lips.

"It could be dangerous," Fuentes stammered. "His heart could stop beating."

Rudolfo's face turned black in the candlelight. He tapped the muzzle of his .45 against the doctor's front teeth. "It will be much more dangerous for you if you do not give the general one more injection," he said quietly, his voice belying the menace behind measured words. "It is your heart that will stop beating unless you do as the general asks." His fingers wound even more securely into the man's hair. "And if General Villa's heart does stop, it will only be a moment before I blow off the back of your head and then your heart will stop also."

"The medicine needs time," Fuentes pleaded, moving only his eyes to look mournfully at Doroteo. "Only a few more minutes."

The doctor seemed so sincere. "I will wait then," Doroteo said, wincing when he shifted position on the mattress. The trip in the hack had been a difficult one, moving so quickly from the cave to this root cellar beneath the Yaqui's house at Santa Cruz de Herrera. But there had been no choice, after the girl had led the American spy to his hiding place below Parral. Bouncing along in the back of the buggy, he regretted not having allowed Fierro to kill the woman. The American cowboy had killed Ramon at a peasant's hut and taken his horse. It was sad, to lose a trusted friend like Ramon. A boy and his mother had assisted the *gringo* for money, and Rudolfo said he could not let it go unpunished or there would be others who might help the Americans for pay. An example had to be made of anyone who betrayed the cause, thus it was unavoidable that the woman and her son had to be killed.

More troubling, the spy had eluded Fierro completely in the dark on the road to Satevo. By now the American army knew of his hiding place. They would be searching the mountains south of Parral, and they would know he had been wounded. As soon as he could travel they had to keep moving farther from this part of Chihuahua before the Americans closed a net around him. He knew he had to stay on the move continually to keep from being caught. If only the morphine would work. . . .

Soft sounds from the night alerted him to danger. "I heard something," he whispered, lifting his head. Sweat beaded on his face; he wiped it away with a soiled shirtsleeve and listened.

Rudolfo released the doctor's hair and went cautiously over to the steps, tilting his head. "I do not hear anything," he said softly. "It is quiet. Diego and Porfirio will let us know if anyone comes too close. They are watching the house from the stable where the horses and the wagon are hidden."

"It is too quiet," Doroteo warned, glancing up at the floor of the house above them. "Something is wrong. I can feel it. I know someone is out there. Perhaps it is the voice of God that tells me there is grave danger close by. God has spoken to me concerning these matters many times in the past."

Rudolfo was ready to come back to the bed when he too heard a distant sound. "Horses," he whispered, pulling a second gun from a holster below his armpit. He put down one .45 and cocked the other. With both pistols in his hands he crept up the steps to peer outside.

Doroteo drew a revolver. His hand shook so badly now

that he had trouble cocking the hammer with his thumb. He turned the gun on Fuentes. "Be very quiet, Doctor, or I will kill you myself with a bullet between the eyes."

Fuentes nodded. "Has the medicine helped?" he asked, whispering.

Doroteo thought about it. "Some, I think. Now be quiet."

Seconds ticked away. No more sounds came from outside the cellar door. Rudolfo had disappeared into the dark, leaving him alone with the doctor. His leg was indeed feeling better, and the medicine was giving him a strange calm, even though he was still in grave danger, barely able to move. He looked to the steps. Who had made the noises he heard before? Were the Americans closing in on him? It did not seem possible that they had found him so soon.

Minutes passed. The candle flickered ever so slightly in the stillness. Where was Rudolfo? The calm he noticed earlier had become a sleepy feeling. His eyelids lowered. When it seemed his head had grown too heavy he rested it on the blanket for a moment. It was so quiet, he thought, struggling to keep his eyes open until Rudolfo returned.

He had fallen asleep and was jolted awake suddenly by the sounds of feet on the stone steps. Remembering his pistol, he raised it hurriedly to cover the doctor, although if the doctor had wanted he could have easily killed him while he slept.

An American soldier in a dusty green uniform came down the stairs with his arms in the air. Rudolfo was behind him, a .45 touching the back of his skull. The soldier had blond hair, the same color as the German woman's, and the boyish face of one who was too young to be of much importance to his army.

"Who is he?" Doroteo demanded, "and why did you bring him here?"

Fierro shoved the soldier across the room until he stood in the candlelight. "He is a scout. He speaks no Spanish, but he will know where the rest of the American army is, where they are going. I thought you would want to ask him about the Americans' plans."

"Yes," Doroteo said, his mind clearing of sleep, "I will question him." He gave the blond boy a closer inspection, then he spoke to him in English. "Where is General Pershing now? I warn you to tell me the truth, or you will be shot immediately."

"At Satevo," the American replied. His arms trembled when he answered, and his uplifted hands shook. Rudolfo kept the gun against the back of his head.

"Where are they looking for me?"

The boy's face knitted. "I'm not sure who . . . are you Pancho Villa?"

Doroteo waited a moment. His silence would tell the soldier the truth about who he was. "Where are they looking?" he asked again.

"Holy Jesus," the boy whispered, glancing toward the heavens as he spoke, then his gaze returned to Doroteo, his injured leg, and the gun in his hand. "We was told you was hidin' close to a place named Parral. That's where we was headed when . . ."

Then it was true, Doroteo decided, that the American spy had escaped and directed Pershing's men to the cave at Parral. More than ever now, he found himself wishing he had ordered the death of Elisa Griensen when he'd had the chance. The stupid bitch had betrayed him to an American agent, and it no longer mattered how beautiful she was. "Who is your commander, and where are you going?" he asked sharply, a wag of his gun barrel emphasizing the need for truthful answers.

"Major Robert Howze of the Eleventh Cavalry is in command. We're headed to Parral, same as everybody else. I was told to scout around that village back yonder, Santa Cruz? Major Howze wanted to know if we'd encounter any soldiers there. I was on my way back to the column when I saw this old house. Two men got the drop on me. I wasn't gonna put up no fight bein' all alone."

The terrible pain was almost entirely gone in his leg, and Doroteo felt much better than he had in days. Keeping a wary eye on the soldier, he sat up slowly, preparing more questions. "How many men are with Pershing in Chihuahua?"

"We ain't supposed to tell nothin' like that, only our rank an' our names. My name's Corporal Bobby Williams. I'm from Fort Oglethorpe, Georgia, and that's all I'm gonna say."

Doroteo lifted his revolver, aiming for the soldier's face. "I will give you one more chance to tell me how many men are with General Pershing in Mexico, Corporal, before I kill you. Do you understand?"

The boy's eyes grew rounder. He swallowed, noticing that the man standing behind him had moved to one side to be out of the way of a bullet. "We was told there'd be eight thousand by the time all the columns moved in. I ain't gonna say anymore. I'm not a traitor to my country or nothin' like that. . . ."

A look passed between Doroteo and Rudolfo. Doroteo lowered his gun. The doctor's eyes were on Rudolfo as he quietly took a knife from his belt.

Doroteo gave a slight nod. An instant later, flashing steel went across Corporal Bobby Williams's throat. The boy from Fort Oglethorpe made a choking noise, hands clawing for his windpipe. Rudolfo stepped back, grinning when the soldier went to his knees with blood squirting between his tightly closed fingers.

Fuentes gasped and started out of his wicker chair at the foot of Doroteo's bed, until Rudolfo turned his automatic on him, motioning to sit back down. He fell back on his rump in the chair, watching the American slump to the dirt floor in a pool of blood that had grown large enough to make a splashing noise when he landed in it.

"I feel much better now," Doroteo said in Spanish, as though nothing of any importance had happened. "This medicine is working. Harness the team and we will move tonight. I must speak to Candelario and Julio at once. If the Americans are truly bringing eight thousand men against us we have no choice but to send our brave men farther into the mountains until the *gringos* grow weary of having no one to fight. They will leave before winter comes, and then we will unite again, when the danger has passed."

Corporal Williams still struggled on the sodden earth floor, his legs kicking, drowning as blood entered his lungs. Rudolfo took his eyes off the dying man with obvious reluctance. "I will tell Diego and Porfirio to harness the horses," he said quietly, starting to turn away.

"One thing more," Doroteo added in a thoughtful voice. "I want you to find the German girl, after we get to the hideout at San Isabel. Find her quickly and kill her, before she betrays me to the Americans a second time."

Rudolfo bowed. "Tomorrow will be a good day," he said, the knife remaining in his fist. The corporal had begun his death throes, and he watched them a moment more before going up the steps.

Fuentes witnessed the end of the blond soldier's life without comment, knowing that he was only one mistake away from a similar fate should anything go wrong with the healing of Villa's leg or their supply of morphine. At last, when the corporal stilled, he took a deep breath and inquired, "How do you feel now, General?"

Doroteo could not answer. He had fallen asleep again.

An hour past dawn, as the hack carried him toward a cave east of San Isabel, traveling back roads through the mountains, Diego informed him that the Americans had struck Santa Cruz de Herrera, engaging several hundred of Carranza's *Federales* in a fierce firefight. It was puzzling news. Why were the Americans fighting the Carrancistas? Had General Pershing been given the order to invade and occupy all of Mexico?

He signaled for the doctor to inject him again. He had grown to like Felix Fuentes, and his medicine made him feel good all over. Perhaps he would make Fuentes his personal physician if the leg had no complications getting well.

General Julio Cardenas and Colonel Candelario Cervantes were the only two allowed into the cavern for this secret meeting. He trusted no one with the information he was about to impart to his most trusted commanders. He was without the services of Rudolfo now, until Fierro could find the German woman and bring back her severed head.

He spoke to Cardenas first. "Go to Namiquipa, to Rancho San Miguelito. Stay in hiding there until I send for you. Scatter your men. Do nothing that will arouse the Americans or make them suspect where you are. This is a time to wait. They are too strong."

He addressed Candelario. "Ride back to Tomochic. The Americans will be gone now, to Parral. I will send for you there when the time is right."

Both men nodded their assent. Candelario was the first to leave, while Cardenas hung back until Candelario was moving up the tunnel. There was something on his mind. Cardenas frowned. "I visited a witch in the mountains. It was at Rubio. She told me the cards revealed that my life is in danger."

"Do you believe her—believe in these cards?"

"Yes. They have always been truthful."

Doroteo did not wish to make light of the man's belief in the witches' magic. He was a brave man, a good leader of men in any kind of situation. "Then it is best to hide until the danger has passed. My plan is a good one. Stay out of sight until you hear from me."

"I will ask the witch to pray for your speedy recovery," he said, backing away from the bed.

He waited until Cardenas's footsteps were out of the tunnel, listening for the return of the doctor with his medicine bag. A twinge of pain had begun near his knee, and the wonderful floating sensation from the morphine had passed, leaving him cold, with his skin crawling as if he were a shedding snake.

Diego came with the doctor. Fuentes no longer had to be prodded with a gun. "Give me another injection," he said, his face wet with perspiration. He lay back and closed his eyes to wait for the good feeling to return.

He thought about how good it would be to see his children, and Luz. It would be nice to spend restful time with them, to stop running, hiding. To truly rest for a while, to play with the children in the little garden, to sleep without nightmares and wake up to friendly faces, to wake up without fear of his enemies.

He felt the needle puncture his skin. "Let me sleep," he told the doctor. "Tell Diego to let no one come in."

Imagining the garden in springtime, he let his mind wander to peaceful scenes. Had he grown tired of fighting? After so many years of battling the tyranny of rich men, was it time to lay down his arms and live in peace?

He wondered if his loyal followers across Mexico would brand him a coward if he abandoned the cause. How could he explain to everyone that, in his heart, he had grown weary of constant war? With the Americans blanketing Chihuahua now, was this a war that could not be won? It seemed the forces being rallied against him would soon be too overwhelming to ignore.

• 31 •

The army surgeon's face was grave, his eyes betraying the fact that he bore bad news. "Both the distal tibia and fibula shafts are hopelessly shattered, Mr. Johnson. Large pieces of the bones are missing, I assume as a result of the projectile —the bullet. The tibiofibular joint is severely damaged. The deltoid ligament is torn from the medial malleolus and is protruding through the skin. I might be able to repair that, but so much bone structure is missing, the talus is also fractured, and I'm afraid any type of procedure must fail. There really isn't much left to work with. I'm sure it is very painful."

"Tell me what you just said in plain English," Will moaned, the effects of the painkillers wearing off. "I hardly understood a damn word of what you told me."

"I'm telling you that your lower leg must come off, and it must be done rather quickly. Gangrene has set in. I judge your wound is at least a week old."

"I guess so," Will replied, gazing up at the roof of the hospital tent. He'd lost all track of time during the long ride to Bachiniva, drugged by the laudanum into a state of half-consciousness that barely permitted him to sit a saddle. At Cienegita, one of the soldiers accompanying him commandeered an automobile belonging to a rancher. Will had been placed in the rear seat for the bumpy though much faster ride north to the medical corps at Bachiniva.

He thought about life without a leg, a lifetime spent on crutches or hobbling about on a wooden peg. "Is there any way to try to save it?" he asked, turning his attention back to the white-haired doctor whose ruddy face was without any trace of sympathy he could detect.

"None, I'm afraid. The damage is far too extensive. Even if we had a bone specialist here, I'm sure there is nothing he could do. Amputation is the only solution. We will give you ether, so you'll be asleep during the operation."

He thought of all the things he could never do again without his right leg. "I can still ride a horse, I reckon," he said, to console himself.

"You can be fitted for an artificial limb as soon as you can be sent back to a hospital. In time, you'll adjust to it and it won't seem so bad. There really isn't any choice."

"How much of it?" Will asked, overwhelmed by despair to the point where he didn't think he really cared how much of his leg remained. As a boy he had seen an old man in a Nuevo Laredo cantina showing off what was left of his leg, which ended just below his hip. Someone had tattooed a parrot on the end of his stump, looking grotesque, night-marish, a green bird perched on a flap of dead white skin.

"A few inches below the knee," the doctor explained.

Will chuckled. "I won't ever need to buy a pair of boots again. Does anybody sell one boot at a time?"

"We'll begin right away, Mr. Johnson. My assistant will put a cloth over your nose and mouth. As soon as you can smell the ether, you'll start to fall asleep."

He closed his eyes. "If for some reason I don't wake up, send word to John Abel in El Paso, so the little white pony can be shipped by train to Laredo in care of Raymond Johnson Jr."

"You'll wake up," the doctor assured him. "There will be some pain afterward, but nothing worse than what you've already been through, I'm quite certain."

"I don't see how it could be any worse. But just in case, make sure the pony gets to Laredo if I don't come out of it. I traded a bottle of good whiskey for that pony, an' my nephew is gonna be real surprised when he finds out it's his."

The doctor walked to the rear of the tent, then there was a

clatter of tin pans and instruments and a few soft-spoken words to his assistants. Another face appeared above the table where Will was lying, a man of about thirty wearing lieutenant's bars, staring at him impassively.

"Sorry to hear about what happened," the lieutenant said, glancing down at Will's leg. "I understand you were very close to Pancho Villa when you were wounded. I'm Lieutenant George Patton, aide to Brigadier General Pershing. When you come out from under the anesthetic, I'd like to ask you some questions. The general would like a full report, and so would I. I only wish I could have been with you, getting so close to him the way you apparently did."

Will was only half listening, sorting through unpleasant images—a man hobbling about on crutches trying to accomplish what were once simple tasks. "Maybe, if you'd been there, it would be your leg they're cuttin' off," he said.

"I understand your frustration, Mr. Johnson. It's most unfortunate to lose a leg. When you have awakened and feel a little better, I'll stop by to talk to you. I made a list of questions. I've been pleading with the general that we're going about this all wrong. There's a better way to chase down Villa and his men, and with the information you can give me, I intend to offer my suggestions to General Pershing for a new approach to this campaign."

Will regarded the lieutenant more seriously. In the background he could still hear doctors readying their tools. "There ain't but one way, an' that's to fight him the way he fights. Break this army into smaller bunches. Forget all that other army shit, like marchin' and haulin' everything all over the place in trucks and wagons. Travel light and travel fast, because that's the way Villa travels, livin' off the land. You'll never catch him unless you learn to think the way he thinks."

Lieutenant Patton smiled, yet there was a curious cold fire behind his eyes. "Exactly what I've been telling the general, Mr. Johnson. This is guerrilla warfare, not some textbook example of the proper employment of military strategy like they taught us at West Point. If we fight the Mexican bastards guerrilla fashion, using Villa's own tactics to hit and run when we find them, we can whip their miserable asses in short order and take Pancho Villa back to Washington in chains before the first of June, if not sooner. There is a significant difference between military strategy and sound military tactics. Strategy is merely how one plans and directs a large-scale military operation. Good tactics, on the other hand, require maneuvers that always gain the advantage. For instance, Villa has a number of trusted officers. We could weaken Villa's army significantly by tracking them down one at a time and putting them out of business."

The surgeon appeared on the other side of the table, a white coat covering his uniform, an assistant in a white jacket at his shoulder. "That will have to be enough for now, Lieutenant," the doctor said, as he folded a small square of cloth and placed it gently over Will's mouth and nose.

Patton stepped back, still watching Will's face. "I'll be back as soon as you've recovered sufficiently to talk. I'd like to hear your ideas, Mr. Johnson."

A tin of foul-smelling spirits was held above the cloth, a few drops falling from it that warmed his nostrils with vapors. As a reflex he held his breath for a time, until the images he saw above him grew fuzzy, indistinct, dissolving before his eyes.

Slipping in and out, vaguely aware of sounds, dim sights too blurred to be recognizable. Pain, far away yet still a part of him, his experience. Voices. Indistinguishable words. Someone moaning. Another sound that could have been a scream. Blurred shapes moving around him. Colors, some vivid, others only dark smudges. Thoughts jumbled, making no sense, a scene or two from his past, ending abruptly. If his eyes were truly open he saw a world he did not recognize. Or was all this a strange dream? A nightmare, something he imagined. There was nothing he understood in this place, wherever he was. The sensation of floating grew stronger. He tried to focus his eyes and his thoughts, only to fail miserably, slipping back into a swirling gray fog.

Someone was seated beside him. He awoke to find himself on a cot inside a large tent, its canvas roof billowing in the wind, making a popping noise above his head. A soldier sat on a stool looking down at him, a face he didn't recognize. Glancing to his left, then his right, he saw the tent was lined with cots occupied by sleeping men. "Where am I?" he asked, his voice gravelly, not his own.

"A field hospital," the soldier replied.

"Who are the others?"

"Men wounded at Guerrero, a few more with minor injuries: a rattlesnake bite, a man who was thrown from his horse. How do you feel, Mr. Johnson?"

"I'm not rightly sure. Like I'm drunk."

"It's the morphine. Dr. Reed plans to keep you sedated for a few days."

It required strength, and a certain amount of courage, to lift his head to look down at his feet. He was clad only in his undershorts, and when he saw one bare leg, the other ending in a blood-soaked bandage, he groaned inwardly and shut his eyes. "I'm a cripple now, a pegleg." He sighed. A dull ache began in his right knee, glowing unpleasantly, although never approaching the pain he knew coming from Parral. "At least it don't hurt all that bad. Not like before."

"If you feel up to it, I'm supposed to inform Lieutenant Patton as soon as you're able to talk. He's to fill out a report for General Pershing concerning your . . . incident."

A low moan came from one of the cots on the far side of the tent. Will turned his head.

"That's Private Heberling," the soldier said quietly. "He has a torn lung from a bullet at Guerrero. The doctors don't think he'll pull through."

"I suppose I oughta feel lucky," Will said, remembering the bright muzzleflash he saw on the mountain just before the slug hit his ankle. "A little higher an' that could be me over yonder with a torn lung."

"Do you feel up to talking to the lieutenant now? He's very eager to hear what you have to say."

"I suppose. I can talk better'n I can walk, so I might as well put the time to some use."

The soldier got up and hurried off through the tent flap. Will lay on his back staring blankly at the ceiling, thinking of the rotten turn his luck had taken. A man with just one leg was about as useless as a shirt without a pocket. He wouldn't be able to help Raymond with most of the ranch chores, or dance with the ladies in Laredo saloons. Breaking young horses, something he was good at and enjoyed, was a part of his past. "I'm in this shape on account of a hundred-dollar-a-month job," he muttered. "I knew better than to have any dealings with the army. I've got Lem Spilsbury to thank for this." It wasn't Lem's fault, he knew, but the mood he was in made him fix the blame on somebody.

Minutes later, Lieutenant Patton hurried into the tent with a notepad under his arm. He nodded politely to Will and took a seat on the stool, removing the stub of a pencil from his shirt pocket. "I'm told you are willing to talk to me now, about the night you came close to Villa. By the way, good to see that you are feeling better."

"I wouldn't say I'm all that much better," Will complained. "In case you ain't noticed, I'm missin' a leg."

"I was speaking of the pain, Mr. Johnson. Out in the field, a soldier has to endure a certain amount of hardship."

Will's eyes narrowed. "I sure as hell ain't no soldier, so don't lecture me about what bein' a soldier is supposed to be like, because I never cared to know. I took this job because I need the money. Got no love for the army, so save your breath."

"I won't mention it again," Patton replied, his cheeks a bit flushed. "It was my mistake—I know you are a civilian scout. I want to know where Villa was that night, where you think he is now. In addition, I'd like to hear your ideas on how we can find him and his most trusted associates. The plan I intend to submit to General Pershing must be comprehensive, detailed. If you know where to look for any of Villa's officers, the most likely places to find them, I'd like to hear about it. You know this area well—better than Mr. Spilsbury, according to Spilsbury himself. He says that if anyone can find Pancho Villa and his most important officers, it is you, Mr. Johnson."

Will studied Patton's face a moment. "I thought it was only generals who decided how an army operates. What makes you think the general will listen to your ideas?"

"I'm one of the general's aides, assistant to Lieutenant Collins. We both have the general's ear. With the right suggestions on how this campaign can be conducted, I'm sure General Pershing will listen. Right now he's frustrated by the terrain, and by Villa's unpredictable moves. Villa refuses to engage us out in the open. The fight at Guerrero was only a lucky guess that we would find him there, and now he and his soldiers have vanished."

"They're still around," Will said. "You gotta know where to look, an' you can't take all day gettin' there."

"That's why I'm asking for your advice on where to look. I know how to get there in a hurry. This campaign is both an end and a beginning, an overlap of the old and the new. This will probably be the last mounted cavalry expedition in history, only because it is Villa's nature to fight this way, guerrilla style. Over in Europe, entire armies are being wiped out by artillery and aeroplanes equipped with guns and bombs. It is a mechanized war, according to all reports, and we have allowed ourselves to fall behind in developing similar equipment. This campaign to hunt down Pancho Villa is a test of our war machine, and quite frankly, thus far, we've failed. Villa is conducting this war on his own terms, and if we intend to win, we must be prepared to fight him that way. If I can propose a plan that will weaken Villa's forces and keep him on the run, using his own tactics against him, I know General Pershing will listen."

Will took a moment to think about what Patton had said. "Villa hardly trusts anyone. He's known to have a few officers who he trusts to lead his men. There's this general by the name of Julio Cardenas from Namiquipa, an' he also favors Candelario Cervantes some. Now that Villa's in hiding, those two will most likely be in charge of what army he has left."

Patton had begun scribbling the names on his pad. "The village called Namiquipa isn't far," he said thoughtfully. "If General Cardenas is there, we could surround the town and conduct a house-to-house search for him, but we'd have to know what he looked like."

"There's your major problem," Will said. "None of the local villagers are gonna help you identify him, and he'll claim he's somebody else."

"We'd need someone who knows him," Patton agreed, "or a good photograph. How about Colonel Candelario Cervantes?"

"Hard to say. He could be most any place. He was born in Namiquipa too, I think. It's always been a hotbed for Villa's recruiting. He's tall. Always dresses real fancy, wearin' a silk vest an' a big felt sombrero with a silk braid. I'm told he has a high opinion of himself."

Patton was lost in thought, "Namiquipa is the key. Two of Villa's top men are natives. They'll have family there, friends, supporters. If we watched the village closely, maybe one or even both of them might return."

"It ain't likely they'd stay in town," Will remarked. "If they do come back, they'll stay out in the mountains an' canyons so nobody can corner them."

"We must have someone who can identify them," Patton insisted. "You tell me the local citizens won't betray their countrymen to us. It leaves us with no choice but to have someone else advise us." He jotted a quick note on the pad, frowning.

A stirring of the tent flap announced the arrival of Major James Ryan and Lemuel Spilsbury. Lem saw Will first and hurried over to the cot. He looked at Will's bandage and lost some of the color in his face.

"They took it off," Lem said quietly, needlessly.

"I'll tell your wife you don't need spectacles, Lem," Will said, trying to sound cheerful.

Ryan came to the other side of the bed. "I'm informed you can discredit the report we have that Pancho Villa is dead," he said, making it sound like he doubted it. He glanced at Will's stump. "Sorry to hear about your leg, Mr. Johnson. One of the casualties of war, I'm afraid."

Will saw no point in hiding his dislike for Ryan. "I never was at war with these people, Major. I was fool enough to get in the way while this slow-footed army looked for a war. I was dumb enough to think that a hundred dollars a month was worth the risk I took. So far, I figure I've made about fifty dollars an' it cost me my right leg. To tell the truth, I can't afford any more of your casualties of war, Major. Wish I'd never taken this job in the first place. As to the report that Villa is dead, it's what Villa wants you to think, so you'll give up lookin' for him. He's very much alive, and he was hidin' in the mountains southwest of Parral. A German woman I know took him food and brought a doctor to tend to his busted leg. I've got no special feelin's for Villa either way, but I hope his luck with legs is better'n mine."

The muscles in Ryan's cheeks were working and his eyes

were slitted, but when he glanced around him at Lieutenant Patton and Lem Spilsbury, he controlled his temper and said, "It's unfortunate. The amputation."

"I got you into this," Lem said apologetically, looking down at his folded hands. "I'm sorry, Will. Very sorry."

Patton surprised everyone when he said, "You're still a very important resource to this army, Mr. Johnson. The information you've given me about Villa's leading officers may be just what the general needs to turn this expedition in the right direction. I intend to discuss what you told me with General Pershing right away, and with his permission, you'll remain with our headquarters company in an advisory capacity, at full pay. I feel sure the general will agree with me. Hunting down Villa's trusted field commanders is the best possible way to weaken him."

Ryan was staring holes through Patton. "All intelligence is to be cleared with me first, Lieutenant," he snapped. "I'm not sure I completely trust everything Mr. Johnson is telling us. I have it on good authority that Villa is buried in a cave not far from Guerrero, and I've given General Pershing this information."

Patton, though somewhat shorter in stature and capable of looking boyish at times, came off his stool and stood stiffly erect, shoulders thrown back. "Begging your pardon, sir, but I'm here on direct orders from General Pershing to question this civilian scout and report back to the general at once. I'll be glad to give you a copy of my written report as soon as it is filed, sir. If you have any questions concerning the matter, I suggest you direct them to the general."

Ryan's face was turning red. "You have an insubordinate air about you, Lieutenant, and I fully intend to report it to General Pershing. I know you are well aware that I am chief intelligence officer for this campaign. You should have informed me that you were sent to question Mr. Johnson."

"I didn't feel it was necessary, sir, since my orders came directly from the general."

Ryan looked askance. "Then I'll take it up with him," he said, with less rancor.

Patton turned his attention back to Will. "Of course it's entirely up to you if you agree to stay on as an adviser, but I think the general will agree that we need your services more than ever now. We need to find Cervantes and Cardenas. Others, if you can think of any. I'm convinced the success of this campaign rests not solely on finding Villa himself—for that could take weeks, even months—but in rendering his army useless. Without capable leadership, they won't pose a military threat to us or to any American border towns."

Ryan's flush only deepened, yet he nodded and asked Lem, "Do you agree that Mr. Johnson's counsel would be valuable to us?"

Lem shook his head, still looking down at Will with deepest sympathy. "He knows this country and most of the right people to ask when something is needed, Major. If anybody can help you find out what Villa and his brigands are up to, this is the man."

"How about it, Mr. Johnson?" Patton asked. "Will you agree to stay on as an adviser?"

Will had been thinking about it, about the money. It was the reason he'd ridden the train to El Paso in the first place. "I can't ride a horse for a spell. It'd be a while before I'd be much use."

"If we provided you with an automobile and a driver?" Patton persisted.

He sighed, contemplating the offer. "Let me think on it for a day or two. See how this damn stump feels."

Patton, although he appeared to do so grudgingly, snapped off a crisp salute to Major Ryan and wheeled away from the cot, hurrying through the tent flap like a man on a mission of the greatest importance.

Lem reached down to pat Will on the shoulder. "I'm so sorry this happened, Will. You will be in my prayers. I'll drop by every chance I get to see how you're doing," he added, sounding as if he could cry.

Will merely grunted, noting that Major Ryan's attention was on the tent flap, his jaw tightly clamped, his lips drawn into a thin, determined line.

· 32 ·

Will wrote a letter home, his spelling aided by Lieutenant James Shannon, the newly appointed chief of scouts from Arizona.

16 April, 1916

Dear Raymond and family,

Hope things are going well at the ranch. The check for $100 should help some. Sure hope it has rained there. It is real dry here. No rain in sight either. We are camped near Satevo. They moved us here after a big fight at Parral with some of Carranza's soldiers. The whole country has turned against Americans. I am afraid the cow-buying business here is over for a while.

I have some bad news. I was shot in the foot. The army doctors took off my leg. But don't worry. I am fine. They gave me crutches. Pretty soon I can ride Poco again. Right now they take me all over in an automobile. Don't know how to drive it yet. Probably can't with one foot. I will get a wooden leg when we get back to El Paso. The army pays for it.

I don't know when I will get home. Villa is wounded. We can't find him. His army broke up. But there is still fighting. We are fighting *Federales* now too. Everyone in Mexico is against us. General Pershing says it is like looking for a needle in a haystack. Nobody knows where Villa is.

Army food is bad. The soldiers are bored. Half the army horses are sick. But Poco is fine. A little thin.

Tell Junior I have a big surprise for him when I get back. I will bring surprises for the other kids too.

Sure hope it has rained there.

Will Johnson

Word of the unexpected battle with Carranza forces and local citizens at Parral had come on April 14, the day after Major Frank Tompkins lost three men, six of them badly wounded, including himself, and more than thirty horses from the Thirteenth Cavalry. Will had been hobbling about camp at Satevo when a courier rode in on a lathered horse to give General Pershing the news.

Working his crutches as fast as he could, he arrived at the general's tent just in time to hear most of what was said: that General Lozano, comandante of the Federal garrison at Parral, had warned Major Tompkins to pull out of town before irate citizens rebelled and took matters into their own hands. Will listened closely as the courier explained how General Lozano had informed Tompkins that the military governor of the state of Chihuahua, General Luis Gutierrez, was demanding that America pull every soldier out of Chihuahua immediately.

Shots were taken at Tompkins and his troopers, who had no choice but to retreat from Parral under heavy fire. A running gun battle resulted in heavy Mexican casualties, both Carrancista and civilian, and the deaths of three U.S. soldiers.

Leaning on his crutches, Will had been expecting just such a turn all along. Venustiano Carranza had only loose control over much of his army. General Lozano was defying the agreement that allowed Pershing to track down Villa. All hell was sure to break loose, open warfare from three sides, with the Americans, the Villistas, and the Carrancistas all shooting at each other.

A day later, Major Tompkins brought his troops into camp at Satevo, the day Will's letter to his brother went north with the rest of the mail by automobile. Frank Tompkins came to the hospital tent while Will was having his stitches inspected by Dr. Reed. The major had been struck twice by bullets, once in the shoulder, once across his thigh.

Tompkins was shown to an operating table by one of the corps surgeons to have his wounds attended, but as he limped past Will he came to an abrupt halt to stare at Will's leg. "I see they had to take it off," he said, beads of sweat clinging to his pale cheeks. "Your name's Johnson, isn't it?"

Will shook his head. "Appears you took some lead poisonin' youself, Major. We heard you had a rough time over at Parral."

"The civilians turned on us first. Someone was riding all over town, whipping them into a frenzy, saying that we would take over and burn the place to the ground, killing women and children the way we had at Guerrero. I tried to tell General Lozano that we were only looking for Villa, but some fellow on a gray horse kept shouting to everyone that we were invading their town, that they would all be American prisoners."

"A gray horse?" Will asked, paying closer attention. "What did the man look like?"

As the doctor removed the major's tunic to have a look at his shoulder, Tompkins frowned thoughtfully. "He had a beard, one of those funny, pointed beards. He wasn't a Mexican. Too light-complected."

"Rudolph Milnor, the German I told you about. He rides a gray Arabian an' has a trimmed beard. I told you I heard rumors that he's a German agent."

"Yes, I remember now," Tompkins said, wincing a little when the bandage around his shoulder was removed. "You also mentioned a German woman. I did see a very attractive blond woman wearing a white dress near the plaza. I remember her so well because she was quite pretty. We beat a hasty retreat out of town when a few citizens and General Lozano's men started shooting at us, and I never saw the man or the woman again."

More wounded from the Thirteenth Cavalry were being carried into the tent on litters, followed closely by Major Ryan, Lieutenant Patton, Lieutenant Collins, and a few more officers. When Patton saw Will talking to Major Tompkins, he hurried through the rows of hospital beds at a fast walk. He saluted the major, then he turned his attention to Will.

"What do you make of it?" Patton asked. "Why did the local people turn against our troops?"

"Probably a handful of reasons," Will replied, a bit uneasy when Major Ryan joined them. "Villa is real popular in this part of Chihuahua, but there was help from that German I told you about the other day. Major Tompkins says that Milnor was ridin' all over town gettin' folks stirred up against Americans."

"Is this true?" Major Ryan asked, interrupting before Frank Tompkins had a chance to speak.

"I saw him, the bearded man Johnson described to me on the night he rode into our camp so badly wounded. Sounds like the same man, the same dappled gray horse. He was shouting anti-American slogans, riding back and forth in the crowds, whipping the locals to a fevered pitch."

"But why would the Mexican militia join forces with them to fight us?" Ryan asked. "We have President Carranza's conditional permission to search for Villa."

When no one answered, Will said, "It's real simple. Those Mexican soldiers are mostly from this part of Chihuahua, an' if they think we aim to take over down here and run them off their farms and take their livestock, they'll forget about any of the promises Carranza made to us. It gets mighty personal when a man thinks he's about to lose everything to some foreign army."

Ryan looked at Will a moment, then at Tompkins. "Do you agree, Major? Is that the feeling you had when they started shooting at you?"

Tompkins thought about it. "It could be, I suppose. At the time we were too busy ducking bullets to consider their motives."

Patton caught Will's eye. "Then we'll soon be at war with the government of Mexico as well as the revolutionary forces if this continues. What do you make of the German, this Rudolph Milnor? What's his stake in this?"

Before Will could answer, Ryan asked, "What would a simple Texas cowboy know about Germany's motives? Why are you asking Mr. Johnson?"

Patton regarded Ryan disinterestedly. "Because he knows these Mexican people, sir, and he may have heard what the

German is telling them about us, about America's plans in Mexico."

Ryan pursed his lips, unhappy with the logic, or the fact that Patton wanted Will's opinion. "Continue then, Mr. Johnson. Tell us what you think the German is up to."

Dr. Reed began to wrap a new bandage around Will's stump, ignoring the talk around him. Will thought about the reasons Milnor might have for stirring the citizens up. "Nobody I talked to knows for sure he's a German spy. It's mostly rumor. He came to Parral many years ago with two small girls. He has plenty of money, a big *hacienda,* knows all the right people in town, but nobody knows what he does for a livin'. In my experience, a man has to make his money some way or another, but none of the locals know how Milnor makes his. I saw him hand the German girl an envelope the day I was watchin' her house. I'm only guessin', but it could have been money to finance another army for Villa."

"But that's only supposition," Ryan reminded. "In fact, we have no proof that Villa is still alive."

"Just what the girl told me," Will said as his bandage was tied snugly around his knee.

A short silence followed. Patton appeared to be thinking. "If you are well enough, Mr. Johnson, I say it's time we took a drive up to Namiquipa. Perhaps some of your sources there know the whereabouts of Villa's officers. General Pershing agrees with me that we are rapidly running out of time down here. We must find Villa, or at least weaken his forces. If you're up to the trip, I can request some automobiles and a squad of men for the drive to Namiquipa."

"I reckon I feel good enough to sit the seat of one of the Dodges," he said. "But the folks I know around there won't be as likely to talk to me if we take along a bunch of American soldiers. Maybe if only a few of us went we'd have better luck findin' out what you want to know."

"I'll clear it with the general," Patton said, turning for the front of the tent after saluting Major Tompkins and Major Ryan.

"Tell me, Lieutenant," Ryan said, halting Patton in midstride. "Just what does General Pershing think of wasting so much time hauling this one-legged cowboy all over Chihuahua in an automobile when we have air reconnaissance and more than two dozen very capable civilian scouts who can ride a horse?"

Patton looked over his shoulder. "He thinks enough of it to allow the use of his personal automobile on occasion, Major. I think that fact speaks for itself."

Ryan hadn't been expecting this answer. He merely grunted and looked the other way.

Will pulled himself up on his crutches, nodding to Tompkins but ignoring Major Ryan on his way out of the tent. Outside, he turned for the horse herd scattered across what remained of last year's corn in a field northwest of Satevo. Swinging his stump, the lower leg of his denims pinned up, he made his way awkwardly, avoiding the curious stares of idling soldiers near their tents. He felt humbled by his lack of mobility, embarrassed by it, sometimes feeling it was worse than the physical pain to endure the sympathetic looks others gave him. He was an object of pity, like some street beggar dressed in rags with a tin cup held out for offerings. Perhaps he'd always had too much pride, like his pa, but the Johnsons always got by with whatever they had despite the fact they were poor. Pity was something no Johnson ever wanted no matter how bad things got, his pa used to say, yet now Will was the object of pity everywhere he went and there was nothing he could do about it. He knew he would see sympathy in the eye of every stranger he met for the rest of his life.

Working his crutches furiously to escape lingering looks from the soldiers, he passed the last row of tents and came to the grazing horses. Resting, out of breath, he leaned on the shoulder pads and whistled through his teeth for Poco. Out in the herd, his little bay raised its head, ears cocked toward the familiar sound. Nickering, Poco struck a trot to the edge of the cornfield, anticipating the tiny lump of sugar Will carried in his shirt pocket.

"You're lookin' thin," he said, smiling unconsciously as the bay nuzzled his palm for the sugar stolen from one of the mess tents. Slobbering, the gelding mouthed the cube, then crunched it softly with its molars. "Wish the hell I could ride you," Will added, rubbing Poco's forelock affectionately. "These damn doctors here say it'll be a spell before I can ride. I hate these damn walking sticks, but I suppose I'll get used to 'em."

It was an odd time, perhaps, to think about the private little ceremony he had down at the creek three days after the amputation. Swinging along on his crutches, he'd carried an object inside his shirt down to the stream, away from prying eyes while the soldiers were at mess. It had come to him that morning as he was dressing, when his gaze kept passing over the empty right boot he would never use again. Seeing it every morning was an unwanted reminder of his disability, not that he didn't have enough already; the empty leg of his pants, the crutches. Thus, perhaps only symbolically, he had hidden the boot inside his shirt and crutched his way down to the stream to forever rid himself of its gloom. He'd meant to toss it into the water in a hurry before anyone saw him, but as he held it, readying his swing, he was overcome by emotion and almost cried. It was, in some strange way, akin to throwing his own leg away forever. He looked down at the boot for a time, fighting back the urge to cry, then he flung it into the middle of the clear-running creek and watched it float with the current, experiencing the saddest feeling he had ever known.

He patted Poco's neck as the memory faded. "You're probably happy that some Mexican bastard got my leg," he said, "on account of you'll never feel another spur on your right side again. But don't take the notion that I'll let you get lazy, because I can still spur like hell with my left foot, just in case you get to where you need it."

He swung around and hobbled away from the cornfield. The bay followed him a short distance and then it lowered its head to graze.

The dusty, twisting road to Namiquipa was pitted with deep potholes, jolting the passengers in both cars violently in spots and causing frequent halts for tire repair by the side of the road. Five days had been required to secure enough gasoline for the reconnaissance trip due to a breakdown of a supply column in the mountains on the way to Satevo, where heavy trucks could not pull the steep grades without overheating. Word had come yesterday that Major Robert

Howze, leading his Eleventh Cavalry, attacked a Villista band at Santa Cruz de Herrera, above Parral. Someone had reported that Villa himself was there, hiding in the basement of an old ranch house, but no one was found alive in the cellar after the Villistas pulled out. Someone had, however, executed an American army scout in the basement, cutting his throat. Howze was following the Villistas' tracks toward Ojos Azules, although Will had his doubts that it was Villa's men Howze engaged. By now Villa would have dispersed his soldiers to keep them from being trapped by much larger American forces.

However, two days earlier, Colonel Dodd and four troops of the Seventh Cavalry finally reached the far side of the Sierras after the fall of Guerrero, encountering a Villista force at Tomochic, where a fierce firefight resulted in heavy casualties on both sides. A report of the battle was flown in to General Pershing by one of the last JN-2s still capable of flight, although it crash-landed with a propeller problem during the approach to Satevo, almost killing the pilot.

There were scattered reports of other skirmishes between Americans and small bands of Carrancista forces. The war was escalating on all sides, and Pershing wanted Villa out of commission desperately, to allow U.S. forces to withdraw from Mexico before all-out war with the Mexican government was declared by President Carranza. Thus when Lieutenant Patton continued to insist that a reconnaissance trip to Namiquipa might yield the location of one or more of Villa's trusted officers, not the least of which could be General Julio Cardenas, Pershing agreed and offered his personal Dodge automobile for the excursion. The stated purpose for the trip was the purchase of corn for horse feed. Accompanying Will and Patton were six privates armed with Springfields and a corporal, all from the Sixteenth Infantry.

Patton drove the lead car, racing along at speeds too great for road conditions, which also, due to the noise, made conversation next to impossible. The two soldiers in the rear seat clung to their rifles, exchanging worried looks when Patton rounded a curve too quickly. Cresting a low rise, they dropped into the Namiquipa valley. Will pointed to a small adobe house at the outskirts of the village. "Stop there," he shouted. "We can ask where we can buy corn."

Patton steered the car for the adobe and braked to a halt in a cloud of swirling dust before switching off the motor. A plump Mexican woman came cautiously out on the front porch, glancing up at the noonday sun, then back to the pair of automobiles.

"*Buenos días, señora,*" Will said. Then he added, in Spanish, "Can you tell me where I can buy some corn for our horses? We will pay a good price, and of course, there will be some money for you if you can direct us to the right place."

She came down the steps hesitantly, looking to the center of town to see who might be watching her talk to the Americans. But as it was siesta time, no one was about and no one had come to a window or doorway to investigate the disturbance made by the automobiles. "*Sí, señor. Puede comprar maíz al Rancho San Miguelito.*" She pointed south, down the road to Rubio. Then she suddenly clasped her hand over her mouth and backed away from the automobile, saying, "*No, señor. ¡Cuidado!*"

Will knew the place, a big *hacienda* where he occasionally bought steers in the past. By her actions, the woman realized she'd made a mistake in sending them in that direction. He turned to Patton. "Give the lady a *peso* or two. I think she just told us more than she intended to."

Patton dug into a pocket for coins. "I heard her mention San Miguelito Ranch," he said, handing Will a silver quarter. "I know the way. . . . I was there once before looking for beeves for the quartermaster. No one would sell me any cattle."

Will tossed the woman her coin as Patton jumped from the car to turn the crank himself. The engine coughed once and sputtered to life.

As they were driving away in a cloud of caliche dust with the throttle open, Patton leaned over in the seat to be heard above the roar of the engine and the rattle of springs. "She let it slip, didn't she!" he shouted. "There's more than corn at that ranch! Maybe this time we'll get to see some real action!"

Real action wasn't what Will had in mind. Holding on to the door handle for dear life, he rocked and swayed with each bump and turn in the rocky road as Patton sped to the crossroads and turned south, skidding the tires across loose gravel, kicking up even more billowing dust as they drove toward Rubio at full speed under a blistering sun. Behind them, cloaked in a layer of white caliche powder, the soldiers in the second Dodge did their best to stay up, driving blind into Patton's choking trail of dust.

San Miguelito Ranch lay in a shallow valley surrounded by hills. Patton drove along a sunken roadway eroded by infrequent floods to a spot near the entrance of a walled courtyard. Inside the adobe wall, a magnificent stone house with an unusually tall roof sat in the midst of a semicircle of smaller huts where ranch workers lived. An old man and a small boy were skinning a steer carcass hung from a corner of the *hacienda,* calmly watching the two automobiles full of soldiers grind to a halt near the front gate, as though nothing there was amiss. Will took his crutches and opened the door as Patton and the others got out. He barely had the crutches under him when Patton rushed around to hand him a cocked .45 automatic pistol.

"There ain't no need for that yet," Will protested, although he took the gun at Patton's insistence and tucked it carefully into his waistband. "I'll ask the old man if they have any corn to sell here at the ranch," he added, looking around the quiet, well-tended courtyard. The boy and the old man continued working on the steer carcass with bloody carving knives, paying little attention to the soldiers.

Patton seemed disappointed by the calm. He let a second pistol he was carrying fall beside his leg. "Ask if they've seen any of Villa's men," he said softly. "I've got a strong suspicion that there's more going on here than it looks like." He turned to the corporal. "Place men at each corner of the house. One of you come with me around to the front."

Will pulled his shirttail over the butt of the pistol to conceal it and started for the courtyard entrance on his crutches, one eye on the pair of Mexican butchers. If there was going to be any trouble here, neither one showed it.

Patton and his soldiers dashed around Will unexpectedly

to spread out inside, rather than outside, the courtyard wall. The old man skinning the steer glanced quickly toward the house and motioned to the boy as the soldiers ran to the *hacienda* walls. Will saw the two Mexicans leap behind a butcher block and cower down, watching two big wooden doors at the front of the house, the same direction in which Patton and the corporal were running. At that very instant, Will knew something was wrong.

Wheeling around as fast as he could, he made for the low adobe wall and barely reached it when the twin doors of the *hacienda* burst open. Three men on horses wearing sombreros and bandoliers heavy with cartridges charged out of the house, their mounts scrambling for footing on tile flooring, then the wooden porch. All three Mexicans carried pistols. The rider at the front swung his gun toward Patton and fired off two quick shots, the explosions thundering off the *hacienda* walls.

The corporal dove for cover as Will drew his .45, leaning against the wall for support when he dropped his crutches. But Lieutenant Patton firmly stood his ground despite the gunshots, bringing his pistol up to aim fearlessly at the riders only a few yards away. Patton's automatic fired three times. The first man to ride off the porch toppled heavily to the ground, the pair on either side of him shooting the moment their companion fell. Bullets screamed through the air while the rumble of galloping hooves moved across the courtyard. Patton swung his gun muzzle to the right, still standing erect without dodging any of the flying lead, and pulled the trigger again. The rider closest to Patton flew sideways, knocked from the back of his horse by a slug at close range. Arms and legs windmilling, the Mexican collapsed in a heap near Patton's feet, rolling over a few times before he slid to a stop on his belly.

The third Mexican to flee the house charged toward the gate where Will stood with his elbows propped on the wall, the borrowed .45 aimed at the rider. Precious seconds elapsed as Will steadied the gun, wondering if he should shoot. He squeezed the trigger reflexively when the man rode down on him with a pistol aimed for his head. The heavy automatic bucked in his palm, spitting out a deadly load that could not miss at this distance. The explosion hurt Will's ears, and he felt himself flinch when the gun went off.

As if in slow motion, the Mexican rolled backward off the rump of his galloping horse, driven by the force of impact when the bullet struck his chest. A second explosion occurred unexpectedly, a shell in the rider's cartridge belt igniting accidentally when Will's slug creased the firing cap. The horse shied, terrified by the noises, spilling the rider off its left flank, swerving to race away from the gate. The man's body went tumbling, arms askew when he landed, his pistol skittering across the caliche.

A movement in the courtyard caught Will's attention. The first Mexican Patton had shot crawled up the porch steps, leaving a red smear in his wake, still clutching his revolver. Patton was looking the other way. One of the soldiers cried out, "Shoot him before he gets inside!"

Patton whirled, firing two shots from the hip just as the wounded man crawled through the doorway. Splintering wood flew from the doorjamb. Undaunted, Patton made a dash for the steps, feet flying across the porch to the entrance, where he skidded to a slippery stop in a trail of blood. Aiming down, he fired one last shot that echoed from the bowels of the house. Then eerily, all was quiet again, as quiet as the moment before the three men had attempted their fatal mounted escape.

· 33 ·

Still a little shaken by their sudden deadly encounter, Will leaned on his crutches, studying the face of the dead man lying in the tiled hallway. Patton's men searched the house, finding four women and seven children hiding in back rooms.

"That's him, all right," Will said, answering Patton's long, questioning look after Will first identified the body. "That's Julio Cardenas. I saw him in a parade one time at Juarez. He's one of Villa's most reliable field generals."

"Splendid!" Patton said breathlessly, almost beaming. "What a splendid stroke of luck!"

Will couldn't understand the lieutenant's excitement over having killed a man, still remembering the Villista he shot near the gate, trying to quell a touch of nausea. "Don't it bother you any to kill someone?" he asked.

Patton's expression did not change. "You want to know if my conscience bothers me? It does not. I feel about it just as I did when I caught my first swordfish: surprised at my luck." He turned to the corporal. "Lash the three bodies to the fenders of these automobiles. I want to show off our trophies when we get back to camp. And remember, when the general questions us about this incident, they fired on us first."

Will took a last look at the death mask frozen on the face of General Cardenas. "I wouldn't drive any too slow goin' back through Namiquipa with him tied to a fender, Lieutenant. Might get us shot at by some of his relatives."

Patton caught Will by the arm as he was about to leave the house. "You don't seem all that pleased with what we've done here today. This could be the blow that causes Villa to give up and surrender."

"I kinda doubt it," Will said thoughtfully, gazing out at the courtyard. "Accordin' to what I know about Villa, he don't care all that much for anyone. He'll find another general or two someplace. As to the surrenderin' part, I'll lay odds that'll never happen. Somebody may capture him one of these days, if they get lucky like we just did. But he won't give up without a fight. He's been fightin' one thing or another most all his life, according to the stories about him. I 'spect he'll finally quit for good when a bullet catches up to him."

On the drive back to Satevo Will's leg started to throb. He ignored it as best he could, also trying to ignore the gruesome jiggle of dead bodies mounted on the fenders like prizes after a deer hunt. The killing of Cardenas was sure to touch off even more anti-American sentiment in the region. Pershing's soldiers could expect more trouble from the citizenry when word of the general's death spread. Cardenas was a local hero of sorts, operating in the shadow of a much larger hero, Pancho Villa. Cooperation from mountain villagers would be slight when Pershing's army sought information, staples, or fodder for their horses. In the back of his mind Will was certain the expedition was destined to failure anyway. Villa would surface again when his leg healed.

A front tire blew out suddenly as they were climbing out of Namiquipa. Patton braked to a halt, pounding his fist on the steering wheel angrily. "We have to make it back before dark!" he cried. "Everyone must have a chance to view the bodies!"

Two privates scurried from their seats to fix the flat.

It was dusk by the time their grisly procession drove into Satevo. Soldiers everywhere stopped to watch the automobiles with bloodied corpses lashed to the front fenders go by. Patton made a special effort to display the bodies in front of as many men as possible, taking the longest possible route to reach General Pershing's tent, driving slowly through growing crowds of curious troopers gathering to watch the macabre parade. Patton's fascination with a public showing of the corpses made Will shudder inwardly. Although the brash lieutenant had demonstrated unusual courage at San Miguelito Ranch, it was the aftermath that made no sense, this preoccupation with exhibiting the result of their skirmish. He wondered how anyone could find a similarity between killing men and catching swordfish.

As soon as the Dodge braked in front of the command tent Will bailed out as quickly as he could, swinging his stump away from the crowds assembling around the automobiles with his face lowered, avoiding sympathetic stares. Today more than ever, he wanted no part of the army. It seemed his life had taken a terrible turn, almost from the day he arrived at Fort Bliss to accept the army's offer. Not much had gone right since then, and if he could somehow alter the course he had chosen for himself by boarding that El Paso train he would still have both legs and some hopes for a modest future in the livestock business.

He avoided the mess tents, finding he had no appetite, nor could he stomach the thought of returning to his hospital tent right then. Something inside him demanded that he spend some time alone, thinking things through. Not that there was all that much to think about, really, for his die was cast now. He had no choice but to continue taking the army's money as long as they would pay him, or until a letter came saying it had rained at Laredo. He had to come to terms with the fact that he was now a cripple, no longer able to totally fend for himself. In the years to come he would be dependent upon his brother for support, he supposed. It was the blackest thought he could imagine.

Outside of camp he crutched to an isolated knoll with a view of the horse herd. It required some effort to struggle to the top where a thicket of slender oak trees would hide his presence. He reached the trees and lowered himself to the ground, badly out of breath from the climb, and rested against an oak trunk. In the fading light he looked down at his legs, the usable one and the horrible stump. After a moment of self-pity he shook his head and looked up at the sky.

"It ain't fair," he said bitterly, addressing some vague presence he felt near him, wondering if it might be God. The only time Will ever remembered his pa discussing the subject of God, Lee confided that anyone with good sense should have some difficulty believing in someone nobody could see. "There's this story my ma used to tell me at bedtime," Lee said, "about somebody called an emperor who thought he had an outfit of brand new clothes. But he'd only been fooled into thinkin' he was wearin' fancy clothes. Everybody else could see 'em, a tailor told him, only he couldn't see the clothes himself, so he took off one day to go to town, naked as the day he was born, believin' he was wearin' them invisible duds. Believin' in some invisible God is 'bout the same thing, Willie. A man with good sense is gonna expect to see somethin' once in a while. I went to church four or five times when I was a kid, an' not once durin' all that time did anybody show up claimin' to be God. There was only this preacher feller askin' for money, passin' a big plate around whilst the congregation was singin' and prayin'."

Remembering his father only saddened him more. Lee Johnson, through good times and bad, had always managed to provide for his family and himself. Johnson pride would never have allowed any other way. What was Will to do with his inherited pride now that he was a useless cripple? How could he swallow his pride to accept help he didn't want when he couldn't function without it?

"I reckon I'm just feelin' sorry for myself," he whispered, resting his head against the tree. Off in the distance, sounds from the army camp reached the knoll on a breath of wind. "I know one thing for sure," he continued, sighing, "I've got to get the hell away from this craziness. I ain't gonna kill nobody else, not for all the money in the world. These silly bastards can go on shootin' each other, playin' soldier all they want, but I won't do any more of it." He had two deaths on his conscience now and they weighed heavily on his mind, despite the knowledge that both men would have killed him if they could.

Gazing off toward the northeastern horizon, in the direction of Laredo, he thought about his brother, Junior, and the ranch. He sat quietly, feeling lonely, his heart harkening to the call of family and home for a while. Later, when darkness was complete, he made up his mind to head back to Texas. Some things were more important than money. If there was a lesson to be learned from his brief experience soldiering in Mexico, it was that life was more precious than most men realized. Three times in less than two months he had come face to face with death, placing himself in front of blazing guns, all for the sake of a few dollars in his pockets. The risk wasn't worth it. Some men, like George Patton and Colonel Dodd, thrived on the excitement, like it was all a game. It wasn't the sort of game Will Johnson belonged in.

Perhaps as another way to punish himself, he thought about Elisa and their tender time together. He told himself that she did not attach the same importance to it, that he was just another man in her bed. After all, she slept with Villa, according to rumor. She was a remarkable woman in many ways, strong enough to stand on her own, make her own choices, not like most of the mewing females he had known around Laredo. But fate had ordained that he could not be with Elisa. She'd probably slept with him on a whim, or, more likely, believing it would further the cause she believed in. He thought about that. Did he truly believe in Villa's revolution?

Elisa wouldn't want a one-legged man anyway.

He cast a curious shadow in the starlight on his way down the hill, that of an incomplete man supported by a pair of thin sticks. When he saw his shadow he was convinced he had reached the right decision to leave the army. An inner voice told him that his shadow was in the wrong place at the wrong time, and unless he took it elsewhere he might well lack the substance to block out the light much longer, for no light was shed at the bottom of a grave.

"You have given us valuable service," General Pershing said, appraising Will carefully from the running board of his Dodge. "I am truly sorry to see you leave. I had hoped you would reconsider. I'll have Lieutenant Collins draft a letter to the commander at Fort Bliss, requesting that your pay be continued for one year. That should give you more than ample time to adjust to the loss of your leg. It was unfortunate, what happened. You acted bravely, going on your own to try to find the location of Villa's hideout. Worthy of a commendation. I hope things go well for you, Mr. Johnson. Corporal Legget will drive you to Columbus in one of the supply trucks and see to it that you get aboard the train."

"I wonder if I can arrange to have my horses sent back, the little bay an' the buckskin," Will asked, resting against the side of a three-ton Jeffrey Quad truck that would take him back to El Paso.

"I'll see to them," Lem Spilsbury said, before the general could speak. "I'm headed back to Colonia Dublan. Got word my wife has a touch of the fever. I'll string the horses to mine and see to it that they get to the shipping pens at Fort Bliss."

"I'd be grateful," Will muttered, thinking of Poco.

Pershing still watched him closely. "What do you think of our chances now regarding the hunt for Villa?" he asked.

"Mighty slim," Will answered truthfully. "But they were slim from the start, and I told you that. Chihuahua is Villa's territory, his backyard. He could be hidin' under that next truck yonder an' nobody'd find him. He knows how to blend in with his surroundings, General, like an Indian, which is what he is. I doubt you'll ever find him."

"I hope you're wrong," Pershing said quietly, looking down at his boots for a moment. "It's going to look bad in Washington if this expedition comes up emptyhanded. Even now, Funston wants to know why he hasn't heard from us. From me."

"I've never been to Washington," Will said. "Maybe folks up there don't know enough about Chihuahua. This place is a hundred years behind the times an' it don't appear to be in any hurry to change. Maybe if you explained that to whoever is in charge of the army, they'd understand."

Lieutenant Patton strode over to shake Will's hand. "I want to thank you personally for what you did at San Miguelito Ranch, Mr. Johnson. You showed courage under fire, and without your help, General Cardenas would still be a thorn in our side. I do wish you would reconsider and stay on with Headquarters Company as an adviser."

He took the handshake and simply wagged his head, not wanting to discuss things further. Turning to the young soldier introduced as Corporal Bob Legget, he said, "I'm ready whenever you are."

Legget, a slender boy from Maryland with gangling legs and ropelike arms, pointed to the front of the line of trucks parked along the roadway and said, "We're awaiting orders to pull out from Sergeant Pike. It shouldn't be long."

Will started for the cab of the truck on his crutches, with a thought to the twisting mountain road to San Isabel, then Agua Caliente, and the long stretch back to Columbus, a distance of almost four hundred miles. He gave the four-wheel-drive truck a sideways glance, hoping it would take him that far without breaking down. As he came to the passenger door, Lem caught up to him.

"I feel just awful about your leg, Will. I thought I was doing you a favor, getting you this job."

"Don't fret over it," Will told him, seeing the hurt in the tall Mormon's eyes. "It wasn't your fault. I followed that woman when I shoulda known better. I'll be obliged if you see to it that Poco and the dun get to Fort Bliss."

"Consider it done, old friend. They will have the best care I can give them."

A shout came down the line of waiting trucks, the order to pull out. With Lem's assistance, Will climbed into the cab of the Jeffrey and laid his crutches beside the gearshift lever.

Corporal Legget cranked the noisy engine, which produced a shivering vibration in the cab that shook the thinly padded bench seat. Trucks ahead of them moved off. Legget climbed in, ground the gears, and let out the clutch. With a sudden lurch the empty truck went forward, accompanied by a whining sound below the floorboard.

Will settled against the back of the seat, preparing for a week of jolting travel inside the hard-tired Jeffrey. The convoy would move slowly through most of southern Chihuahua due to the terrain. It would be a test of a lifelong horseman's nerves getting used to the bouncing and the drone of an engine. Right then Will found himself wishing for a bottle of good whiskey.

"Maybe later on," Legget shouted above the noise, "you'll tell me about the time you got shot. I've been worrying about getting shot myself ever since we got down here. I'm sure it hurt like the dickens. What's worrying me most is I'll find out what it's like to die, or get wounded real bad the way you did."

"It was mighty painful," Will remembered.

The truck bounced over a pothole, springs cracking, swaying the cab. Legget cursed and changed gears.

"They call these roads. Back home, we wouldn't call this a satisfactory ditch. It's no wonder the trucks keep breaking down. Mexico has got to be the roughest, ugliest place on earth. I sure hope we get to go back home pretty soon."

Will gazed out the window. He'd always found the Sierras beautiful, but then he'd never been to Maryland to make a comparison. Looking through the front windshield, the line of trucks crept away from Satevo into the mountains, canvas tops swaying back and forth over the uneven ruts toward San Isabel. Dust rose from the tires, spiraling into cloudless skies. He wondered if it was raining anywhere in the world.

The column stopped unexpectedly near the top of a mountain pass almost an hour later. Corporal Legget leaned out the window to see what was causing the delay.

"A flat tire on one of the other trucks," he said, switching off the motor. "We'll be here a while. Might as well get out and stretch your legs." He looked down quickly at the floorboard, realizing what he said. "I'm sorry, Mr. Johnson. I plumb forgot about . . . your other leg."

"It's okay," Will said, seeing the boy's embarrassment. "I might as well get used to it. And call me 'Will' from now on. All that 'mister' stuff ain't necessary. I'll get out an' stretch what I've got while they're fixin' the tire."

Legget seemed relieved. "Call me 'Bobby.' I'll fetch us a drink of water from the back while we're waiting."

Will had some difficulty climbing down from the cab with his crutches, but he made it. A muscular soldier came down the line, his campaign hat at an angle, inspecting the rest of the vehicles with a cold, unfriendly stare.

"That's Sergeant Pike," Legget said, handing Will a tin cup of tepid water. "He's looking for any excuse to chew ass among the drivers. He's the hardest man to please I ever met. He'll find something to gripe about when he gets here."

Legget's prediction came to pass as soon as Sergeant Pike came to the truck. "That goddamn hood isn't latched!" Pike snarled, aiming a blunt finger at Corporal Legget. "If you're too goddamn lazy to fasten a simple latch, Corporal, then I'll find another driver and you can pull sanitary duty!"

"I'll fix it, Sergeant," Legget said, hurrying around to the front of the Jeffrey.

The sergeant gave Will a stern look, his square jaw jutted belligerently. "What the hell are you staring at, mister?" Pike bellowed.

The tone of the question struck Will the wrong way. "I reckon I'm lookin' at a two-legged jackass, soldier boy. There ain't no law against lookin', is there?"

Pike's face flashed bright red. "If it wasn't for those crutches, I'd teach you some manners," he said, balling his hands into fists.

"Don't let that stop you," Will snapped, ready to face any challenge now that his dander was up. "I've still got two hands, an' if I get the chance, I'll use 'em on you. I don't have to take any shit off some stuffed-shirt son of a bitch in a uniform, soldier boy. I ain't a part of this damn army."

The sergeant took a step closer, his chin turned to granite. "I can whip your ass with one hand tied behind me," he said evenly, hooding his eyes.

Legget stepped between them. "I wouldn't do that, Sergeant. This man is a personal friend of General Pershing. It could get you court-martialed. Besides that, I wouldn't stand by and let you do it. I'd have to try to stop you. This man's only got one leg."

Pike glared at Legget, then at Will. His fists relaxed. "I never pick on a cripple anyway," he said, spitting the words out like they had a bad taste. He pointed to the hood latch. "Don't ever let me find anything wrong with this vehicle again, Corporal." At that, he marched off with his shoulders squared, boots grinding over small pebbles in the road.

Will watched the sergeant's back a moment. "I've taken a real dislike for that bastard," he said, his temper cooling.

"You've got plenty of company," Legget said quietly, also looking at Sergeant Pike. "Every soldier in this outfit hates him. One of these days, somebody's likely to suffocate him in his sleep."

Half an hour later the column started to move again. Will stared through the windshield, nagged by a disconcerting thought. It was something Bobby Legget said that put him to thinking. How many boys like Legget would die or be seriously maimed if fighting in Mexico continued? By refusing the army's offer to stay on as an advisor he supposed it could be said of him that he felt he had no duty to his country to help stop a border war that might some day threaten Raymond's ranch and his family. And it was old Es Ki Ben De who said that he would feel differently if bandits had burned his own house or killed members of his family. The innocent people who died at Columbus had no stake in the Mexican revolution, yet it made no difference to whoever led the attack.

It was all so confusing. He was not accustomed to having thoughts dealing with notions like patriotism or duty. Wasn't it enough that he had lost a leg to such foolishness?

He found he was forced to consider the possibility that he might be doing the wrong thing by leaving now.

• 34 •

Deputy Chief of Staff Tasker Bliss and almost everyone else at the War Department was dreading this hurriedly called meeting like the arrival of the black plague. President Wilson's reaction to Pershing's first written appraisal of the future of the punitive expedition was, as Hugh Scott put it, predictable as the coming sunrise. Pershing's report, wired to General Funston at Southern Command headquarters in San Antonio, contained a proposal that would escalate Wilson's growing concerns to the breaking point. This morning's meeting with cabinet members and Wilson's key military advisers to discuss Pershing's bold plan could have only one outcome: Pershing would be relieved of his command. A proposal to General Obregon, Carranza's new minister of war, was being drafted by the State Department at Wilson's request, to suggest that a joint conference take place between Obregon, Hugh Scott, and Fred Funston, to find ways to end growing hostilities between American forces and Carranza's soldiers. Wilson believed that Scott could persuade Obregon peacefully, whereas Pershing's plan called for action that was sure to leave Mexico with no choice but to issue a declaration of war against the United States.

Woodrow Wilson entered the room, flanked by Secretary of State Robert Lansing and the secretary of war, Nelson Baker. It was quite clear the three had talked privately before the meeting. Admiral Josephus Daniels, secretary of the navy, was seated at one end of the conference table with his head bowed meekly, a sure sign that his vote would be cast in Wilson's favor, a vote against Pershing's suggested strategy. Ever since the admiral's bungled handling of the incident over the prisoners taken from the U.S.S. *Dolphin* by Huerta's Mexican troops at Tampico, Secretary Daniels could be counted on not to make waves in Wilson's foreign policy. Senator Henry Cabot Lodge and a number of others in Washington stood behind the navy's ultimatum to release the prisoners and hoist the American flag over Tampico with a twenty-one-gun salute. But the affair had incensed Wilson, forcing him into a position he felt he had to defend publicly. After things cooled down with the fall of Huerta to the Carranza revolution, Secretary Daniels was summoned to the president's office to face a broadside from which he never recovered. Daniels could be counted on to vote for anything the president wanted now, even if it meant turning the U.S. Navy into a fleet of recreational fishing vessels.

Hugh Scott walked in briskly from a rear door with a copy of Pershing's report in a dog-eared folder. Everyone in the room had seen the report a dozen times yet Wilson would require that it be real aloud, thus to attack it item by item, piece by piece. Scott dropped the folder unceremoniously on the table beside Bliss and took out his handkerchief to clean his glasses while the others present pulled back chairs and sat down. Bliss began to feel uncomfortable. A general's military career was on the line this morning, and Bliss was feeling more than a little culpability. An army, an entire wartime industry, had been mobilized to hunt down just one man, apparently the wrong man, on foreign soil, and the campaign was failing miserably. Now the manhunt was on the brink of becoming a war between neighboring nations, and only one man present at this meeting knew the truth: The hunt for Pancho Villa had been launched based on misinformation. The whole thing was a terrible mistake, a fraud perpetrated by someone in the de facto government of Mexico, possibly Venustiano Carranza himself. The deception was about to end the promising military career of John Joseph Pershing, a man he truly liked, and there was nothing Bliss could do to put a stop to it without exposing his own role in it, his own negligence.

President Wilson, always austere, watched Hugh Scott clean his eyeglasses and then sit down. "Gentlemen," Wilson began in his usual monotone, "we have come to consider a very grave matter of no small importance to the future of this country. As you know by now, Pershing has submitted his initial summary of the punitive expedition thus far, and I must say it is dreary, at best. General Scott, please read from Pershing's wire to Fred Funston where he proposes the course of action he wishes to pursue."

Scott put on his spectacles and read silently down the page until he came to the final paragraph. " 'In order to prosecute our mission with any promise of success it is therefore absolutely necessary for us to assume complete possession, for the time being, of country through which we must operate; and establish control of railroads as means of supplying forces required. I therefore recommend immediate capture by this command of city and state of Chihuahua, also the seizure of all railroads therein.' "

Wilson looked down his nose. "Pershing proposes a military takeover of one of Mexico's largest and richest states in order to lay hands on a lone bandit, Pancho Villa. Such an action will mean all-out war with President Carranza and the people of Mexico. We must not become embroiled in a war along our southern border. War looms larger in Europe than ever before, with Germany calling for unrestricted submarine warfare on the high seas. What Pershing suggests is a very dangerous policy. We simply must find another course."

"I agree," Nelson Baker said, fixing Scott with an accusatory stare. "We went along with the recommendation that Pershing lead this campaign, however we must not let him set policy. He may be a competent soldier, but he clearly lacks statesmanship. Diplomacy is called for, not a military takeover of an entire region while we look for a rogue bandit. What Pershing proposes here is preposterous. Let's look for a better solution."

"Well said," Secretary Daniels muttered, unable to look down the table at his army counterparts. "Let us use diplomacy first, until all peaceful avenues have been exhausted."

Hugh Scott dropped the report in front of him, pursing his lips, fingering his mustache while his cheeks were turning red. "I can assure you that if John is calling for a seizure of the railroads it is necessary to the success of his mission."

Wilson had begun shaking his head before Scott was finished. "The Mexicans are now demanding a complete withdrawal of American forces. Our reaction to their latest demands cannot be a seizure of their railroads and full military occupation of the state of Chihuahua. Pershing appears to be wandering rather aimlessly across the desert, skirmishing with Carranza's forces when he is unable to locate any of Villa's men. On the surface of it, one might conclude that Pershing is looking for a fight anywhere he can find one."

Bliss decided to come to Pershing's defense. "General Pershing has always shown the best of judgment. He would not provoke any difficulties with Carranza soldiers. On the other hand, we know full well Carranza is quite capable of saying one thing while he does something else behind our backs, His record speaks plainly for itself."

"He is unpredictable," Baker agreed, "but we can't let our frustrations with Pershing's failure to locate Villa influence us to start a war with a neighboring country. The defense of our shared border would become a monumental task, and the American people would have a strong negative reaction to a policy of war with Mexico. The votes would not be there in Congress for a declaration. There has been enough grumbling the way things are now."

"Let us hear what General Scott proposes," Wilson suggested, "which I am sure will be more in keeping with our wish to remain in a firm neutral posture."

Scott scowled at the head of the table, which Bliss knew might be mistaken for displeasure over something when in fact it was simply that he was squinting to see.

"We have three options," Scott began. "We can act upon Pershing's recommendations and drive straight through by force, taking over the railroads in Chihuahua, but this will not result in the capture of Villa, who can go clear to Yucatan if he wants. Pershing could, on the other hand, concentrate his forces to the north, near Casas Grandes, where he could protect our Mormon colonists there and have water and forage for his horses and men. We could maintain these forces there indefinitely as an incentive to Carranza forces to kill or capture Villa. Our final option is to withdraw the expedition altogether, which would clearly be an international embarrassment. The second option seems best, if we can secure the agreement of General Obregon that there will be no clashes between our forces and his."

"I have mixed feelings about remaining in Mexico at all," Baker said quickly. "I'm in favor of pulling Pershing out before something else goes wrong. Quite frankly, Pershing's attitude frightens me. We undertook this campaign as a police action to bring a criminal to justice, and now Pershing is calling for a full-scale military occupation of Chihuahua. I'm sure we all expected the punitive expedition to meet with early success, but in view of Pershing's repeated failures to locate Villa, I feel we run too many risks by leaving him there any longer."

"Withdrawal now makes us a laughingstock," Scott argued. "I will confer with Funston and then meet with General Obregon at the earliest possible date." He peered at Secretary Lansing. "When will you have the proposal ready to send to Obregon?"

Lansing rubbed a hand through his silver hair, worsening a mass of tangles he seldom bothered to comb. "As soon as the president has approved it, we could get it off as early as tonight."

Wilson squirmed uncomfortably in his chair. "I'm worried about what might happen in the meantime. Pershing seems bent on having his way. If we can only restrain him from any further engagements with Mexican regulars we may avoid an ugly incident that could propel us into a war no one wants. By no means shall we authorize Pershing to take over Mexican railroads or occupy any cities in Chihuahua. Inform him of that immediately through General Funston. Arrange a conference with General Obregon at the earliest opportunity and convey to him that we wish to avoid any difficulties with his soldiers. America does not want war. Our agenda continues to be domestic reforms, not international intervention. It would be the irony of fate if my administration had to deal chiefly with foreign affairs when there is so much to be done within our own borders. I have promised the voters that we would break up the trusts and the interlocking directorates to get these dollar diplomats out of Washington. I no more than set foot inside the door of the White House and found I was confronted with a possible war in Europe and now war with Mexico. I shall not be pushed into a war, gentlemen. Let us go about the business of finding another way to accomplish our objectives."

Secretary Baker was still unhappy. "There are those who say America has already declared war against one man, a single bandit who is hardly worth serious mention on an international scale. If we pull out now and admit our folly, we will have shown the rest of the world that we are a civilized nation earnest in our pursuit of peace."

Hugh Scott's face was scarlet. "Peremptory withdrawal now would be disgraceful. Driving forward could mean war. My compromise solution does neither. We order Pershing back to Casas Grandes and wait for Villa to surface. He is badly wounded, so we have been told, making him less likely to be a nuisance for the time being. I will confer with Obregon and persuade him of our intent to conduct the search for Villa without any disruption of Mexican politics. Mexican leaders are, as a general rule, like bantam roosters who feel they must crow a lot and perform a good deal of ritual posturing. But when the chips are down, they seldom are as tough as they wish to appear, mostly feathers and hot wind. Villa may be the one exception to this rule. I truly believe he is every bit as tough as he acts, and certainly he is clever."

"He has gall," Lansing remarked, mussing his locks again. "Or he could be certifiably insane, attacking Camp Furlong the way he did, with fewer than five hundred inexperienced men who appear to have been armed with little more than slingshots. His actions may have been those of a madman driven over the brink of reason."

Tasker Bliss unconsciously sank lower in his seat upon hearing a recounting of the Columbus raid. Six of those men Lansing said were armed with slingshots that night still had the potential to bring down any number of Goliaths in Washington until Major Frank Lawson carried out his special assignment.

Hugh Scott pushed back his chair. "I can assure you Villa is not mad. Brash, perhaps, but he knows what he is doing, and I am sure this is why John is experiencing so much difficulty finding him."

Wilson cast a worried look out a window, pinching his brow, a habit worsened by the duties of high office. Everyone on the Hill knew he was a domestic reformer without experience or skill at international diplomacy. Tasker had been a witness to his indecisiveness on countless occasions, but as time passed he only became more unsure of his position on world events.

"While he may not be insane," Wilson mused, "he has shown a decided tendency to disregard all logic at times. Attacking an American town fortified by a military base with only a handful of poorly equipped rabble rousers is hardly the mark of a man in full possession of his senses. I simply cannot understand why Pershing is experiencing so much difficulty finding him. We have put ten thousand men afield at Pershing's disposal, and they seem to be unable to locate him."

"They almost had him at Guerrero," General Scott said, still fuming over Secretary Daniels's refusal to take a side with the military on what was clearly an issue calling for a military solution.

Wilson glanced down the table at Scott. "When I was a boy I almost landed a magnificent speckled trout, a ten-pounder to be sure. I had him almost to the bank when my line broke and it got away. Anyone can see there are two versions of this tale—mine and the trout's. I almost caught a fish and the trout almost got caught, however the net result is the same. I had a bowl of oatmeal for my supper and the fish, perhaps a bit wiser, remained free."

Scott was not interested in fishing stories. "The rainy season will begin soon in Chihuahua, and this will render all roads impassable. We won't be able to supply Pershing without the use of the Mexican Northwestern Railway from Juarez to Casas Grandes. A decision must be made."

Wilson sighed. "Confer with Obregon as soon as possible. Your second option seems to be the only course we have. Notify Pershing at once that he will be pulled back to Casas Grandes."

At the president's signal everyone got up. Bliss felt a bit queasy as he and Hugh Scott walked out of the room. Was a time bomb ticking somewhere that could rattle the foundation at the War Department? Today he felt like the little Dutch boy with his finger in a leaking dike. Until Frank Lawson completed his task and the punitive expedition came to some sort of conclusion, he dared not wiggle the finger. Scott was worried about a disgrace if the expedition was withdrawn. Only Bliss himself had reason to ponder the enormity of an international embarrassment if it were learned that American military leaders had failed to find out who their target should be before wielding a vengeful sword.

The meeting had produced one favorable result: For the present, Scott's second option put most of Wilson's worries to rest, saving Pershing's ass. Now if Pershing would only behave himself and cease his demands for a military take-over, Wilson might leave him in command long enough for a face-saving miracle to occur.

When Tasker returned to his office he found an envelope

marked "Confidential" resting on his desktop. He opened it with some misgivings, until he noted that the message came from Major Frank Lawson:

Major General Tasker H. Bliss

Our six "guests" have departed by merchant vessel from the port of Galveston, bound for the fishing village of Celestion in the Bay of Campeche at the southernmost tip of Yucatan. It is most doubtful they will ever be heard from again. I am quite sure we persuaded them that a return to the north of Mexico will be contrary to their continued good health. Each was given a small amount of money from my discretionary fund. The deputy sheriff in El Paso has willingly accepted a position with the U.S. Border Patrol, at a substantial increase in pay, which he assures me will help him forget the El Paso incident entirely.

Tasker folded the message and put it into an inside pocket of his coat. Frank Lawson had stamped out the last sparks of a potentially dangerous fire. A catastrophe of grand proportions had been narrowly averted.

He let out a satisfied sigh.

• 35 •

George Dodd aimed a boot at the empty tequila bottle and gave it a swift kick. Glass shattered, sprinkling over the two blanketed forms sleeping beneath a pine tree. Captain Shaw flinched and looked the other way, dreading the next order from his commander. Tired cavalrymen stood red-eyed from lack of sleep beside their spent horses. A man groaned softly at the rear of the column, slumped in his saddle, one of the four wounded from Tomochic who had suffered the agony of another forced march in spite of a bullet hole in his thigh.

"Maybe General Sherman was right," Dodd muttered, turning away in disgust when he could not rouse Es Ki Ben De or Loco Jim from a sound slumber. His gaze went to Captain Shaw. "Sherman said the only good Indian is a dead Indian, and today, finding our scouts in this deplorable condition, I'm inclined to agree with Sherman. Were it not for the fact that I would face dire consequences for my actions, I would order them put before a firing squad this very minute. Have someone lash these poor creatures to the backs of their horses, Captain, before I change my mind and shoot them myself. Even that would seem a waste of perfectly good ammunition."

"Yessir," Shaw said, beckoning to Corporal Eddings and his squad. "Tie those Apaches to their horses!" he shouted. "And be quick about it!"

Dodd walked stiffly to his horse. When the scouts had not returned yesterday he suspected foul play and doubled the guard around their camp. Learning that the Indians had merely gotten too drunk to find their way back from Parral was almost more than he could take. Indians had never proven to be all that reliable in the service of the army, in his judgment, but Pershing wanted them in spite of their numerous faults, a lazy nature being their most prominent feature. And, they had no tolerance for alcohol. He meant to ask Pershing for the cowboy named Johnson when they got back to the main column. Will Johnson had shown savvy and good natural instincts while leading them over the mountains to Guerrero. In private, Dodd mistrusted any soldier who was not white. In his opinion, Negroes were often dull-witted and could not be hurried, Mexicans were never to be trusted, and Indians were generally too slovenly to adapt to army life. What he knew about Chinamen was not all that promising. An all-white regiment, well trained and properly equipped, made the most dependable fighting force.

As two soldiers attempted to lift Es Ki Ben De over the back of his horse, he awakened from his stupor and began to struggle. "Put me down!" he cried, making one feeble effort after another to free his arms and legs. "Where you take me? Gimme whis-key!"

Dodd shook his head and climbed woodenly into the saddle. It was no wonder Pancho Villa eluded them so effortlessly, when they were forced to depend on a couple of drunk Apaches to find his tracks. Villa would continue to run loose forever at this rate. Dodd was reminded of his hollow promise to Pershing, that he would deliver Villa on a silver platter before the first week was out. Almost three weeks later, there had not been so much as a glimpse of Villa's ass by anyone wearing an American army uniform. "The boys in Washington will be steaming," he said under his breath, wondering how long Pershing could survive as the commanding officer of the expedition if this should continue.

Loco Jim awakened with a start before he could be lifted off the ground. He saw Dodd watching him from the back of his horse and batted the soldiers' arms aside to sit up on his blanket without assistance. Closing one eye, weaving, he tried to focus on Dodd and said, "Don't go to Parral. There was a big fight. The people and the Mexican soldiers say they will shoot every American who comes there. We don't go to Parral."

"Who told you this?" the Colonel demanded, doubting the veracity of anything coming from a drunken Indian, a man who could scarcely sit up.

Es Ki Ben De vomited when he was hoisted belly-down over his saddle. With his head dangling he began to strangle, kicking so fiercely that his legs could not be tied to a stirrup. Loco Jim saw this and said, "Let him go! I will hold him on his horse."

"Who told you about the fight at Parral?" Dodd persisted, ignoring the old Indian's struggle for now.

"A storekeeper who spoke English where we bought the Mexican whiskey. Now tell them to put the old man down or he will choke to death."

Dodd gave Captain Shaw a nod of approval. "You say it

was Mexican regulars who fought our troops?" he asked carefully.

"Yes, and the people from the town shot at them also. The storekeeper said no American soldiers are being allowed to come there. He warned us to ride away quickly, before the *Federales* learned we were with the American army."

Dodd glanced over his shoulder. His men were exhausted, and their horses had nothing left. There was no choice but to turn north, seeking the main column for fresh mounts and a few days of rest, awaiting further orders. Pershing would be in a fix, finding he was at war with the Mexican Army as well as Villa's men now. The campaign in Mexico was beginning to crumble.

"Order the men to mount," he told the captain. "We will look for Pershing or any reinforcements we can find. Send a man ahead of us to the north, and tell him to watch out for any sign of Mexican regulars or we could find ourselves caught in a crossfire."

The plain west of Satevo was alight with campfires where Headquarters Company was bivouaced. Guards patrolled the perimeter in pairs. George Dodd sipped whiskey from a tin cup as a westerly wind rustled the command tent behind them. Pershing was in an understandably somber mood tonight. Major Robert Howze's Eleventh Cavalry had won a superb victory earlier in the day at a place called Ojos Azules, northwest of Satevo, killing forty-two Villistas and capturing nineteen more. It had been the sort of action the expedition needed desperately to report to Washington, a successful engagement among a long list of failures. Later that same afternoon a courier drove in from El Paso with orders from General Funston at Southern Command, calling for a complete pullback of all the expeditionary forces to Casas Grandes by order of the president, leaving hard-won territory to the south open to Villistas again.

"I asked for permission to take over the railroads," Pershing said quietly to Dodd, growing more melancholy. "That may have been the straw that snapped Wilson's back. We can't whip Villa like this, striking here and there at random, never knowing where they may turn up next, having no control over the territory, avoiding the cities, denied all use of the rails. It could go on like this forever. I suppose I'll be recalled over it.

"We should never have interfered in Mexican affairs without complete resolve to see it through to completion. Wilson and Baker are apparently satisfied to have a limited war here. We are asked to make a show of our muscle without employing it to any useful purpose, criss-crossing back and forth with our hands virtually tied behind our backs. It's a senseless exercise to go on like this, dragging along enough firepower to blast Mexico City off the face of the earth while heeding Wilson's instructions as to where it may not be used. Without control of the railroads we are powerless to move to our best advantage and we must plug along over these godforsaken roads at a snail's pace.

"I'm afraid Villa is teaching us a very valuable tactical lesson from which we may never profit. He jumps up here or there and then vanishes, only to reappear somewhere else. It reminds me of our efforts to outwit Geronimo, something we never truly did. And now Venustiano Carranza, being the astute observer he is, has begun to sense Wilson's indecision over our purpose here and is throwing out his chest, making demands that we not go to this place or that, which is often the most logical place to conduct our search. His troops have begun firing on us when they enjoy numerical superiority. Frank Tompkins was lucky to get out of Parral alive."

"I feel like I've let you down, John," Dodd said. "We did the best we could. Those goddamn mountains south of Guerrero are almost impassable. We damn near killed every horse we had trying to get to Tomochic, and somehow Villa and Cervantes got away in plenty of time."

"You and your men performed above and beyond duty. I could not ask for more from mortal men. Villa seems almost inhuman at times, like the way I remember Geronimo's frequent disappearances when it looked like he could vanish altogether. Villa is at the very least a brilliant tactician, managing to make us look foolish." Pershing paused and took a breath. "I honestly never thought I would see the day when I became too confounded by an enemy's tactics to be able to counter his next move at some point. But I must admit, Villa has me stumped. Now that my orders are to pull back to Casas Grandes, I have no delusions. This expedition is a failure, George, and I have failed along with it. My advance in rank has been thwarted by a clever Mexican hellion. Any dreams I had of leading an American expeditionary force to the battlefields of Europe have been thoroughly dashed by this debacle in Chihuahua."

"You sound like you've given up, old friend."

"Perhaps I have," Pershing remarked a bit sadly. "I fear we have lost the moment. You almost had him at Guerrero, and the civilian scout, Johnson, all but discovered his hiding place near Parral. Yet at just the right time, Villa is able to sense the trap closing around him and he moves without leaving a trace."

"I might have found him again, only I was hamstrung by your beloved Indians, Johnny. I sent our civilian guide ahead to Parral and that left me with two drunken Apaches. If you would give me Will Johnson and fresh horses in the morning, we might be able to pick up Villa's trail before he gets too far away."

Pershing sipped coffee, listening to the wind. "Johnson lost a leg to one of Villa's sharpshooters. He left the service and went back to the border, but not before he led Lieutenant Patton and a six-man troop to General Julio Cardenas near Namiquipa. I asked Johnson to stay, but he wanted no part of it. He isn't a soldier at heart. No spirit for this sort of life, I suppose."

"He knew this desolate place," Dodd remembered.

"You'll have to make do with the Apaches, or you can have your pick from the other civilian guides. But it really is too late for that now. Our orders are to withdraw to the border area at Casas Grandes."

Dodd downed a generous swallow of whiskey and waited for the burning to subside in his throat. "We can't do anything from there. We may as well call it quits and go home."

"Precisely my judgment on the matter. We shall end it in utter disgrace, returning like a dog with our tail between our legs. I wonder now if I might have been too rigid from the very beginning. I wanted to crush Villa soundly, decisively, in one powerful stoke. Our purpose may have been better served if I had deployed a greater number of small companies across a much wider region, a fine-toothed comb that could travel quickly, needing less in the way of supply and heavy armament. Hindsight is, as you know, always clear."

"Too bad about Johnson's leg," Dodd said. "I liked him. I felt we could trust his instincts."

"We differed in that regard," Pershing remembered. "When I first met him I found him unpleasant, uncouth, crude in mannerism and speech. Likewise, he had no fondness for the army and he made that plain from the beginning. Men like him are seldom swayed to another viewpoint. I believed he was incorrigible, a simple cowboy poorly suited to our purposes."

"He knew Chihuahua and he understood Mexicans, which is more than I will ever be capable of. I despise the cocky bastards. I would have truly enjoyed bringing Villa down."

Pershing gave him a half-hearted smile. "You should strive to achieve a more tolerant attitude, George. You dislike Indians and all Mexicans, by your own admission, and I doubt you have any real love for Negroes. The world is changing. Old attitudes toward the races are disappearing. Men of other colors have done more than simply prove their worth. They make excellent troops in the field—I cite my record with the buffalo soldiers during the Indian wars and in the Philippines."

"I suppose I'm old fashioned. From what I hear around camp, your all-Negro Tenth hasn't done that well here in Chihuahua."

"Colonel Brown has been a disappointment during this campaign, I'll freely admit. I had hoped they would distinguish themselves. As to your admission to being old fashioned, I now wonder if the same will be said of me after this fiasco comes to an end. Will history say that John Pershing was too old fashioned to correctly employ a mechanized army in the field? Was an old horse soldier too outdated to know how to use modern weaponry to its fullest advantage?"

"This wasn't your fault, Johnny. No one was prepared for what this terrain would be like. Chihuahua is the most inhospitable place I ever saw, hardly fit for scorpions and lizards. I find it hard to imagine why anyone would fight over it. There isn't any farmland to speak of. About all they can raise down here is hell and cactus."

Pershing was gazing across the flat plain to the dark outlines of the Sierras. "A hell of a bad place to try to further a man's military career, it would appear. I was quite convinced I could accomplish our mission. On paper, we had insurmountable numbers and mechanical superiority, yet it wasn't enough. In the planning stages, I saw no way we could lose."

Dodd finished his drink and put the cup down. "Too bad about Johnson's leg," he said again, fastening his chinstrap so his hat would not blow off in the wind on the way to his tent to go to bed. "On the ride up here from Parral I told myself that if I had Johnson, and fresh horses under my men, I could trace Villa from Parral to wherever it was he went. I don't suppose we'll ever know if I was right. Going back to Casas Grandes, we may as well try to enjoy our picnic. We sure as hell won't be seeing any more of Villa until his own leg gets well. Good night, John. I hope you get some sleep."

"Good night, George," he heard Pershing mumble, as he trudged off the hill to retire for the night. He had never seen Pershing's spirits so low.

· 36 ·

Elisa watched the crowd for familiar faces, speaking to the few people she knew well, but a vague uneasiness made her cautious. Passengers had begun to board the train. Her trunk was loaded in the baggage car, her goodbyes already said to her sister, Christina, at the ranch. She was bound for war-torn Germany with only an address in Berlin to help her locate her brother, an address she took from a file in Herr

Milnor's desk when she ransacked the big *hacienda* looking for money. She scarcely remembered having a brother, for he was only a tiny infant when she and her sister were taken from the orphanage for the voyage to Cuba, then Mexico. That had been so long ago, and she had trouble remembering any of it. But she did have a brother in Germany—she knew that. Fritz Griensen was being held prisoner by someone close to the foreign secretary as leverage, forcing Elisa to do Herr Milnor's bidding. She had been told countless times that Fritz would be executed unless she did everything asked of her. It was deeply disturbing to know that if she were to refuse any of Milnor's wishes a small boy, a brother she never knew, would be killed. She often tried to imagine what he looked like. As the years passed she developed a mental image of a blond boy ten years her junior, with her same eyes and skin, a face similar to hers. But he lived only in her imagination, for she had no real memories of Fritz beyond a poorly defined recollection of a baby swaddled in a dirty blue blanket who cried all the time as though he was always hungry. The address in Berlin was all she had to guide her once she reached Germany. And even when she found him—if she could find him—she had only a loose idea of what she would do. She still carried the pistol in her handbag. Given the chance, perhaps she could kill whoever was holding Fritz captive and then bring the boy back with her to live at the ranch with Christina and Pedro.

The train whistle sounded. Steam hissed from the couplings and pistons on the sides of the locomotive. More people were boarding, and it was time for her to find a seat. She got up from the bench beneath a wooden canopy covering the depot and looked both ways along the busy loading platform. She saw nothing that should cause her to worry, yet she did worry. It was as if eyes were watching her, but when she tried to find them in the crowd she saw no one who was looking at her, no face she recognized. She wondered if it might only be that she was not yet accustomed to being free of Herr Milnor's unrelenting control.

Soldiers were patroling the depot. General Lozano's men were not paying attention to her. No one had reason to suspect her of Herr Milnor's death, for it appeared he had been killed during the wild shooting spree when the American army was driven from Parral. Nor did she know where Francisco was now, only that he was still in hiding until his leg healed. She had done everything he'd asked of her, bringing the new doctor, Felix Fuentes, to his bedside. She felt no real sorrow leaving Francisco now, no regrets, even though she cared for him a little, though not the way she once did. More times than she cared to recall he had given her nothing but rough treatment in return for her devotion. All of that was behind her now, a part of the past. Francisco would be easy to forget, for she had never truly loved him. He had been the one who picked her from his many women, making her his favorite. It had not been something of her own choosing, although it suited Herr Milnor's purposes almost from the beginning.

She started across the platform, still feeling as though she was being watched. From the corner of her eye she glanced in both directions and found nothing, no reason for alarm. People stood near the railroad cars talking, saying their goodbyes. Why did she have the nagging sensation that something was wrong?

She came to the iron steps leading into the car and grabbed a handrail to climb aboard, keeping her face hidden below an old sun bonnet she wore to the train. Before her foot was planted on the first step she heard a voice calling her name.

"Señora Griensen!"

She froze and barely turned her head. General Ismael Lozano walked along the tracks flanked by two of his aides. Lozano wore his best dress uniform, dark blue with crimson shoulderboards and red fringe, a tall officer's cap with a black peak that glimmered in the midday sun.

"General Lozano," she replied, turning to greet him, offering her hand.

"Are you leaving Parral?" Lozano asked, frowning slightly. "One of my men informed me that you purchased a ticket to Tampico this morning."

"Yes. I am visiting a friend. I will only be gone a few weeks."

The general seemed to relax. "I had hoped . . . you would visit me again. I enjoyed your company."

She did her best to keep her face from coloring. "Perhaps when I return, General."

"Then I shall look forward to your return, *señora,*" he said, smiling now. He patted the back of her hand. "I am sure you are deeply grieved by the death of your close friend *Señor* Milnor. I was so sorry to learn that he had been killed by the Americans, for he was a fine gentleman, an upstanding member of our community. Please accept my condolences. He shall be missed."

"It was a terrible thing," she said quietly, with an appropriate touch of sorrow in her voice. "I do hope those dreadful Americans will be gone by the time I return to Parral."

Lozano gave her a knowing look. "We intend to drive them from Chihuahua if they will not leave on their own. Orders have come from General Obregon that we will issue an ultimatum to the *gringos,* having them withdraw completely from Mexican soil or war will be declared. Now that it is rumored that Pancho Villa is dead, there is no reason for the Americans to remain here. I believe they mean to occupy our country. General Obregon will not stand for it!"

"The general must do what is best for Mexico," she told him politely, casting a look down the platform when the train whistle sounded again. She slowly drew her hand away from Lozano's and was turning to climb into the passenger car when she got a brief impression of someone, a dark silhouette standing in the shade of the canopy at a corner of the depot.

She caught her breath suddenly. A tremor shook her arms and she clasped her handbag tightly, trying to conceal her fear. She recognized the man standing in the shadows. Rudolfo Fierro was watching her. A small voice told her why he was there.

"That man!" she gasped, reaching quickly for General Lozano's sleeve. "The one with the dark mustache—please make him stop! He means to harm me!"

Lozano wheeled around. "Which man, *señora?"* he asked, looking through crowds departing from the platform.

"At the corner of this building, General—the tall man over there."

The general spoke to his aides. "Bring him to me at once!"

Elisa had no doubts about what the Butcher would do when he saw the two soldiers coming for him. "I must board my train," she whispered to Lozano. "Please keep that man from finding me!" She did not wait to hear what the general said in reply, climbing the steps into the passenger car as quickly as she could. At the top step she glanced over her shoulder without pausing at the threshold. Fierro was staring at her. He had a terrifying expression on his face, a look she had seen before when his orders were to kill someone for Francisco.

She started up the aisle at a fast walk with her shoulders bent in haste. Passing the first two rows of seats, suddenly a windowpane exploded beside her. Glass shards flew across seated passengers and the floor, showering her with broken glass. The fading echo of a gun's roar was quickly muffled as passengers started to scream. Elisa reached into her handbag as she broke into a run between the seats.

A burst of automatic gunfire followed her the length of the car. Windows shattered, popping almost in unison, spraying the inside of the train with razorlike bits and pieces of glass. A shrieking woman was knocked from her seat with a stream of blood spouting from the side of her head. Glass swirled around Elisa, accompanied by the thud of a gun pounding from the platform. Screams and frightened wails all but drowned out the explosions and the crash of breaking windowpanes erupting around her.

Gripping her Mauser, she ran to the end of the aisle and came to a stop when the gunshots ended abruptly. Outside the car, people were running in every direction, shouting wildly. A lone pistol shot cracked near the depot, then it was answered by another stuttering burst of automatic fire, and somewhere a voice cried out in agony.

Panting, her heart lodged in her throat, she crept to the edge of a half-closed boarding door overlooking the platform, to peer cautiously through a broken remnant of windowpane. Someone in the aisle behind her was choking, someone else sobbing softly. Voices outside moved farther away. She cocked the Mauser and steadied it as best she could, waiting, listening, looking for Fierro in the darkest shadows beside the building.

To her right, she saw a uniformed man sprawled facedown on the platform, surrounded by a pool of blood. Ismael Lozano had taken only a few steps away from the train before he died. A man in cotton homespun lay crumpled against the depot wall, whimpering, holding a bloody smear down the front of his shirt, staring blankly at the side of the train. Another soldier had fallen on a suitcase near an empty baggage cart, a pistol dangling limply from his hand, as dead as General Lozano with a huge hole in the back of his head, a plug of brain tissue exposed where his hair was missing.

Elisa told herself there was no time to be afraid. Fierro was coming after her. He had been sent to kill her, and like some dumb animal he would do exactly as Francisco dictated. She would have just once chance to kill him first, before he emptied one of his automatics at her. In order to get a clean shot he would have to approach the train quickly, before gunfire was heard all across Parral, attracting the rest of General Lozano's soldiers. Summoning courage she did not realize she possessed, she steeled herself for the moment when Fierro rushed the car. She had found the courage to kill Herr Milnor somewhere, somehow, and she would kill again if she had to, in order to be free.

A woman in a bloodstained dress swayed to her feet in the aisle, tears streaming down her cheeks, sobbing so loudly that Elisa could hear nothing else. "Shut up!" Elisa screamed, only taking her eyes from the platform a moment. "He is still out there! Lie down and shut up or he will kill us all!"

The words had no more than left her mouth when a man dashed across the platform to the train—she saw him only as a blurr, but she was sure of his identity. Swinging her gun to the aisle where the sobbing woman stood, she cried again, "Get down!" just as a darting shape jumped into the opposite end of the passenger car.

A pair of thundering explosions rocked the train. The woman standing in the glass-littered aisle jerked twice, keeping time with the banging gun as though she meant to dance to the quickening beat of a drum. Her left breast erupted, turning the front of her yellow dress red, and she seemed to float toward Elisa without her feet touching the floor.

At the back of the car Rudolfo Fierro grimaced, trying to see past the rows of seats, past the staggering woman, for this one brief moment unable to find his target in the confusion. It was the hesitation Elisa needed, just enough time. She raised the Mauser and took hurried aim before she pulled the trigger.

Her gun banged three times, recoiling, ejecting empty brass shell casings that went spinning through the air to the floor of the train. Her ears were ringing, and she couldn't quite hear a noise from the back of the car—a cough or an angry roar. She saw Fierro sway, gritting his teeth; he knelt suddenly behind the last row of seats.

The Mexican woman in the red-and-yellow dress collapsed in the aisle on her face, groaning, her arms and legs rubberlike when she fell. Instinct warned Elisa to move. She crouched down behind an empty seat and held her breath, trying to calm the tremors in her hands.

Footsteps thumped outside the car, irregular, a limp moving away from the train. Elisa raised her head a little and looked over the sill of a shattered window. Fierro, holding his thigh, hobbled toward the depot leaving a bright red trail on the adobe brick platform.

Indecision made her pause too long. Before she could think to aim and shoot him in the back, Fierro limped around a corner of the building and disappeared.

She let out a breath and sagged to her knees, shaking from head to toe. The gun fell from her hand, banging on the wooden floor of the car. In the distance she heard shouts and the dim rattle of horseshoes. Closing her eyes, she gave silent thanks that her life had been spared. The Butcher was getting away and she did not care. She was alive.

Later, when dozens of soldiers and curious people rushed to the depot, she got up and hid the Mauser in her handbag. Two women lay dead in the passenger-car aisle. An old man in a dark business suit was slumped over in one of the seats with blood trickling from his right ear. Light-headed, feeling giddy, a whirling sensation weakening her legs, she walked calmly to the steps and climbed down to the platform where groups of soldiers stood around General Lozano's body. A soldier began questioning her. She knew she had to answer carefully if she wanted to avoid being detained.

The train rocked gently through the night, wheels clicking rhythmically over joints in the rails. Elisa sat with her face to the window, unable to sleep, watching dark mountains in the distance. She was thinking about the cowboy. Will Johnson was the only man she had ever known who knew how to be gentle with her. She had sensed his kindness. When she gave herself to him in a rare moment of self-indulgence, their lovemaking had been even more than she dared hope, awakening feelings inside her that she never knew existed. All her life, men had used her. Making love was a duty, a means to an end. Just once, in the arms of Will Johnson, she had known what it was like to feel differently.

But in the end he had betrayed her, proving what she had known all along: A woman's body was merely a tool, an attraction to lure men into giving her what she wanted. Sleeping with Will had been a mistake, a mistake she would never make again, letting her heart rule her head. He would be the last man ever to take advantage of Elisa Griensen. Experience was a harsh taskmaster, but its lessons were not easily forgotten.

• 37 •

Captain Charles Boyd stood at attention, listening to General Pershing outline the reconnaissance mission to Villa Ahumada. Boyd would command Troops C and K of the Tenth Cavalry. Pershing deemed Boyd the most aggressive black officer he had, the type who could get the job done and follow orders without dalliance. Boyd was a solid West Pointer and had recently published a book on tactics, making him the most likely and trustworthy officer from the Tenth for a sensitive undertaking.

"We have been told that a large force of Carrancistas has detrained at Villa Ahumada. I want you to verify the report and observe any troop movement. Obtain as much information as you can regarding their strength. This is a reconnaissance mission only, and you will not be expected to fight. In fact, I want you to avoid a fight if at all possible. Do not allow yourself to be surprised by superior numbers, but if wantonly attacked, use your judgment as to what you should do, having due regard for the safety of your command."

"Is that all, sir?" Boyd asked.

"Take Captain Lewis Morey and his men from K Troop. I have assigned Lem Spilsbury as your civilian guide. Pick up Spilsbury on your way through Colonia Dublan. He's there now, seeing to his ailing wife. That will be all, Captain. Be sure of your position at all times. Report back to me as soon as you have learned anything. We will be coming north to set up a base camp at Casas Grandes. Keep me fully informed."

Boyd saluted and marched away from the line of automobiles. For reasons hard to explain, Pershing had an uncomfortable feeling about Boyd's assignment. Something big was going on to the east of Carrizal at Villa Ahumada and he needed to know what it was. One report said as many as four hundred Carrancistas were camped between the two villages. Why were so many *Federales* being deployed so close to the border? Was it to flank the American column as it pulled back to Casas Grandes, making it appear the expedition was being ushered out of Mexico by Carranza's troops?

George Dodd came toward the front of the column chewing the stump of a cigar, wearing his perpetual scowl. George had gotten into a heated argument with Major Ryan this morning: Like everyone else camped with Headquarters Company, his nerves were frayed by the sudden arrival of orders from Washington to withdraw to the border. Dodd called Major Ryan a bumbling idiot for having sent Loco Jim and Es Ki Ben De ahead to reconnoiter along the road to Namiquipa and Las Cruces. "They'll be able to find every goddamn saloon and whorehouse, without a doubt!" he shouted, his face florid. "If you had read my report you would know those two are nothing but drunks. Anyone who trusts intelligence gathered by that pair is a bumbling idiot. Having Apaches gather intelligence is an outright contradiction. All they'll bring you is drunken nonsense!"

Lieutenant Patton saw Dodd coming. "The colonel is on the prod this morning. He got into it with Major Ryan after breakfast. What's eating him?"

Pershing noted Dodd's purposeful stride. "He's still mad at the Indians I gave him, I suppose. I suspect the underlying cause for his restlessness is the same as mine: frustration over the latest developments in Washington."

Patton chewed his lip thoughtfully. "Major Howze's victory at Ojos Azules hasn't set well with him either. Colonel Dodd is desperate to see some action. He was sorely disappointed when the search for Villa ended at Parral."

"We all feel the same regrets," Pershing said. "The matter has been taken out of our hands now. President Wilson prefers to get along peacefully with our neighbors, even when our neighbors spit in our eye."

Dodd arrived at the front of the column where the procession was halted to add water to steaming radiators at a crossing over Rio Santa Maria. By the deep color in Dodd's cheeks, he was still fuming as much as an overheated radiator himself. Captain Boyd's black cavalrymen trotted down to the river and began fording. Dodd watched them silently for a moment. "You could be making a mistake there, General," he said, addressing Pershing formally in the presence of others. "That Boyd is a hothead. He aspires to higher rank. He even wrote a book about his notions for better ways to run the army."

"It was a book dealing with tactics," Pershing replied, as the last pairs of cavalrymen from C Troop entered the river.

Dodd shook his head. "When I saw them riding off I felt I had to come forward and speak my piece. I hope you won't regret sending them to Carrizal."

Pershing was rapidly losing patience with Dodd's prejudice. "I have every confidence in Captain Boyd. He understands his orders and his men are well disciplined."

"My men are rested and ready to go," Dodd offered, clamping his teeth around his unlit cigar. "If you should change your mind, or decide to augment Boyd's forces, we can be ready to ride in less than an hour."

A truck convoy rattled down to the river crossing from the north, four gasoline tankers and four Jeffrey Quads loaded with supplies. The lead truck ground to a noisy halt at the edge of the water, waiting for the men of the Tenth to ride across. Pershing noticed that a civilian in a shapeless cowboy hat got out of the first tanker, a man wearing faded denims and using a pair of crutches.

"It's the scout," Dodd declared. "He's missing a leg. . . ."

Pershing was more than a little surprised to see Will Johnson. "I wonder why he came back?" he asked himself aloud.

"It's possible he learned something he thought we ought to know," Lieutenant Patton suggested hopefully. "Maybe he found out where Villa is hiding, or he may have learned the whereabouts of Candelario Cervantes, or Sergio Lujan. Major Ryan received a report that Lujan is in this vicinity, trying to recruit men for Villa."

"He may have decided he needs a job after all," Dodd said. "His leg won't stop him from being useful to us."

Pershing turned to his overheated automobile and driver. "Drive me across so I can find out why he's here. The Dodge can cool down just as quickly over there."

"I'll ride along," Patton said, climbing onto the running

board without waiting to be asked. "Johnson may know something we all need to hear . . . possibly where Villa is hiding now."

After two failed attempts with the crank, the Dodge belched loudly and lurched into the river with Pershing and Colonel Dodd in the rear seat. The general kept an eye on the civilian guide while the wheels bumped over submerged rocks and hidden obstacles buried in the riverbed. Had Johnson learned something about Villa or one of his field commanders? Why would he return to the column when he seemed so bitter toward the army over the loss of his leg?

The automobile rolled out of the river and braked to a halt beside the tanker. Dodd climbed out of the back seat before Pershing got his door open. Johnson was regarding them with no real interest. Resting his weight on the armpads of his crutches, he shook hands with Dodd and Lieutenant Patton before Pershing made his way around the Dodge.

"Sorry to learn about that leg," Dodd remarked.

"We're all surprised to see you," Pershing said. "I thought you were on your way to Fort Bliss."

Will shrugged. He thumbed his sweat-stained cowboy hat back on his forehead. "I reckon I had a change of heart, General." He looked at Patton, then at Colonel Dodd. "We stopped off at a little cantina in Bachiniva to wet our whistles while your soldiers were coolin' the trucks down, an' that's when I heard a couple of things I figured you oughta know. First off, there's a big batch of *Federales* just east of Carrizal. I was told there was better'n five hundred camped at the edge of the village under the command of General Frederico Gomez. Gomez is a feisty son of a bitch, so they tell me. He ain't sayin' why he's there, but the foreman out at Santo Domingo Ranch, ol' man McCabe, told me that Gomez is settin' up barbed wire an' diggin' ditches, like he aims to be in one hell of a fight pretty soon. Now, what don't make a hell of a lot of sense about that is that Villa has sent his men into the hills until his leg gets better an' damn near everybody in this part of Mexico knows it, so Gomez can't be figurin' on fightin' any Villistas. That don't leave nobody else in this neck of the woods to fight 'cept you, General."

Colonel Dodd made a half turn to look at Pershing.

"Carrizal is where Boyd and his men are going. They'll be riding into a trap if we don't warn them right away."

"There's one thing more," Will added, talking to Patton now. "I found out that Colonel Candelario Cervantes is just north of Namiquipa, hidin' out at this little pueblo called Las Cruces. I was told he's still there—McCabe saw him just yesterday. If you took some men and surrounded him, he wouldn't put up much of a fight. I'd say Colonel Cervantes is probably the most dangerous of Villa's officers, now that Julio Cardenas is dead."

Patton whirled around. "I could take a small squad. Las Cruces is only a day away."

Pershing was still appraising Will carefully, ignoring both Patton and Dodd for the moment. "I'm curious as to why you came back to tell us these things, Mr. Johnson. I assumed you meant what you said, that you wanted nothing more to do with the army."

Will nodded. "That's for sure what I said, General, only I got to thinkin' about some things. If I went on home, knowing something that might save the lives of some of your soldiers, I wouldn't feel good about it. If you're gonna keep on payin' me, even if I have got just this one leg, I figured the least I could do to earn my money is find out everything I could about what's goin' on in this part of Chihuahua. All I did was ask questions. Besides, me an' that Sergeant Pike wasn't gonna get along all the way to the border. A one-legged man has still got pride, and in my book I don't figure nobody oughta have to take the kind of horseshit Sergeant Pike dishes out to his men. If you'll pardon me sayin' so, General, a man like Pike ought not to be wearin' no kind of uniform, or givin' orders to anybody else. If I'd had two good legs under me I'd have already whipped his ass the time we stopped outside of San Isabel, after he lit into that boy who was drivin' me, Corporal Legget, for not havin' a latch fastened down on his truck. No sense in talkin' to another man the way Pike did. I understand that a soldier's gotta take orders, but he don't have to take 'em from some asshole who's screamin' at the top of his lungs. You take that uniform off Pike an' he's nothin' but an asshole with too much wind. So now that I've said my piece about Pike and what's wrong with this army, I'll show you the way to where

Colonel Cervantes is hidin', if somebody'll take me in one of those automobiles."

"What about Captain Boyd?" Colonel Dodd asked, before Pershing or Lieutenant Patton could speak. "Someone has to inform him of what is going on at Carrizal before he leads his men into trouble."

The general frowned, considering options. "Boyd has his orders to avoid a fight if at all possible. If we could capture Candelario Cervantes, it might make a favorable impression in Washington and silence our critics. I agree with Mr. Johnson, that Cervantes is the most able and desperate of Villa's leaders. With Villa out of commission, the downfall of Cervantes could accomplish a major victory for us— something we could give the newspapers. For the present, locating Cervantes has top priority." He ignored Patton for the moment and spoke to Dodd. "Assemble a troop of your men and take four automobiles. Be sure to include a couple of men from the machine-gun troop. And invite the two newspapermen along, Elser and Gibbons, so they can get their stories firsthand. It's time the American public got a taste of what we are up against here. I'm taking the lid off the press for this one, George. Give Elser and Gibbons something to write about. Find Colonel Cervantes and, if possible, make us some headlines."

Patton looked as if he were about to burst at the seams. "I earnestly request permission to accompany them, sir," he said.

"Permission denied, Lieutenant. We have other more pressing business to attend to, seeing to the movement of these columns to Casas Grandes forthwith. You are needed here."

"But sir, Lieutenant Collins is quite capable of—"

"That will be all, Lieutenant. Have four of the automobiles brought across the river for Colonel Dodd and his men, and be sure to include Elser's Ford." Dismissing Patton, he gave Dodd final instructions. "Make sure of your quarry, George, before you start shooting." Then he looked at Will. "I want you to know I am grateful for what you've told us. I understand that you don't always agree with my methods, but we do have the same objective. As to the sergeant . . . I believe you said his name was Pike, I intend to make sure his behavior is modified as soon as we get to Casas Grandes. Giving orders is necessary in an army, Mr. Johnson, however I will not tolerate a bully." He offered his hand. "Glad to have you with us again."

They shook. Behind them, wading angrily through waist-deep water to the south bank of the river, Lieutenant Patton began barking orders to soldiers who went scurrying off to assemble a motorized troop bound for Las Cruces.

28 May
We have been ordered back to Casas Grandes and I fear all is lost for the campaign. Talks between Hugh Scott and Obregon have come to nothing. Carranza forces are building up all around us, and I have a strong sense that there will be war between the United States and the de facto government of Mexico. The civilian guide Will Johnson has returned and I am sincerely thankful. He says he knows where Colonel Candelario Cervantes is hiding, and if so, I may be able to save face to some degree. George Dodd and a squad of men are heading to Las Cruces at this hour to try to corral Cervantes. I sent Elser and Gibbons along, hoping to provide grist for their mill if Cervantes is captured. We must have some form of measurable success soon or I will be devoured by my critics in Washington. Without some tangible result of a military nature in the near future, I will be coming home.

· 38 ·

Lance Corporal Marksbury hurried the Dodge over danger-ously uneven roadbeds at speeds that could easily dislodge a loose tire or throw a passenger from his seat, and even then, Colonel Dodd continued to demand that Marksbury drive faster. Private Hulett, an expert marksman from one of the machine-gun units, held fast to the bottom of his seat with white-knuckled hands, keeping his eyes tightly closed. Will hunkered down behind the windshield to keep his hat from blowing off. Every now and then, when Corporal Marksbury slowed down for a curve, the colonel shouted, "Speed up! Can't this goddamn contraption go any faster than this?"

Careening around sharp bends, plunging down steep slopes to long stretches of straight road only to climb again, the automobiles sent a roostertail of dust high above them as they raced away from Namiquipa on a rutted lane leading to Las Cruces. At the back of the procession, Frank Elser and Floyd Gibbons did all they could to keep up in the slower Ford. Will wondered if he would soon regret his decision to come back to scout for the army. It was beginning to look like he might lose his life when an automobile overturned, rather than dying from a gunshot wound. Colonel Dodd was obsessed with reaching Las Cruces in time to capture Candelario Cervantes. For Will, accomplishing nothing more than surviving the trip was coming into question now.

Along the way, shouting to be heard above the roar of the engine and the rattle of springs, Dodd told him about the recent order from Southern Command to withdraw to the border region near Casas Grandes. According to the colonel, leaders in Washington were already calling the punitive expedition a failure. Unless some dramatic turn of events transpired quickly, General Pershing and all expeditionary forces would be recalled to Fort Bliss and then dismantled. Everyone involved was destined to obscurity in some remote military outpost, becoming forgotten men who would fade into the woodwork for the balance of their army careers.

"If we could have gotten our hands on Villa," Dodd said, a sour expression puckering his mouth.

"I 'spect he'll be too slippery to let himself get caught where he knows the lay of the land," Will offered, feeling the Dodge sway around a precarious turn, slewing rocks from the tires. "Until his leg gets well he ain't likely to surface. He could be hidin' out in Sonora or Durango by now. But if we can round up Candelario Cervantes, that'll cripple the hell out of his revolution. Things should quiet down for a spell."

"I only pray we aren't too late," Dodd said, squinting into the heat haze blanketing the empty mountains and canyons in front of them.

Will omitted mention of his belief that if prayer worked it might serve a better purpose asking that members of Dodd's party be allowed to survive the trip in speeding automobiles down roads barely navigable by burro cart.

Sunset was less than two hours away. If Will remembered the region correctly, Las Cruces lay just beyond the next low hills.

The small house was hidden at the back of a dry canyon. A lone cottonwood tree marked a shallow well where inhabitants of the adobe hut drew their water. Dodd sent Marksbury and Hulett to the west side of the canyon, armed with a rifle and a machine gun. Six men under the command of a boyish captain named Shaw crept along the east wall of the canyon where rocks and brush provided cover. Colonel Dodd was perched on the running board of the Dodge, watching the house through a pair of field glasses. Will sat in the front passenger seat, waiting for the crackle of gunfire to begin. He declined the offer of a gun, having made himself a promise that he would not kill anyone else for the army's sake. He had enough dead men on his conscience.

"The place looks deserted," Dodd said. "I don't see any horses in the stable or in any of the corrals."

"A horse has got sense enough to stay out of the sun durin' the day, Colonel," Will replied, watching a pair of windows at the front of the adobe. "Somebody's there. I smelled smoke when we came up the canyon. They've doused their fire, soon as they heard our automobiles and saw our dust. I 'spect the shootin' oughta start most any time now."

"You seem very sure of it," Dodd remarked, like he wasn't of the same mind.

Will noticed that Marksbury and Hulett were crossing an open stretch of hardpan to reach a pile of boulders. Hulett cradled a Benet-Mercies machine gun with its forks extended. "Right about now is when I figure we'll hear . . ." The roar of a gun blasted from a window of the hut. The explosion sent Hulett and Marksbury diving for cover. From the east, Captain Shaw's men opened up with a barrage of rifle fire, guns banging in unison.

The stuttering concussion of a machine gun came from the rocks where Hulett and Marksbury took up positions. A second rifle banged. Bullets sprayed the sides of the adobe, showering the surrounding area with dust and spent lead. Someone took off at a run from the rear of the house, a man in a white sombrero and a silky tunic with a sash tied around his waist. Two more figures dashed away from the building, dodging back and forth to reach the stable.

"Yonder goes Cervantes!" Will cried, ducking down behind the dashboard when a bullet sizzled over the top of the automobile.

Private Hulett stood up quickly, bringing his Benet to his shoulder, feet spread slightly apart to accommodate the kick when his gun went off. He drew a careful bead on the fleeing Mexican and fired a rattling stream of bullets.

The man wearing the sombrero, in full stride racing toward the corrals, was instantly staggered when Hulett's Benet exploded. He ran a few steps more on wobbly legs and then collapsed on his knees in the dust. Head bowed, spilling his sombrero to the ground, he knelt with his hands over his stomach until the next chattering string of slugs from Hulett's machine gun struck him in the back. His torso jerked. A second later, Shaw's soldiers began firing as rapidly as they could. Bullets riddled the Mexican's body from half a dozen angles at once, tearing him this way and that—as he started to fall one way a bullet sent him reeling in another direction, so that from a distance it appeared a puppeteer was pulling strings to keep him from falling down.

Finally the gunfire slowed when the Mexican toppled over on his face. The other two men reached the safety of the barn and began firing back sporadically with small-caliber pistols toward the rocks where Captain Shaw's men were hidden.

"I reckon that's one gent who oughta be dead enough to suit anybody," Will said during a brief lull in the shooting, when the bullet-riddled body of the man he had identified as Candelario Cervantes lay motionless between the house and the barn.

Colonel Dodd merely grunted at first, until he lowered his binoculars. "Nothing wrong with making sure of it," he said, a frown knitting his forehead. "I'd trade a whole goddamn truckload of ammunition for a corpse I knew was Colonel Cervantes."

A stray pistol shot fired from a corner of the stable struck the side of Frank Elser's Ford with a resounding crack. "Jesus Christ almighty!" Floyd Gibbons shouted, leaping from the front seat where he had been sitting to watch the affair, his forgotten notepad and pen tumbling to the running board. Gibbons raced around to the back and ducked down behind the rear of the automobile.

Corporal Marksbury chose this opportunity to make a run for the trunk of the cottonwood tree beside the well. Private Hulett dashed from the brush, zigzagging his way toward the rear of the adobe house in a running crouch. Guns erupted from the stable. Tiny spits of dust arose from shells fired at Hulett and Marksbury until they both found cover. Then a heavy silence came to the canyon, and for a time the fighting stopped.

Frank Elser peered above the back of his Ford. "Is it over now?" he asked in a loud voice.

A gun popped at the stable. The windshield of Elser's Ford erupted in a maelstrom of swirling glass fragments, sprinkling the fenders and seats, sending Elser diving to the ground with the answer to his question echoing off the canyon walls.

"Son of a bitch!" Gibbons shouted, cowering behind one of the tires. "We'll all be killed unless you keep your mouth shut!"

Captain Shaw's troops unleashed a staccato of rifle fire aimed at the stable. Private Hulett opened up with his Benet. A muted scream came from inside the building, barely audible above the roar of the guns, then a man staggered away from the barn holding his right ear. He took two more uncertain steps before his knees buckled. He went down heavily on his belly with blood pouring from the side of his head and he did not move again.

The third Mexican tossed out his gun. *"¡No más!"* he cried.

The fight was over. Will sat up in the seat. Men in green uniforms surrounded the sole survivor of the battle to usher him toward the automobiles at gunpoint.

Colonel Dodd stepped down from the floorboard of the Dodge. He had been standing in plain sight during the shooting, with no apparent thought to the danger.

"Come have a look at the body, Mr. Johnson," Dodd said. "I want to make damn sure it's Cervantes before we breathe easy."

Will struggled out of the seat onto his crutches. "Maybe kinda hard to tell, Colonel, after your boys shot him up bad as they did. From what I saw of it, I ain't gonna be surprised if it looks like he's been run through a meat grinder."

"I'm bleeding!" Floyd Gibbons whimpered, picking slivers of glass from his forearms and hands. "Why'd you park so goddamn close, Frank? Looks like you'd have known this could happen."

Will made his way over to the body. Despite the fact that the dead man's left cheek had been blown away, he recognized him. "That's Cervantes." He sighed, closing his eyes briefly. Never in all his life had he seen so much blood. He knew from experience that on any given day things were kept tidier on the killing floor of the Laredo slaughterhouse.

Colonel Dodd knelt down, reaching inside the dead man's tunic. He took out a bloodied envelope and scowled to read its inscription. "It's addressed to Colonel Candelario Cervantes," he said, motioning to Captain Shaw. "Cover him with a blanket and put him in the back seat of my automobile. We've got something to show John now." He waved to Elser and Gibbons. "Bring your cameras, gentlemen. I want you to take a photograph of a dead Villista field commander, none other than Colonel Candelario Cervantes himself. He's just about the last of Villa's henchmen. Write your stories quickly and get them ready for a courier to El Paso. I hope you can assure General Pershing of big headlines for a story like this. I know the general will want this to reach your newspapers in a hurry." He turned to Will. "If you like, we can have your picture made beside the body, Mr. Johnson, and make sure that mention is made of your role in showing us the way to Cervantes's hideout."

"No thanks, Colonel," Will mumbled, wheeling away from the blood-soaked ground where the mangled corpse was already attracting blowflies. "I'd just as soon not have my name mentioned at all. To tell the truth, this ain't the sort of thing I'm too awful proud of." He crutched his way over to the Dodge, for the moment wishing he'd continued his journey back home to Laredo. He only hoped that having led the soldiers to Cervantes would help spare the lives of young men like Corporal Bob Legget.

General Pershing seemed to be pleased. He examined the body in the dim lamplight and then covered it with the blanket. "Nice work, George," he said, yet there was something missing in his voice when he said it. "Our howling critics will now have less to cheer about. I am expecting a report from Captain Boyd before morning. Let us hope his reconnaissance mission brings back news as hopeful as what you brought us tonight. When the prisoner has been questioned thoroughly, bring me the details. Perhaps he'll tell us where Villa is now, or something about his present condition."

Will was slouched against the fender of the general's car, listening to what was being said. "I asked the prisoner what he knew about Villa's leg. He told me that gangrene set in and that's the reason Villa sent everybody home for a spell, until his leg gets better. There's a doctor travelin' with him. Villa's in a lot of pain."

Pershing eyed Will carefully. "Does he know where Villa is recuperating?"

Will nodded. "I 'spect he does, only he'd rather somebody cut off his own leg than tell us where Villa is. In case you haven't figured it out, General, you're up against somethin' that's a lot stronger than any of those politicians up in Washington figured. It's the spirit of these Mexican people. When they believe in somethin', don't matter whether it's right or wrong to anybody else, they're ready to die for it, if that's what it takes. The folks who believe in Villa's revolution would die themselves before they tell us where he's hidin'. Unless we get lucky and stumble on him ourselves, I'll wager we don't see hide nor hair of Villa 'til he's ready to start shootin' up this part of Chihuahua again."

Pershing frowned. "I'm inclined to agree that we seriously underestimated the spirit of nationalism in these people. But on the other hand, I don't see how we could have ignored Villa's attack on Columbus or the killing of innocent American citizens."

Will folded his arms across his chest, balancing on his one good leg while resting against the general's Dodge. He looked up at the stars. "It hasn't been proven to my satisfaction that Villa led that raid in the first place. Some folks who oughta know are inclined to agree that Villa wasn't there. But since he hasn't come out and denied it, I suppose the army did the only thing it could by goin' after him like this. Either way, he's made quite a name for himself across Mexico, takin' on the American army and Carranza's *Federales* all at once. Makes a man wonder if that isn't what he wanted all along."

• 39 •

Doroteo watched his eldest daughter play with her puppy in the walled garden of a *hacienda* belonging to Abrain Gonzalez, a rich benefactor who always offered him refuge when he needed to rest. The house was close to Chihuahua City, making it a particularly brash spot in which to hide, since a large *Federale* garrison was quite close, less than five miles away. From the top of the hill where the *hacienda* sat Doroteo could often see patrols scouring the countryside, and it amused him to think they were looking for him. But then, that was the best possible place for anyone to hide, he knew, a place where no one expected to find him. He had learned this from his father, Augustin, when he was very small, for his father was Indian and he knew the ways of *los indios.* Many years later, when Doroteo was seventeen, he left home to join the bandit gang of Ignacio Parra, and it was from Parra that he truly learned the finer art of hiding where no one would think to look. During that time with Parra he had changed his name to Francisco Villa, he remembered. Those had been such wonderful years, full of excitement and adventure. And there had been so many beautiful women sharing his bed!

Luz came over to his chair to offer him a gourd dipper of sweet lemonade. She had grown darker, he thought, and so much fatter. She was a lovely woman of even temperament, yet she was no longer beautiful, and that displeased him. What would others think if he possessed a plump wife? Fat women were not desired by other men. A fat wife did not fit his image, and the people of Chihuahua might think less of him for it.

He took the lemonade. "Thank you, my dear," he said. He gazed across the garden where his son and daughters played in the late-afternoon sun and shade. "It is so good to see you and the children again. They have grown."

"They missed you, Francisco," Luz said. "They ask for you almost every day, and sometimes the girls cry when they think of you at night."

He stared thoughtfully across the walled courtyard where the children played. "Perhaps it is time to end this revolution and spend time with my family," he said later, in a gentle voice that he only used with his daughters on some occasions. "I have grown weary of all the running. Venustiano only grows stronger with the passing of each week. My men are being hunted down like dogs, and there are traitors everywhere these days, telling Carranza and the Americans where we are. And now there is my leg. Never in all my life have I known so much pain. Were it not for the doctor's medicines I would have surely gone mad with the agony of it."

"The gangrene is getting better," Luz observed, peeking at the edge of his bandage. "The worms are healing your wound, my husband, not the medicines."

He did not wish to admit that Luz could be right. An old *curandera's* methods, applying maggots to the rotten flesh where gangrene decayed it, seemed to be doing more than anything Felix Fuentes did for him. The maggots ate away the rotten skin and muscle, although they had to be removed as soon as they came to healthy spots. But the shots of morphine the doctor gave him made him feel good, and now he could no longer make it through an entire day without several injections. "The doctor's treatments are making me well," he said with a note of finality that he knew Luz would not ignore, risking his wrath.

"Yes, Francisco," she whispered, lowering her face meekly.

He continued to think about his possible retirement from the revolutionary struggle. What would the people—his people—think of him? So many of the poor had given him their undying loyalty and trust. Would they see his retirement as a betrayal? "I now wonder what the people would say if I stopped fighting," he asked his wife in a faraway voice, as though he was truly considering it.

Luz waited an appropriate length of time before she gave her answer. "Everyone knows how hard you fought against the tyranny in Mexico City, my husband. Who could blame you if the fight has become impossible to win?"

He turned to her then, reading her expression. "But what would the people say about me?"

Tears formed in Luz's deep brown eyes. "They will say you still have the heart of a lion, Francisco. You are the hero of the revolution, and nothing will change that. But even the most courageous lion must rest. The children and I miss you so very much, my darling. At night, when the sky is dark and full of stars, I look toward the heavens and pray that God will send you back to me. Sometimes I worry that you will not come home again, that you will be killed, or that you may find . . . another woman you love more than you love me."

"This will never happen!" Doroteo snapped. "You must know by now that there can be no other woman for me! You are my wife, and these are my beloved children. No woman on earth can give me what you have given me. How can you even think such a thing?"

Luz started crying openly. "I hear some people say that you have many other women in other towns. I pray it is not true!"

He stiffened and leaned forward in his chair, knitting his bushy eyebrows. "Tell me who has said this and I will have them killed immediately!" he cried. "I will shoot them myself for telling my dear wife such terrible lies!"

Luz covered her face with her hands. "Sometimes at the marketplace I hear people whisper these things," she sobbed.

Doroteo lowered his voice. "It is not the truth," he stated flatly. "You must not listen to what my enemies say about me. I love no one but you, darling Luz. Whoever is saying otherwise is telling lies about me." He reached for her hand and held it in his own until she stopped crying. "There now," he said softly, smiling warmly when she looked up at him through her tears. "I have told you the truth: There is no other woman. Now stop all this foolish crying and get me something to eat."

Luz nodded and got up, drying her eyes on the sleeve of her dress. "I will sleep soundly at night, knowing you have given me your promise that there is no other woman you love," she said.

"I swear it on the lives of my children!" he replied, making his voice sound impatient. "I love no one else. Now go! Fix me something to eat!"

She turned away quickly and hurried into the house. He did not move in the chair or change his fierce expression until Luz was out of sight. Then słowly, his face softened into a faint smile and he let his eyes wander to the children again, knowing he had not given Luz a false oath. He didn't love any of the others at all, nor did he truly care for them the way he cared for his wife. A woman was something he needed from time to time, the way men often needed good horses when another went lame. While he was away seeing to the business of the revolution, he required the services of a beautiful woman—several beautiful women—when the need arose. But he did not love any of them. They merely served him as his soldiers did, giving themselves to the cause of freedom. It was not wrong, to make love to more than one woman. *Machismo* was expected of him. How could he let his followers think he was in any way unmanly? God made men in this way, with a need for more than one woman, for God was himself a man. It was Eve who tempted Adam, God's own creation. Why should any more be expected of a humble man like Doroteo Arango?

Staring absently at his children, he considered retirement from the fighting for a while. If he stayed in hiding for a year or two, everyone would stop looking for him, perhaps even give him up for dead.

"I have many fresh worms," the old woman said, holding forth a handful of squirming maggots. "See how hungry they are?"

Felix Fuentes shook his head. "There is the strong possibility of infection," he warned again.

The *curandera* ignored the doctor's remark. "You will be completely healed in a few days, General," she promised.

Doroteo pointed to his open wound. "Put the maggots in and watch that they do not eat too much." He looked at Fuentes. "I need another injection. The maggots are better than your medicines. See how much better my leg is now?"

"I admit they do seem to be removing the bad flesh, but I am concerned that they will do more harm than good."

"Give me the injection," Doroteo snapped, resting his head against the back of the chair, feeling shaky without morphine in his body. "Then see to Rudolfo's wound, but do not give him my medicine. We have so little, and without it I will surely die."

Rudolfo Fierro sat in a chair beside Doroteo with a bloody bandage around his thigh. He listened to what was being said and said nothing until he was spoken to.

"Tell me about the German woman," Doroteo said quietly, "and be sure Luz does not hear what you are saying."

"She escaped," Rudolfo began bitterly, his expression one of pure hatred. "She got on the train with the help of General Lozano and his soldiers. She told them about me and told them I was there—she knew I was sent there to kill her. I shot Lozano and two of his soldiers, but the woman shot me in the leg and I was forced to run for my life with Lozano's soldiers after me. I could not go back, *Jefe.*"

"Someone must look for her. She must be silenced."

"When my leg is better I will go."

"Where was the train going? What was its destination?"

"Tampico."

"Tampico? Why would she go there?"

"She took everything from her house. It did not look like she meant to come back again. She sold her horse and saddle at the stable."

Doroteo's mind was racing. "At Tampico she could get on a boat bound for Germany. Maybe there is nothing to worry about. Find out if she booked passage on a boat to Germany as soon as you are able to ride."

"Yes, *Jefe.*"

He watched the maggots being placed into the hole below his knee. The old woman did it carefully, one worm at a time. He spoke to Rudolfo again. "We will be leaving soon, to the place at Cumbre Pass. Meet us there. Diego is making the arrangements now. But find out about the woman first. If she has not left the country, she must be put to death."

The *curandera* flinched when he said this and he knew she too would have to be killed when her services were no longer needed, for she would know about Cumbre Pass and she might betray him to the *Federales* or the Americans.

"I bring more bad news, *Jefe,*" Rudolfo said.

"Tell me," he urged softly as the doctor's needle went into his arm.

"Candelario has been killed by the Americans. They found him at Las Cruces. Hipolito is also dead. Gonzalo was taken prisoner and he will talk if they torture him. Gonzalo is weak."

"Candelario . . . is dead?" Doroteo whispered.

"It is true. There is no mistake."

He swallowed, wishing the morphine would hurry into his veins. "How can this be? Candelario was always so careful."

"He was betrayed. The American *vaquero* who followed the German woman to the cave was with the soldiers. He seems to know many things. I was able to learn his name. He is called Johnson, and he is a friend to Pedro Alvarado."

"Then Pedro must be executed without delay. He must be the *vaquero's* source for information about us. Kill Pedro and look for the *vaquero* as soon as you are well enough to ride. We must silence the traitors around us, Rudolfo. If one of them is left alive, our enemies will find us."

"I understand, *Jefe.* When the doctor fixes my leg I will go to Parral and silence Pedro Alvarado. The American may be more difficult. He is always with the American generals. He has only one leg, and I am told he does not leave the army camp alone."

"You must find him and kill him. Somehow, he is able to learn things about us. He has led the Americans to Julio, and now to Candelario. He has to be stopped."

He watched maggots wriggle deeper into the hole, swarming to the putrid flesh surrounding his bones. Speaking to the *curandera,* he said, "Make certain you take all of them out when they are finished feeding, old woman. If I find even one of them in my leg tonight I will have someone cut off your head."

Doroteo's infant son toddled across flat patio stones with

a baby turtle in his chubby fist. When Doroteo saw this, he smiled and beckoned to the boy. "Come here, my son. Show me what you have found."

The boy brought him the turtle, holding it forth for Doroteo to see. "It is for you, Papa, so you will stay with us. We are sad when you go away."

His son's words touched him the way no others could. "Then because of this wonderful gift of a turtle, I will stay with you forever. I will take you and your sisters to a secret place in the mountains where we can catch many fish and go swimming. I will never leave you again, my son. Go and tell your mother the news. We are leaving for the mountains in the morning."

Beaming, the boy hurried off to find Luz. Doroteo waited until his son was out of earshot. "Join us at Cumbre Pass when it is finished," he said to Rudolfo. "I am thinking that, for a time, we will rest. I have grown weary of this war." He let the thought sink in, that he would end the fight with his old enemies in the government for a while. It would be good, to sleep soundly at night and get to know his children.

Two weeks later Doroteo was informed of Rudolfo's death when he drowned crossing a rain-swollen river on a horse. Among the Butcher's personal effects was a passenger manifest from a ship of German registry showing that Elisa Griensen was aboard, bound for Germany.

Doroteo mourned the loss of Fierro for a time, however he gave no more thought to the woman. There would always be another to take her place.

• 40 •

General Pershing summoned his ablest field commanders and every scout, civilian and Apache serving under Lieutenant James Shannon for a meeting of the utmost importance at the new command post west of Casas Grandes. Present were Frank Elser and Floyd Gibbons who were still glowing over the stories they filed with *The Times* and the *Tribune* the day before, reporting the killing of Colonel Cervantes. Pershing had called the meeting to brace everyone for what he felt was an important and potentially threatening development, about which he was appraised by a wire from General Funston. President Carranza's foreign minister, Candido Aguilar, had just delivered a note to Secretary of State Robert Lansing demanding that all American troops be withdrawn from Mexico at once or war would be declared by the Republic of Mexico. Mexican troops were being rushed toward the border at this hour. War was imminent. Pershing had been advised to be prepared for open hostilities unless a touchy situation could be defused.

"I want regular patrols moving from Casas Grandes every hour around the clock," Pershing said gravely, pacing back and forth. "Send scouts riding circles for a radius of fifty miles day and night along our southern flank. Any sign of troop movement by Carranza forces is to be reported to me at once. I do not intend to budge from our position here unless we receive new orders. Be prepared for war, gentlemen . . . a war with Mexico. Villa is no longer our primary problem or concern. It would appear President Carranza wants war with the United States, and we have been instructed to oblige him should any of his armies initiate hostilities with us." He looked past the assembled officers and scouts to a faint dust cloud moving across the flat plain beside the Casas Grandes river where Headquarters Company and units from the Seventh, Tenth, Eleventh, and Thirteenth Cavalry were setting up camp. Companies of the Fourth Field Artillery had started setting up gun emplacements around the site. There was still no report from Captain Boyd's C Troop concerning the activity near Carrizal, and early this morning, Pershing had sent Lieutenant Patton and Will Johnson by automobile toward Santo Domingo Ranch to find out why. He wondered if the dust could be Patton and Johnson coming back with news of Boyd's reconnaissance mission. "So I urge each of you to be observant over the coming days. We are on the brink of war, and I have no doubt someone will try to shove us over the brink."

He could make out an automobile now below the dust boiling into the eastern sky. "Stand by for further orders," he added, "and have your men ready to move at a moment's notice. That will be all, gentlemen."

Floyd Gibbons, his arm bandaged after the close encounter with windshield glass at Las Cruces, hurried toward the general as the meeting broke up. "Do you believe President Wilson will finally meet Mexican aggression with force?" he asked, out of breath. "Our readers will want to know what you think, General, about the prospects of full-scale war with Carranza."

"I haven't the slightest idea what Wilson will do," Pershing replied, "and I doubt he does, either, which is a sad commentary on the leadership of this country, if you ask me. Only you may not ask me that kind of question, Mr. Gibbons, for it would seem insubordinate for me to give you that sort of reply concerning my commander-in-chief." He could see the automobile clearly now in the distance; a report of Boyd's recent activities was coming at last. He frowned when he saw another civilian in the seat of the Dodge, wondering who he might be, why he would accompany Johnson and Patton back to Casas Grandes.

The automobile roared up to the general's command tent where the engine died, steam boiling from its radiator cap. Patton jumped out of the Dodge ahead of Will Johnson and the stranger.

"I have terrible news," Patton said, glancing to the newsman standing at Pershing's elbow. "We should talk in private. The man with us is W. P. McCabe, foreman of Santo Domingo Ranch, and he has a story to tell you. Captain Boyd is dead."

"Bring McCabe inside," Pershing said quietly, fearing the rest of the news Patton bore could be far worse. "Then start from the beginning and leave nothing out."

"I'll let McCabe tell you in his own words, General," Patton replied, waving Will and McCabe toward the tent. "He saw the whole thing."

W. P. McCabe, an elderly rancher from southern Texas who had been managing an American-owned ranch in Chihuahua for a number of years, shook hands with General Pershing when they were alone inside the canvas walls. "The nigger soldiers you sent to Carrizal are damn near all dead or wounded, General," he began.

Pershing pursed his lips. "I would ask that you refer to them as 'Negroes,' Mr. McCabe. Please continue."

McCabe, a smallish man with deeply bowed legs, showed brief annoyance. "That Captain Boyd, he rode up to Carrizal where a Meskin general by the name of Gomez had his troops deployed. I went along because of Lem. Lem's an old friend from way back an' he wanted me to be there, 'cause I knowed General Gomez. So I went, only now I wish I hadn't. This Boyd, he got real smart-mouthed with Gomez, sayin' his orders told him not to ride around Carrizal like Gomez wanted. Instead, Boyd said he was gonna ride straight through. Gomez told him that if he did, he would have to do it over the bodies of five hundred dead Meskins. Boyd said he was comin' anyways. Right then I told Lem he'd better scoot or he could wind up dead as a fence post, 'cause Gomez meant what he said and I knowed it."

"Then what happened?" Pershing asked, feeling quite sure that he already knew.

"Boyd commenced to lead his troops straight at Carrizal, and I heard him say something to the effect that he was about to make history. That's when all the shootin' started. Captain Boyd got killed right off, an' so did his assistant, Adair. I hollered for Lem to follow me away from there, only he didn't. I never heard so much shootin' in all my life. Last count I took, there was at least fourteen American soldiers dead and nearly forty wounded. Twenty-five, includin' Lem, got taken prisoner. There was dead soldiers all around town, Meskins and niggers . . . Negroes, hardly any survivors 'cept for the prisoners the Meskins took. It was over before a man could sneeze. Captain Boyd led his men straight into General Gomez's guns, like he went crazy all of a sudden. Gomez was ready for a fight, with trenches and cannons all over the place. Boyd had to be the dumbest soldier who ever lived, if you ask me. He got his men killed, leading that dumb charge straight at Carrizal like he did. Hell, all he had to do was ride around it."

"Where are the American survivors?" Pershing asked, doing a quick mental tally: There couldn't have been many left unharmed.

"Scattered all over the damn place," McCabe replied sadly, wagging his head. "Damn near all of them are afoot. They got their horses shot out from under 'em during the first charge. I saw a few runnin' like hell for the underbrush. Some was wounded mighty bad. General Gomez got killed himself, so there's no way to know who's in charge at Carrizal now. But I saw a bunch take Lem and the others prisoner, herdin' 'em like sheep toward the middle of town at gunpoint. I watched what happened from the top of this hill west of town. I took off when I saw that it weren't no use to stick around."

"We found Mr. McCabe as he was coming back to the ranch," Patton said. "He told us about the disaster, so I asked him to come with us so you could hear about it from a witness. Someone should be sent back to look for stragglers, General. The survivors, what few there are, are on foot somewhere between Carrizal and Santo Domingo Ranch."

Pershing's jaw remained clamped for half a minute of silence as he considered what the massacre would do to negotiations between Washington and Mexico City. All hell was sure to break loose now, and the fault lay with the disobedience of the late Captain Charles T. Boyd. Fourteen dead, forty wounded, and twenty-five taken prisoner, the worst blunder of the campaign. Nothing could prevent his detractors from chewing him up over this debacle—and it would make no difference that Boyd had disobeyed his orders. Pershing knew he would be blamed. Instead of being chosen to lead an American expeditionary force to glory on the battlefields of Europe following a successful Mexican campaign, his military career would be in ruins. "This is the spark that will touch things off," he said in complete resignation, quite suddenly near the point of exhaustion. "Nothing can prevent a war with Mexico City now. I will have allowed my country to become embroiled in a war no one wants, battling a neighbor nation over a dispute of the most minor insignificance. We came here to look for Pancho Villa. What we have found is a senseless war over nothing of any consequence."

Will Johnson adjusted his crutches to better support him. "I found out from a railroad engineer I know at Villa Ahumada that General Obregon has ordered ten thousand fresh troops to Chihuahua, and that more are headed this way."

McCabe agreed and said, "Meskin troops are movin' all over the place lately, the past week or so. Trains full of soldiers have been comin' through on the way to Juarez, and Laredo, so I don't figure the fight is gonna be confined to Chihuahua pretty soon."

"I think we should retaliate immediately," Patton suggested, "by sending cavalry to Carrizal to wipe out what is left of the troops Gomez commanded. With Vickers field guns, we will be able to decimate any Federal forces there. Artillery could easily level the town in an hour."

Pershing was half listening, thinking about what would go on in Washington when news of Boyd's folly got there. "Many innocent citizens would be killed, Lieutenant, as well as our men who are prisoners there. Blasting a sleepy Mexican village into oblivion is not the answer. Captain Boyd was at fault. I'll have to get a wire to Fred Funston without delay, explaining how this happened. I only hope all-out war can be averted through diplomatic channels before it's too late."

Patton's flush only deepened when he heard the general's reluctance to act, and without thinking he blurted out, "We can't let them get away with this, sir! We can't let them slaughter our troops without some form of retaliation."

As Pershing was about to give Patton a terse reply the sound of boots came to the tent. Colonel Dodd burst through the flap with fire in his eyes.

"What's this I hear about our men getting whipped at Carrizal?" he demanded, ignoring protocol by omitting to salute his superior officer.

Pershing sighed, forgiving Dodd the intrusion. "Captain Boyd and his troop was wiped out by Federals. It means we will go to war with Mexico, I'm afraid."

"What's being done about it?" Dodd cried, looking at faces around the tent.

"Nothing now," Pershing replied softly, wishing Dodd hadn't been so quick to learn about it. "I'll contact Funston and ask him what we should do."

Dodd seemed on the verge of exploding. "I don't need Freddy Funston to tell me that we ought to kick their asses!" he bellowed. "Surely we aren't just going to sit here!"

Pershing's own temper was set to flare. "That is precisely what we will do until my orders come, George."

Patton continued to push for an advantage, hoping to seize the heat of the moment. "We should demand the release of our prisoners, and if they refuse, we have every justification to bombard Carrizal with artillery. When they see we mean to turn their town to rubble, the prisoners will be released."

"Not now," Pershing said again. "Not until someone higher up makes the decision."

Dodd looked at Patton and Patton looked at Dodd, but neither man would say a word upon hearing the steely tone in the general's voice.

Pershing motioned to Patton. "Take a message. Have it delivered to Columbus for immediate transmission to Southern Command. Then assemble a detachment to go to Carrizal to look for survivors, and I want it understood that no fighting will occur—not one shot is to be fired until our orders come."

Outside, a distant rumbling took Pershing's attention from the message to Funston. He walked to the tent flap and peered outside, discovering a bank of dark clouds forming to the south and east. A bolt of lightning arced down from the clouds, then thunder rumbled again.

"It's going to rain," he said absently, his mind a thousand miles away at a meeting room at the War Department where his fate would be decided in the coming days, perhaps only a few hours from now.

Will Johnson hobbled to the opening and looked up at the sky. "The rainy season is gonna start," he said. "The road to Columbus will turn to mud. Anything carryin' a load heavier than a sack full of goose down will get stuck. You won't be able to supply your men with wagons or trucks much longer. Mules will be the only way."

"One more problem I don't need right now," Pershing said, as more chains of lightning flashed across the horizon.

"Worst mud to stick I ever saw," Will continued. "Worse than when we was stuck in that sand comin' down here."

"There is a strong possibility now that we will be going home anyway after what took place at Carrizal."

"Sorry to hear 'bout your troubles, General. But like I tried to tell you from the beginning, this ain't no real hospitable place to start with. I don't reckon I need to be reminded that I ain't got a military mind, but this place don't hardly seem worth fightin' over, if you ask me."

Pershing let out the breath he was holding, listening to the faraway thunder a moment longer. "More and more, I'm finding that I am inclined to agree with you, Mr. Johnson."

18 June
Captain Charles Boyd committed the most serious blunder of the campaign by attacking Carrizal. War with the de facto government of Mexico will surely result, and I will be blamed. I thought Boyd to be a courageous man, but not foolish. After my conversation with him I felt confident that he fully understood the importance and delicacy of his mission. No one could have been more surprised and chagrined than I was to learn that he had become so seriously involved. I have only high praise for George Dodd and Robert Howze—the Seventh and the Eleventh Cavalry have performed well. But as to the other officers, they have done nothing of value from a military standpoint since being with the expedition. They know little of service in the field, or

else they care nothing about their responsibilities. Most have had their regiments reported for more delinquencies than any reasonable man should be asked to tolerate. Some of them have been utter failures down here, without the least practical ability. Men of their kind should make way for those who are efficient. One of my lieutenant colonels whom I will not mention by name is quite simply asleep. He takes no interest in anything, lacks initiative, and is, upon the whole, hopeless as a regimental commander. The sooner the army gets rid of men like these the better off it will be. Their failures will surely reflect on me. At the onset of this expedition I was quite hopeful, looking forward to a chance to prove my worth. Now I am faced with a disaster from which I must somehow extricate myself personally. I am reminded of the mouse who no longer desires the cheese, merely wishing to be set free of the trap. Not only are we no closer to finding Villa, we now face the likelihood of war with a neighboring country, a war no American wants. Wilson is nearing reelection and, fearing a campaign against Charles Evans Hughes, will strike no blows that could pull America into a fight.

The rains have begun. We face even more impossible obstacles in a desert turned to mud. The men are already showing signs of ennui, and in order to placate them I will grant permission for a whorehouse in camp, under the closest of supervision. Patton has devised all manner of drills to keep the men from boredom. He is most adept at every type of detail and has the men marching back and forth in the mud so often that they will surely develop webbed feet. I have wholeheartedly recommended Patton for a promotion, which is his just due, although his quick temper will prove to be his undoing, I fear. He still broods over my refusal to send him along on the mission to capture Colonel Cervantes. I am still disappointed that the death of Cervantes was given such small notice back home, for I sincerely believe the loss severely cripples Villa's future efforts to raise Cain here. However, in light of recent develop-

ments, Captain Boyd's disastrous misadventure at
Carrizal, Villa assumes less importance. Somehow we
must avoid a war with Carranza. Otherwise I will
surely spend the rest of my career in this unholy place
battling an enemy whose spirits cannot be broken.
While Mexicans are poor soldiers in the main, they
make up for any deficiencies with bloodlust and sheer
determination. In George Dodd's succinct summation
of our situation here, he is of the opinion that Mexicans
of all persuasions are unreasoning fools who, when
provoked, can be very difficult to thoroughly extermi-
nate.

• 41 •

The artificial leg freed him from dependence upon crutches
and gave him back most of his mobility. A doctor from Fort
Bliss came down to treat some of the more seriously
wounded from Carrizal, and while he was at Casas Grandes,
landlocked by a sea of mud surrounding the army's base
camp after the rains began, he fitted Will with a wooden leg.
Thus he was able to maneuver in reasonable fashion and
suffered only minor pain where his stump was encased by a
leather collar supporting him above the piece of polished
pine. The leg was carved with a foot at the end, and he now
regretted having tossed his previously empty boot into the
stream at Satevo. The quartermaster provided him with a
new pair of cavalryman's high-topped boots. Other than for
an awkward limp necessary to swing the artificial limb into
place for each step he took, Will allowed as how he was
almost as good as new while he waited, along with the rest of
the soldiers, for a war with Mexico to begin.

Captain Boyd's disastrous charge at Carrizal had resulted in the hurried formation of a joint high commission between Mexican officials and representatives from Washington. General Pershing's worry that he would be recalled as commander of the expedition did not come to pass. And now, as torrential rains came to Chihuahua, turning the land into a sticky morass, all eyes were on the meetings between governments. Mud prevented any more hostilities from taking place for the present. The encampment at Casas Grandes became an unnavigable quagmire of souplike clay. Motor-driven vehicles were rendered useless. Hopelessly mired trucks and automobiles were scattered all over the muddy plain, abandoned to the sea of sucking, bottomless slop as more heavy rains pelted northern Chihuahua. Horses and mules provided the only means of reliable transportation. Swollen creeks quickly became rivers of watery mud. Soldiers were confined to their tents. Those who braved the storms resembled drowned rats while slogging about camp doing routine duty. Engineers struggled to make the road to Columbus passable, succeeding only by slow degrees in what amounted to progress of barely a few yards of solid roadbed each day. Boredom quickly set in among the waterlogged soldiers. Gambling and fistfights resulted when too many idle men were thrown together by inclement weather. Will found himself housed with C. E. Tracy, the cowboy from Arizona, to wait out the downpour and perhaps the commencement of war. Days were spent sitting on folding cots staring out the tent flap at sheets of dark rain. Will's thoughts were with Lem Spilsbury most of the time. The prisoners taken at Carrizal were being held as a form of ransom by the *Federales* until a negotiated settlement was made for the complete withdrawal of American troops from Mexican soil.

"Hell of a way to make a payday, ain't it?" Tracy mumbled, his face to the opening where row upon row of tents sat in the midst of a gray deluge. He was playing solitaire on his cot.

Will had begun a letter to Raymond, finding the piece of paper so soggy that his pencil tore through it. "I reckon it beats dyin' of thirst, maybe."

"That Lieutenant Patton is an out-and-out son of a bitch, makin' men march in this shit. Makes me glad I ain't in the army or I'd have to bust his jaw with my fist when he tried to order me out to march in this miserable rain. An old-fashioned country ass-whippin' is what he needs."

"He marches in the rain himself. Kinda hard to fault a man who is willing to do what he asks the rest of 'em to do."

"He's plumb crazy if you ask me." A mounted courier came from the direction of Columbus, distracting Tracy for the moment. "Somebody's comin'. Maybe there'll be word about that commission meeting so we can all go home."

Will watched the waterlogged courier dismount in front of General Pershing's tent. "I'll walk over and see if I can find out anything—any news. Been aimin' to talk to Pershing anyway about goin' home to Laredo. This army sure as hell don't need me here now." He got up and shouldered into his slicker, tugging his hat down for the slippery trek across the mud.

"Let me know if we're headed back," Tracy asked. "I need the money, but I'd rather earn it someplace else."

Shoulders rounded, he walked out in the rain as darkness came over the camp, dodging larger puddles, testing his balance, not quite fully accustomed to the wooden leg. Like Tracy, he needed the army's money, but not enough to endure much more of this endless monotony. He crossed the sodden ground without much difficulty and halted in front of the general's tent just in time to meet a badly drenched courier departing. He spoke to General Pershing before noticing that another soldier was inside. "If I could have just a word . . ."

"Come in, Mr. Johnson," the general said. "Major Young was just leaving."

A black officer from the Tenth stood up from a folding stool and put on his campaign hat. "I only wanted to say how sorry I am that it had to be one of my men," Young said in a hushed voice that was hard to hear because of raindrops falling on the canvas roof. "I thought Captain Boyd was a good soldier with a promising future. Apparently he had another side, one I couldn't see."

"The Tenth cannot be blamed for the actions of just one

man, Major. The responsibility was his, not yours, to follow direct orders. It is obvious he ignored them."

"Thanks for your understanding. Good night, General. I'll be going now."

Pershing dismissed the major and indicated the stool when Will hesitated near the tent flap. "Sit down, Mr. Johnson. It has been a long day for both of us, I am sure. Waiting can be hard on a man's nerves." He reached into a footlocker and took out a bottle of brandy. "Would you care to join me for a drink? I seldom ever imbibe, but today has been a difficult one."

Will slouched on the stool and took off his hat and slicker. "Don't mind if I do, General. I wanted to talk to you a minute, if you've got the time."

"It would seem I've got nothing but time. However, there is one bit of cheerful news. The prisoners taken at Carrizal will be released at Laredo in the morning. A deal has been worked out between Minister Aguilar and General Scott to let them go while talks continue, so our mutual friend, Lem Spilsbury, will soon be a free man, as will the others."

Pershing poured brandy into tin cups and handed one to Will. "I'm glad for Lem's sake," Will said. He took a sip of liquor and swallowed slowly. "What are the chances that we will go to war with Carranza?"

Pershing settled into his seat, frowning at the contents of his cup. "No one really knows. Carranza has shown a tendency to back down on those rare occasions when Wilson takes a firm stand. I'm informed that Wilson refuses to withdraw our troops completely. He's activated the National Guard and in a few weeks, over a hundred thousand soldiers will be guarding twelve hundred miles of border from Nogales to Brownsville. I predict we will merely be engaged in more of the president's watchful waiting policy. The next move will be up to Carranza, and the brass at the War Department do not believe Carranza wants an open war with us, with the Mexican economy in ruins. We have what amounts to a stalemate. I fully expect we will be here in this same posture throughout the winter, perhaps even next spring, unless Villa can be found."

Will toyed with his drink. "I'm pretty sure we won't find

him. He's gone into hiding until his leg is well, then he'll come back as troublesome as ever. His people will hide him from us and make it nigh onto impossible to sniff him out."

Pershing looked at Will a moment, his face illuminated by a kerosene lantern hanging from a tent pole. "I confess I misjudged you, Mr. Johnson. I believed you were overconfident in the beginning, thinking yourself to be an expert on matters you knew very little about. But now I find I have been wrong about you. You have keen insights into our dilemma."

He paused and took a sip of brandy. "I have long suspected this expedition was in actuality a covert military exercise devised by my superiors to prepare our troops for the war in Europe. While it is true we are testing motorized transport, it is failing rather dismally under these difficult conditions. However, the most dramatic failure has been with our leadership. My officers, for the most part, are pampered tin soldiers with no common sense. I suppose I'm from the old school. Responsibility has an obligation. Soldiers under my command risk their lives based on my decisions, my judgment of situations. I endeavor to keep this in mind at all times, for when the scales of justice are balanced, I should be willing to take the same risks as those I ask of my men. I have a job to do here, and for the life of me, I simply cannot get it done with the men and equipment I have at my disposal. Our aeroplanes won't fly, our vehicles continue to break down, and our quarry, Villa, is never where we believe him to be by the time we get there. He has thumbed his nose at us from the moment we arrived, and nothing seems to deter him. Now President Carranza has ordained even further restraints on how and where we may look for Villa. I find myself in an impossible situation, and now this weather threatens to intervene even further."

Will took a sip. "Chihuahua can be a tough place to look for anything besides a rattlesnake—and I don't mean the two-legged variety. What you set out to do here most likely couldn't have been done by anybody. Villa is a hero to these people, mostly because he don't appear to be afraid of anything or anyone. Tryin' to chase him down in his own backyard wasn't the most sensible undertaking in the first place. An' like I told you before, Villa probably wasn't the one who attacked Columbus, accordin' to what I hear. If I was in your shoes I wouldn't take it too hard that Villa gave you the slip. I doubt anybody could have found him."

The general stared blankly at the floor. "My failure here has probably ruined my military career," he said. "It seems things have taken a turn for the worse since . . . the fire."

"Somebody told me you lost your family, General. Must've been hard to put it out of the way to come down to Mexico so soon after it happened. I never had a wife or kids, but I've got a nephew, an' he means the whole world to me. That's one reason I came over to talk to you 'bout headin' back home. I miss the boy somethin' awful and I don't see how I'm doin' you any good just sittin' in a tent watchin' it rain."

Pershing gazed out at the storm, silent for a while, as if his thoughts were a million miles away. "It has to stop raining one of these days. I wish you could be here when it does finally stop. I need men who know how to conduct themselves, and I find I am seriously short in that category. When it stops raining, if God is willing, I intend to make a determined effort to hunt down Villa wherever he is. I'd feel better if you were here to help us decide where to look."

Will took another drink, warmed by the burn. "Then I reckon I'll stay a bit longer. But I wouldn't count on hearin' about Villa again until he's raised another army. I'll stay on for a month or two, so long as there's no war between us and Carranza. If there's gonna be a shootin' war with the *Federales,* I won't be hangin' around to see if my luck has changed any when it comes to bullets. I just wasn't made to be a soldier. Killin' another man is somethin' I ain't too good at. Besides, you've got plenty of boys in this outfit who are lookin' for a fight if Carranza decides he wants one."

"If only they knew how . . ." Pershing said thoughtfully. "I suppose we have come to a crossroads. My best officers have been trained for combat in a form that no longer exists. Horseback campaigns are no longer really viable. Aeroplanes and motor-powered vehicles are the future of warfare. Personal courage will mean very little when an aeroplane drops bombs on enemies the pilot cannot actually see. German U-boats sink vessels with hundreds of people on board by the simple act of aiming a torpedo at a ship on the horizon. War is no longer a conflict between men. Machines will be pitted against each other, and the side with the best machinery shall be the victor. If I am to win battles of this nature, then Congress and the president will have to provide us with the best war machinery on earth. Rattletrap vehicles and aeroplanes that are scarcely airworthy will not suffice in modern combat. If this Mexican campaign has taught me a single lesson, it is that we are totally unprepared to go to war against a power armed with better war machines."

"Villa has no machinery at all," Will said, "but he's smart enough to know that he can't win against what you've got if he comes out in the open to fight. He'll stay out of sight, pickin' his spots, striking where nobody figures he will when your back is turned. Makes him that much more of a hero in the eyes of his followers, that he can make bigger armies look foolish when they can't find him to whip him."

"Guerrilla warfare, Mr. Johnson, and I confess that Villa is quite good at it, far better than I first supposed. Add to that the grim fact that we have blundered so often, and now we find ourselves in a most untenable position. With ten thousand men at my disposal and the best wartime machinery this country has, I cannot so much as locate or fully engage the object of my mission here.

"It would appear, however, that we are not the only ones stymied. Yesterday's courier brought me a copy of *The New York Times.* A war correspondent describes what the Allied forces are confronted with in Europe. Battlefield conditions are worse than anyone imagined in France. Continual rains have flooded trenches, and neither man nor machine can move across the mud, not even the new armor-plated tanks equipped with field cannons that move on hinged steel tracks. Both sides are stuck indefinitely. Dead bodies cannot be removed due to the inability of the medical corps to reach them until the rains stop, and corpses have begun to rot, spreading disease. The Germans are similarly entrapped by the bottomless ooze. Neither side can advance. It is a stalemate. Nature has rendered both armies helpless while men are suffering under the most extreme conditions. It sounds like a field commander's nightmare, asking his men to hold a line in driving rains that have turned the battleground to slop. Had America joined the Allied effort, we would be similarly immobilized, and I have no doubt our casualties at this point would be horrendous. No strategy can be successfully employed when men are unable to move, which is the situation we find ourselves in here, now that these rains have begun. How can we possibly look for Villa until these monsoons have ended?"

Will drained the contents of his cup. "I'm sure glad we ain't over there in France," he said. "Your boys figure they're mighty miserable, marchin' around in all this mud, but the one thing they ain't is dead. Soon as this rain stops, I'll do whatever I can to help you find Villa, just so long as nobody is shootin' at me while I'm about it. Well, thanks for the cup of brandy. G'night, General."

"Good night, Mr. Johnson. And you have my gratitude for agreeing to stay with us a while longer."

Will put on his slicker and hat before trudging out into the cold rain. On his way back to the tent he thought back to the talk with General Pershing, discovering that he had grown to like the man. Odd, that he found a soldier he truly liked. Pershing was so very different from most military types. He had the best interests of his men at heart.

"If I had to be a soldier," he muttered, slogging through inky mud puddles in the dark, "I reckon I'd want to be in his outfit if I had a choice. Just so I didn't have to be over there in France, wherever the hell that is."

• 42 •

Blistering heat turned the railroad depot at Laredo into a furnace. A hot wind lifted dust from barren earth along the tracks. Will watched dust devils form beside the rails as he sat on a bench in the shade below the depot roof, holding the *El Paso Times* he had been reading until railroad crews unloaded his horses. He'd been reading about the latest events befalling the Pershing expedition, mostly misfortune. The paper editorialized that America was now on the very precipice of war with Mexico. Secretary of State Lansing, Secretary of War Newton Baker, and President Wilson were deciding what should be done.

Will gazed off at the rooftops of Laredo, remembering the battle scenes he witnessed at Guerrero, the Villista he killed on the mountain, and the man he shot at San Miguelito Ranch. When he left for El Paso back in March he would hardly have called himself an innocent, growing up on the border, accustomed to its often brutal struggles. But now, so many months later, he could add two killings and the loss of a leg to a bushwhacker's bullet to his troubles. He could never have imagined any of this happening to him before-hand, not in his wildest dreams. He had only wanted the army's money, payment for telling Pershing which roads to travel, showing them the way. It all sounded simple enough, a job with minimal risk to life and limb. Yet he had almost lost his life a number of times, and he did lose a limb in the process. Had he known what awaited him in Chihuahua, he would have stayed in Webb County no matter how dry it got.

He thought back to Elisa. On the slow train ride back to Laredo he'd had plenty of time to examine the way he felt about her, and he had finally come to the conclusion that he

350

might have grown to care for her, even though he didn't really know her. It hadn't mattered that she shared a bed with Villa at the time, or that she was probably involved in some sort of spying for the German government. He felt he understood those things, for he was no stranger to difficult circumstances and hard times. She was doing what she felt she had to do, and whether he agreed or not, he knew some small part of him still wanted to see her again. Perhaps when the war was over he would write to her at Parral.

He looked down at his wooden leg. At a hospital in El Paso, army surgeons had fitted him with another artificial limb. A wooden foot fit snugly inside his right boot, a new pair of boots he'd bought with money he got from the paymaster at Fort Bliss. He walked without crutches, and could ride a horse, even walk without all that much of a noticeable limp when he really put his mind to it. Things weren't so bad, considering.

He watched the trainmen lead Poco and the white pony down a slanted loading chute. Getting up from the bench slowly, still not quite used to balancing on his artificial leg, he tucked the newspaper under his arm and picked up his new war bag with the clothing he'd bought in El Paso folded inside. He'd traded the dun for a used saddle with John Abel, telling him about the expedition and how he'd lost his leg. John allowed that there were now almost a hundred thousand National Guardsmen from all across the country watching the Mexican border, according to the *Times*.

Walking stiffly at first, he came to the end of the platform and went carefully down the steps. He could almost see Junior's face when the white pony arrived. There were gifts for everyone, a new dress for Rosa, toys for the younger kids, and a shirt for Raymond with snaps instead of buttons. It would be good to see the ranch again, even as dry as it was this October.

A member of the unloading crew looked up as he approached, and he tried as best he could not to limp. Poco's ears cocked forward, then the little bay nickered softly.

"Need any help gettin' saddled?" the man asked, taking note of Will's awkward shuffle.

"I can manage," Will said, believing that he could.

* * *

He rode through the gate at an easy trot, thankful to be home. Their old spotted dog left the front porch wagging its tail, recognizing both the man and the horse from a distance. Pastures along the Las Minas road had been sad sights, the grass almost nonexistent. Razor-thin cows stood in scant shade below mesquite trees, existing mostly on mesquite beans to stay alive and nurse their calves. It wasn't a very pretty picture, the ranch and the herd in the middle of a drought, but there was something about it that touched a soft spot in Will's heart, and he felt better now being there.

He looked at the old house, unpainted boards cracking in the sun, having withstood almost forty years of dry weather since Lee Johnson erected it with his own hands. A steeply slanted tin roof that made wonderful pattering sounds when it did rain was beginning to fall apart. Raymond and Will had added the roof years before, when crumbling wood shingles no longer turned water. A leaky roof was a problem they both would have enjoyed this year, he thought, guiding Poco up the lane with the pony tied to the saddlehorn. He watched the front door, waiting eagerly for the boy to come out. It was then that Will noticed how badly the front porch had begun to sag, bowed in the middle, badly in need of repair.

A handful of calves stood in the cow lot beside the shed in back of the house, calves that needed milk from a pail when their mothers grew too thin and weak to nurse them. Conditions at the ranch were no better than when he left, but it was home. With the money he got from the army they could buy corn and hay until it rained—if it ever rained here again, an unlikely prospect when Will glanced up at a cloudless sky and a merciless midday sun.

The old dog barked, a friendly yelp alerting everyone in the house that someone was coming. Poco quickened his trot, pulling the pony up a rutted, tree-lined lane.

The screen door opened. A small boy walked out on the porch in his bare feet, shirtless in the heat, squinting in the sun's fierce glare. Then his face broke into a wide grin.

"Uncle Will!" the boy shouted in a tiny voice, running down the steps, scattering Rosa's chickens pecking about the grassless caliche yard. Bare feet pounded over the hardpan, sending up tiny puffs of dust when Junior ran toward him, a sight Will had longed to see for many months in the desolate Sierras.

He reined Poco to a halt and got down before Junior raced up to him. The boy flung himself at Will's neck, arms outstretched, his face bright with joy.

"I been waitin', Uncle Will!" he shouted, as Will stooped down to scoop him into his arms. "Pa told me you was bringin' me a big surprise!"

Junior hadn't noticed the pony yet, thinking his present might be in Will's gear. He hugged Will's neck with all his might and then leaned back, grinning from ear to ear.

"What did you bring me?" he asked, peering around to see the canvas bag hanging from Will's saddlehorn. "How big is it, Uncle Will?"

The screen door slammed again when Rosa came out with Johnny and her daughter. Will waved to her, then he spoke to the boy. "Nearly as big as a horse. Almost that big, anyway."

Junior frowned. Will's war bag wasn't large enough to hide a big present. He was about to ask another question when he saw the white pony. His dark eyes, the same color as his mother's, rounded in genuine surprise. His frown melted. "The pony?" he asked breathlessly.

"He's yours," Will answered quietly. "He's real gentle, but you'll have to learn a few things before you can ride him off by yourself. I've been tryin' to think of a name for him, only I decided on the way out here that it's your job to come up with a name."

The boy squirmed to be free of Will's arms. "Put me down, Uncle Will," he cried, small feet churning before he reached the ground.

"Take it easy or you'll spook him," Will warned, a warning that went unheeded. The boy ran to the pony, halting near its muzzle, holding out a palm so the little horse could catch his scent, the way Will taught him to approach horses.

The pony lowered its head and flared its nostrils, nuzzling Junior's hand with its ears pricked forward, snorting once at the boy's unfamiliar scent.

"He's so beautiful, Uncle Will. White as cotton. That's what I'll name him. 'Cotton' is gonna be a perfect name."

" 'Cotton' suits me," Will said, listening to Rosa walk up to them as Junior began to stroke the pony's neck.

"Hello, Will," Rosa said, smiling when he turned around to greet her. She tucked her infant daughter in one arm and put the other arm around his neck, tears glistening in her eyes. "We have been so worried since we got your letters."

He embraced her warmly and kissed her forehead. "I'm fine," he replied, reaching down to tousle three-year-old Johnny's dark hair. "I brought you somethin' too, Johnny. I brought presents for everybody. Where's Raymond?"

"He has ridden to the pastures," Rosa said, "checking for more calves that must be bottle fed. There is no grass. Some of the older cows will die soon. The money you sent was a help, but it was not enough. The price of corn is so high . . ."

"I brought more money," he told her, noticing that Johnny had eased away from them to join his brother beside the pony, a look of wonder on his face. "And one more mouth to feed, I'm afraid. I got the pony in El Paso. It'll make a perfect first horse for the boy. A kid his age needs a horse so he can start learnin' how to help me an' his pa around the place."

"He will be so proud of it," Rosa whispered, watching Junior rub the pony's neck and withers. Little Johnny inched closer and stuck out a finger to touch the inquisitive gray muzzle lowered near his face.

"How is your leg?" Rosa asked. "Your letter said they had to take it off."

Bending down, he rapped his knuckles on the artificial shin above his boot top, grinning when it produced a hollow sound. "I got to be careful not to stand too close to the fire this winter or I'll smoke up the room," he said. "It's healed, pretty much. Still hurts some late at night or if I walk around too much, but I can sit a saddle." He remembered the other presents and took down his war bag. "Here's a new dress for you," he told her. "I hope I got the right size." He gave her another package, a doll for her daughter, then he took out a bright red wooden fire truck, and when Johnny saw it he hurried over on his short little legs crying, "It's mine, it's mine!"

"There's a shirt for Raymond when he gets back," Will added, as Johnny set the truck down in the dirt and started to push it, imitating the sound of a motor by blowing through pursed lips.

A movement caught his eye when Junior, standing up on his tiptoes, put his arms around the pony's neck. "I love you, Cotton," the boy said, keeping his voice low. "I'll feed you real good and brush your mane and tail every day. Promise I will."

"You might give both those horses some water," Will said.

Junior turned around, and in the sunlight, despite the smile he wore, his eyes were watering a little. "I sure will," he promised. He came over to take Poco's reins, keeping his face to the ground until he stood before Will. Then he looked up and his face was beaming. "Pa was right when he told me what your letter said, Uncle Will, about how you were bringin' me a big surprise. A pony is what I've been wantin' for a long, long time, only Pa said we didn't have enough money this year. Didn't have enough last year, either. This is the best surprise in the whole world. I'll say thanks a hundred times, if you want."

"Once is plenty. Now go take 'em to water, before they dry up an' blow off in this heat."

Before he turned away, Junior tilted his face thoughtfully. "You think 'Cotton' is a good enough name, Uncle Will? I want his name to be somethin' real special."

"'Cotton' is a fine name."

The boy glanced at Will's new boots. "There was somethin' in that letter wasn't true," he said. "Pa told me you said they cut off one of your legs on account of you got shot by somebody."

Amused, Will hoisted the right leg of his denims until his wooden leg showed. "They took it off just below my knee, so I'll have to be real careful that the wood ants don't get in it when I ain't lookin'."

Some of the color left Junior's cheeks. "It's just painted wood," he said softly, like he couldn't quite believe it. "I bet it still hurts somethin' awful."

"It don't hardly hurt at all. Besides that, I won't ever have to worry 'bout gettin' a cactus needle in my foot, or worry that a scorpion got in my right boot overnight. Run along now, and see to those horses before they die of thirst."

Junior bobbed his head and led Poco toward the well at

the back of the house, the pony obediently following the pull of its lead rope.

"We are so glad to have you home again," Rosa said, the package containing her new dress still unopened. "Raymond will be so glad to see you. He has been worried ever since you left, and when the letter came telling us about your leg, it only made things worse—for all of us. Come in the house and I will fix you something to eat."

"I want a pony too," Johnny said, although he continued to push the toy fire truck over the bumpy ground.

Will chuckled. "When you're a little older. Maybe in a couple of years."

He followed Rosa to the house, hearing the familiar creak of the front steps when they bore his weight. The black-and-white dog trotted beside him, begging for an affectionate pat before he walked in. He stroked the dog's neck and went inside, stopped a few feet inside the door, examining the front room as though he was seeing it for the first time: a threadbare sofa, hidebound chairs, small tables, shaded oil lamps for reading at night, the dark fireplace, a mantle lined with faded photographs behind dusty panes of glass. Lee Johnson's old Sharps hunting rifle above the fireplace, resting on wood pegs. The vague smell of ashes in the hearth, coal oil in the lamps, and a sweet scent he couldn't identify coming from the kitchen.

"I baked a peach pie," Rosa said, placing her daughter in a rocking crib. She stopped before entering the kitchen. "Did the soldiers find Pancho?" she asked. "Is that the reason you have come home?"

He sighed and took off his hat, the Stetson he purchased in El Paso. "No," he answered in a faraway voice, suddenly reminded of the expedition, the hardships, the futility. "He's still on the loose somewhere in Chihuahua. I came back because I'd had enough of the army. I had to shoot two men, Rosa. I killed them. I still see 'em in my sleep sometimes, their faces. Bein' with that army, I was likely to have to kill more men, an' to tell the honest truth, I didn't have the stomach for it."

"I understand," Rosa whispered, coming across the room. She took his hand and held it tightly. "You are needed here,

Will. We are all so very glad you came back. Raymond has not been the same since you left, always quiet, his thoughts always with you in Chihuahua. Many nights he could not sleep."

"I was thinkin' about this place a lot too," he admitted, "and 'specially about you folks. You're all the family I've got, an' when they started shootin' at me, I suppose it made me come to realize how much I wanted to be back here with you. I got to missin' the boy somethin' awful, Rosa, like he was my own. I wanted to be back here, fixin' a stretch of fence, or fishin' for perch with Junior down at the Rio Grande." He walked past her into the kitchen and stared out a window at the well trough where Junior was bucketing water for the horses. His voice had thickened when he spoke again. "I was missin' this ol' place and the five of you the whole time, Rosa. I was homesick, I reckon. I saw all those soldiers gettin' killed an' I figured I could wind up bein' the next one to die. . . ." His voice trailed off.

Junior poured a final bucket of water into the stone trough, then he set the pail down and came over to the pony's withers to begin rubbing its coat with the palm of his hand. Will cleared his throat as though he meant to speak, then he shook his head and turned away from the window with an odd tight feeling in his chest.

Rosa was staring at him. "Welcome home, Will," she said. "Perhaps now Junior will stop asking about you. While you were gone, he asked about you every single day."

He left the window to embrace her, and for the first time he noticed how much larger the child inside her had grown. Standing in the kitchen of the old house where he had grown up, surrounded by its familiar sights and smells, he closed his eyes briefly. It was even better than he imagined to be back home.

He was resting in the old porch swing listening to the soft creak of rusted chains around the rafters while he swayed gently back and forth, idly watching the boy brush his pony in the late evening shade below a live oak tree west of the house when he saw a rider in the distance. Skirting dense thickets of mesquites, a man on a dark grullo gelding rode toward the ranch. Inside the house, Rosa cooed to her little daughter between spoonfuls of chicken soup. Johnny played in the yard with his new fire truck. Will halted the movement of the swing to watch the horseman, and by the way the man sat a saddle and the color of his horse, he knew who he was.

He got up carefully, reminded to test his balance before he went down the porch steps. He could hear the approaching hoofbeats grow louder. One at a time, he descended the steps and started across the yard toward a pasture gate to open it for his brother, doing his best not to limp too noticeably.

Raymond saw him and heeled the grullo to a lope in spite of the heat. His sun-blackened face broke into a grin. He rode to the gate and reined to a sliding stop, swinging down before the horse came to a complete halt within a swirl of chalky dust.

In the instant before they embraced each other, Raymond looked down at Will's right leg. Still grinning, he hugged Will fiercely and patted his shoulders. "Damn glad to see you," he said, taking a half step back to examine Will's face.

"It's good to be back," Will replied, trying not to show the emotion he felt."

Raymond frowned a little. He was a few inches taller than Will, heavier by a few pounds, his hair beginning to thin on top where he thumbed back his hat. "You're back earlier than we had it figured. On account of the leg, I suppose." He glanced at Will's right leg again.

"It's made out of wood. Got a natural-shaped foot and everything. I'm almost as good as new."

Raymond clapped him on the shoulder and led his winded horse through the gate. "We've been keepin' up with Pershing in the newspaper the best we could. Sounds like it's one hell of a mess down there."

"It is," Will replied, "an' I 'spect it's gonna stay that way until they finally give up an' come back. They'll never catch Villa. Never in a million years."

Raymond grunted as he was closing the gate, latching it with an old horseshoe fastened to a piece of rusted wire. "They're lookin' for the wrong man in the first place," he said, stopping on his way to the horse shed when he saw the white pony.

"That's the same thing John told me before we went down to Chihuahua," Will said absently. "The pony was a gift from John Abel. I asked John how much he wanted for it. When he found out it was for Lee's grandson, all he wanted in exchange was a bottle of whiskey. It's real gentle, gentle enough for the boy."

Raymond watched his son brush the pony's coat a moment more, then he smiled. "Junior's been askin' for you. He hardly went a day without askin' when you'd be home."

"I missed him too," Will said. "Missed all of you. I knew I'd seen enough of that army. I had to kill a couple of Villa's men when they came after me, and it kinda got stuck in my craw, like sand."

"They've been chasin' the wrong man the whole time," Raymond said again, like he knew something about it.

"That's what I heard from a couple of folks. John said it wasn't Villa at Columbus, and so did this German woman I know at Parral."

Raymond took a bandanna from his pocket to wipe sweat and grime from his face and neck. "Do you remember Luis Vela?" he asked, peering under Will's hat.

"Sure. He's the man who used to run the Santo Domingo Ranch before Bill McCabe down at Carrizal. Pa used to buy steers from him a long time ago. He was a saddle maker."

Raymond nodded thoughtfully. "I saw Luis over in Nuevo Laredo last month, while I was buyin' corn with some of that money you sent. We shook hands an' talked about old times for a spell. He asked about you, and I told him you were down in Chihuahua with Pershing, actin' as a scout. That's when he told me somethin' you oughta hear firsthand."

"What's that?" Will asked.

"We'll ride over to his house tomorrow, so you can hear it for yourself. I'm hungry, little brother. Let's find out what Rosa has for us to eat."

"A peach pie," Will said, following Raymond toward the barn. "I already sampled it. Best peach pie I ever tasted in my life."

On the way to the horse shed, Will wondered what Luis Vela could tell him that he didn't already know.

"Look, Pa!" Junior cried, pointing to the pony excitedly when they came around the house. "Look what Uncle Will brought me!"

Raymond led his horse over to the shady spot below a live oak where the boy was brushing the pony. "He's a mighty fine animal, son. The best part is that your uncle got back home safe an' sound. We'll be a family again, like we used to be."

Junior put down his brush and came over to Will. "Sure am glad you're home," he said, toeing the ground with one bare foot, looking down like the admission embarrassed him a little. "I had this real bad dream while you was gone, Uncle Will. I dreamed that somebody shot you, only you was dead when they found you. I woke up cryin' in the middle of the night. Ma came in when she heard me. She told me it was only a bad dream. It was the night after your letter came, tellin' us how they cut off your leg."

"I was lucky," Will told him, putting a hand on his shoulder. "That bullet was lower'n it was meant to be. Besides that, I had some real important business to tend to back at Laredo, so I wasn't gonna let anybody kill me right then, not 'til I got that business done."

The boy looked up at him. "What business was that, Uncle Will?" he asked, his face dark and serious.

Will's gaze drifted to the white pony. "It had to do with a little horse I got in El Paso. I promised I would deliver it in person to its new owner."

Junior stood a little taller. "That's me, Pa," he said, sounding older than his years. "I'm the owner of that pony, in case you didn't know. Uncle Will gave him to me. His name is 'Cotton'. I'm the one who named him."

Raymond nodded, admiring the little horse. "I 'spect your uncle will be teachin' you how to ride pretty soon. Now go wash up. It's time for supper."

Will watched the boy lead Cotton toward the corrals while Raymond worked the pumpjack at the well, thinking how remote, how meaningless, all his troubles down in Chihuahua seemed now. He had come within a whisker of dying there for a hundred dollars a month. He understood now, more than ever before, that the only truly meaningful things in his life were right here—his family, and a section of dry land bordering the Rio Grande. William Lee Johnson would never take them for granted again.

• 43 •

They had ridden through one of the poorest sections of Nuevo Laredo to reach Luis Vela's tiny house, past a stinking slaughterhouse where swarms of flies hovered above piles of cattle bones and stacks of curing hides. Rows of huts and adobe shacks were crowded together along chug-holed dirt streets away from the central business district. Unwashed children played in front of ramshackle houses, pausing long enough to beg for a coin or two when Will and Raymond rode past.

At the end of a quiet lane, Raymond stopped his horse in front of a one-room adobe and swung down, tying his reins to a cast-iron ring affixed to a corner of the house. Will tied off Poco and followed Raymond to the front door.

A soft knock produced the question, *"¿Quién es?"*

"Raymond Johnson. My brother's with me."

The thin plank door opened inward. Will saw a haggard face stubbled with black beard growth, sunken eyes beneath a shock of wavy salt-and-pepper hair. He barely recognized Luis he was so skinny, so pale, looking half starved.

Luis grinned and bowed to them, stepping back to allow them to enter. He wore ragged cotton pants and sandals, and a shirt discolored by too many washings. "Come in, my friends," he said in English. He looked much older than Will remembered as he showed them into the musty, sweltering room.

Luis pointed to hand-hewn wood chairs with rawhide

bottoms around a cluttered table. *"Sientense,"* he said, using Spanish when he couldn't recall the English word he wanted. Then he offered his hand to Will.

They shook. Luis seemed strangely uncomfortable with their presence. Will and Raymond took chairs.

"I only have pulque to offer you," Luis apologized with a helpless shrug.

"No thanks," Will replied, as Raymond wagged his head.

"I want you to tell Will what you told me," Raymond began, watching Luis take a chair opposite them, "about that raid at Columbus. Will has been scoutin' for the U.S. Army down in Chihuahua. Somebody told him the same thing you told me that day, about how Pancho Villa wasn't the one who led the raid."

A guarded look crossed Luis's face, as if a veil had fallen in front of his eyes. "I do not remember telling you anything," he said, looking down at his bony hands folded on the tabletop. "You must be mistaken, *Señor* Johnson. How would I know about such things? Could it have been someone else you spoke to?"

"It was you," Raymond insisted, although he said it gently, without reproach. "I know you served in the army, Luis. You were a member of the *Federales.* You told me you joined them because of the pay when the cattle market turned sour. Nobody was buyin' any saddles. Cattle prices were down. It's okay to talk in front of my brother. He don't work for the American army anymore."

Will turned in the chair and hoisted his right pants leg. "I got shot in the ankle, Luis. They had to cut off my leg just below the knee. I've got no love for the army on either side of this trouble, so you don't have to worry about what you say. I won't repeat anything you tell me."

Still uncertain, Luis shrugged again and looked askance. "I know nothing, *señors.* It is true, I served a short time with the *Federales.* But I know nothing about what happened at Columbus. I was discharged for failing to obey my orders. Now I receive no pension. *Nada,* nothing at all. As you can see, I am a very poor man. There is never enough to eat at my house. My wife left me while I was away with the army, taking *los niños* with her, and I will never see them again. It is a disgrace, to be discharged from the *Federales* without a pension. *Mis amigos* avoid me, and no one will speak to me when I walk the streets. Everyone knows I was dishonored by *mi comandante*, being discharged for not obeying the orders. *¡Dios!* Every day I go to the rubbish heaps to look for food like many of the orphans. It is a sad time for me."

Will gave Raymond a sideways glance. "I'll leave you a few dollars for food," he said, reaching into a pocket for coins. "I made some money workin' for the army." He placed six new silver dollars and some small change on the table in front of Luis. "Go on an' take it, Luis. Sounds like your troubles are a whole lot worse'n mine."

Luis stared at the money. *"Muchisimas gracias,"* he whispered, although he left the coins where they were. He looked at Will, then at Raymond. "In exchange, you want me to tell you *la verdad*, the truth, about Columbus?"

"I'd like to hear it," Will said. "You've got my word that I won't tell anybody else."

For a moment Luis remained undecided, glancing at the money, then to the men across the table. His hands were shaking noticeably, and he started blinking. "I will be killed if *el comandante* learns that I talked to *Americanos* about what happened on that night, *señors*. My life will be in your hands. *Los otros*, all the others who were there, were sworn to secrecy. No one talks, for they know what will happen to them. The others still receive good pensions. Some are still *Federales*, earning the rank of officers for what they did. I was the only one, *solamente*, who refused to obey when they ordered us to . . ."

Luis reached for the coins. He held them in a gnarled hand and stared at them for a moment, trembling.

"What did they order you to do?" Will asked, coming to the edge of his seat, wondering what could have been so terrible to frighten Luis this way. Was he really afraid to tell them what he knew about Columbus? Could he have been there himself? A sixth sense told Will he was about to hear something he would remember for the rest of his life.

"We were ordered to kill the woman," Luis said a moment later, his voice so strained that it sounded like he was genuinely in pain. His fingers curled around the money, then his hands disappeared below the table as he started to cry. Deep sobs sounded in his chest and he closed his eyes.

"She was wearing a wedding dress when we found her. Hector cut off her husband's head with his machete. She started to scream, and that is when *mi capitán* ordered me to silence her with my machete. *¡Madre!* I could not do it! I could not kill a woman! There was blood all over her! Her husband's head lay at her feet and she would not stop screaming! I begged her to be silent, so I would not have to kill her! But she could not hear me!"

Will swallowed, envisioning the grisly scene Luis described. "You were at Columbus?" he asked softly. "You said you were a *Federale?* . . ."

Luis's entire body shook, wracked by violent sobs. He gave a weak nod, his eyes still tightly closed, tears streaming down his sunken cheeks. *"Sí.* I . . . was there. We came . . . at midnight. We wore no uniforms. Some who rode with us were only children. They were told we were members of Villa's *Dorados,* and General Villa himself would pay them in gold and silver if they came with us that night to attack the Americans. Some came from as far away as Chihuahua City, believing they were to fight for Villa's revolution. They were too young to know they had been deceived. They did not know we were *Federales.* Papers were given to them, a letter they were told was signed by General Villa, asking them personally to fight for him. So many were only *niños* who knew nothing about guns. Some had only a few bullets. So many of them were killed that night, slaughtered like cattle, unable to defend themselves from the machine guns."

Will found Raymond looking at him while Luis was drying his eyes on a soiled shirtsleeve. The story Luis told was incredible. The Columbus raid was staged by a *Federale* force disguised as Villa's Dorados, strengthened by young recruits from parts of northern Chihuahua who were tricked into believing they fought for Villa's cause. The letters Luis described explained the papers found on the bodies of dead raiders the next morning. It was all a part of the plan to make the raid look like Villa's handiwork.

"I refused to kill the screaming woman," Luis said, choking when he said it. "Capitán Ponce drew his *pistola* and said he would kill me unless I followed his order. I threw my machete on the floor and ran from the house, barely escaping the bullets coming from the army camp and the city. I escaped with my life, running all the next day and night to Juarez, hiding in the brush when I saw *soldados,* both *Federales* and Americans. I knew no one would believe my story. And who was I to tell? We were sworn to secrecy. If any of us told the truth, Capitán Ponce promised us that we would be executed. I deserted from the *Federales,* so I could not go back or *mi comandante* would shoot me. It was only much later that I learned *Capitán* Ponce was killed at Columbus." Here Luis stopped to take a deep breath. "I came back home. I was afraid to tell anyone about our secret mission. I went to the *Federale* garrison here in Nuevo Laredo, saying that I got separated from my division when my horse went lame in Chihuahua, pretending to know nothing of what happened at Columbus. They told me to come back in one month. I went back, and they told me there was no job for me in the army, and I would get no pension. Nothing."

"They want to forget about you," Raymond offered. "They hope you'll just go away an' keep your mouth shut. Maybe the commander here doesn't know about your secret mission. To him you're nothin' but a deserter, a nuisance."

"It's one hell of a story," Will said, digesting everything Luis told them. "It probably means Venustiano Carranza was behind the Columbus raid all along, maybe in cahoots with the Germans, if what Elisa told me is the truth. They want to keep Pershing busy in Mexico so Germany can win the big war over in Europe. If they can keep Pershing chasin' shadows in Chihuahua, America ain't as likely to join the fight over there."

"¿Quién sabe?" Luis asked, wondering if anyone knew the whole truth. "Those of us who followed Capitán Ponce that night were only told the attack was necessary to keep the Americans from invading Mexico. We were reminded of Vera Cruz, when the American army came ashore to capture the town. *El capitán* said that the Americans were planning to invade Chihuahua. If we killed them and took their weapons, pretending to be Villa's Dorados, the American government would seek to punish Villa. No one would know that we took the machine guns and bullets for ourselves."

"Only things didn't work out that way," Will observed.

The attacking Mexican force had been decimated, more than a hundred killed, while eighteen American lives were lost during the fight.

"No," Luis said gravely, remembering, fingering the money underneath the table, rattling the coins. "No one expected the American soldiers to fight so courageously. Their machine guns gave them the strength of ten thousand men. I was frightened. I knew I was going to die. Flying bullets were everywhere, like hailstones, coming from every direction at once. Dying men were screaming, begging for water. My rifle had no bullets. I had only my machete. My horse was killed. I prayed to the Blessed Virgin that *Dios* would spare me. When Capitán Ponce ordered me to kill the screaming woman, I could not do it. We came on her wedding night."

Will gave his brother a silent nod.

"You've told us enough," Raymond said quietly, pushing back his chair and standing up. "Buy yourself somethin' to eat before you starve plumb to death, Luis. Later on, if you get hungry, come to the ranch. There's enough to go 'round."

"Gracias," Luis said humbly, bowing his head.

"An' don't worry about what you told us," Will added as he came to his feet with the aid of the tabletop. "We'll keep your secret. If it matters, in my opinion you did the right thing that night when you were ordered to kill the woman. I couldn't have done it either."

They walked out silently, leaving Luis sitting at his table with the money clenched tightly in his fist. Will mounted Poco without too much difficulty and reined away from the hut, heeling his horse to an easy trot toward the river.

Raymond rode up beside him for the ride back through Nuevo Laredo. "I wanted you to hear it for yourself, Will. I didn't think you'd believe it unless you heard it from him."

"It fits with everything the German girl told me. She said the Germans are workin' both sides of the fence, tellin' Carranza they supported him while they secretly give money to Villa so he can keep up the fight. The Germans want to keep us busy over here so we won't join the war in Europe. Maybe they suggested the idea of the Columbus raid to Carranza an' told him it would be a good idea if they made it look like Villa did it."

PANCHO AND BLACK JACK

"I figure we'll be at war with Mexico before too long," Raymond said, thinking out loud, gazing across the rooftops of the Mexican city. "It could spell trouble for us out at the ranch, bein' right on the border."

"Maybe," Will remarked, wondering himself. "I suppose it kinda depends on what happens to Pershing in Chihuahua. If he gets crossways with the *Federales* again the way they did down at Carrizal, there won't be much choice. If a war starts, I'll be out of the cow-buyin' business for sure, rain or no rain. The border will be closed. We'll have to make do with what calves we can raise on six hundred an' forty acres."

Raymond frowned. "Dry as it is, that won't be much beef," he said sadly. "Right now there ain't hardly enough grass to keep a herd of jackrabbits alive."

"We'll manage. I'll get a hundred a month from the army for the rest of the year. We'll get by."

"Sounds cheap, for givin' up one of your legs, little brother. I sure as hell wouldn't take that for a leg of mine."

Will recalled the night he got shot. "I had it comin'. I took a big chance, a chance I didn't have to take. When a man gambles, there's always a chance that he'll lose."

Riding out on the north bank of the Rio Grande, Will looked over his shoulder in the direction of Chihuahua. Somewhere down in Mexico, General Pershing was still taking chances with the lives of his men while searching for Villa, but there was a big difference: Pershing knew what he was doing. He was a trained soldier—he understood the risks.

A steady rain pelted the tin roof, the most welcome sound he ever remembered. It had rained endlessly for three days and nights, turning pastures into swampy marshes. The Rio Grande was on a rampage, flooding the valley all the way to Matamoros. The rains had come unexpectedly late in April, too late to provide good spring grazing, yet holding promise of a bountiful grass crop later this summer. Will watched the steady downpour from the front porch of the old house, tilted back in a hidebottom wicker chair, taking infrequent sips from a bottle of tequila to help ease the boredom of inactivity. Daydreaming now and then, he thought back to the ill-fated expedition in Chihuahua when he ran out of other things to think about.

Pershing's columns were out of Mexico since the middle of February, the Laredo newspaper resting on his lap said, ending the punitive expedition in predictable failure after almost a year of fruitless searching for Pancho Villa. Villa had resurfaced, up to his old tricks again, fully recovered from his broken leg, raiding Carrancista garrisons with renewed fury and hundreds of well-armed fresh recruits. Until fate dealt him a losing hand. A Carrancista general, Antonio Mugica, had engaged Villa north of Torreon around the first of January and crushed his new army, capturing or killing all but a handful of Villa's aides. A full-scale war between the United States and Mexico had been narrowly averted after months of unsuccessful sensitive negotiations between General Hugh Scott and Carranza representatives. Villa was no longer seen as a threat. America could pull out of Chihuahua and still have its dignity intact. The fearsome Lion of the North had now been reduced to a harmless kitten, the newspaper said, running from his pursuers with his tail between his legs again.

Will gazed across the sodden pastures in front of the house, remembering the expedition, the battle he witnessed at Guerrero, its bloody scenes forever etched in his memory, and his own terrible agony when he lost his leg. Worse than a recollection of his personal pain was the pain he felt when he remembered what it was like to kill another man. Two men, in fact. Sometimes at night he saw their faces floating before him, awakening suddenly bathed in a cold sweat. He told himself over and over again that he had no choice but to kill them, yet they still came to haunt his dreams, robbing him of sleep, ghostly reminders of a split second in time when the simple act of pulling a trigger had turned him into a killer.

He thought about Elisa then, as he had several times since his return to Laredo. There were moments when his heart ached to see her. Then he would tell himself how foolish it was, to feel that way about a woman he never really got to know. He knew enough about her to know they lived very different lives. Their brief time together had been the result of circumstance, then they had gone their separate ways. Will supposed it was the way things were meant to be.

The newspaper said Pershing was headed to France at the head of the American Expeditionary Force. America had finally been drawn into the conflict in Europe, declaring war on April 6—the result of a telegram from Arthur Zimmermann, minister of foreign affairs in Berlin, to the German minister in Mexico City, Heinrich von Eckhardt. The wire had been intercepted by British Naval Intelligence. It called for an alliance between Mexico and Germany to make war on the United States. In return for its help, Mexico would be given thousands of square miles of "lost" American territory—parts of Texas, New Mexico, and Arizona—when America was defeated. The telegram had been enough to convince President Wilson to declare war on Imperial Germany. John J. Pershing was the only general with actual field experience when Wilson declared war, making him the logical choice to head the AEF in France. After reading the article in the *Laredo Times*, Will found himself hoping Pershing could accomplish in Europe what he was unable to do in Chihuahua: lead American forces to victory.

The Zimmermann telegram also explained Elisa's connection to Germany through Rudolph Milnor. She had been a part of the conspiracy to involve Mexico in border conflicts with the United States: She was the German conduit to Villa, providing money to keep him an irritant in Chihuahua. The Germans wanted to keep America busy with problems on its doorstep, too busy to join the Allied effort in Europe. Will wondered if Elisa had merely been an unwitting tool of Milnor and the Germans, believing she was helping Villa without truly understanding how she was being used. He supposed it made no difference now.

He thought about John Pershing as he watched the rain. It had been raining in France when Pershing told him about the war from the story in *The New York Times*. Perhaps the mud in Chihuahua and countless other difficulties Pershing experienced there would be a help when he got to Europe. One thing Will was sure of: Pershing was the most dedicated soldier he had ever known. If dedication could win a war of the kind being fought in France, then John Pershing could whip the Germans.

A distant roll of thunder rattled across the brushlands from the south. Raindrops pattered on the tin roof like the beat of a thousand tiny drums. It was the sweetest sound a cowman in south Texas could hear, a signal that the drought was over at last. It was lousy weather for fighting a war, but it sure as hell grew a lot of grass.

· Author's Note ·

This is historical fiction. For the most part I have tried to be faithful to the facts of the Mexican revolution: the major battles, the political conflicts, the characters of such people as Pancho Villa (whose real name was Doroteo Arango), John Joseph Pershing, George Smith Patton Jr., Venustiano Carranza, Alvaro Obregon, Rudolfo Fierro, and Elisa Griensen, who led the citizens of Parral against the punitive expedition when Major Frank Tompkins first arrived. Will Johnson, whom I knew personally in the 1960s, was with Pershing as a scout and had lost a leg during the campaign. Other characters are real: Candelario Cervantes, and Julio Cardenas, who was killed by Patton in the manner portrayed. The German connection with Elisa Griensen, however, and Rudolph Milnor are speculation and creation on my part, respectively, and Major General Tasker Bliss is innocent of any wrongdoing concerning the El Paso prisoners and probably did not know of their existence until years afterward.

What is not mere speculation is a serious question over whether or not Pancho Villa led the raid on Columbus. Until his death in 1923, Villa denied it. Will Johnson told me on several occasions he knew two men personally who were with Villa the night of the raid and that Villa was not at Columbus, nor did he authorize the action. Dr. R. H. Ellis, writing in *Pancho Villa: Intimate Recollections by People Who Knew Him* (New York: Hastings House, 1977), claims he was with Villa on the day of the raid more than three hundred miles from Columbus. Dr. Ellis was an observer for President Wilson on the border, writing that "after the Columbus raid, Carranza soldiers were captured in uniform at Columbus by National Guards. Placed in federal detention they made statements in writing pleading guilty, and admitting that they were Carrancistas under the direction of Obregon and the German agent, Luther Wertz." Wertz was later apprehended and, under a death sentence, exonerated Villa in a written statement of all blame for the Santa Ysabel massacre and the Columbus raid, although Clifford Irving writes, in *Tom Mix and Pancho Villa* (New York: St. Martin's Press, 1982), "I have been unable to find any such statement." Dr. Ellis wrote that the statement "is in the files at Washington, D.C.," yet Irving was unable to locate it.

Most historians have concluded that Villa attacked Columbus, but there has never been real proof of it. Villa's own denial, long after any risk of retribution existed, may speak louder than what has been written about him by those who would blame him. He stood to gain nothing either way, it would seem.

Villa was gunned down on July 20, 1923, while at the wheel of his Dodge touring car on Calle Juarez in Parral by six gunmen led by Jesus Salas Barraza. Barraza was given a twenty-year sentence for his crime, however Obregon had him released from prison after serving less than one year. Villa was buried in a pauper's grave at Parral. A year after his burial his coffin was opened and his corpse was decapitated by persons unknown. Rumors still abound over who has custody of Villa's skull.

John Joseph Pershing died in 1948 at Washington D.C.'s Walter Reed Hospital at the age of eighty-eight, suffering from deteriorating health the final years of his life. His son, Warren, survived to attend Yale and serve in the U.S. Army Corps of Engineers in W.W. II. Pershing's grandson Richard was killed in Vietnam on February 17, 1968, holding the rank of Second Lieutenant, ending the line of this prestigious military family.

I was importing wild horses from the Yucatan in Mexico in the 1960s when Will Johnson told me the fascinating tale that Pancho Villa did not lead the infamous raid on Columbus, New Mexico. Johnson was almost eighty, living in Laredo, yet his memory of the expedition was clear. He knew several men who were with Villa on the night of the Columbus raid, and, though usually bedridden, he took me to Colonel Arturo Vela, who insisted that Villa was innocent of the attack. According to Vela, Pancho Villa was more than three hundred miles away at the time. Thus the basis for this story was there, from the recollections of two old warriors who took part in the conflict.

Will Johnson died of old age in Laredo, Texas in the early 1970s, leaving two sons and a daughter, maintaining until his death that Villa was framed for the Columbus raid by Obregon and agents of the German government.

Like many ghosts from our past, shadows of doubt linger over events surrounding enigmatic figures in history. Was Billy the Kid killed by Pat Garrett? Or did he die of heart failure at Hico, Texas, in 1950 under another name, as noted historian Dr. C. L. Sonnichsen seems to suggest in *Alias Billy the Kid* (Albuquerque: University of New Mexico Press, 1955)?

Was Villa at Columbus? I doubt we'll ever really know the truth. Villa is a part of legend now, and the ghosts of legends don't like to be disturbed.

In addition to the aforementioned sources, I'm indebted to the following histories of the Villa/Pershing conflict: Haldeen Braddy's, *Pershing's Mission in Mexico* (El Paso: Texas Western Press, 1967); Herbert Mason's *The Great Pursuit* (New York: Random House, 1970); Richard Goldhurst's *Pipe Clay and Drill: John J. Pershing, the Classic American Soldier* (New York: Reader's Digest Press, 1977); Frank Tompkins's *Chasing Villa* (Harrisburg, PA: Military Service Publishing Co., 1934); Barbara Tuchman's *The Zimmermann Telegram* (New York: Viking Press, 1958); and to the marvelous film documentary *The Hunt for Pancho Villa*, produced by Hector Galan for Galan Productions, of Austin, Texas, and PBS in 1993.

THE BEST WESTERN NOVELS
COME FROM POCKET BOOKS